Charley was hurrying hom[...] [...] was her state of euphoria. *He* had been more wonderful than ever before in this play called *Progress*.

He had portrayed an older man and had whitened the wings of hair at his temples, but he was still by far the most handsome man on the stage.

Charley sighed and paused in her headlong rush for home as she pulled a card out of her pocket. She had succumbed to temptation, something that was becoming a habit and for which she had a decided aptitude, and had expended a valuable sixpence on a photograph of her hero.

And as her sisters maintained a vigil by their mother's deathbed, Charley was gazing adoringly at the lean, classically beautiful profile of Vere Cavendish.

Also by Carolyn Terry

King of Diamonds
The Fortune Seekers

My
Beautiful
MISTRESS

CAROLYN TERRY

WARNER BOOKS

A *Warner* Book

First published in Great Britain in 1997
by Little, Brown and Company
This edition published by Warner Books in 1998

A CIP catalogue record for this book
is available from the British Library.

ISBN 0 7515 1810 7

Set in Sabon by M Rules
Printed and bound in Great Britain by
Clays Ltd, St Ives plc

Warner Books
A Division of
Little, Brown and Company (UK)
Brettenham House
Lancaster Place
London WC2E 7EN

To Roy, again

Prologue

The little tableau on the stage was posed so perfectly that it might have been arranged by the great Irving himself, but the theatricality of the setting was deceptive. There was nothing artificial about the body spreadeagled on the bare boards. The blood that seeped from the man's shattered skull, to mingle with the wine and the shards of the champagne bottle, was real.

Three beautiful young women were huddled together at one side of the stage, one of them in such obvious distress that she had collapsed on the floor, the group achieving an effortless symmetry and grace, which riveted the gaze of the two men who had just entered the auditorium.

In an atmosphere attuned to sound and movement, the silence and stillness were eerie and the two men from Scotland Yard paused at the back of the stalls.

'Not exactly your common-or-garden murder scene, eh, Sergeant?' the older man said, with a note of satisfaction in his voice.

'A bit early to be assuming that it's murder, isn't it, sir?'

'Well, laddie, it's my considered opinion that Vere Cavendish didn't happen to walk into a bottle by accident and, to the best of my knowledge and belief, this ain't a favourite – or even feasible – method of suicide. If he was killed with that champagne bottle, one of the lovely ladies hit him over the head with it.'

'But they are the Leigh sisters,' protested the sergeant in awed disbelief.

'A beautiful woman is as capable of murder as a plain one.'

'Yes, but the three *Leigh* sisters . . . !' Despite his best efforts to remain detached, the sergeant could hardly contain his excitement at being involved in a case concerning these goddesses.

'There was another one,' his colleague said reminiscently, 'but she died.'

'I didn't know that you were a theatre-goer, sir.'

'I'm not. My dealings with the Leighs have been purely professional. I first came across them ten years ago, and I attended the death, and the funeral, of the fourth sister quite recently. It's odd how they keep cropping up – more drama in their lives off the stage than on.'

He lingered a moment longer, watching the sisters as they comforted each other, but it was difficult to say whether his hesitation was due to reluctance to disturb the tableau, and the sensibilities of its charming components, or to an assessment of each woman's expression and demeanour.

Something was bothering him and he did not know quite what it was.

'Best get on with it,' he said gruffly and began to walk slowly towards the stage. And then it came to him. He could have sworn that when he first met these girls ten years ago, there had been five of them: three brunettes, a redhead and a blonde. He had seen one of them buried but, looking at the three on the stage, they had lost another one somewhere along the line. Oh well, and the inspector gave a mental shrug. In his line of business he met a great many young women, and it was quite likely that his memory was playing tricks.

He reached the front row of the stalls and looked up at them.

'I did not expect to have the pleasure again so soon,' he remarked, and then he elaborated slightly on their previous encounters.

'If you want to come up to the stage, Inspector, you will have to use that side door,' one of the sisters said, pointing the way, 'and go through the office.'

'I expected to find the stage door open.'

'So did we but, like you, we came in through the front entrance.'

'Still,' the inspector went on, 'if I had come in from the side, I would have missed the full impact of the Leigh sisters on stage.' And he named them, one by one, giving each in turn a courteous nod of his head. 'Now, before I do join you, let us clarify the situation. Even from the back of the stalls it is clear that Mr Cavendish collided with a bottle. It would save a lot of time if you told me which of you ladies hit him over the head with it.'

There was a slight pause and then the young woman slumped on the floor raised her head. 'I did,' she said.

My
Beautiful
MISTRESS

Part One

Chapter One

She woke early, that Saturday morning in spring, with a
sick feeling in the pit of her stomach, which twisted
into a knot of misery when she remembered what the day
had in store. However, by the time she had braved the
cold linoleum and was wriggling into her best dress, her
mood had changed to one of seething resentment.

Stooping slightly under the sloping ceiling of the little
attic, Charley glared at the floorboards as if her stare
could penetrate to the three rooms below, one occupied by
her invalid mother, another shared by her elder sisters,
Marion and Frances, while the third was the domain of
the twins. Yet, when she had answered Marion's peremptory summons the previous afternoon, for a brief moment
Charley had known a wild spurt of hope.

Marion had been holding a letter and Charley recognised the handwriting.

'A letter from Father . . . is he coming home?' But
Marion shook her head and, engulfed in a wave of disappointment, Charley interpreted the expression on her
sister's face. 'He didn't send us any money either, I suppose.'

'He wants *us* to send *him* money,' Marion said bitterly.
'I simply do not understand how he *dares* . . . What does

he think we live on, for heaven's sake? Fresh air? We certainly don't live on anything *he* provides.'

'What about the time his stake in that Mexican silver mine – or was it in Texas? – paid off?' Charley challenged, rushing to her hero's defence.

'Oh yes, we lived like kings for six months,' agreed Marion drily, 'until he sank everything into Zmyrna railway shares and lost the lot.'

'The railway shares were an unfortunate investment,' Charley was forced to concede.

'Investment! Father's schemes do not deserve the dignity of that description. He isn't an investor, he's a speculator. What's more, he's a *failed* speculator and it's about time he faced up to that fact and came home to do a decent day's work.'

With an absentee father and an invalid mother, the responsibility for the family rested on Marion, who, at twenty years old, was the oldest of the five sisters. She took this responsibility seriously but handled it with complete self-confidence. Oldest equalled first equalled best, in Marion's estimation, and she never doubted for a moment that she was stronger and smarter than her siblings and that, with her mother's blessing, her word was law.

For Charley, who had guessed what was coming, the blow finally fell.

'You must go to Uncle John tomorrow and ask him for a loan.'

'Why *me*?' Charley burst out rebelliously.

'Someone has to go – we cannot pay the rent.'

'But why is it always me? It isn't fair!'

'Frances and I have other duties.'

'Like going to Mudie's for the library books. Tell you what – I'll swap with you. I don't mind going to Mudie's, in fact I would absolutely love to go to Mudie's, and you can go begging to Uncle John.'

'It isn't begging,' Marion said sharply.

'What else is it? Oh, I know you call it a "loan", just to make it sound better but, believe me, it *feels* like begging when you have to do it! Besides, if Uncle John's contributions are loans, why do we never pay him back?'

Marion winced. 'Uncle John likes you,' she said feebly.

'But he would absolutely adore the twins, given the chance to see them. Imogen could do the talking as usual, and one glance from Arabella's baby blue eyes is enough to bring blood positively gushing from a stone.'

'The twins are too young to make the journey across to the City on their own.'

'They are eleven years old and you were sending me on that journey, alone, when I was that age.'

'It was different for you. You could cope, and you have always seemed older than your years.'

'I wonder why,' Charley said sarcastically.

'Charley, Uncle John genuinely likes you best. He is Father's brother and you are a Leigh through and through.'

Coming from Marion, this was not a compliment but this morning, as she finished dressing and the ordeal came another step closer, Charley hoped that it was true. She wanted desperately to be like her father and different from the others. Making her way down the narrow uncarpeted stairs to the lower landing and then down the main staircase to the hall, Charley felt an emotion perilously close to hate for her mother, blaming her for the horrid prospect of asking Uncle John for money. All very well for *her*, Charley thought mutinously, pretending to be ill in order to avoid her responsibilities. Much simpler to lie in bed all day and be waited on than have to face up to life's problems. Taking the easy way out, that was all Mother ever did; and then the others had the nerve to blame Father for their difficulties, when any fool could see that Mother had driven him away. Frankly she, Charley, did not blame him one little bit; given half a chance she would be off like a shot herself.

The coat selected for today's expedition belonged to Frances and so, Charley being much the tallest of the family, it was too short. Mind you, even a good-length coat would have failed to conceal the wrinkles in Charley's stockings and the several inches of petticoat sagging beneath the hem of her brown woollen dress. Glumly she jammed a much-detested high-crowned, squashy felt hat on her head and picked up a pair of leather gloves. She was ready, a very tall, thin, untidy fifteen-year-old with her father's russet hair and blue-green eyes set in a bony, paper-white face. With a sigh and a final silent glare up the stairs, Charley let herself out of the front door.

At first she took little interest in her surroundings as she headed south from Kentish Town, walking briskly through the streets of terraces, each virtually identical to her own, with their smoke-blackened brickwork, small corner shops, pawnbrokers and public houses. She jingled the coins in her pocket, donated by Marion for an – unspecified – 'emergency', or for an omnibus should weariness prostrate the traveller. But Charley was acutely aware that she would miss lunch as well as breakfast and had allocated her pennies to the purchase of buns. Only when she reached Bloomsbury did she slow down slightly, in order to catch her breath and absorb the gracious atmosphere of the quiet squares and superior houses.

When Father comes home we'll be able to live in a place like this, she thought loyally, and allowed herself to imagine the glorious day when her father did return, bringing his buoyant spirits and unquenchable optimism. She could almost feel the strength of his arm around her and hear the warmth of his voice as he greeted 'my boy Charley'. Oh, if only she were a boy! She ought to have been a boy! The length of her legs, the skinniness of her narrow-hipped, flat-chested frame, and the ease with which she achieved academic excellence, all proved the enormity of Nature's mistake. Best of all, when Father did come home, she would not be alone any more. At the moment, with Marion and Frances being close allies on the one side, and the twins inseparable on the other, Charley was stranded in the middle of the family, without a friend in either camp.

The sight of John Leigh's office, situated in a narrow lane off Cheapside, brought on another attack of nausea and a dryness in her throat. Already she was envisaging the cool reception she would receive, the supercilious glances from her uncle's employees, who would guess the reason for her visit, but it had to be done. Charley pushed open the door and went in.

A crescendo of noise blasted her ears, although only two of the four big machines at the back of the room were operating. At desks near the door two shirt-sleeved men were working on big sheets of typescript, while behind them another man was setting up a document in type. Each of the machines was supervised by its own operator, and at a long workbench against one wall a boy was tying up bundles of completed papers into neat parcels. This was John Leigh's printing works. He did not handle big projects such as books or regular issues of newspapers and magazines but had built up a steady jobbing trade based on the requirements of City offices, legal firms and shops, as well as orders from private individuals. On this particular Saturday his staff were engaged on the production of a religious pamphlet, a number of advertising bills, a batch of business cards, a theatre programme, a share prospectus and a small collection of poems by 'a lady' for personal circulation.

Seeing Charley, one of the shirt-sleeved men stood up, lifted his jacket from a nearby hook and put it on, then came towards her. Her uncle, he informed her, was in the back office and he would let Mr Leigh know she was here. Charley waited, trying to ignore the irritating whistling and impudent glances of the boy. It was almost a relief when she was beckoned through to the dreaded confrontation.

The family resemblance was obvious immediately. Sitting behind the desk was a lean, spare man with grey streaks in his red-brown hair and an exasperated expression on his handsome face, an exasperation that deepened when he set eyes on Charley's unkempt appearance.

'Good God, Charlotte, you look as though you have been sleeping in the park!'

'Sorry,' said Charley humbly. 'Oh Lord, I've lost a coat button – Frances will kill me – and this hat has always been useless.' She removed the offending headgear and made valiant, if fruitless, attempts to push her hair into some semblance of order.

John's pale, ascetic features softened as he looked at the tumbling mass of russet hair, the candid eyes and tall, thin frame, for his niece had more of the Leigh in her than any of his own children.

'Sit down, sit down,' and he waved her into the chair opposite him. 'I assume that I owe the pleasure of this visit to the fact that your father has not struck gold yet.'

'Diamonds,' Charley said seriously. 'He is looking for diamonds, not gold, but actually he has not found either. But he will, Uncle John. He will prove them all wrong, I know he will!'

'Then you are a fool,' her uncle replied but, because he knew the attitude adopted by the rest of the family towards his brother, he found her loyalty touching. He waited for her to continue, thus deliberately making it difficult for her. John was not a cruel man but he was genuinely irked by the perpetual demands of his brother's family on his own limited resources.

'We received a letter yesterday but he sent no money and we cannot pay the rent and so we, that is Marion, wondered . . .' Charley floundered, looking at her uncle in the hope that help might be forthcoming. She found him implacable, and took a deep breath. 'We should be most grateful if you could spare us the rent money. Of course it would only be a loan and we will pay you back at the first opportunity.'

'Did you hear that noise?' and John cupped his hand to his ear in an exaggerated gesture. When Charley shook her head, he smiled grimly. 'That, my dear, is the sound of pigs' wings flapping as they swoop over our heads like eagles.'

'I am really very sorry to bother you,' and her voice trailed into a whisper of hurt and humiliation.

'Have you approached your mother's family?'

He knew this was a silly question. When, twenty-one years ago, James Leigh had eloped with Fanny, she had been rejected by her wealthy and respectable family, and that rejection had been firm and final. Her parents had not wavered in their resolve to disown her and, after their death, Fanny's siblings had been content to continue the tradition, particularly as they had a shrewd idea that a reunion could prove an expensive drain on their purse. Only an old aunt, with a special fondness for the girl, had been unable to cast her off completely and had bequeathed her a small annuity; and it was this, paid meticulously each quarter by the solicitor, that was largely responsible for putting food on the Leigh table. Worn out by disappointment, money worries and child-bearing – nine children in twelve years, but all the boys had died – the birth of twins had been a turning point. Fanny Leigh put up her feet on the sofa and declined into delicate ill-health before graduating to bedridden invalidism.

'But you still receive that quarterly allowance from the aunt?' John went on.

'Yes, but it doesn't go very far, although we try to be economical.'

'Your father believes that the income from that source is more than it actually is. He is convinced that the moment his back is turned, your mother's people shower you with sovereigns. How is your mother?'

'Poorly.'

John snorted impatiently. 'So poorly that her nearest and dearest are kept running round after her, all day every day, when they could be out supplementing the family income! And in the meantime Miss High-and-Mighty Marion and Miss Prim-and-Proper Frances get you to do their dirty work.'

This coincided so exactly with Charley's personal opinion that she was awed into silence.

A slender volume was lying on his desk and, as he drummed his fingers thoughtfully on the polished mahogany, his gaze alighted on it. 'Hm,' he murmured, 'I wonder . . .' The finger-drumming increased in intensity and tempo and then he seemed to come to a decision. 'Tell Marion that this lady,' and he began to write down a name and address, 'is interested in the arts – I am printing a little book of her poems for private circulation – and holds cultural soirées at her home. I understand that a feature of these evenings is a reading from a book or a play, so perhaps she might consider allowing Marion to participate.'

Every evening, for as long as Charley could remember, Marion had read aloud to the family. Their taste was catholic and although poetry, history and biography featured in their entertainment, novels were consumed with avid enjoyment. They had recently embarked on Thackeray's *Pendennis* and last night had reached the point where the hero pays his first visit to the theatre. Marion had a tremendous talent for bringing every scene and character to life, and Charley had been riveted as the Fotheringay – the 'stunner', the 'crusher' – made her entrance on the stage.

'Does this lady pay people?' Charley asked bluntly.

'The fee would be small at the outset but I believe that established readers, chiefly professional actors, can receive as much as five guineas a night for their services.'

Charley was impressed. 'Marion is awfully good,' she said magnanimously. 'Will you tell the lady to expect her?'

'No, Marion must introduce herself.'

'That would amount to virtually asking for the job and the money . . . Oh, I see,' and Charley grinned involuntarily as she perceived how her uncle was turning the tables on her sister.

After handing over the piece of paper bearing the name and address of Marion's proposed benefactress, he took a key from his pocket and, to Charley's immense relief, turned towards the safe. However, at that moment they were interrupted because John Leigh's presence was required in the outer office and so Charley's agony was prolonged. He was gone for some time, long enough to warrant an explanation, although not an apology, when he returned.

'It is impossible to get reliable staff these days,' he

muttered irritably, opening the safe. 'I'm two short today and goodness knows how many deliveries to get out.'

'Could I help? I don't have anything else to do.'

He looked at her, noting that she had made a fairly good job of neatening her appearance during his absence from the room. 'I don't suppose you go anywhere near the Strand – hardly on your way home, is it?'

'I can easily go that way,' Charley assured him eagerly.

'In that case you could deliver a package for me. Thank you, Charley, you are a good girl and you deserve better than that pack of harridans at home.'

Unexpected tears stung her eyes at this unprecedented sympathy and she looked away, hoping that he had not noticed.

'Tell Marion that this is all I can spare,' and he handed her a bag of coins, small but reassuringly heavy, 'but it will keep the wolf from the door for a few months. And now let's find that packet for the Lyceum.'

In the main office he led the way to the workbench. The boy had disappeared, presumably on another errand, but a large parcel was ready on the counter.

'You may have to go to the side entrance,' John instructed, 'and be sure to tell the doorkeeper that the goods are from me and that Mr Stoker is expecting them.'

Charley carefully pushed the bag of coins as far down into the depths of her pocket as it would go, and picked up the parcel.

'Charley, do you always take all the money home when you leave here?'

'Of course.' She looked astounded by the question.

'You do not appropriate a bit of it for yourself – a little tip for your trouble in fetching it?'

'No.'

'More fool you,' and with a teasing smile John Leigh returned to his desk.

Her uncle had referred merely to 'the Lyceum', but when Charley approached the imposing pillared portico at the corner of Wellington Street and the Strand, she realised that she was destined for the Royal Lyceum Theatre. A crush of people milled about on the pavement and part of the crowd was forming several distinct queues but Charley, seeing no obvious recipient for the parcel, followed instructions and walked round the corner into Exeter Street. Here, eventually, she found an unprepossessing entrance, in marked contrast to the pillared grandeur at the front. This turned out to be the stage door and she was able to leave the packet with the doorkeeper.

Retracing her steps, she loitered for a while among the crowd outside the theatre. A large notice proclaimed the imminent performance of a benefit matinée of *The Merchant of Venice* and revealed that Shylock would be played by Mr Henry Irving and Portia by Miss Ellen Terry. Charley had never heard of either of them. She had heard only of the Fotheringay and, oh yes, of the Crummles and the Infant Phenomenon from the pen of Charles Dickens. The theatre was never discussed in the Leigh household although the works of Shakespeare were read. Charley frowned, trying to recall *The Merchant of Venice*, but she had only a vague memory of it and did not think it numbered among her favourites.

Slowly she walked away along the Strand, bought two large buns and munched them thoughtfully. For some reason her feet did not want to move towards Trafalgar Square; they wanted, as desperately as the rest of her, to enter the Lyceum.

Entirely against her better will and judgement she

walked back. The idea was ridiculous; for one thing, a theatre ticket was bound to be expensive. But, she reasoned, Uncle John had virtually *told* her to take a bit of the money for herself. An inspection of the seat prices revealed stalls at ten shillings, dress circle and upper circle at six and three shillings respectively – all out of the question, of course – while the pit cost two shillings and the gallery one shilling. Charley felt the weight of the money bag dragging on her pocket. She could afford a shilling, she thought.

The other reason for hesitation was the certainty, although she did not know why she was so sure, that her family would disapprove of the theatre. If they found out that she had seen a play, they would be shocked. But need they find out, and what was so shocking about it? Charley watched the fashionably dressed ladies and their escorts descending from their carriages and sweeping through the front entrance and decided that the theatre attracted a very superior sort of person. However, she had the common sense to realise that these society people were destined for the expensive seats and therefore she scrutinised the queues lined up for the gallery and the pit, admitting reluctantly that there was a distinct difference between the two. At that moment a woman and three younger women, all plainly but neatly dressed, joined the queue for the pit and Charley was attracted to them immediately. They could so easily have been her own family that she was quite sure that, extra shilling or not, where they sat was where she ought to sit. She hurried across and stood behind them, extracting a florin from the money bag as unobtrusively as possible, and managed to tag along with them past the box office, into the auditorium and finally into a seat beside them. Thus protected, Charley took her very first look at the interior of a theatre and gaped at its magnificence.

The great arc of the auditorium, painted in sage green and turquoise blue, swept round to the ornate boxes by the stage, while above her the tiers of the circles and gallery towered to the sky-blue and gold ceiling, the bright house lights gleaming on gilded figures, lamp brackets and decorative panels. A green baize curtain obscured the stage and, invisible to Charley, an orchestra was playing a medley of operatic arias. The plain wooden bench on which she sat seemed a long way from the stage, compared to the rows of midnight-blue velvet stall seats in front of her, and she began to worry that she would not be able to see much through the forest of elaborate hats and bonnets. Then, as the house lights dimmed slightly and the footlights on the stage glowed softly into life, the ladies in the audience, as one, removed their hats. Charley followed suit, clutching it in both hands as she leaned forward slightly in her seat, eyes fixed on the green curtain as it rose.

Having no idea what to expect, she watched the first scene carefully, heart thumping with excitement, trying not to miss anything important, trying to reconcile this vivid picture with Marion's reading of the play. But then, *then*, came the second scene and the entrance of Portia – glorious, golden-haired Ellen Terry in a gown of gold brocade, gliding like gossamer – and Charley's heart was lost.

Chapter Two

Hours later, having been immersed in magic, Charley wandered out of the theatre and stood, dazed, in the dark street among the milling crowd. Someone dropped a programme and she picked it up, folded it and placed it in her pocket with infinite care. Slowly she walked down the street, oblivious of her surroundings, wrapped in a glow of happiness, detached from the demands of the real world. Vaguely she was aware that she was very late and so she steered a path towards Trafalgar Square with the intention of taking an omnibus as far as Euston.

Her whole being was saturated and ablaze with the play, with its entrancing scenery and gorgeous costumes, with its poetry so beautifully spoken, with the gaunt pathos of Shylock and, above all, with the gaiety and charm of Portia. Flashes of the performance re-enacted themselves in her mind's eye: Shylock's unsuspecting return to his empty house after the elopement of his daughter; Portia's pretty by-play in the Casket Scene; Portia's 'Quality of Mercy' speech in the Court Scene, and then her verdict and Shylock's reaction to it.

Somehow, mechanically, Charley negotiated her way to Euston and began the trudge home. Part of her regretted being unable to share this experience with anyone, but another part of her rejoiced in hugging it to herself. Groping in her pocket for reassurance that the programme was safe, she was reminded about the money and hesitated, wasting precious seconds, as she pondered her next move. Then, swiftly, she took ten shillings from the bag, wrapped it in a handkerchief and pushed the money and the theatre programme into her dress pocket. Ten whole shillings – five visits to the theatre! Thank heavens she had a room of her own, a private place where she could hide her little hoard of shillings and her secrets.

It was just a pity that she could not run straight to this refuge now.

'Where the hell have you been?' Marion was waiting at the door of the house and pulled Charley inside, pushing her into the back parlour, her handling of the girl as rough as her speech. 'We have been worried sick about you.'

'I'm all right.'

'Evidently.' Seeing Charley sound in wind and limb, Marion was furious about the worry she had caused. 'You ought to have been back hours ago.'

'You have lost a button off this coat,' Frances accused, plucking at the loose threads where once the button had been, 'and where is your other glove?'

'I must have dropped it. I really am sorry but I have been very busy, which is why I am late. Uncle John gave me this,' and Charley handed over the money bag with a virtuous air. 'He told me to tell you that it was all he could spare.'

In the ensuing lull, while Marion and Frances counted the money, Charley hardly dared breathe for fear that the remaining sum would be deemed insufficient and her pilfering suspected. However, her sisters seemed perfectly satisfied, even pleased, with the amount and Charley was more than ever convinced that her uncle had included a bit extra, which he had intended her to take.

'Uncle John was short-staffed today so I offered to help him,' Charley continued, her air of saintliness increasing. 'I delivered a lot of parcels, which was jolly hard work but I thought it would help to repay our debt,' and she gazed innocently, but pointedly, at the columns of coins piled on the table.

Her sisters stared at her in astonishment, stunned into uncharacteristic silence, but then Marion collected herself.

'It was a very good idea, Charley, and I do concede that you could not let us know that you would be late.'

'I told Uncle that I would help him again. He said,' Charley added angelically, 'that I was a good girl.'

'There is a first time for everything,' Marion said drily.

'Oh, and he asked me to give you this.' Charley fished out the piece of paper bearing the poet's name and address, gave Marion the message and escaped triumphantly to her room with her secret intact.

With only a year between their ages, Marion and Frances often felt that they were nearly as close as the twins, and they looked so alike that they might almost be taken for twins. Both had inherited their mother's black hair, big blue eyes and flawless complexion, and both were of medium height and slim, with the same graceful walk and hand movements. In family matters Marion took the lead and discussions between the two sisters tended to be a matter of Marion thinking aloud, rather than a genuine exchange of opinions. Still, Marion liked to think that Frances was her chief confidante, comfort and support, and Frances liked to think so too.

However, there were differences between them. Frances's personality paled beside the strength and vibrancy of Marion, and she appeared inhibited in comparison with the great blaze of her elder sister's energy. Marion's hair was blacker and glossier, her complexion creamier, her eyes of deep violet more alluring than the blue-grey of Frances's, her beauty so arresting that people turned to stare at her in the street. Frances was very lovely but the delicacy of her features, which could be so charming in repose and so piquant when she laughed, were too often set in a thin, pinched line of discontent. A conformist to the core, Frances cared deeply about 'appearances', propriety and social niceties. And it was these differences that came bubbling to the surface as the two sisters stared at the name and address on the note Charley had given them.

'I wonder what would be the best day to call on Lady Melton.' Marion's eyes were sparkling with excitement. 'Not Sunday. Monday, perhaps . . . yes, Monday. You could cope with Mother for a couple of hours on your own, couldn't you?'

'Of course I could,' Frances said impatiently, 'but surely you cannot be giving this proposal serious consideration!'

'I most certainly am. Money for jam. I think I might even enjoy it.'

'But calling on her without a proper introduction is like begging for work!'

'Nonsense,' Marion said robustly, although inwardly she quailed at the prospect. 'I shall send Charley with a note tomorrow – she can take a cab for the last part of the journey, it will make a better impression – so I will be expected. Besides, I am not too proud to seek work of this kind. It seems a perfectly ladylike arrangement.'

'But you might have to mix with these professional actors that Charley mentioned!' Frances wailed, clearly outraged.

'I do not suppose they will contaminate me unduly,' Marion said lightly, 'but it is a risk I must take. We need the money, and this is a heaven-sent opportunity to earn some in a way that need not disturb our domestic routine unduly. Now, I wonder what I should wear. I think I will ask Mother, because I have the feeling that she will approve thoroughly of the whole idea.'

She was right. For once Frances, to her dismay, found herself isolated and out-of-step with the rest of the family.

'Perhaps you would be good enough to read a passage for us,' said Lady Melton, 'so that Mr Druce and I may assess your suitability for our little entertainments.'

Marion had come prepared for such an eventuality, with several pieces that she considered safe choices for the unknown taste of her audience. Her mouth was dry and she wished that she dared ask for a glass of water, but instead she tried to clear her throat, coughed delicately and began to wobble through a piece of Wordsworth. She was intensely nervous and aware that she was not giving her best, but performing here, in this beautiful drawing room in this elegant house in front of these extraordinary people, was very different from reading in her own home for the benefit of the family.

At the end of the piece she looked up inquiringly, wondering if they had heard enough. Lady Melton was leaning back in her chair, eyes closed, an expression of rapt attention on her face but Mr Druce indicated that she should continue and, bless his cotton socks, as Marion said afterwards, gave her the most charming smile of encouragement. Accordingly her voice gained strength in the Shakespeare and by the time she embarked on Tennyson's 'The Lotos-Eaters' she had found the full range of her rich, flexible voice.

'Thank you, Miss Leigh,' and Lady Melton stirred languidly into life. 'Please leave us for a moment.'

Marion rose, dropped a polite curtsy and walked through the door that Druce held open for her, still too nervous to be indignant over her casual dismissal and the knowledge that they were discussing her in her absence. The small salon where she waited had several ornately framed mirrors on its walls and dismally Marion confronted her reflection. She had always admired herself in this cuirass-style jacket of dark brown wool worn over a narrow skirt draped into elaborate, vertical pleats at the back but she felt a complete frump beside the utterly unexpected style of Lady Melton.

Her ladyship was wearing a garment the like of which Marion had never seen before, a flowing, softly draped gown of brocaded silk in subtle shades of green and yellow, with puffed sleeves and no discernible waist. Her hair was such a mass of loose curls that the term 'frizzy' sprang irresistibly to mind. Yet the style made an impact. If, Marion thought, her ladyship – a woman of mature years and no great beauty – could look like that in such an ensemble, what would the fashion not do for *her*?

The door opened and Mr Druce beckoned her to rejoin them, but as Marion reached the entrance the main door of the drawing room was flung open and the butler announced: 'Mr Cavendish, m'lady.' And Lady Melton was transformed; eyes brightening, expression animated, she sparkled into life as surely as if someone had switched on a light inside her.

'Show him in,' she ordered. 'Eddie, take Miss Leigh out this way,' and she propelled Druce and Marion back into the little waiting room and closed the door on them, leaving Marion staring at her companion in some confusion.

'Don't mind the Mellie,' he said confidently, opening another door, 'it's just her way.'

Marion did not trust herself to comment but walked out of the room in silence, wondering if all aristocrats were this discourteous or if Lady Melton had a natural talent for it. Emerging on to the landing, she glanced back along the passage in time to see a man entering the drawing room. She saw only his back but the tall, broad-shouldered figure in a beautifully tailored suit, and the cut of the thick dark hair shaped smoothly into his neck, were enough to explain Lady Melton's enthusiastic welcome.

'Mr Druce,' she said as they descended the stairs, 'before we go any further, would you mind telling me if I passed the test?'

'Passed the . . . ? Oh yes, absolutely. You're in, that's if you want to be, on Sunday. Sorry, I had forgotten that you did not know.' Collecting his hat and cane in the hall, he smiled at her again, a handsome young man, about six feet tall and lightly built, with wavy brown hair, hazel eyes and eyelashes to kill for. Outside in Lowndes Square he raised his face appreciatively to the sunshine. 'Not a lot of warmth in the sun but a walk in the park might be pleasant while we discuss matters.'

'I would not wish to put you to any trouble,' Marion said anxiously.

'No trouble at all.'

'I feel that I have disrupted your morning enough already.'

'But you are the reason I am here.' He stared at her in puzzlement, but then his brow cleared and he burst out laughing. 'My dear Miss Leigh, I am not a friend of the family, I'm the hired help, like you. The Mellie – and I certainly do not call her that to her face – employs me to organise her theatrical entertainments.'

'Why did she choose you?'

'You mean that my charm, good looks and talent are not sufficient reason?' he teased, but then smiled and shrugged. 'My father does a bit of legal work for Lord Melton and I suppose one day they compared notes on the black sheep of their respective families. Mind you, I shouldn't think that the Meltons can produce anything to compare with me in the disgrace stakes. The *stage* is about as low as one can go.'

So her 'contamination' by the acting profession had begun already. Marion wondered if she dared tell Frances, and decided not. 'For such an outcast from society, you seemed on extremely good terms with Lady Melton.'

'She has been rather decent,' he agreed, 'and that helped a lot at home. My people have resigned themselves to my fate, even if they haven't given me their blessing. They even came to see me last week – I'm with the Kendals at the St James's, you know.'

Marion, her ignorance of theatrical affairs being the equal of Charley's, did not know, but she adopted what she hoped was a suitably interested and impressed expression.

'Does Lady Melton always look like that?' she asked.

'The frock, you mean. Absolutely. Fancies herself no end in aesthetic dress although there are those unkind enough to mutter "mutton dressed as lamb" under their breath.'

'I thought that perhaps she had dressed up because she was expecting Mr Cavendish.'

Mr Druce laughed again, a most attractive laugh, making fun of his subject but without malice. 'I have little doubt that her ladyship chose to wear her most recent and alluring acquisition in the hope that Mr Cavendish would call. As do most of her friends and acquaintances, who will be greener than the brocaded silk when they hear that she was the one favoured with his presence this morning.'

'Evidently Mr Cavendish is a popular man?'

'Is Christmas in December?' Druce exclaimed, flinging wide his arms in a wildly theatrical gesture.

They were strolling at a leisurely pace past the Serpentine and Marion permitted a pause in the conversation, hoping that Druce would elaborate, but when he seemed disinclined to do so, she could contain her curiosity no longer.

'Forgive me for asking,' she said diffidently, 'but who is Mr Cavendish?'

A wooden bench happened to be unoccupied and Druce collapsed on it in another actor-ish display of exaggerated surprise. 'You don't *know* . . . ? Miss Leigh, you are a treasure! Your innocence is charming and *so* refreshing!'

Having tried to assume an air of sophistication all morning, Marion was anything but charmed by this reaction. However, she sat down on the bench beside him and smiled politely.

'Vere Cavendish is the newest addition to the ranks of our actor-managers,' Druce explained. '*Very* important and influential people, are actor-managers, and although Cavendish is not in the Irving class yet, or even up there with the Bancrofts and the Kendals, he's getting there and some say he'll outclass them all one day. Vere Cavendish has . . . how should one put it? . . . presence.'

Yes, Marion had gathered that. One brief glimpse of the back of his head had been enough to sear an image, uncomfortably and indelibly, on her mind.

'He made his name with the Bancrofts, at the Prince of . . .'

'I really do not need all the details,' Marion said hastily.

'Knowing he is an actor is quite enough, thank you. Now, you said something about Sunday?'

Druce fished in his pocket and produced a sheaf of tightly folded papers. 'Part One will comprise recitations from her ladyship's latest volume of verse. These are yours, so have a read-through during the week.'

Marion took the sheets of paper, read a few lines, and looked up at Druce with eyes wide with horror.

'Utter drivel,' he said candidly, 'but you ain't seen nothing yet! Here is Part Two of the entertainment – although I dare say the more discerning guests will have another word for it – a dramatic piece that flowed from her ladyship's pen during one of her more inspired moments. This is your part,' and he handed her another bundle of papers covered in a spidery scribble.

'It doesn't look very long, and it doesn't seem to make much sense.' Marion turned over the pages doubtfully.

'Those are only *your* lines. Couldn't copy out the whole thing for everyone – take me hours and hours.'

'Oh, I see . . . but in that case, ought we not to practise, rehearse I mean, in advance?'

'The cast meets at Lowndes Square at six o'clock for a run-through – the Mellie provides rather a good cold collation, and we usually starve all day in order to do justice to it – and then we hang around until summoned.'

'What should I wear?'

'Something pretty, but not too pretty,' was Druce's enigmatic and not very helpful reply.

'Mr Druce, why does Lady Melton want me for her play? Surely London is full of actresses who would perform it with more distinction than I can hope to achieve.'

'Yes, but you are a lady.'

'I don't understand.'

'The stage is becoming more acceptable as a profession

but,' and he hesitated, biting his lip unhappily, 'more so for men than for women.'

'Actors are socially acceptable but actresses are not.'

'Damned unfair, of course, but old prejudices die hard. Lady Melton would not welcome a professional actress in her drawing room, but she does require a lady with a refined voice and manners to play the beautiful *ingénue* in her play and you fit the bill perfectly. Look the part, too, if I may be permitted to say so.'

'Thank you for the compliment,' Marion said demurely, 'and for your encouragement. I will be at Lowndes Square at six o'clock on Sunday evening.' And she walked on through the park towards Marble Arch, wondering if it really had been Marion Leigh sitting on a park bench on a Monday morning, in such relaxed conversation with an attractive stranger. A new way of life was opening up and she loved it, and she was nearly home before she realised that she had loved it so much that she had completely forgotten to ask how much she would be paid.

The whole family – even Fanny, propped up with pillows on the sofa – waited up for Marion on Sunday evening. It had been a strange day: Marion refusing to eat anything; Frances helping her to dress; everyone trying to settle into a semblance of their usual routine after she had gone, with Frances playing the piano and singing, and Charley taking over *Pendennis*, miserably aware – even without the scornful glances of the twins – that she fell below Marion's high standards. They were a sleepy little group when they heard the sound of hooves heralding the arrival of the cab, and then into the house swept Marion, wide awake and bursting with excitement, and it was as though they had never seen her before. After so short an absence, they had forgotten how beautiful she was.

For once it had been Fanny who had solved the chief problem: what to wear. Sending the girls to the attic room adjacent to Charley's, she had told them to open an old trunk and bring down the dresses that had lain in scented darkness for twenty years.

These were the gowns of Fanny's girlhood, the one possession that her family had sent on to her, their silks, satins and velvets too fine for the family's present circumstances, the sight, smell and feel of them too painful a reminder of a previous existence. But for Marion's sake, Fanny had made the effort: her daughter would walk into Lady Melton's drawing room looking like a lady, as well as behaving like one.

They pored over the gowns for hours, stroking the silk with wondering fingers, trying them on, but there was one to which Marion's longing eyes returned time and time again: a dress of violet silk that brought out the beauty of her eyes. She was taller than her mother but, the dress having been designed for wear over a crinoline, there was ample material for refashioning and updating the style and fit. The result was a triumph and now the girls and their mother stirred sleepily into life, gazing in astonishment at the vision of Marion, her upswept dark hair shining, her huge eyes sparkling and her skin gleaming against the folds of violet silk, and the black velvet of the evening cloak she had also appropriated from Fanny's treasure chest. They did not need to ask if the evening had been a success; it was evident in her whole demeanour and in every movement she made.

Exhorted to start at the beginning, she described her arrival in Lowndes Square and the gathering of the 'participants', as she phrased it tactfully, in an ante-room on the ground floor where they 'ran through' the play.

'They were the most amusing people I have ever met!

We laughed and laughed, and I've never had so much fun in my life.' She smiled, her lovely face transfigured with happiness, blind to the mixed reaction that this statement received. 'And the *food* . . .' She depicted the cold collation in such detail that Charley's mouth watered. 'Then we were summoned upstairs . . .' Marion paused and decided to omit the details of how Mr Druce had offered her his arm in order to escort her into Lady Melton's drawing room and how he had looked at her with the most ardent admiration. 'I think they liked my recitation,' she said modestly, 'and it was surprising how much better the play sounded when we were doing it seriously than when we were fooling around.'

'Did you remember your words?' Charley wanted to know.

'Yes, thank heavens, *and* I managed to avoid bumping into anything or anyone!' She got up and tried to re-enact a scene for them but the area available in the Leigh back parlour was so much smaller than in the Melton drawing room that the restriction was irksome and she subsided into her chair with a troubled frown.

'How much did they pay you?' Frances asked. 'And do they want you again?'

Proudly Marion produced two guineas and waited for their torrent of praise and incredulity. Two guineas for a few hours' work!

'And yes, they do want me to perform again. Lady Melton and Mr Druce both have my address and as we were leaving the butler brought me this,' and with a flourish she waved a card in the air, 'from one of Lady Melton's guests, asking me to call on her later this week regarding another engagement.'

'Can we go to bed now?' asked Imogen. 'Arabella is tired.'

Impulsively Marion bent her head and kissed them both, before shooing them upstairs. Then she realised that bedtime meant divesting herself of her finery, and the shabbiness of her surroundings and the mundanity of her everyday existence overwhelmed her. Exposure to the world of society, to the luxury and elegance of the Meltons' home, to the cultivation and refinement of their guests, to the wit and colour of her fellow 'participants' had made Marion dissatisfied with her home, and even with her family. Raising her eyes she looked at her mother, who was watching her with a knowing sadness, and at that moment Marion understood her mother, what she had sacrificed and what she had suffered, as she had never understood her before.

However, the sentiment that was uppermost in her mind when at last she lay, wakeful, in bed, was the disappointing absence of Vere Cavendish from the soirée. Unfortunately she had failed to take particular note of the presence, and the singularly appraising scrutiny, of Lord Melton.

Chapter Three

A year after that first engagement, Marion disposed of the day's quota of Jane Austen and escaped from her client as quickly as possible without giving offence, before hurrying to the park where a familiar figure was waiting for her.

'How is *Persuasion* progressing?' Edward Druce inquired.

'Galloping along, thank you. That tiresome Louisa Musgrove has just fallen on the Cobb at Lyme, but our heroine was equal to the crisis and was the first to suggest summoning a surgeon.'

'Do I detect a certain dryness of tone? I thought you were an admirer of Miss Austen's work.'

'I am a most fervent and sincere devotee of her novels,' Marion assured him, 'but even the great Jane's heroines deserve a prod with a parasol occasionally. They can be a trifle passive.'

'And easily persuaded.'

'By the wrong people.' Marion laughed. 'I am being unjust. One cannot expect the women depicted in books written so many years ago to behave as we do today.'

'And there I was hoping that you could be easily persuaded,' Druce said, with a smile and a mock sigh.

'To do what?'

'Have you read any of Miss Braddon's novels?' When Marion shook her head, he continued: 'So you are not familiar with *Lady Audley's Secret*, which was adapted for the stage. Same type and vintage as *East Lynne*.'

'Which was too melodramatic for me,' Marion said firmly. 'Give me a woman with spirit any day.'

'Lady Audley is a "woman with a past", although I do not think you are ready to play her yet.'

Marion glanced at him sharply. 'I was not aware that I was being considered to *play* anyone.'

'Ah well, that is what I was hoping I could persuade you to do. Only in an amateur capacity, of course,' he added hastily. 'A friend of mine – a barrister, mad keen on everything connected with the theatre – is planning a production of *Lady A.* and is looking for three ladies to take the female roles. Rest assured that the entire enterprise is utterly respectable.'

'But not respectable enough to permit your friend's sisters, or the sisters of his friends, to participate in this venture?'

'He does not have a sister but I take your point. Look,' and his eyes met hers candidly, 'he and his group want to put on a public performance – in a hall, not a commercial theatre – and sell tickets for admittance. Therefore they need support from ladies,' and he emphasised the word subtly, 'who can give a good account of themselves, who are of professional or semi-professional standard, not little girls who giggle over charades at a country-house weekend.'

Half of Marion was longing for the excitement, while the other half was filled with doom-laden fears for her reputation, and that was only part of the problem.

'It embarrasses me to raise the matter,' and she avoided

his eyes, 'but does this friend pay these ladies . . . ?'

'You would be paid for the performances, of which
there will be five, including a Saturday matinée, but not
for the rehearsals.'

'In that case I will not be able to do it.'

He heard the sigh in her voice. 'Why not?'

'I could not possibly tell my family what I was doing,
and I could not account for my absence from the house
without bringing home some wages.'

'I could lend you something to tide you over,' he said
diffidently. 'You could pay me back out of the performance fees, which, I assure you, will be generous.'

'I could not possibly take money from you!'

'Yes, you can. Marion,' and he took her hand in his, 'I
know what it is like to be short of money. When I first
went into the theatre, my people cut me off completely
and for a while I thought I'd starve! They have relented,
thank God, but I have not forgotten those days and I
think it is only right that I should help others as once
others helped me.'

He made it sound more a Christian duty than a sin,
but for a brief moment Marion felt that she was stepping
on to a very slippery slope and that she might not get off
it again. In the ensuing silence she allowed him to keep
hold of her hand, even though she knew that he might
read more into this gesture than she intended. It had
been obvious from the start that Edward Druce adored
her, but Marion was not sure how she felt about him.
He was excellent company, good-looking and charming, and at first he had appeared to be sophisticated,
very much a man of the world, but she had come to
realise that this impression was due merely to the fact
that he inhabited a very different world from hers. He
was not, she judged, more than a couple of years older

than herself and there were times when she felt vastly more mature and experienced. However, in matters concerning the theatre and their little entertainments, Edward remained the fount of all knowledge and – and here Marion admitted that this was why she was allowing him to tighten his grip on her hand – a useful source of additional work.

'I appreciate the delicacy of your position,' he said gently, placing his own interpretation on her silence. 'You are reluctant to borrow from me because I am a man and you are saying to yourself that, although I may have accepted money from other actors, I would only have taken it from a fellow. Well, you would be wrong. I overcame my pride and accepted loans from several women. Do not believe all you hear about professional actresses, Marion. Most of them are kind, generous *and* virtuous.'

'But . . .' prompted Marion, in a no-smoke-without-fire tone.

'There are a few girls whose reputations would not stand too close a scrutiny,' he admitted unhappily, 'but they tend to be those from the poorest backgrounds, with the smallest acting talent.'

'And with no one to lend them the rent money,' Marion murmured. Driving home after late-night engagements, she sometimes saw these girls standing under the lamps, lingering on street corners, and she was terrified by the narrowness of the gap between their station in life and hers, and by the ease with which she, or one of her sisters, might slip through that gap. It was a memory that heavily influenced her decision.

'I earned seven shillings and sixpence this afternoon, reading *Persuasion*, and therefore I should be extremely grateful if you could advance me a similar sum for each rehearsal of the play. How many rehearsals are there likely to be?'

'Not many.' Druce looked rather flustered. 'The play is to be staged the week after next.'

'The week after . . .' Marion stared at him in amazement. 'Is there something you aren't telling me?'

Druce admitted that the production had been planned for some time, but one of the ladies had dropped out at the last moment and his friend, Peter Frith-Tempest – more an acquaintance actually, a bit older than him, but they had been at the same school and their fathers knew each other – had approached him in the hope of finding a replacement.

'I understand perfectly.' But she would not allow pride to stand between her and the money she needed, or between her and the experience she now ardently desired. 'We must hope that my ability to act, and to memorise the lines at such short notice, are equal to the challenge.'

Arriving home, Marion found Frances leaning against the wall in the hallway, eyes closed, a smile softening her face. However, only minutes before, giving Imogen a piano lesson, Frances's mood and demeanour had been very different.

'Stop!' Frances covered her ears, wincing. 'Start again at the beginning and this time *concentrate*.'

Dutifully Imogen moved her fingers across the keyboard, but the resulting discord was no improvement on her previous attempt.

'I cannot bear it! The only explanation, and the only charitable excuse I can find, is that you are not trying. And when I think,' Frances went on through gritted teeth, 'of all the little girls who would be glad to have a competent teacher like me, I wonder what fate burdened me with an ungrateful, useless article like you.'

Frances was a highly talented musician, possessing a fine technique and a sureness of touch and, above all, instilled with a feeling for music that was quite out of the ordinary. In addition, she was blessed with a magnificent singing voice, a pure, strong soprano whose power surprised those hearing her for the first time and who were deceived by the slightness of her frame. Several years earlier, when the family had been briefly in funds, Frances had taken singing lessons from a professional teacher and had attended the Guildhall School of Music for twice-weekly sessions with a piano-master. So good was her progress, and so highly was her potential rated, that the master believed she had an excellent chance of winning a three-year scholarship to study music on the Continent. Then disaster, in the shape of the Zmyrna Railway, struck and wiped out the wherewithal to pay the tuition fees. Frances had never forgiven James Leigh for this blow. She did not say much, did not criticise him as openly as Marion, but she did not forget what might have been, and perhaps this repressed passion contributed to the fact that the normally inhibited Frances poured her heart into her music.

Had she been able to take up that music scholarship, a career as a concert pianist would have been a distinct possibility; and several times her singing teacher had insisted that she might achieve fame as a concert, or even operatic, soprano. But Frances had not the slightest wish to perform. No dreams of fame and fortune enlivened, or disturbed, her sleep. Frances resented the severance of her music studies because she wanted to excel, to learn everything there was to know, to be respected and then to pass on her knowledge and her love of music to others, for

Frances was the sister most likely to conform, the sister most typical of her time and generation.

'Doubtless this will come as a dire disappointment to you,' she told Imogen drily, standing up, 'but I have had as much of your violation of the piano as I can stand for one day. I have a headache and I should think that Mother has had a relapse. Stay there and keep quiet until Charley and Arabella have finished.'

In the tiny hall she took a deep breath, leaned against the wall and closed her eyes. She genuinely had a headache. The house was quiet, except for the slight drone of voices in the back parlour as Charley, who had taken over the task from Marion, conducted Arabella's daily elocution lesson, so it seemed that Fanny had not been unduly disturbed by Imogen's ham-fisted manipulation of the keys. Then, very softly, from the front room, stole the strains of the melody that Imogen had been practising; but now it was played to perfection, not with any great feeling, true, but with effortless technical accuracy. And that was the moment when Frances smiled. She could cope with a pupil's intransigence, it was the failure of her tuition that she found impossible to bear.

'Everything under control?' Marion asked gaily. 'How is Mother? Have you started preparing supper yet? I must tell you the funniest thing that happened . . .' Hardly pausing for breath, in a state of perpetual motion – hanging up her hat and coat, smoothing her hair, hurrying into the kitchen – Marion had a momentum that Frances felt powerless to resist.

Silently Frances followed, and listened to her sister's chatter. She watched as Marion reached up for the tea-caddy on the kitchen shelf and counted into it the seven shillings and sixpence she had received for her afternoon's work.

'Were you paid today?' Marion asked, inspecting the contents of the caddy with satisfaction before replacing it on the shelf. Frances nodded. 'How much?'

'Half a crown,' Frances muttered, feeling the modest contribution from her piano lessons belittled by Marion's largesse. 'But I could earn much more if I was not constantly tied to the house.'

'Of course you could, dear,' Marion said absently, her mind on *Lady Audley's Secret*.

'Someone has to look after Mother while . . .'

'I have been so fortunate, Frances. Mr Druce knows a girl who does similar work – reading, I mean – and she only receives three-and-six for each session. I must remind Charley to tell Uncle John again how grateful I am for the introduction to the Mellie.'

'Tell her now – she is in the back room giving your elocution lesson to Arabella instead of doing her own school work.'

'What has got into you?' demanded Marion, her sister's sharp tone penetrating at last. 'The sight of that caddy, half full, ought to cheer up even the worst pessimist. You must admit, Frances, that we are better off financially than we have ever been.'

The trouble was, Frances thought, as Marion left the room in order to speak to Charley, *she* was unhappier than she had ever been. The hairline crack that had opened in her relationship with her beloved sister on the night of that first soirée – because Frances above all had been hurt by those thoughtless remarks about the very amusing people and having so much fun – was widening imperceptibly, but steadily, day by day. Frances missed the rapport, the sense of mutual aims and achievements, the shared responsibilities that had bound them together to the exclusion of everyone else. Now she felt that strangers were experiencing a closer relationship with Marion than she was, and that Marion was enjoying a life full of experiences and fulfillment while she, Frances, was left with the drudgery.

'I suppose that you were with this Druce person after your reading engagement this afternoon,' she snapped when Marion returned, 'which is why you are so late.'

'And what if I was? He is a very valuable contact and brings me extra work. Why, only today he . . .'

'You do not need to explain, or excuse, yourself to me. I only hope that you know what you are doing, and that you are not allowing any improprieties to take place between you and this . . . this *person*.'

'Don't preach at me,' Marion exclaimed. 'I am the oldest and I will decide . . . Good heavens, *now* I understand! You're jealous! You are jealous because I have an admirer and you don't.'

'If I wanted an admirer, which I don't, I hope I could do a great deal better for myself than some person with no discernible means of support and nothing better to do than loiter on park benches every afternoon.'

Marion grimaced but decided that it was best if Frances remained in ignorance of Edward Druce's profession. 'There is more to it than that,' she said slowly. 'For a long time I have thought that you were not interested in my work and in the news and stories I bring home, but the truth is that you are jealous of where I go, and what I do and who I meet.'

'Don't be ridiculous.'

'You know the solution – come with me one night.'

'No, thank you.'

In her heart of hearts Marion had no wish to have Frances tagging along; she was afraid that her sister would not fit in with friends like Edward Druce and that

Frances's presence might cramp her own style. However, the supreme sacrifice must be made. 'I could mention your musical talents here and there, and see if there is a place for you in the programme.'

'Don't put yourself out on my account,' said Frances haughtily. 'Anyway I would not dream of standing up in front of a crowd of strangers and making a spectacle of myself.'

'Meaning that I do?'

The new edge in Marion's voice was unmistakable and the two sisters, who had never quarrelled seriously before, stared at each other in sudden consternation and stepped back from the brink.

'I'm sorry,' Frances apologised awkwardly. 'I am feeling rather tired, and I have a headache. Imogen . . .'

'You need a change,' suggested Marion. 'Why not go out one day while I stay at home?'

Frances thought quickly. 'I have been planning a little excursion and was hoping that you could hold the fort.'

'By all means,' Marion agreed magnanimously. 'Any time, any time at all. So, when?'

'Not this Saturday, but the Saturday after. All afternoon.'

'Ah. Now there is a slight problem there . . .' A very large problem, actually, in the form of *Lady Audley's Secret*.

'Go on, surprise me,' Frances said sarcastically.

'I have a little engagement, nothing out of the ordinary, of course, but I must maintain my reputation for reliability. And, it being Saturday, Charley will be going to Uncle John . . . Must it be that Saturday?'

'Yes,' said Frances firmly, because it had become a point of principle. 'I have arranged to visit my old singing teacher,' she lied, 'and it is the only time she is free.'

'In that case, certainly you must go,' Marion decided, 'and Charley shall go to Uncle John as usual. Unfortunately my engagement is a lengthy one – in fact, I shall be unusually busy all that week – but I will be as quick as I can. The twins are old enough to manage on their own for a few hours. Imogen can be perfectly sensible when she wants to be, and it isn't as if Mother needs much looking after.'

They exchanged a meaningful, and fearful, look. Fanny was fading away before their eyes but no one admitted it or talked about it. There seemed to be no rational explanation for her gentle decline; it was as if proof of Marion's strength and success had been the sign for which she had been waiting and, feeling that her girls would now be safe in those capable hands, she was gratefully loosening her already tenuous hold on life.

'You and I cannot always be here,' Marion reasoned, 'twenty-four hours a day, seven days a week, indefinitely.'

For Charley, that Saturday was a theatre day.

Impecuniosity prevented her from going to the theatre every week, but her duties at her uncle's printshop were another factor. Mostly she worked until early evening and returned home genuinely tired from her exertions. At the beginning she had packed parcels at the long workbench and delivered them to various addresses in the City and West End, using her peregrinations around London to familiarise herself with its famous landmarks, learning the location of its theatres, and the names of the actors and managers.

However, John Leigh did not leave her to this monotonous, and comparatively simple, task for long. Impressed by her willingness to work, the speed with which she picked up knowledge and the efficiency with which she carried out her duties, he promoted her to reading the proofs and personally taught her the marks used to indicate corrections. When Charley proved adept and reliable in this important area, he taught her book-keeping and she would pore happily over the ledgers for hours, fascinated by this insight into the business world and how it worked. Away from the atmosphere of her home, Charley gained in confidence as well as knowl-edge, and even her appearance improved because she took care to be neat and tidy, as befitted a representative of the company.

For many weeks she had refused payment for her ser-vices, reiterating that her contribution should be offset against the family's debt, but after a while John insisted that she accept a few shillings for her trouble, shillings that were occasionally taken home to Marion and occasionally pocketed for her own purposes.

Not that Charley had more than one purpose: her sole dream was, and remained, a visit to the theatre. Often she would think wistfully of attending an evening perfor-mance, which would widen her choice of entertainment, but she had been unable to evolve a plan. So her stolen pleasure in the afternoon had to suffice and she continued to frequent the pit – except at the Haymarket, where the Bancrofts had ripped out the pit seats and replaced them with plush stalls at ten shillings and sixpence, and where a shilling perch in the gallery was all Charley could afford.

Today being theatre day – and every now and again she reassured herself that her precious two shillings nestled at the bottom of her pocket – Charley danced down the street with light feet and a light heart because she was going to see *him* again. Charley had found a favourite, one among all the actors in London who fired her with a passion of which she had not known she was capable, a tall, dark and handsome hero whose classic profile was imprinted on her heart and whose deep voice sent a thrill of excitement shivering through her.

With all the raw and untried emotion of her sixteen-year-old heart, Charley was in love.

Invited to take another piece of cake, Frances's companion eagerly cut a second generous slice of the iced confection that Frances had brought for their tea, and ate it with swift, delicate movements of her remarkably beautiful hands. Frances had always admired those hands, fancying that her own rivalled them in shapeliness and grace, but certainly any physical resemblance between the two women ended there. Even the most fervent devotees of Miss Maria Scarlatti were prone to doubt the authenticity of her name, but everyone agreed that she looked the part, and that this assumed identity suited her to perfection. Her black hair was scraped back severely from its centre parting and twisted into a thick crown of plaits on top of her head. The dark eyes were small, bright buttons in the fleshy face and a shapeless black dress attempted to disguise the enormity of the bulk beneath. From within this ample form there emerged a voice of such power that it seemed to resonate in her very ribs, and when Maria was in full flow Frances's admiration was tinged with concern for the disturbance being caused to the other inhabitants of this modest dwelling.

'And now,' Maria announced when her plate and teacup were empty, 'you will allow me to judge the extent of the deterioration of your voice.'

Nervously Frances sat down at the piano. She had known that she would be subjected to this test and it was the main reason for her visit; she wanted the truth but knew that the truth could hurt. However, there was no going back and so, her long, sensitive fingers rippling lightly across the keys, she began Mendelssohn's 'On Wings of Song', gaining in confidence as she hit the high notes strong and true. When she had finished, Maria said nothing for such a long time that all Frances's fears resurfaced.

'How bad was it?' she asked anxiously.

'It was a miracle considering the lack of guidance and proper practice. Yours is a God-given talent, my child, which is being wasted, *tragically* wasted.'

Relief made Frances generous. 'It is not wasted entirely. I entertain my family and they appreciate it very much – most of the time, anyway.'

Miss Scarlatti dismissed such appreciation with a wave of her hand. 'I wish I could give you free lessons, but I regret that circumstances do not permit,' and another expressive gesture drew attention to the shabbiness of the room and its occupant, 'so we must devise another plan.'

'There is nothing to be done,' Frances said despondently. 'My family circumstances have not changed, so there is not the slightest hope of finding the fees.'

'And there is no hope of finding a rich husband?'

Frances smiled ruefully. 'Not a chance of any husband, let alone a rich one.'

'Why should that be? You are a most attractive young woman.'

If this meeting achieved nothing else, it was making Frances feel really good about herself. 'I never meet any men,' was her simple answer. 'You cannot begin to imagine what my life is like, Maria, just how restricting, how dull every day.'

'Then change it.'

Frances shook her head vehemently. 'I cannot leave my

mother. Even getting away today was more difficult than you could believe!'

'One cannot argue against a girl's duty to her mother. But,' and Maria paused, 'one can amuse oneself, and dream a little, by thinking what one would do if the opportunity presented itself. So, Frances, of what do you dream – the concert platform or the opera house, perhaps?'

'Heavens, no, don't you start! I have enough trouble convincing Marion that I am a teacher, not a performer, by nature and that the idea of standing on a stage gives me nightmares!'

'Yet it was my reputation as a serious concert singer that brought the pupils, and their fees, to my door when I began to teach,' Maria pointed out. 'Some professional background and qualifications are needed to teach at this level, and I do not need to tell you that my spiritual and financial rewards are far greater than those of the drudges who take in run-of-the-mill pupils with no interest and even less aptitude.'

'I am one of those drudges, but my only alternative is a position as governess to a family who have musical daughters.'

'But that is still not the stuff of dreams! Come, let your imagination fly!'

'A school of my own,' Frances said slowly, 'in a lovely old house with vast rooms overlooking gardens, and enough space for all of us to live there and take in a few boarding pupils as well as day girls. Marion could teach English, history and the Bible, and Charley could do the mathematics classes and other odds and ends, while I took care of the music and singing and dancing, with a really good piano. And perhaps you could be persuaded to teach Italian!'

'I can think of a better dream than that, *cara*. Imagine that house, with its well-dimensioned rooms and beautiful gardens, and populate it not with pupils but with that rich husband and a family.'

'And there is a music room,' Frances sighed dreamily, 'where I sit in the evenings, gowned in silks and velvets, entertaining my husband's friends and neighbours to an impromptu recital.'

'So you do not object to performing on a domestic stage?'

'Of course not, such a recital would be in perfectly good taste. I would be known throughout the length and breadth of the county, people would flock to my drawing room and vie for my attendance at theirs, the gifted and beautiful Mrs . . .' Stuck for a name, Frances's voice trailed away, the smile fading from her face and the light dying in her eyes. 'I don't think that I like these dreams, Maria. It is so cruel when one has to wake up.'

'At least you now know what it is you really want.'

'Not a lot of help when it is so far out of reach. Let's face it, Maria, my best hope is to be a governess.'

'Maybe, maybe not, but remember that the least you should expect is the dignity of making your own decisions. Your loyalty to your mother is admirable but do not permit yourself to be persuaded that such loyalty extends to all your family.'

This warning was still ringing in her ears when Frances rounded the corner and came within sight of the house. A carriage was standing in the street, and surely it was the doctor's brougham, and surely it was standing right outside . . . Frances picked up her skirts and began to run.

'Reggie and I have known Peter Frith-Tempest since he was so high, haven't we, Reggie?'

'He is my godson,' Lord Melton reminded her.

'Is he? Well, if you say so – between us we've so many sons and daughters, nieces and nephews, godchildren and general hangers-on that I tend to lose track. Anyway, Miss Leigh, with all the proceeds of Peter's little play going to charity, we had to come along and do our bit. *Such* a worthy cause.'

As she talked Lady Melton was surveying her fellow play-goers with the bewildered, faintly baffled, look of someone who rarely mixed with 'ordinary' people *en masse* and never ceased to be amazed that they should exist at all. It was with visible relief that she caught sight of an acquaintance and hurried away with almost indecorous haste.

However, her husband, a big, ruddy-cheeked man of about fifty, with thinning grey hair, was in no hurry to leave Marion's side, and indeed the moment his wife's back was turned his behaviour changed markedly. Moving a step closer, he stared at Marion intently, his smile and his eyes expressing open admiration.

'Quite a crowd this afternoon,' he remarked affably. 'Has the play been doing good business every day?'

'The hall has been full all week. Mr Frith-Tempest and his friends must have worked very hard to sell the tickets.'

'Nonsense, everyone's come to see you. Particularly the men.'

Marion flushed and lowered her eyes, unaware that the sweep of her dark lashes against her magnolia skin created an effect of demure innocence that was an irresistible challenge to a man of Melton's mettle.

'They certainly didn't come to see the play,' he continued. 'Damn silly piece, and I told Peter so. And that part he gave you did not do you justice.'

'You are very kind, but I am afraid that I am vastly inexperienced as an actress and . . .'

'Inexperience is nothing to be ashamed of,' and his voice dropped to a murmur, 'as it allows some lucky man to teach you the hows and whys and wherefores, as it were . . . of the role, of course.'

Of the role, my foot, thought Marion furiously, being in no doubt about the performance that Lord Melton would like her to give. Hemmed into this corner with him, literally and metaphorically, her every instinct was to brush past him and walk away, but Lady Melton was her patron and she could not afford to alienate such a valuable source of custom and contacts. She was still wearing her costume from the last act of the play and was thankful that the dress was not immodest.

'I ought to be going home,' she said desperately. 'I am expected . . . my mother . . .'

'And that dress doesn't suit you,' Lord Melton went on, evidently pursuing some private line of thought. 'Like to see a bit of flesh meself, but I will say that you were a stunner in that riding habit.'

Yes, Marion had adored the ravishing blue habit with its jaunty feathered hat and she had handed it back to its rightful owner with infinite regret. Needless to say, the dress she was wearing now was her own. But she was amazed that this man dared to speak to her in this way and could only presume that men felt licensed to overstep the mark with actresses.

'You ought to go on the stage professionally,' his lordship drawled. 'You're good enough, you know, as well as being so awesomely decorative.'

Somehow Marion forced a smile. 'Thank you for the compliment, but my father would never allow me even to consider the idea.'

'You have a father?' His heavy eyebrows rose in what seemed to be genuine astonishment.

Biting back a caustic rejoinder of a Biblical nature, because she could see no way of avoiding the word 'virgin', Marion indicated that indeed she was the fortunate possessor of a male parent. 'He has been away, but we expect him home any day now,' she lied.

'Does his return mean that Lady Melton and I will lose our favourite performer?'

'I am unlikely to step on a stage again,' Marion prevaricated.

'You have ruined what was a highly successful and enjoyable occasion,' complained Peter Frith-Tempest, overhearing the last interchange as he joined them. 'Miss Leigh cannot desert us now, can she, Uncle Reggie? We have only just discovered her.'

'Your Aunt Barbara positively relies on her.'

'I am sure that I could continue my association with *Lady* Melton,' Marion emphasised.

'Talking of whom, sir, she has been trying to attract your attention for some time,' Peter remarked cheerfully, 'and is beginning to show signs of losing patience.'

Lord Melton glanced guiltily over his shoulder, his florid face turning a deeper shade of purple as he caught his wife's eye, and he moved to her side with a swiftness remarkable in someone of his bulk.

'Poor old Uncle Reggie is in for an ear-bashing but I am sure it was worth it.' Peter Frith-Tempest, sandy-haired and of medium height, with an impeccable upper-class accent, smiled disarmingly at Marion. 'Aunt Babs is a charmer, but I freely confess that I would prefer your company to hers any day.'

'Believe me, Mr Frith-Tempest, I was not trying to detain Lord Melton. Quite the contrary.'

'Like that, was it?' He glanced at the big, broad figure of his godfather with renewed interest. 'Didn't think he had it in him. Ah, correction – didn't think Aunt Babs would *allow* him to have it in him. Keeps him on a pretty tight rein.'

'It cannot be too tight for my liking,' Marion said, with considerable feeling, but then she laid an anxious hand on his arm. 'I'm sorry . . . Lord Melton was very kind and I am sure that he did not intend . . .'

'I bet he did intend. Don't worry,' and he patted her hand reassuringly. 'I am the soul of discretion. Look, Mr Leigh won't really come the heavy father, will he? Because I . . . we . . . all of us . . . are terribly keen to work with you again.'

'Lord Melton was suggesting that I should become a professional actress and I was merely trying to indicate the impossibility of such an idea.'

Frith-Tempest frowned, as a very ugly reason for his godfather's proposition crossed his mind. 'You have all the prerequisites for a highly successful career, Miss Leigh, but of course I agree that such a step is out of the question. However, might we not tempt you back into the theatre in an amateur capacity?'

'Are you planning a new production?'

'*Lady Audley* has been a tremendous success and it was only intended as a trial run. What we . . . Do have another glass of wine while we talk.' He plucked a glass from a tray carried by a passing waiter and offered it to her.

Marion hesitated. 'I am late as it is, but . . . Oh well, just one little glass.'

Here was an admirer who would be the envy of Frances, who would be the envy of virtually anyone, she thought a trifle smugly. Perhaps he was not quite as handsome as Edward Druce, but Peter Frith-Tempest was more mature and, being a barrister, infinitely more respectable. Growing accustomed to male admiration, and becoming more adroit at handling it, Marion was also aware that her addiction to this new strata of society made her reluctant to leave a gathering such as this. To exchange such company, and the attention she received here, for the dull routine and lack of appreciation at home was becoming increasingly difficult.

'What we want to do,' Peter continued, 'is take a theatre, preferably in the West End. Either we will use one that specialises in amateur productions or wait for one to close for the summer break.'

'But society people leave town when the Season ends,' Marion objected. 'I assume that is why big managements tour the provinces in the autumn.'

'We do not need to rely on socialites,' Peter asserted confidently. 'A couple of years ago Irving did not tour, but opened an autumn season in September.'

'So we can do the same,' Marion said drily. 'In fact, anything Mr Irving can do, we can do better.'

'Not exactly,' and he smiled at her gentle sarcasm. 'But if we keep prices down, we can attract the people who would like to go to the theatre but cannot afford to do so. And the railways are bringing in middle-class people from the suburbs, and even further afield than that, just for an evening's entertainment.'

'Am I good enough,' she said seriously, 'for a real theatre? There were times, particularly in rehearsal, when I felt so dreadfully stiff and awkward, and I simply didn't know what to do with my hands, how to stand, how to move. Come on, admit it. I was the most appalling stick.'

'But you learned so quickly.'

And she liked him for that, for not immediately denying her early woodenness but assuring her that she had overcome it.

'And then I dried,' she persisted. 'Last night. It was the

most embarrassing moment of my entire life.'

'Apart from that one mistake, you were word-perfect and that was a blooming miracle, considering how late in the day you were introduced to our venture.'

'Which play have you chosen for your next production?'

'The decision rather depends on you. Yes, I'm serious. If you will participate, we will select a piece that suits you.'

'The reason I ask is that I was not completely happy with Alicia. Such a passive, whining sort of girl. When I had to utter the immortal words: "Robert! Robert! my father is dead. Oh, pity me! pity and protect me!" frankly, I did not know how to keep a straight face.'

'You would have preferred to play Lady Audley?'

'She is somewhat extreme – a bigamist *and* a murderess – yet there is a spirit in her that makes her not only more interesting to play but more attractive to the audience. Be honest, given the choice between spending an hour with Alicia and an hour with Lady Audley, who would you choose?'

He smiled and shrugged. 'If you put it that way . . .'

'I do. I am reminded most strongly of the works of Wilkie Collins. In *The Woman in White* the heroine is a feeble creature called Laura Fairlie, who drifts helplessly from one disaster to the next, completely dependent on others to rescue her from her latest plight. In fact, the real heroine is the stout-hearted and courageous Marian Halcombe, who fights back.'

'I am familiar with the work and agree that it is sensational stuff. I also confess that I would much prefer to spend an hour with Marian Halcombe, despite her professed lack of good looks, than linger in the decorative but drooping presence of Laura Fairlie.'

'There you are then,' Marion said robustly, downing

the last drops of wine. She swayed slightly. 'I mention it because there is a slight resemblance between *The Woman in White* and *Lady A.*, in that both works deal with a substitution of identities. However, I also mention it because I think I would prefer to play a heroine with the merest, just the slightest, dash of wickedness about her.'

'We intend to do the thing properly this time. We will pay you for the rehearsals, just as if you were a professional.'

Marion smiled and did not share the information, acquired from Edward Druce, that not all professional managements paid their actors for rehearsals.

Being so late, she took a cab all the way home, suddenly remembering the lip-rouge applied for the performance and scrubbing at her mouth with a handkerchief. She was, she had to admit, ever so slightly squiffy.

Imogen opened the front door. 'You are only just in time,' she said reproachfully.

'She's asleep.'

'I know that, silly. I should think the whole street can hear her.' As soon as the twins were left on their own, Imogen had tiptoed into her mother's room and peered cautiously at the invalid. Fanny's snoring was stentorian, but the girls were unsure whether or not this was a normal manifestation of their mother's afternoon nap. The volume was such that they suspected it was not normal, but they were so relieved she was asleep that they tiptoed out again.

On the landing they looked at each other, and then looked at all the doors and the staircases leading up to the attic and down to the hall, considering the various options open to them. Stealthily, still half-expecting to be challenged, Imogen pushed open the door to the room shared by Marion and Frances. Idly the two girls picked over the possessions strewn on the dressing-table, meticulously replacing each item exactly as they found it, before opening the wardrobe and examining the silk dresses that Marion wore for her evening engagements.

'You try the green and I'll have the blue,' Imogen decided, thrusting billows of emerald silk into Arabella's arms.

Raven-haired Imogen had inherited the same colouring as her mother and eldest sisters, but beauty had passed her by. Her strong, square little face with its heavy dark eyebrows showed determination, even pugnacity, but it was unremittingly plain and, according to Marion, one just had to hope that the child would improve with age. But Arabella . . . Arabella was the changeling of the family, the thick heavy waves of bright hair forming a sheet of gold across her back. She was only twelve years old but already her beauty seemed fully formed, her exquisite face dominated by immense sapphire eyes fringed by long, dark lashes and framed by the high arch of her brows. The wide curve of the mouth was usually closed because Arabella said little, allowing Imogen to speak for them both, and now – as always – she gazed at herself in the mirror expressionlessly, apparently without vanity. If one wanted to carp, one could find fault in the slight plumpness of her young cheeks, but when the lines and planes of her face were sculpted, Arabella's beauty would be devastating.

This was the reason for Marion's insistence on a strict regime of music lessons and instruction in elocution, deportment and etiquette after the twins had finished their schoolwork. Marion was determined that Arabella would be a perfect lady and a bride fit for a prince. She would walk, dance and speak like a duchess, sing like a diva and be able to converse in a cultivated fashion. For Marion nothing was too much trouble, no sacrifice too great, for the securing of Arabella's golden future.

Of course the other twin had to be included, even though it was a waste of everyone's time and effort, and unfortunately the highly intelligent Imogen understood the position perfectly, which was why she deliberately made life difficult for her tutors. However, what Imogen really resented was the way that, in her view, Marion tried to control, to own, Arabella. No one seemed to realise that Arabella belonged to her, Imogen, and to no one else, and that she never would belong to anyone else.

With handkerchiefs and scarves stuffed into their bodices, creating impressive *embonpoint*, the twins next proved adept with brush and pins and soon two replicas of Marion's upswept chignon were gleaming on two tiny heads. Trying not to trip over the long skirts, they paraded solemnly up and down the landing, in and out of the bedrooms, and even dared attempt a few dance steps. A shaft of sunlight pierced Arabella in mid-pirouette, transforming a precocious little girl dressed up in her sister's clothes into a mysterious sea nymph, with a pale, pale skin and golden hair, and eyes that took on a tinge of turquoise.

After changing back into their own clothes, they prepared their mother's tea tray in the kitchen as Marion had shown them and carried it upstairs. The snoring had stopped, but Fanny did not move or acknowledge their presence so, after placing the tray on the bedside table, the twins stood by the bed and stared down at her. She was half-sitting in the bed, supported by pillows, her head tilted back. The black hair was streaked with grey but her face, white as marble, was strangely unlined and youthful.

Imogen leaned forward and listened to the shallow, irregular breathing.

'We might as well let her sleep a little longer,' she decided. 'Sleep is good for invalids, isn't it? Let's take a quick look at Charley's room and then wake Mother before the tea goes cold.'

But at the top of the stairs the adjacent attic room looked more inviting than Charley's, and they ventured in among the boxes, trunks and portmanteaux. Ignoring the items with which they were familiar, such as Fanny's diminished collection of gowns, they searched for something new to interest them, until eventually Imogen unearthed a dusty chest hidden under a pile of junk in the corner. Eagerly Arabella helped to clear a space round it and to heave up the lid, but as soon as she saw the contents she shrank back, her expression a mixture of fear and disgust.

'There's nothing that'll bite you,' Imogen said reassuringly, placing an arm around Arabella's shoulders and giving her sister a comforting squeeze. 'These are only Father's *things* – they cannot hurt you. I expect Marion threw all this stuff in here the moment his back was turned – out of sight, out of mind. She and Frances hate him nearly as much as we do.'

'But for different reasons.'

'Yes.'

They were silent for a moment, sharing their thoughts as well as their embrace.

'Perhaps he won't come back at all, ever,' Imogen suggested bracingly.

'Not even Father can have failed this time. *Everyone* makes money on the diamond fields.'

'Not everyone. It stands to reason that some people do not find diamonds, because otherwise there would not be enough to go round.' Imogen's logic seemed irrefutable. 'Besides, he left it too late. He only went to the Cape after hearing the success stories.'

'Long after,' Arabella agreed and then she smiled. 'I heard Marion say that Father could buy shares in the Royal Mint and still lose money.' She mimicked Marion so perfectly that an outsider would have found it uncanny, but Imogen was accustomed to this talent of Arabella's and merely grinned at the sentiment expressed, glad that her twin was feeling better.

They went back to an examination of the contents of the trunk.

'He must have brought back this necklace from one of his journeys.' Arabella held up a rope of brightly coloured beads. 'Do you suppose it might be valuable?'

'Marion would have pawned it if it was. There isn't anything interesting, it's mostly old clothes and, ugh, they smell of *him*, and of whisky and tobacco . . .'

'And these papers refer to his old schemes,' said Arabella, throwing sheaves of letters and share certificates on the floor, 'but here is some more jewellery. I wonder where this came from?'

Imogen inspected the bracelet thoughtfully. 'Mexico?' she hazarded, 'and perhaps this did, too.' She picked up an ornately tooled leather belt, nearly long enough to wrap round her waist twice. Then, with a sudden exclamation, she dropped the belt and reached into the chest to retrieve an object from the very bottom.

Arabella was examining a fan with a mother-of-pearl handle and parchment painted with wreaths of flowers and charming figures in eighteenth-century costume.

'That's pretty,' said Imogen. 'You ought to keep it. And I shall keep *this*.' Under Arabella's startled nose, she brandished her treasure – a dagger with a wickedly curved blade. 'Isn't it the most beautiful thing you ever saw? It goes with the belt – see, the knife goes into this leather pouch, which slides on to the belt, like so. But look at the carving on the handle and at the pattern on the blade!'

'I don't want to keep anything that reminds me of him.'

'How can a fan remind you of Father?' scoffed Imogen. 'And if we have another opportunity to dress up, it could be very useful.'

'Which is more than can be said for that horrid knife.'

'It's mine,' Imogen said defensively. 'I found it and I am going to keep it.'

They repacked the chest and were replacing any items they had disturbed in the attic when suddenly they heard a loud crash. They froze and looked at each other. The noise had come from below, but from exactly where they could not tell.

'I'll go,' hissed Imogen. 'You bring the treasure trove and hide it in our secret place.'

On the first-floor landing Imogen leaned over the banister and listened. The house was quiet, which meant that neither Marion nor Frances had returned, which in turn meant that . . . Heart thumping, Imogen peered into Fanny's room and let out a muffled shriek.

Fanny had slumped sideways so that she was half in, half out, of bed. She had knocked the tea tray to the floor and, evidently unconscious, was struggling for breath.

Imogen ran to her room, where Arabella was pushing their trophies into a drawer beneath piles of petticoats. 'I'm going for the doctor. No, don't go in there,' and she propelled Arabella past their mother's door and down the stairs. 'Don't do anything. Just wait in the kitchen until I get back.'

Arabella waited for what seemed an eternity, sitting on the kitchen chair, arms wrapped round her body, gripping herself so tightly that her knuckles were white and her fingers left red weals on her pale flesh. No sound came from upstairs and she started with fright when she heard the knock at the door.

The doctor and Imogen found Fanny lying in the same position, her breathing hoarse and laboured, her pulse weak. An unpleasant stench overpowered the room and, under the doctor's supervision, Imogen changed the sheets, washed her mother and dressed her in a clean nightgown.

This was the scene that greeted Frances – the doctor sitting by Fanny's side, feeling the faint flicker of her pulse; Imogen gathering up an armful of stained, foul-smelling linen.

'I should have been here,' Marion whispered when she came home, and closed the deep blue eyes for the last time. 'I will never forgive myself for not being here.'

Charley was hurrying home but felt that she was floating, such was her state of euphoria. *He* had been more wonderful than ever before in this play called *Progress*.

He had portrayed an older man and had whitened the wings of hair at his temples, but he was still by far the most handsome man on the stage and how that silly chit, Eva, could have preferred that young nincompoop to him beggared belief. Mind you, how he could have been attracted to Eva was equally inexplicable, for she was such a weak, vacuous creature with nothing to recommend her, and not nearly as pretty as Marion or Arabella. But he had been so noble in his treatment of her, when he relinquished his own hopes and put her happiness first . . .

Charley sighed and paused in her headlong rush for home as she pulled a card out of her pocket. She had succumbed to temptation, something that was becoming a habit and for which she had a decided aptitude, and had expended a valuable sixpence on a photograph of her hero.

As her sisters maintained a vigil by their mother's death-bed, Charley gazed adoringly at the lean, classically beautiful profile of Vere Cavendish.

Chapter Four

The day after Fanny's funeral, the sisters gathered round the table in the back parlour in order to discuss the outcome of Marion's interview with the solicitor.

'The position is precisely as I feared,' Marion began. 'Mother's income died with her. We will not receive one more penny from her aunt's estate.'

The girls looked at each other and shifted uneasily in their seats. The regular payments, received quarterly in advance, had not been much, but how were they to manage without them?

'We received the last quarter's allowance only a month ago,' Frances said suddenly. 'Must we pay back the money covering the time between Mother's death and the end of the quarter?'

Marion shook her head. 'No, he said that would not be necessary. Which is,' and she sighed, 'something to be grateful for, I suppose.'

'Who receives the money now?'

'Mother's relatives. The solicitor was not specific.'

'Whoever it is, I guarantee they do not need the money as much as we do,' Frances said bitterly.

'Talking like that doesn't get anyone anywhere,'

Marion said firmly. 'We must make plans for the future and stop crying over the past. As you know, I cabled Father last week but until he returns, and we must remember that the Cape is a long way away, we have to survive somehow and that means increasing our earning capacity.'

'What do you mean "until he returns"?' Frances asked sarcastically. 'You cannot seriously imagine that our finances will improve the instant Father walks through the door. Quite the contrary – we shall have one more mouth to feed, and a mouth that can eat as much as the rest of us put together, at that.'

Charley jumped to her feet. 'You are being beastly and unfair,' she accused. 'I bet he makes you eat your words. I bet he walks in absolutely dripping with diamonds and I hope he doesn't give any to you! In fact, I'll make sure that he doesn't because I will tell him . . .'

'Sit down, Charley, and shut up,' Marion ordered. 'I was about to say, and your outburst has only served to emphasise the relevance of this, that the most important thing is for the family to stick together. We must help each other as much as possible and, if the necessity arises, make sacrifices for each other.'

Under the table Imogen's foot found Arabella's and nudged it. Then she made a retching noise, as if she was going to be sick, but skilfully camouflaged it into a cough.

Marion glanced at her sharply but decided to let it pass. 'Mother would want me to keep the family together in this house until Father comes home and assumes responsibility for us. Therefore, our first priority is raising the money to keep this roof over our heads and food on the table.'

'Guess who will be sent to the pawnshop,' Charley muttered *sotto voce*.

'Fortunately my recent earnings enabled us to redeem all our pledges at the pawnbroker's so we can take them back again,' and with a dramatic gesture Marion unfastened the pearl necklace that she wore and laid it on the table, 'starting with Mother's pearls. Frances, you will collect the other things together and Charley will take them to the shop tomorrow.'

'Surprise, surprise,' Charley said, louder this time, and received glares from her two elder sisters.

'Unity, Charley, unity,' Marion reproved. 'Instead of making snide remarks, you should be thinking of ways in which you can make a larger contribution.'

'At the funeral Uncle John said that he would pay me more,' and Charley bit her lip. Uncle John's offer was generous but it meant that she would have to work all day every Saturday. It meant no more visits to the theatre.

'Good, we are getting off to an excellent start.' Marion assumed a tone and a manner full of false heartiness, and turned her attention to Frances. 'Now that you are able to leave the house more frequently, can you find additional pupils?'

'I will try, but I wondered if you could inquire among your rich friends for any opportunities.'

'Do I take it that you have had second thoughts about giving public performances?'

'Certainly not! Naturally I meant teaching opportunities.'

'I can ask, I suppose,' Marion agreed dubiously, 'although anyone with young daughters already employs the very best music masters.'

'The sacrifice of your time and effort will be much appreciated,' Frances said sweetly.

'So, as I expected, it looks as if I will be the chief wage-earner. Fortunately . . .'

'What about us?' Imogen interjected. 'Don't Arabella and me get to help?'

'You will be at school.'

'But,' and again Imogen kicked Arabella under the table as she fixed serious blue eyes on Marion, 'we thought that we could run errands for people . . .'

'. . . or work in a shop,' contributed Arabella.

'. . . or take in washing,' Imogen continued.

'Take in washing! Have you gone mad?' The colour rose in Marion's face, but then she saw the suppressed giggles that were shaking the shoulders of the twins. 'Very funny, Imogen, although I would have appreciated your support rather than an example of your warped sense of humour. As I was about to say, fortunately I have a very full diary and there is some new work in the offing, which . . . which I may discuss with Frances later on.'

Frances glanced at her inquiringly but hers was not the only curiosity to be aroused. Charley, too, sensed something unusual in Marion's tone and manner and was sufficiently interested to take steps to find out what it was. Knowing from experience that Marion always waited until bedtime for such important conversations, Charley did what she always did when she wanted to know the truth about various goings-on: she crept down her attic stair and sat on the lower steps in the darkness, only inches from the bedroom door that Marion habitually left open, in case her mother or the twins called for her in the night.

'I wondered how long it would take you to get round to telling me just exactly what is going on,' Frances was saying.

'Nothing is *going on*, as you put it.' Marion, hanging her dress in the wardrobe, averted her face.

'You were not reading to a client the day Mother died. You came home after dark and there was the smell of drink on your breath.'

'I had one glass of wine, for heaven's sake. Good Lord, not much gets past you, does it!'

'With a father like ours, I have had plenty of practice.'

'Kindly do not place me in the same category as Father. So maybe I did have a drink, but I *had* been working.' Marion sat down at the dressing-table. 'If you really want to know,' she said off-handedly, 'I had been acting in a little play – for charity, of course. There were five performances, which was why I was so busy that week, and it was such a success that they want me to do it again.' Marion took a deep breath. 'In a theatre.'

'*Theatre!*'

Frances's shriek was so piercing that Charley was sure she could have heard it upstairs in her room. She nearly shrieked herself, with the excitement and the unbelievable revelation that there must be more to Marion than met the eye.

'You wouldn't . . . you *couldn't* . . . not in a theatre!'

'I fail to see what the fuss is about. The previous production was very genteel and respectable, in aid of a charity – of which Lord Melton is patron – and I see no reason why the next production should not be equally acceptable.'

'Rubbish – you see every reason, which is why you kept quiet about it for so long. You seem to have taken leave of your senses, Marion, but surely you have a grain of intelligence left with which to see that acting in a theatre is a very different matter from mouthing poetry in Lady Melton's drawing room.'

'I do not see why,' Marion maintained obstinately.

'You will have to act better than that if you decide to go

through with this preposterous scheme, because I can see that you are lying. You know very well why. You know as well as I do that the theatre is an immoral place, and that actresses are no better than . . . than . . .'

'Say it, Frances. No better than prostitutes is what you mean, isn't it! Are you really so naive as to believe that because a girl plays the part of a woman who deceives her husband in the play, she must be a harlot off the stage?'

'Not as naive as you, because apparently you believe that you can retain your good name and reputation even when lending yourself to such doubtful undertakings, and when mixing with illiterate, ill-bred and light associates.'

'You have been reading *Pendennis* again,' Marion snapped. 'As it happens, I am mixing with barristers and diplomats, all of whom treat me with the utmost respect.'

'But not enough respect to invite you into their drawing room as a guest,' Frances said shrewdly. 'Only the sort of attention that they show to actresses, when they hang around stage doors looking for pretty girls to seduce.'

'No one is trying to seduce me,' Marion shouted, 'and if they did try they would not succeed. All they are doing is encouraging a talent of mine and, incidentally, paying me very well. I hate to remind you, Frances, up there on your fluffy little cloud of righteousness, that down here in the real world we happen to need that money and need it rather badly. And don't tell me that you would rather starve than take tainted money earned in the theatre, because let me assure you that you wouldn't, and you certainly would not like to lose this roof over your head.'

'Very well, go ahead and act in your theatre but don't come running to me when things go wrong. To think of you, displaying your person on a stage, in front of a crowd of leering men . . .' and Frances buried her head in a pillow to hide the hot, angry tears that started to flow down her face.

'I'm sorry, please don't cry.' Marion patted her sister's resistant shoulders. 'I must go through with this, Fran, really I must. I promised, and we do need the money so desperately, but I tell you what I'll do – I will make sure that I play a sympathetic part, a young woman of impeccable character, if that will make you feel better,' and Marion sighed for the spirited, dramatic heroine she really longed to play. 'I will compromise with you that far, but I cannot give up . . .'

Charley did not hear any more. Her head reeling, and resisting the urge to cheer Marion on, at first she assumed she was mistaken when she thought she heard a noise downstairs. But, no, there it was again. It sounded like the front door opening. Charley tiptoed across the landing and peered over the banisters into the darkness below. A candle flame flared into life, making Charley's throat go dry, but then she saw a man's face illumined in the tiny pool of flickering light and she let out the most almighty yell.

'*Father!* At last, at last . . .' and she hurled herself down the stairs and into his arms, nearly setting her nightgown on fire as James Leigh hastily set down the candle on the hall table.

'Charley, my boy, is that you? Good Lord, you've grown into a big chap. Let go, there's a good fellow, you're strangling me.'

As Charley reluctantly disengaged herself, James looked up the stairs to where two points of light burned against a background of white nightgowns, revealing the blurred, startled faces of Marion and Frances.

'Come down, you two,' he said impatiently, 'and bring the twins, but don't disturb your mother.' Suddenly he seemed to recollect that the front door was still open. 'There's a cab outside – fetch me five bob, Charley.'

Grabbing the candle, Charley hurried into the kitchen, took five shillings from the tin and watched her father hurry into the street and come back into the house carrying a carpet-bag.

'I don't suppose there's a decent drink in the house, Marion?' he said, dumping the bag in the hall and closing the door. 'I'm parched.'

'We have a little brandy, for medicinal purposes, but I will try to rouse the kitchen fire and boil a kettle for tea.' Marion was still staring at him as if she had seen a ghost.

'The brandy will do, and don't look at me like that, it's most unsettlin'.'

'I am sorry, Father, but I do not see how you could have got here so soon. I only cabled you last week.'

'Cable? What cable?' In the back parlour he took the brandy bottle that Frances had fetched from the kitchen and poured himself a generous tot, tossing it back in a single gulp as Charley lit the lamps. 'Where are the twins? Don't they want to welcome home their father?'

'Here we are.' Imogen, in a long white nightgown like her sisters, was standing in the doorway, her arm protectively around Arabella whom she had wrapped in an eiderdown.

'What took you so long?'

'We came as quickly as we could.'

The two girls were hanging back and James looked at them irritably as he sat down. 'Come in, come in, what's the matter with you girls tonight? There's only Charley who knows how to welcome home the wanderer. It is customary to kiss your father and tell him how pleased you are to see him.'

Imogen advanced slowly towards him, brushed his cheek with her lips and said dutifully: 'We are very pleased to see you.'

'We? *We?* Cannot Arabella speak for herself? Hasn't she a tongue in her head?' He stretched out a hand towards Arabella, half-beckoning, half-entreating her to come closer.

Obeying with obvious reluctance, and hampered by the voluminous folds of the eiderdown, Arabella inched across the room and pecked him on the cheek. She tried to pull away immediately but James kept hold of her hand, his gaze never leaving her face.

'Even though there isn't a tongue in your head, it is such a pretty head that we will have to forgive you,' he said teasingly, 'and as the youngest you shall have pride of place – you can sit on my lap.'

But Arabella slipped out of his grasp, leaving him holding the eiderdown, and ran to Imogen.

'We are much too old to be treated as children,' Imogen said belligerently, 'and we do not sit on men's laps.'

James stared at her, utterly taken aback, but after a moment he threw back his head and roared with laughter as he emptied the contents of the brandy bottle into his glass.

'You must have left the diamond fields weeks ago,' Marion said quietly, 'so you never received my cable. You do not know that Mother is dead.'

Suddenly grave and attentive, he listened as Marion recounted the events of the past few days and then shielded his eyes with his hand in a grief-stricken gesture.

'Fanny,' he murmured quietly but audibly, 'my dearest Fanny.'

Four pairs of blue eyes regarded him distrustfully and cynically; only Charley was convinced of the sincerity of his grief and knelt beside him, leaning her head against his shoulder. His profile was nearly as handsome as that of Vere Cavendish, she thought, his face so lean and bronzed, the deep russet hair streaked becomingly with white at the temples.

'Leave me now,' he said, his voice choked with tears. 'We will talk in the morning.'

He slept late the next day and when he did come downstairs his demeanour was that of a grave and sober widower.

'I should be most grateful, Marion, my dear, if you would remove your mother's clothes and other possessions from the bedroom. I find the sight of them intensely painful.'

'I will see to it at once.' Marion had left her mother's room exactly as it was, almost like a shrine, but now she loathed to think of it being defiled by his presence, let alone by his touch.

'Except the silver-backed brushes, and the mirror and comb that make up the set,' he decided. 'I do not believe I could bear to part with those.'

'They were going to the pawnshop today,' Frances informed him bluntly.

A look of surprise, followed by a brief frown of concern, flashed across his face but in an instant he was himself again, giving Frances an injured, even pathetic, look. 'Surely I am entitled to keep a small memento of a most beloved wife?'

'Of course, Father,' Marion replied, hoping against hope that he had forgotten about the pearls.

'Mind you, now that I come to think about it, your

mother's pearls were her pride and joy. Perhaps . . . but no,' and he smiled benevolently at Marion, 'you must have the pearls, Marion. Your dear mother would have wished it.'

Marion did not know what to believe, or how far she could trust him. In the past she had given him the obedience and respect due to a father from a dutiful daughter, but now she realised how much that conventional, unquestioning subservience had owed to her mother's existence in the house. Without Fanny, without the need constantly to protect and cherish that still, small calm presence, nothing stood between Marion and her father. Suddenly she felt strangely exposed and vulnerable as she stood on unfamiliar territory, facing the unexpected necessity of re-negotiating the relationship.

'I should be glad if someone could see to the heap of dirty linen I've turfed on to the bedroom floor, or I shall not have a shirt to my back,' he said and bestowed his most disarming smile on Charley when she eagerly offered to do his washing and ironing from now until eternity. 'And while on the subject of clothes, I hate to raise the thorny question of money, but I shall need a mourning suit, several shirts, some footwear and a few other odds and ends. You have a little put by, I'm sure, Marion, to tide me over?'

'Tide you over until when?'

'Until I have realised my assets . . . a parcel of diamonds . . .' and he was interrupted by a triumphant whoop of joy from Charley. 'Merely a matter of priorities, Marion. Obviously I need to be properly dressed before I pay a visit to Hatton Garden,' and he indicated his threadbare attire with an apologetic gesture of explanation.

'Can I see the diamonds now, Father? Please, I'm dying

to see them.' Charley tugged at his sleeve, fairly dancing up and down with impatience. 'Tell me where they are and I'll fetch them.'

'They are right here,' and to Charley's astonishment he pulled a handkerchief out of his pocket, untied it, and displayed a handful of dull, dirty pebbles.

Charley picked up one of the stones and turned it this way and that, holding it up to the light, her face a picture of confused puzzlement and disappointment. 'It's a joke,' she said uncertainly, 'isn't it? You have the real diamonds in your bag upstairs.'

'These are diamonds all right, but they are unpolished stones, which is why they look different from what you expect.'

'But I thought diamonds were white. These look yellow; a sort of brownish-yellow, actually.'

'Yes, well, the quality is not all I would wish.' James gathered up the stones swiftly and a touch defensively. 'But they are worth something, and they are all legit. Every single one from my own claim.'

'Are you seriously telling us that all you have to show for years of work is that pathetic heap of pebbles?' Marion shrieked.

'And my fare home. I paid my own way here, which is more than some fellows can say, I'll have you know!' James exclaimed indignantly. 'Some fellows had to walk all the way from the diamond fields to Cape Town, a distance of six hundred miles.'

'And then again some other fellows made a fortune.'

'It is the luck of the draw.' James spread his hands expansively and smiled confidently at his daughters. 'A diamond rush is a gamble. You cannot choose your claim in advance, it all happens in the heat, noise and dirt of the moment. The centre of a Kimberley diamond mine is richer in good stones than outlying claims, and so there are winners and losers.'

'Let me guess – you were a loser,' said Marion, 'and therefore you sold your claim to a newcomer who did not know any better.'

James looked at her sharply, surprised by her acumen. 'You are not far wrong,' he admitted, 'but by then things were looking bad for the small digger, and the share market was looking distinctly iffy.'

'And we all know what a shrewd operator you are on the share markets, don't we!' Marion snapped, thinking of the trunk full of defunct share certificates in the attic.

His face darkened and for a few moments James fought to control a temper that threatened to put Marion in her place, forcibly if necessary. 'Dear Marion,' he said, after a tense silence, 'never one to miss an opportunity of reminding a chap of past misfortunes.'

'Missed fortunes, in your case.'

'Very witty.' He laughed and patted her shoulder approvingly. 'Incidentally, while on the subject of shares, I trust that my papers and other personal items are safe?'

'I packed your things myself and put them in the attic. You will find your possessions intact, down to the last tawdry bead necklace.'

'Due only to your dislike of anything that reminds you of me, plus your innate honesty and the fact that the pawnbroker would not give you tuppence for the lot.'

They stared at each other with thinly veiled animosity and Frances felt that the sparring match had gone far enough.

'I do hope, Father, that if we advance you the money for new clothes, you will put them to good use by wearing them in search of work.'

'But of course.' James looked astonished that she could even think it worth mentioning.

'We have been working very hard but badly need additional income.'

'And now I am here to look after you,' James assured her expansively. 'In fact, looking after my five girls is my chief, indeed my only, aim in life and I shall not rest until I am able to meet all the household bills from my own efforts. However, just as a matter of interest, what sort of work have you been doing?'

He listened to Charley's account of her Saturdays with John Leigh, and exclaimed that she was a good lad, that he must call on his brother without delay, and that he would not dream of preventing her from continuing this arrangement as she evidently enjoyed the work so much. He assured Frances that he had no objection to her pupils practising in the house and that their presence would not disturb him in the least, as doubtless he would be out a lot. When it came to Marion's turn, he seemed fascinated by her entrée into the best circles and questioned her closely about her patrons and acquaintances. She answered him tersely, worried that his enterprising brain was already busy with new schemes in which he would try to involve these wealthy and influential contacts.

Then Frances took the one, and only, advantage that she saw in her father's return. 'Marion has not told you everything, Father. You have returned home just in time to save her.'

'From the shocked tone of your voice, Frances, I assume that Marion is mixed up with – dare I say it – a man?'

'Worse than that,' Frances said triumphantly. 'She wants to act in a theatre. I could not stop her, but you can.'

'A theatre, eh?' He looked speculatively at his eldest

daughter and nodded. 'Yes, I can imagine that you would do very well. How much are they paying you?'

'It is only an amateur production,' Marion said, flushing under his scrutiny of her face and figure, 'but I believe the fees could be as much as ten guineas for the entire week.'

'Ten guineas . . . Good God! That is more than I . . .' James stared at her in genuine astonishment. 'Good God,' he exclaimed again, 'it's a proper little gold mine. Perhaps we ought to look into this theatre lark, eh? Good-looking girls, all of you, although I says it as shouldn't. Damn it, if Arabella sat on a stage reciting her ABC, people would pay just to stare at her.'

Not trusting herself to speak, Frances walked out of the room and, joining Charley who was washing her father's shirts in the scullery, astonished her sister by the venom with which she attacked the dirty linen.

'I think there is probably a bit more to it than that,' Marion said in a carefully controlled voice. 'Certainly Frances considers the stage to be a fate worse than death. Charley has no knowledge of, or interest in, the theatre. I shudder to contemplate the havoc Imogen would wreak and, as for Arabella . . . I am sorry, Father, but I will *not* have Arabella involved in the theatre.'

'So Frances did strike a chord,' he remarked knowingly.

'Arabella is destined for something better, something so much better that not a hint of gossip must touch her name.'

'In that case, how is she to explain away a sister with theatrical connections?'

'This is only an amateur production! And, if need be, I will guide Arabella from the sidelines and then disappear totally from her life.'

'The ultimate sacrifice! By God, Marion, your mother

did a good job with you. You look like her and you sound so like her that I am beginning to believe in reincarnation.'

At that moment they knew they detested each other, yet one mark of respect remained: to Marion, James was still her father and therefore she must guard her tongue, while James saw in her a spark of animation and determination which had never manifested itself in his wife. The girl had gumption and even though she made him feel uncomfortable, he admired that.

Chapter Five

For a month or two the household jogged along fairly peaceably. The girls went about their daily routine much as before, the only difference made by their father's return being the vast increase in laundry, in the food to be provided and, as they had feared, in the money required to maintain him.

As for James himself, he remained in resolutely good humour, constantly complimenting his daughters on their looks and character, praising Marion for the supply of guineas with which she replenished the tin on the kitchen shelf, Frances for her culinary skills, Charley for her intelligence and general *bonhomie*, and treating the twins with a paternal benevolence that gradually eased the tension in their bodies and the wariness in their eyes. In his new clothes he gave an impression of bluff cheerfulness, a big, handsome, open-handed, gregarious man, the sort of man who was liked by his friends but not entirely trusted, and certainly not expected to make anything of himself.

He appeared to be as good as his word, sallying forth each morning in search of work, always optimistic that his luck was about to turn. True, no work materialised and he tended to be vague about the actual avenues he was exploring, but his spirits were so unquenchable and infectious that even Marion refrained from criticism. But, as May blossomed into June, an essential vigour seemed to ebb slowly out of him. He began leaving the house later in the day – ten o'clock became eleven, then it was noon, and then afternoon, until there were days when he only went out for a few hours in the evening. On one such evening he came home to be confronted by Marion, grimly holding the family money-box.

'I have suspected for some time that you were taking money from this tin,' she snapped, 'so this morning I counted it very carefully and this evening I counted it again. As I expected, I was a guinea short.'

He seemed to be about to deny the charge but, seeing her face, changed his mind and shrugged. 'So what?'

'Is that all you have to say for yourself? How dare you steal the housekeeping money! Haven't we been more than generous . . .'

'*Steal* . . . did you say steal?' He moved a step closer to her, glancing down at her from his superior height. 'This is my house and I am entitled to take anything I want.'

'Not when you have contributed nothing.' Marion stood her ground courageously. 'Two months you have been here and not a penny has come out of your pocket into the tin. The movement of coins is entirely in the other direction. What happened to all your fine words? What happened to those supposedly fine diamonds?'

'If you must know, Hatton Garden would not take them,' he said sulkily, turning away. 'Had the bloody nerve to tell me – *me*, who slogged away on the damned diamond fields and who handled more diamonds than they've had hot dinners – that the quality wasn't good enough. Fat lot they know.'

'What have you done with the stones?'

'They are upstairs in my room. Don't you worry your

pretty head, my dear, I'll offload them soon enough.'

'The sooner the better,' Marion said coldly. 'It is high time you started to pay for your own keep, even if you cannot provide for ours. And you can keep your charm for those who appreciate it. Unfortunately, Father, you are wasting your breath on me, particularly when that breath stinks of whisky.'

'So I'm not allowed a little drink now? For God's sake, it is the only pleasure I have left! Besides, I was out on business.'

'In the pub? Paying for the drinks with my money?' Marion gathered up her skirts and prepared to retreat with dignity. 'I must insist that tomorrow, and I do mean tomorrow, you replace the money you took from the tin.'

That night she slept with the money-box under her pillow and found a new hiding place for it the next day. In the evening a reproachful and superbly dignified James deposited an impressive number of coins into her palm, shaming her into unquestioning acceptance of his largesse.

Only a week later did she discover that he had pawned Fanny's silver-backed brushes and mirror. The diamonds were never seen or mentioned again.

Charley was happier than she had been for years, but she was beset by anxiety that her father was not doing himself justice and that he was, as usual, much misunderstood. Since her father's homecoming, Marion had closed her bedroom door firmly each night, thus depriving Charley of her chief conduit to the heartbeat of the house. So all she could do was reassure her father constantly of her undying love and devotion and help him make the most of his many fine qualities. Alone of all the sisters, she showed unflagging interest in his various money-making schemes and pored for hours over advertising material, pamphlets and pages of notes on grandiose projects that were never pursued.

'This is the best idea you have ever had,' she enthused, pointing at a picture of a Remington Standard typewriter. 'The information says that a new development, called a shift-key, enables the machine to produce small letters as well as capitals.'

James looked at the leaflet doubtfully. 'Do you really think it would catch on? Looks a bit laborious to me. Surely it is quicker just to dash off a note by hand?'

Charley shook her head. 'No one "dashes off" business letters. Uncle John is most particular that all his letters are written in the clerk's best handwriting and without any mistakes. Not only that, but he always keeps a copy. Honestly, Father, it takes ages.'

James grunted but did not respond.

However, Charley was warming to her theme. 'The typesetters are constantly complaining that they cannot read people's writing – think how pleased they would be if their rough "copy" was typed clearly.'

'Probably put them out of business.'

'No, I'm sure that the uses for the typewriter are quite different, but you could speak to Uncle John about that. Then you could write to these Remington people in America and tell them to send you some machines to sell here.'

He smiled at her simplistic view of the business world and sighed. 'Any arrangement with Remington would require capital, Charley, and that is a commodity I do not possess.'

'Someone would lend it to you. The bank. No? In that case, ask Uncle John. You could go into partnership – the typewriter business would work very well alongside the printshop.'

Again James sighed. He supposed that she was right but he was certain that his brother would turn him down flat. They looked alike, but in temperament they were poles apart. To James, John was plodding and dull, whereas his own world was full of excitement and endless possibilities where the sky was the limit; to John, James was an irresponsible ne'er-do-well, whereas he was steady and successful. They had met only once since James returned from the Cape and the interview had been acrimonious, John making it clear that he had assisted the family more than enough during his brother's absence and that no further financial help would be forthcoming. But now there was something about Charley's dog-like devotion that made it impossible to let her down, so James gathered up the leaflets and took a cab to the City – it was all very well for Charley's young limbs to walk that distance but he could not be expected to do it – strolled into his brother's office and, rather apathetically, dumped the leaflets on the desk.

John scanned the papers quickly and then pushed them back across the cluttered mahogany desk-top. 'I think Charley was right – in fact, she usually is. Best of the bunch, that one.'

'That isn't difficult,' James responded wearily. 'Bloody women!'

'But even if you were to be first in the queue for a Remington agency, the venture would take more capital than I could raise.'

'So you don't want to help me.'

'It isn't a matter of not *wanting* to help, it is a fact that I *cannot* help. I am doing tolerably well here and I have a few expansion plans, but I have no assets to spare. And don't suggest that I approach the bank because, believe me, I am mortgaged to the hilt as it is.'

'Mortgaged? You don't know the meaning of the word.' Morosely James leaned back in his chair 'You've never had to struggle, not like me. You married the only daughter of an ailing printer and took over the business. Had it made.'

'The business was ailing as well as the man and I had to build it up from scratch,' John said sharply, 'and you could have done equally well if you'd had the sense to marry into trade and not the gentry. But, oh no, not you – aspirations above your station as usual.'

James gloomily acknowledged the truth of this, twisting his brother's actual meaning so that the words confirmed his heartfelt belief that Fanny was to blame for all his problems. 'If she had handled her family right,' he maintained, 'everything could have been different. As it turned out . . . well . . . and five daughters! Strewth!' He was silent for a moment, fiddling with a pencil and moodily tapping it on the leaflets in front of him. 'Five millstones, more like.'

'Obviously you are not surprised by my refusal,' John commented, 'but I did expect you to be more disappointed.'

'Not really my line of country, is it, office equipment? Cannot see myself touting typewriting machines from door to door, nothing but a bloody salesman.'

'Too much like hard work, perhaps,' John suggested drily.

'I need to get fired up by an idea, to feel that this is what I want to do, body and soul, that at last this is the big one . . .' He paused, his face animated. 'I need space and action and excitement, and I am sure that I know where to find it. This time I know exactly how to get it right – I must go to America.'

He got up and prowled restlessly round the room,

searching for a way to make his brother understand. 'The Americans I met on the diamond fields were tremendous fellows, real go-getters, like me. Soul-mates, that's what we were, sharing the same attitude to life, determined to live it to the full and grasp its opportunities. And, believe me, brother, being stuck in a back-street London terrace with a house full of complaining women is not my idea of an opportunity.'

'You could not go to America without them,' John said flatly.

'No, I don't suppose I could. That's what I mean about millstones . . . Damn it, if only I was free . . .'

That was the day James began drinking in earnest. Instead of going straight home, he called in at the local public house and spent the evening cadging drinks off anyone naive enough to listen to his traveller's tales. When he finally opened his front door, the house was in darkness. Slowly he groped his way up the stairs and stood, swaying, on the landing.

Arabella and Imogen had lowered their guard in recent weeks, lulled into a sense of security by their father's good behaviour, and lately they had even dropped off to sleep before he came upstairs. However, tonight was different. He did not come home for supper. He had still not come home when Marion sent them to bed and they could hear her talking angrily to Frances, hear the words 'pub' and 'drink', and so the twins lay awake, praying that history would not repeat itself.

Charley came to bed, and then Marion and Frances, and surely it must be closing time by now. They tensed as they heard the front door, and their throats went dry as his footsteps inexorably mounted the staircase and they both held their breaths as those footsteps paused on the landing, and then a floorboard creaked right outside their room and the door opened.

By now Imogen was in Arabella's bed and, as James stared down, he saw a misshapen mass of heads and entwined limbs. His eyes growing accustomed to the dark, he identified Imogen and flung back the bedcovers. 'How many times have I told you to sleep in your own bed,' he growled, carrying her to the other divan.

Sitting down beside Arabella, he hugged her rigid but unresisting form tight against him, stroking her silky hair. 'You're not a millstone, are you, pretty Arabella,' he murmured, his drink-sodden breath fouling the air. 'You would come with me to America and you would be a good girl, wouldn't you? You would do things to make me happy. You want me to be happy, don't you?'

While one arm still held her tightly against him, his other hand slid underneath her nightgown and began stroking the slender, pubescent limbs as his breathing grew heavier. In the other bed Imogen shut her eyes and curled into a foetal ball, clasping her knees so tight that it hurt.

'All good girls do things to make their fathers happy,' James was crooning persuasively. 'All I want you to do is touch me . . . here . . .' and he guided Arabella's little hand to his groin and pressed it against the hard lump in his trousers. 'You'll like it, darling Arabella, you liked it when we did it before, I know you did, I'll undo . . .'

Suddenly the creak of stairs made him pause and he cursed under his breath as a soft voice called: 'Father, is that you?' Moving hurriedly to the door, he saw Charley on the landing.

'I was saying good night to the twins,' he said awkwardly. 'Shouldn't you be asleep?'

'How could I sleep without knowing what happened?'

Charley peered at him anxiously. 'Uncle John said no, didn't he!'

'I'm afraid so. Now, go to bed, there's a good lad and we'll talk in the morning.' And James went to his room.

The house was quiet, but only after Imogen had crept across the landing, and listened at her father's door to the resounding snores within, did she dare to return to her sister's bed, hold close a trembling Arabella and drift into sleep.

From then on the twins were alert every night, waiting in the dark with their guilty secret and their fear. For a week or so nothing happened. The footsteps reached the top of the stairs and went in the opposite direction, straight to his own room. But on the tenth day that floorboard creaked again and a gasp of terror escaped Arabella's lips. Then, just as he was pushing open their bedroom door, Marion's voice said sharply: 'For heaven's sake, Father, what do you think you are doing? Are you so drunk that you cannot find your way to your own room? You should be ashamed of yourself.'

The reprieve lasted for two weeks, long enough for his fear of another interruption to fade. Next time he succeeded in forcing Arabella to touch him, but after he had gone Arabella was violently sick and Imogen had to summon Marion. Again James maintained the pattern, deeming it wise to leave them alone for a while.

In the meantime Marion was rehearsing the new play with Peter Frith-Tempest and his friends. *Masks and Faces*, a comedy by Tom Taylor and Charles Reade, had been chosen as the vehicle for their West End venture and in it, honouring her promise to Frances, Marion had elected to play the virtuous wife. It was not an insubstantial part, in that the lady had several lengthy scenes, but it was milk-and-water compared to the real meat of the starring role of Peg Woffington, the honest actress with a heart of gold. However, Marion made the best of the situation and overcame her disappointment by emphasising, off the stage more than on, the social gap between her amateur status and that of the professional actress who had been hired to play Mrs Woffington.

Several days before opening night Marion came home late, flushed and excited after a rehearsal that had gone well – too well, according to Peter Frith-Tempest, who felt that if a whole host of disasters did not occur now, they would certainly manifest themselves in their thousands on opening night.

'Opening night,' she groaned to Charley, who ran downstairs to meet her. 'I know that I will be terrible. I will forget my words, bump into people or, most likely, freeze to the spot in pure terror.'

'You will be wonderful,' Charley reassured her, taking the bag containing the incomplete costumes and lifting out the travelling dress, hood, cloak and silk gown that Marion wore during the two acts of the play. 'I'll help you finish these tomorrow, if you like.'

Still ignorant of Charley's theatrical interests and ambitions, Marion looked at her sister in surprise. 'Thank you. I'd be grateful if you would. Frances refuses to touch anything connected with the stage – presumably she thinks the contamination is catching! And I need these costumes for the dress rehearsal the day after tomorrow.'

'And tomorrow you rehearse in the theatre for the first time.'

'I wonder how it will feel,' Marion said slowly, 'whether it will be a lot different from the hall where I played in *Lady Audley*. I dare not ask anyone because I do not want to admit that I have never set foot inside a theatre before.'

I have, Charley wanted to say, and it is the most wonderful, magical place in the whole wide world.

'Neither have I,' said James as he entered the room, 'not in London anyway. A music-hall, yes, many times, but not a theatre. About time we rectified that, don't you think? But then, of course you will be providing me with a ticket for your opening night, won't you, Marion?'

The thought had never crossed her mind. She stared at him wildly, trying to think of a cast-iron reason why it was impossible.

'You wouldn't enjoy it,' she said feebly.

'Who says I wouldn't? Besides, that is not the point. I am your father. Ought to chaperone you.'

'All the tickets for the opening night have been sold.'

'I find that difficult to believe but, if it is the case, I will come another night.'

She thought quickly. Opening night was out of the question, because she could never cope with the strain of that occasion and her father as well, but if he would not be fobbed off . . . 'Closing night.'

'Please, please, can I go too?' Charley begged, hanging on to her father's arm and looking beseechingly at Marion. 'I will be good for ever and ever if you let me go.'

'Very well,' Marion agreed, after her father had shrugged his indifference as to whether or not Charley accompanied him. With luck, Charley might prove a restraining influence.

Charley settled into her seat with a wriggle of delight and anticipation. Heaven, she decided, was being at the theatre, with her father beside her, and wearing a very grown-up green silk dress, a reject of Marion's that she had altered herself. All week Marion had improved in spirits and confidence and there could be no doubt that the play, and Marion's performance, were being well received.

Beside her, James pulled a hip flask out of his pocket and surreptitiously took a quick swig from it. Oh dear, she did wish that he would not do that. For one thing, it meant that he had found the latest hiding place for the money-box and there would be a terrible row; for another, he had had several drinks before they left home, and he had stopped off for another on the way.

However, as soon as the curtain went up, her attention was focused so intensely on the stage that she became oblivious of her father and his frequent use of the flask. Completely caught up in the action, Charley laughed at the jokes and worried about the characters' feelings, but also found herself watching some points with an almost critical interest. Lily Palmer, the young woman playing Peg Woffington, was awfully good, better than Marion actually, but that was to be expected; and to Charley's immense pride and relief, Marion was truly charming in the part of Mabel Vane. Occasionally she was rather stiff and awkward, and from time to time she seemed nervous and uncertain, but her inexperience suited the naïvety and trustfulness of the part and she looked so beautiful that the audience gladly forgave any minor shortcomings. She received a tremendous ovation at the end and bowed in the most stately and ladylike way, quite putting Miss Palmer in the shade.

'Not bad,' was James's answer to Charley's rapturous effusions of praise for the production and for her sister's performance. 'Marion really could make a go of this if she put her mind to it. Right now I am more interested in going backstage and finding some liquid refreshment.'

Charley's heart sank. His face was flushed and his speech had taken on that slurred sound that meant he had had too much to drink already. 'Shouldn't we go home?' she suggested.

'Absolutely not. Bound to be a party to mark the closing of the show and it is my duty to ensure that no one molests my little girl.'

'But I would prefer to go home,' and then Charley realised that the little girl to whom he referred was Marion and that he must be even more drunk than she had feared.

On the brilliantly lit stage, out of sight of the auditorium, Marion was receiving the congratulations of her admirers and her colleagues.

'Well done, Marion.' Generously Lily Palmer shook Marion's limp and unresponsive hand. 'You deserve every "bravo" and every bit of applause that you received.'

'As indeed do you, Miss Palmer,' Marion said graciously and with more than a touch of hauteur. 'May we hope that you will soon be returning to the professional arena?'

'Got an audition on Monday. Hold thumbs for me, eh?'

'If you are successful, I shall certainly make up a party and come to see the show,' Marion said in her most refined tone of voice.

'D'you know something, Marion?' and Lily came closer, a petite blonde with highly rouged cheeks and a vivid slash of lipstick. 'You're a better actress than I thought. You nearly had me fooled in the last scene when Mabel tells Woffington: "Let me call you sister." For a moment, even I thought you might mean it.'

'I have four sisters, Miss Palmer, and four is quite sufficient.'

'And Woffington goes on to say: "You do not know

what it is to me, whom the proud ones of the world pass by with averted looks, to hear that sacred name from lips as pure as yours."' Lily struck a flamboyant attitude, but her eyes were alert, cynical and cold as ice. 'Remember, proud Marion, that not all women can be born ladies like you, but that all women are sisters under the skin.'

As Lily swung away with a toss of her head, Marion felt her face flaming. This was all Frances's fault, she told herself angrily. It was Frances who made her feel that she must show her superiority to the theatre and all its works, that she must demonstrate that she was more Frith-Tempest than Palmer. But she wasn't, was she? She must apologise to Lily immediately, or at least as soon as she could escape from Lord Melton, who was heading purposefully in her direction.

'My dear Miss Leigh,' Lord Melton bowed over her hand, holding it a lot longer than was necessary or fitting. 'Words cannot express how much I have admired your performance, but perhaps my actions will convince you of my sincerity. I have,' and he leaned over to whisper in her ear, 'attended this theatre every night this week, incognito and in secret.'

She was so surprised and horrified that before she could help herself, she had blurted out: 'Why on earth did you do that?'

'Well, it wasn't to see those chaps poncing about as Vane and Pomander, and Lily Palmer used to be a dear little thing but she's got a trifle overblown, ain't she! So that leaves you, my dear Miss Leigh. I came every night in order to feast my eyes on your beauty.'

'And did Lady Melton come too?'

He seemed to find that extremely funny. 'Not often that Barbara and I come together,' he said, shaking with laughter, and the sight of Marion's uncomprehending eyes seemed to both amuse and delight him. 'Good Lord, no, my wife thinks that I was out on business or at my club so, you see, you could make life very difficult for me if you chose to tell her. You have me in your power.' Apparently he found the image of being in Marion's power even more delightful, because his eyes took on a glazed look. 'I still say that you could turn professional. I know someone in the business – Cavendish, perhaps you have heard of him?'

'I believe that I have heard the name mentioned.'

'Have a certain amount of influence with him, actually, a financial interest in his enterprise, if you understand me. I could put in a word.'

Marion stiffened. 'Your interest in my welfare is greatly appreciated, Lord Melton,' she said coldly, 'but there is no question of me becoming so attached to the theatre.' She used every nuance at her command to spit out the word 'theatre' as if it were poison. 'I am always prepared to give my time to a charitable cause, and I freely admit that unfortunate circumstances have placed me in a position of charging for my services . . .'

'Just name your price, Miss Leigh.'

'. . . in literary and theatrical pursuits among *ladies*, but if you think that my family, who are gentlefolk, impoverished through no fault of their own, would ever . . .'

She could not complete the sentence. From the darkness of the wings into the brilliant light lurched James, followed by an anxious Charley, having talked their way past a reluctant stage doorkeeper. In that awful moment Marion saw him exactly as he was: a bluff, brash, red-faced 'spiv' in a cheap suit with the smell of whisky on his breath. She watched in horror as he homed in on Lily Palmer.

'I say, but you're a little cracker! What are you doing, wasting your time with this bunch of has-beens. Correction, they're not has-beens, they're never-will-bes, get it?' And he slipped an arm around her waist and attempted to kiss her.

With practised ease, Lily escaped. 'Now then, someone's been at the sauce and the party's only just begun,' she admonished good-humouredly.

'You and I could have a bit of a party,' and he tried to grab her again. 'How about it? A couple of drinks and then you and I get out of here.'

'Dream on,' but Lily saw Charley's unhappy paper-white face, and refrained from saying any more.

'When I say "never-will-bes", naturally I exclude my little girl.' James helped himself to a glass of wine and lurched towards Marion. 'A toast to the star of the show – my little girl, Marion, the best and most beautiful actress in town.'

For Marion, the contempt in Lily Palmer's eyes was bad enough, but it was nothing to the look on Lord Melton's face, a thoughtful, knowing, appraising look as he 'placed' her, so he thought, in the social hierarchy and calculated how far he could go with her. Her lady-like façade demolished in that one brief moment, Marion knew that her father had placed her at an unutterable disadvantage in her future dealings with this man.

During the drive home, Charley sat mute while her father and Marion hurled insults at each other. 'I have never been so humiliated in my life' . . . 'Just like your mother' . . . 'How dare you show me up in front of my friends?' . . . 'I'm your father and I will do as I bloody well please.' And so it went on, all the way home, until Charley covered her ears in a futile attempt to shut out the unpleasantness.

At this late hour the twins were in bed and Frances, ostentatiously displaying her disinterest in the evening's activities, had also retired. Charley escaped immediately to her room, leaving Marion to a final acrimonious exchange. Lighting the lamps in the back parlour, for the first time she noticed the bulge in James's jacket pocket. She pounced and found the hip flask.

'I thought so! I suppose you have hidden a whisky bottle in here,' and after throwing the flask at her father in a fit of fury, she bent down and opened the sideboard door.

Suddenly she was pulled upright. Glaring at his inter- ference, she raised a hand as if to strike him but, surprisingly coolly for a man so drunk, James imprisoned both her hands and held them tight. It was Marion's first experience of the overwhelmingly superior strength of a man and, after one brief attempt to break free, she stood still and looked up at him, into a face so implacably stern and angry that for a moment she was afraid. Then, as he released her and stepped back, she recovered herself. He was her father and in this year of 1881, he was lord and master in his own house.

Deliberately James removed a half-full whisky bottle from the cupboard and placed it on the table. Marion turned on her heels and left the room without saying another word.

To Imogen and Arabella the hours of waiting seemed endless. Their fears were heightened by the atmosphere in the house; the threat was always greatest when he was drunk and in a bad mood. As the footsteps started up the stairs, Arabella gave a great sobbing sigh and Imogen tried to swallow but her throat was too dry, because both of them remembered what he had said he wanted Arabella to do with him next time, and now both of them were sure that this was the next time . . .

Marion had lain awake for some while, trying to control her restlessness so that she would not wake Frances, even though she was almost certain that Frances had not been asleep when she came to bed. At last she had fallen into an uneasy doze but remained only in a shallow sleep and therefore woke at the first scream. 'Mother? I'm coming . . .' and then she remembered and paused, puzzled, until another agonised scream propelled her out of bed and into the twins' bedroom. The screams continued, but in the darkness she could not tell which twin was making the noise, huddled so close were they by Imogen's bed on the far side of the room.

Then she saw the dark shape on Arabella's bed and Frances came in, candle in hand, to cast light on the confusion.

'Father?' Marion shook him hard. 'Are you so drunk that you have fallen asleep? Get up, damn you,' but his body remained limp and, as Frances lit another candle and held the lights over him, they saw his staring, sightless eyes and the dark stain spreading over the bedclothes.

The doctor said that in such cases the police had to be informed and so the sisters waited, Marion and Frances distraught, Charley in floods of heartbroken tears, Imogen and Arabella absolutely silent. The twins had not spoken to anyone, not even to each other, since uttering the screams that had marked their father's death.

The sergeant was not long out of uniform, a detective in the recently formed Criminal Investigation Department and attached to the local division. He looked at the huddle of distressed and immensely beautiful womanhood and his eyes softened. As he murmured to his junior colleague, this was evidently an incident that required diplomatic handling, and where heavy-footed policemen should tread softly and not cause undue distress. However, the fact remained that unpleasant questions had to be asked, because James Leigh was lying dead on the little girl's bed with a dirty great dagger sticking out of his ribs.

Gently he questioned first Marion, then Frances and Charley, piecing together the story of the evening's events and then, with great reluctance, he said that he was sorry but there was no help for it, he had to question the little ones.

'Imogen,' prompted Marion, 'can you tell us what happened?'

But Imogen only stared at her, eyes huge in her white face, and to Marion's astonishment it was Arabella who replied.

'I can tell you what happened, but I will have to tell you upstairs so that I can show you.'

'But, miss, the body . . . I mean, your father, is still there.'

'I know,' said Arabella, 'but it's all right, I saw it before,' and with eerie composure she led the way upstairs.

'We were in bed, me here,' and she pointed to the bed nearest the door where James was still sprawled in a pool of blood and vomit, 'and Imogen over there. We were asleep but a funny noise woke me up, and Father was in the room sort of staggering about.'

'Did that alarm you?' the sergeant asked.

'Oh no, it wasn't the first time.'

'I caught him opening your door one night,' Marion exclaimed, 'but I did not realise he had actually been in here. Why didn't you tell me?'

'It didn't seem important,' Arabella shrugged. 'We assumed that he turned the wrong way at the top of the stairs because he was drunk. But tonight it was different; he was waving his arms about and he seemed to be holding something in his right hand. In the dark I couldn't make out what it was, but now I realise it was that knife.'

'Could you bear to look a bit closer, Miss Leigh?' the sergeant asked Marion, 'and tell me if the knife is familiar. Distinctive handle. Not one that you would forget if you had seen it before.'

Gingerly Marion bent down and inspected the part of the dagger that protruded from her father's chest. 'Yes, it is a souvenir from one of his journeys. I packed it in a trunk in the attic when he went to the Cape.'

'And did Mr Leigh, or anyone else, unpack that trunk when he came back?'

'None of us did, but Father knew where his things were, because he specifically asked me about some papers he wanted.'

'So it is feasible that he went to the attic in search of the papers and found the knife?' The sergeant nodded. 'Go on, Miss Arabella.'

'I was frightened and I climbed out of bed and went over to Imogen,' and again she indicated the far side of the room, 'and no sooner had I moved than Father staggered again and seemed to trip, and he fell over on the bed and made an awful noise, not exactly a scream and not exactly a groan, but . . .'

'Yes, miss, thank you, that's quite enough,' the sergeant said hastily, feeling that the lovely little thing had suffered enough for one night and that if she had to relive this dreadful business she might never get over it. 'Drank a lot, did he, your father?'

'I know for a fact that he drank half a bottle of whisky

after we came home,' said Marion, 'because the empty bottle is on the table downstairs. And I am afraid he had the rest of it earlier.'

The sergeant nodded. The room smelled like a distillery.

'You won't have to question Imogen, will you?' Arabella asked anxiously, making full play of her innocent eyes in that heart-shaped, heart-stoppingly beautiful face. 'She was terribly upset.' And she smiled as the sergeant gruffly assured them that, apart from a quick visit to the attic, his inquiries were at an end.

As Marion showed him to the attic stairs, Arabella succeeded in closing a drawer in the chest that stood in the corner of the room, a drawer full of petticoats, without anyone noticing that it had been open. Then, being careful not to soil her clean white nightdress, she pushed two blood-spattered nightgowns further out of sight under Imogen's bed.

'Terrible accident,' the sergeant said to his colleague as they drove home. 'Just shows you the perils of the demon drink.'

Part Two

Chapter Six

The table in the Melton dining room had been set with only eight places, but apparently the occasion warranted the very best china and glassware, and Lady Melton was supervising the finishing touches with a relentless eye for detail.

'Not expecting the Prince of Wales, are we, Aunt Babs?' Peter Frith-Tempest teased, strolling into the room and kissing her affectionately on the cheek.

'Royalty does not receive special treatment in my house. All my guests receive equal honour and courtesy.'

'Except that Vere Cavendish is rather more equal than the others! Only joking, Aunt Babs, honestly! And is that a new dress?' He made a show of subjecting her elegant gown to close scrutiny. 'Very fetching, but you shouldn't have gone to all that trouble for me!'

'You are a young rascal,' Lady Melton admonished, laughing in spite of herself, 'and what's more, your place is in the drawing room, entertaining Eleanor.'

At the mention of his hosts' eldest daughter, Peter's brow creased into an anxious frown. 'Nothing will give me greater pleasure. I'm frightfully fond of Eleanor, you know, but sometimes I worry that I may not be quite as fond of her as you and Uncle Reggie, and my people, hope.'

'If it is any comfort to you, Eleanor feels much the same way.'

'Oh.' Taken aback, Peter digested this piece of news but still felt impelled to explain himself further. 'I do hope that everyone understands that it's nothing personal – Ellie is perfect in every way, truly – but I don't feel ready to commit myself, or settle down, just yet.'

'No one is putting any pressure on you, Peter. Besides, by the time you do want to settle down, Celia will be ready.'

'When I arrived, she was loitering on the upstairs landing in her dressing-gown, looking about eight years old.'

'Celia will be fourteen next birthday, but still requires a lot of work,' Lady Melton said with a sigh.

In the drawing room Peter, taking more interest than usual in Eleanor as a result of finding that she was not interested in him, found to his chagrin that she was looking particularly handsome this evening. She greeted him coolly, her eyes fixed on the door behind him.

Oh no, thought Peter, not Eleanor, too! Because it had to be *him* for whom she was waiting; she was hardly likely to sit on the edge of her chair, so upright and self-conscious, hazel eyes shining with excitement, in anticipation of her mother entering the room. All the other guests had arrived: sitting on the sofa were his parents, Sir Charles and Lady Frith-Tempest; Lord Melton was standing in front of the fireplace; and in an armchair was the dapper figure of Ernest Meyer, the financier, said to be close to Ernest Cassel, who was close to the Prince of Wales. There was an air of suspended animation, which the arrival of Lady Melton did nothing to dispel, but then . . .

'Mr Vere Cavendish,' the butler announced.

Peter knew it was probably a tired old theatrical cliché, but it was as if the curtain had risen on one of the drawing-room dramas in which Vere Cavendish excelled and, with his arrival, the entertainment could begin.

No need to ask what the ladies saw in him: Cavendish was the most crashingly handsome bastard in London. No need to ask why Lord Melton and Sir Charles Frith-Tempest had invested in The Cavendish Theatre: both gentlemen were susceptible to the glamour of the theatre, and both had wives who were susceptible to Vere Cavendish. But Ernest Meyer was another matter: a hard-headed businessman and a bachelor, the least likely man in town to be carried away by dreams of sipping champagne from coryphées' slippers, his participation in the enterprise proved that Vere Cavendish was taken seriously. Meyer believed that, behind the attractive and charming façade, there lurked a talent and an acumen that could make money for them all.

And the really sickening part of it – because Peter did not list himself among the man's admirers – was that Cavendish was living up to everyone's expectations.

'To the next season at The Cavendish Theatre.' Lord Melton made the toast at dinner. 'May it be as successful as the last.'

'What do you do, now that the theatres have closed for the summer?' Lady Frith-Tempest inquired. 'Do you take a long holiday until September, Mr Cavendish?'

'If only I could.'

The voice was deep and resonant, the most musical voice on the London stage, a voice that Cavendish used knowingly, cleverly and to full advantage. There were those who said he intoned rather than spoke, that he committed the ultimate sin of listening to his own voice and luxuriating in its beauty but, if he did, who could blame him? Its effect on a theatre audience was amazing; its impact on the dinner guests was devastating.

'Unfortunately, Lady Frith-Tempest, my holiday will comprise precisely one week by the sea, so that I can rest my voice and revitalise myself, and then I shall return to London in order to prepare the next season's programme.'

'Why are you not touring?' inquired Ernest Meyer, in his clipped, precise tones. 'It seems to me that many managements do better business in the provinces than they do in town.'

'In future years I do intend to tour, but this has been our first full season.' Cavendish leaned forward, addressing himself to Meyer and to him alone. 'I, and my leading lady, are well known in the provinces and have a following there but, before I tour, I need to build up a company and a repertoire that can hold their own in an increasingly competitive market.'

'Irving is touring this year,' Meyer said flatly.

'But it is the first Lyceum company tour,' Cavendish pointed out, 'and he has been there a damned sight longer than I've had the Cavendish. He is taking *nine* productions, with all the scenery and props, *and* he has Ellen Terry. Now, I am pleased to say that Arlene Sidley is staying with me next season and she has an enthusiastic following, but she is no Ellen Terry.'

'She is rather old, isn't she?' suggested Eleanor.

'Arlene Sidley, old? Nonsense,' scoffed Lady Melton, only too aware that the Sidley was several years younger than herself.

'Miss Sidley may be slightly past her prime,' Cavendish said delicately, 'but her talent remains undiminished. However, find me the next Ellen Terry, gentlemen,' and he looked at his three backers in turn, 'and our fortunes are made.'

'If you are looking for fresh talent, there is a young woman of our acquaintance who might interest you,' Lord Melton said quickly. 'Barbara's protégée, actually – I am thinking of Miss Leigh, my dear.'

'I am not at all sure that I want Marion Leigh turned into an actress,' Lady Melton objected. 'She is useful to me as she is.'

'But with her father's unfortunate death . . .'

'You mean, with her unfortunate father's death! Oh well, I suppose you are right, Reggie. Mustn't stand in the girl's way. Yes, indeed, Mr Cavendish, the young woman has talent and you should look her over.'

'I shall be delighted to interview her,' Vere Cavendish said courteously, with a barely detectable sigh. Finding parts for the protégées of wealthy patrons was one of the crosses that an actor-manager had to bear.

Peter laid down his knife and fork, his appetite unaccountably gone, and drained his glass of wine. Suddenly he felt depressed and disappointed. The prospect of Marion Leigh on the stage as a professional actress was not something he cared to contemplate and the reason, he had to admit, was that he cared about her. He had managed to push that ghastly scene with her father to the back of his mind and had reinstated the image of Marion as a heroine – noble and virtuous – gallantly succouring her little sisters. To see this paragon slip into the world of the theatre, where danger lurked at every turn, was almost more than he could bear. Yet, being an intelligent man, he was aware of a paradox: outside his work, the theatre was the love of his life and he could sit at table with Vere Cavendish without a qualm.

However, he did feel a qualm at the idea of Cavendish being close to Marion. Who was Vere Cavendish anyway? No one knew anything about him – where he came from, who his family was, or what school he had attended. Cavendish had appeared from nowhere. Suddenly, one day, there he was on the London stage and in the decade since he had grown in stature, popularity and good looks, and had women falling over themselves merely for a glance from those burning dark eyes. Look at Aunt Babs and Ellie trying to catch his eye now, and Celia had nearly fallen over the banisters in her anxiety to attract his attention as the party crossed the hall *en route* to the dining room. But give the man his due: he had bowed to Celia with grave courtesy and looked up at her with an avuncular twinkle in his eye, and at table he was giving Aunt Babs exactly the right amount of preference over her daughter.

Someone had asked him if he had settled the programme for the new season and he was explaining, yet again, his policy for The Cavendish Theatre.

'There are two options – either go for the Bancroft, Wyndham, Hare and Kendal approach of keeping to one style of acting and one type of play, or emulate Irving by introducing repertory. I tend to favour the latter course. I feel there is a place for a company with a range of plays – modern, poetic, melodramatic and classic, including Shakespeare.'

'I thought Shakespeare spelled ruin,' Peter remarked.

'Try telling that to Irving,' countered Cavendish.

'But if Shakespeare sat in the Lyceum stalls, he would hardly recognise his own work! Irving has adapted the plays to fit his personality, using them to provide magnificent parts for himself, and settings that display him and Ellen Terry to advantage.'

Cavendish nodded in agreement. 'I want to follow the texts more closely, and I continue to maintain most strongly that classic English plays should have a place in our theatre – a theatre which I intend shall have such a good name and reputation for excellence that mothers may bring their daughters to our entertainments with complete confidence.' And he bowed deferentially, first to Lady Melton and then to Eleanor. 'So I have decided to put on *Richard II* as my first Shakespeare production – important to choose plays not annexed by Irving! Then I thought that the success of Robertson's *Progress* last season could be followed by his *Birth* . . .'

Here Lady Melton gave a little cry of rapture, and exchanged an ecstatic glance of approval with Lady Frith-Tempest, before returning her undivided attention to Cavendish.

'I have someone working on a new adaptation of *David Copperfield*,' he went on, 'because *Nickleby* went down very well, but I have not settled on a fourth choice. Miss Sidley is very keen to do *Masks and Faces* . . .'

'Then you must see Miss Leigh,' Lady Melton declared and proceeded to explain Marion's familiarity with the piece.

He listened politely but without obvious enthusiasm.

When the ladies had withdrawn and the gentlemen were left to their port, Meyer became businesslike again.

'There was an item in the accounts that surprised me,' he remarked, leaning back in his chair. 'The expenditure on the refurbishment of the theatre.'

'Surprised me, too,' agreed Sir Charles. 'Devil of a lot of money.'

'On the contrary,' and Meyer was watching Cavendish closely. 'Having been to the theatre on several occasions, and taken a particular interest in the décor and accoutrements, I am astonished that you achieved such results for such a modest outlay.'

'I do assure you that I used only the very best materials.'

For the first time Cavendish looked flustered and uncertain. 'I think it is very important to have the best in every department, right down to the programmes, and the cloakrooms. The auditorium has received many compliments . . .'

'You misunderstand me, Cavendish. The auditorium is absolutely splendid, a symphony of crimson and gold magnificence, while reducing the number of pit seats and increasing the stalls makes sound business sense. No, my point is that the plushness of the auditorium must surely have cost all, or nearly all, the sum debited in the accounts, thus leaving nothing, or next to nothing, for behind-the-scenes improvements.' Meyer sipped delicately at his port. 'Are we to assume that you inherited all the machinery and the gas, and countless other gadgets in perfect working order?'

A muscle tightened in Cavendish's cheek but he managed a confident smile. 'Indeed we did. We were very lucky there. Well, there are one or two minor, *very* minor, adjustments that I would like to make when we are more established, nothing that cannot wait.'

'I do hope your judgement is correct,' Meyer said softly. 'Of course it is more satisfying to spend money on the auditorium, which is in full public view every night, but it is not sound business sense to skimp on the invisibles, especially in an area where safety is paramount. We do not want anyone hurting themselves, do we, or the place going up in flames?'

Cavendish made a gesture of acquiescence.

'A business, and perhaps a theatre in particular, lends itself to comparison with a handsome woman, or man.' Again Meyer leaned back in his chair and watched Cavendish from under hooded lids. 'However handsome the exterior, however glossy the hair and creamy the skin, however exquisite the bone structure, if the heart and lungs are not sound, if the blood is not pure and free from infection, an early and possibly painful death can ensue.'

'Usually at the most inopportune moment,' contributed Sir Charles. 'I remember . . .' and he launched into a ribald anecdote about an acquaintance, sadly deceased, which caused Peter to look at his progenitor in an entirely new light, while Cavendish smoothed back his glossy hair and rested the exquisite bone structure of his face on one hand, relieved at the change of subject.

As they rose to rejoin the ladies, Lord Melton laid a restraining hand on his arm.

'Cavendish . . . Vere, old man . . . if you could find a berth for Marion Leigh, I would be very, and I mean very, grateful.'

'I see, or I think I do. Pretty, is she?'

Melton groaned. 'Gorgeous. Black hair, blue eyes . . . a pair of breasts to drive a man wild. God, the mere thought of her gives me a hard-on. I'm getting one now.'

'And you think that, as a professional actress, she will be more easily seduced.'

'Goes with the territory, doesn't it?'

'I will see her,' and deliberately, but he hoped not impolitely, Cavendish avoided answering the question, 'but I cannot promise to engage her. If the girl is a stick, she will not please the public and Meyer will have both our guts for garters. I cannot afford to have him jump ship.'

'Understood,' and Melton pumped his hand enthusiastically, 'but you won't be disappointed, believe me.'

Overhearing the exchange, Peter's depression deepened. He supposed that he could not blame Uncle Reggie, Marion *was* gorgeous, and what was the point of having one's own theatre, which is how his godfather would view his investment in The Cavendish, if one could not avail oneself of certain facilities? Black hair and blue eyes – but Marion's hair was ripples of black silk, her huge eyes were pools of violet, her skin the cream of camellias, and her lips rose-red. Marion Leigh was ebony, ivory and roses but – and Peter's heart lurched – he, too, had longed to cup those breasts, and to caress the shapely ankles that flirted with the hem of her dress, ankles that became calves and knees and then thighs . . . Politely allowing his elders to precede him from the room, Peter leaned against the dining table and tried to get a grip on himself.

His pursuit of Marion, as yet academic, was impossible; he could not offer her marriage but admired her too much to make her his mistress. To complicate matters further, Uncle Reggie considered himself first in the queue, but had he given enough thought to the brooding, dark sexuality of Vere Cavendish? Given a choice between the two, it would take a very mercenary woman indeed to plump, and Peter used the word advisedly, for Lord Melton.

If Marion joined the company at The Cavendish Theatre, the future was strewn with pitfalls.

Peter wondered if he ought to warn her.

'I don't know why you are asking my advice. You will do what you want to do, in any event.'

'Frances, that isn't fair. I have no one to guide me and I would have thought you could spare a few minutes for an open, frank discussion.'

'Very well, my open, frank opinion is that you should thank Lord Melton kindly for his trouble but tell him that you are perfectly happy as you are. In other words, Marion, tell him to tell Mr Cavendish to get stuffed!'

'*Frances – language!* The twins will hear,' hissed Marion and outside, sitting on the stairs, Charley trembled in case her sister closed the bedroom door. 'I do think that at least I should find out what Mr Cavendish has to say. He might not offer me a job but, if he did, it would be interesting to know what kind of money he would pay.'

'Thank you, Marion, you have just proved my point better than I could hope to do in a thousand years – as I say, you will do whatever you want because you always do. Anyway, I don't care what sort of fool you make of yourself, because I will not be here to see it.'

'Why not?' Marion asked sharply. 'Where will you be?'

'I intend to find a suitable position as a governess, preferably with a family as far away from here as possible!'

'But you cannot do that,' wailed Marion, panic-stricken. 'You are needed here, to look after the house and the twins while I am working.'

'I knew you would say that! "We must look after the family" . . . "The family must come first" . . . "The family must stick together" . . . You say these things over and over again like a parrot. But all you ever do is *talk* about it, while it is me who has to *do* it. Well, I'm sick and tired of doing what you say. I'm going to do what I want, for a change.'

'You have been talking to that dreadful Scarlatti woman again. She has been putting ideas into your head.'

'If I have talked to her, it is only because the sister in whom I used to confide is hardly ever in the house and, when she is here, is interested only in her own affairs,' Frances riposted angrily. 'As for having ideas put into my head, that is rather a case of the pot calling the kettle black.'

'You might do me the courtesy of admitting that it is me who has the burden of financial responsibility, and that I have carried it pretty well so far. A position as a governess – sounds frightful to me, but if that's what you

want – could keep you but would not enable you to contribute to the household expenses.'

'There would be one less mouth to feed, and moving to
a smaller house would reduce the rent. You could earn
enough by your reading and so on to pay those expenses
and still be here for the twins after school.'

'What about the school holidays? Anyway I am not
prepared to move to a smaller house – Mother would
have a fit if we slid any further down the social scale.'

'That's a bit rich coming from an aspiring actress.'

'Mother would want you to help me with the twins.'

'The twins, the twins, what is so special about the
blasted twins!'

On the stairs Charley hugged her knees exultantly – it
was about time someone challenged Marion's obsession
with her own extreme sense of responsibility. The trouble
with Marion was that she tended to confuse her role as
protector with the power that she so much enjoyed wield-
ing. But oh, how Charley wished that she could join in the
conversation and urge Marion to go ahead with the audition. How could she hesitate about an opportunity to
meet Vere Cavendish? Charley had not seen him on the
stage for ages, and felt a lot more grown-up than the girl
who had secretly purchased his photograph. But she still
quivered at the prospect of encountering him again, as
surely she would if her sister was in the Cavendish company.

'You are very selfish, Frances. Mother would want you
to think of the welfare of the entire family, not only of
yourself.'

'*Me*, selfish. That's a laugh!' But Frances knew that
she was not going to escape. Three times Marion had
mentioned their mother, and three times Frances
reminded herself that her loyalty had been to her mother

alone, and that she must not be persuaded to extend that loyalty to the entire family. The trouble was that she was discovering that her loyalty, and responsibility, to her mother had not died when her mother did. She capitulated. 'I don't know why we are arguing. You know, and I know, that you will see Mr Cavendish and that I will stay here as cook-housekeeper and maid-of-all-work. Just remember that I am not prepared to do so indefinitely.'

Marion kneeled beside the bed and held her sister's hand. 'I will make it up to you, truly I will! But this is an opportunity I cannot afford to miss, not with Father gone and no steady means of support. Hundreds of girls would give their eye-teeth for an introduction to Vere Cavendish – Edward Druce told me that starting in the profession is terribly hard, even though there is a new publication called *The Stage*, which carries job advertisements.'

Charley crept quietly up the stairs to her room and sat down on the bed. A great wave of self-pity overwhelmed her, sending hot tears coursing down her face. Not once, during the whole conversation, had she been mentioned. Not once had she been considered, let alone consulted. No one cared about her. She did not count. The only person who had cared about her was her father, and now he was dead and she missed him terribly.

The tears stopped but, still sniffing and feeling achingly lonely, she moved to the tiny attic window and gazed out over the rooftops. She could not see much, the surrounding houses being huddled close together and all much the same height, but somehow the scene never failed to bring a sense of perspective and of wider horizons. Surely somewhere out there was a place for her, somewhere where she would be appreciated and noticed and would count for

something; somewhere where there might be companionship and laughter, a sense of purpose and of belonging.

Out of her next week's wages Charley bought the most
recent edition of *The Stage*.

The pillared portico of The Cavendish Theatre fronted
on the Strand, but Marion made her way round to the
stage door situated in an inconspicuous alley at the back.
Her tentative assertion that she had an appointment with
Mr Cavendish did not make the anticipated impression on
the doorkeeper, who indicated, with a jerk of his head,
that she should proceed down the dark passage beyond.
Reaching the greenroom, packed with a score of young
women, she stopped to ask further directions from a man
standing at the door with a clipboard in his hand.

'Name?' he barked.

'Marion Leigh. I have an appointment with Mr
Cavendish. Would you be kind enough to tell me where I
can find him?'

He was running the tip of his pencil down the list in
front of him and made a large tick beside one entry. 'Sit
down over there with the others,' and he pointed into the
room.

'You don't understand. I have an appointment . . .'

'Yes, dear. Just wait your turn.'

Self-consciously Marion sat down in the empty chair
nearest the door and looked around her, to find twenty or
so pairs of eyes staring back. She had been foolish enough
to assume that she had been granted a private interview
with the great Mr Cavendish, instead of which this was a
public audition and presumably all these girls were vying
with her for the position. Perhaps, she hoped, as she compared the ages, looks and dress of her rivals with her own,
more than one vacancy existed. At least her dress bore

favourable comparison; without Edward Druce to advise her – he was out of town, touring the provinces – she had been in an agony of indecision about what to wear, and the hot August weather had not made the choice any easier. In the end she had selected a simple day dress in the polonaise style, its cool ice-blue silk poplin decorated with tiny bows, the skirt finished with pleated flounces at the hem, and the tight-fitting bodice topped by a narrow white collar. There was no prettier gown in the room and Marion's confidence rose an infinitesimal notch.

The man at the door disappeared and, after an interval of five minutes or so, bustled back to his post announcing: 'They're ready' and sending a *frisson* of excitement through the room. Calling out a name, he directed the first girl towards the stage.

Unsure how long it would be before her name was called, and not liking to ask, Marion opened her Shakespeare and, the book shaking slightly from the tremble in her hands, went over the speech she had memorised. She had spent nearly as long deciding what pieces to present to Mr Cavendish as she had deciding what to wear: *Romeo and Juliet* and, for luck, the same Tennyson and Wordsworth that she had read during her successful interview with Lady Melton. Surely he would not want more than three.

The names were called in alphabetical order, so when a Miss Knight was summoned, Marion braced herself, smoothing a strand of hair under the little white hat and straightening her dress. Then it was her turn and, clutching the books, she walked unsteadily through the wings, panicking suddenly as she saw that the stage was empty. Quickly dumping the books on the prompt table, she wobbled to centre-stage with a lot less dignity than she had planned and stood blinking under the lights. The

auditorium was bathed in the soft glow of the half-light
that was fashionable in London theatres, enough illumination for the patrons to see each other and be seen, but
not enough to distract attention from the stage, and
Marion could make out a group of men sitting in the
centre of the stalls. There were three of them, so surely the
big man in the middle must be Vere Cavendish, but it was
the white-haired man, on the left as she looked at them,
who called out 'Name?' and then 'Begin'. Nervously
Marion embarked on: 'Farewell! God knows when we
shall meet again, / I have a faint cold fear thrilling through
my veins, / That almost freezes up the heat of life . . .', an
apt opening if ever there was one, and she hoped that the
tremor in her voice would be taken as artifice.

They heard her through in disconcerting, unresponsive
silence and when she had finished she hesitated, wondering whether to launch straight into 'The Lotos-Eaters' but
the man with the clipboard joined her on the stage and
handed her a script.

'Read Sarah,' he said, 'and I will do the rest.'

'And speak up,' called the white-haired man from the
stalls.

Taking the script, Marion blessed her hours and hours
of sight-reading to family and clients and launched into
the dialogue with enthusiasm. After two pages, the man in
the stalls called: 'Thank you. Next', and she was ushered
off. Told to wait with the others in the greenroom, she
resumed her seat and, once again finding herself the focus
of curious eyes, tried to calculate whether her audition had
lasted longer than any of the others. One or two of the
girls were chatting, but tension mounted when the last
girl came back and, as the clipboard man reappeared, the
silence was complete.

'These six stay,' he said, 'you . . .' and he pointed at

each of the chosen six in turn as he read out the name. One, two, three, four, five, and 'Miss Leigh.'

The unsuccessful candidates departed, some in tears, and the lucky ones smiled at each other nervously as the first girl was recalled to the stage. Remembering that she had left her books on the prompt table, Marion walked softly to the wings in order to retrieve them. The clipboard man was standing there and raised a finger to his lips as he saw her. Indicating the books, Marion managed to linger long enough to ascertain that the current candidate was standing alone on the stage, apparently answering questions from the men in the stalls.

So Marion, who was called last, thought she knew what to expect. She stood still and waited. Then the tall figure, in the centre of the little group in the stalls, disengaged himself from his fellows, moved to the end of the row and began to walk up the aisle towards her. He stopped at the front row of stalls, so that there was only the width of the orchestra pit between them, and looked up at her.

Now she could see him and her heart missed a beat as she looked at that impossibly handsome face, the chiselled features, the wide, cruel mouth and the eyes dark as midnight, although from this distance and in this light she could not tell whether they were dark brown or a very deep blue.

'Turn round,' he said, but Marion hesitated, taken by surprise and half-hypnotised by his voice. 'Turn round,' he repeated impatiently.

So Marion turned her back on him and waited.

'Walk round the stage. Go on, right round . . . and again. Now, do a few movements – a curtsy . . . a bow . . . sit down . . .'

She turned to find that a chair had been placed on the

stage behind her and sank on to it gracefully, or so she hoped.

'Take off your hat.'

Startled, she hesitated again, noticing for the first time that his companions in the stalls had disappeared. She was alone with Vere Cavendish.

'Do I have to say everything twice, Miss Leigh?' he said wearily. 'Take off your hat – I want to see your hair.' After she had complied, he stared at her intently and indicated that she should stand up again and turn a full circle in front of him. Critically he assessed every angle of her profile. 'Let down your hair.' Stupefied into silence, Marion obeyed, pulling out pins and releasing an ebony cascade. 'Now do it up again.'

'But I have no mirror.'

'It is not the hair I am interested in at this moment, so the end result is immaterial. I want to see how you use your arms.'

So Marion did up her hair and waited again, but nothing that had gone before prepared her for his next command.

'Lift up your skirts.'

She glared at him, outraged, but he merely stared at her with a dispassionate, world-weary look.

'As high as the knee.' And he sat down in the front row of the stalls, leaned back and folded his arms.

When still she did not move, he smiled sardonically. 'Do you want to be an actress, Miss Leigh? Your presence here today would seem to indicate that you do, and part of being an actress is to undertake what we in the profession call "breeches parts". In other words, Miss Leigh, you walk out on to the stage with your – to save your blushes I will call them *nether limbs* – clad only in a pair of tights. Thus it is incumbent on me to judge whether or not you possess the requisite attributes.'

Marion remained frozen to the spot. Out of the corner of her eye she could have sworn she detected movement in the wings.

'Perhaps you are confusing The Cavendish Theatre with a burlesque show or a music-hall,' he drawled. 'You tested our patience earlier with your rendition of Juliet. Are we to assume that you do not aspire to Viola or Rosalind?'

Slowly, her face flaming, Marion raised her skirt to the knee, displaying a slim and shapely pair of stockinged ankles and calves that would have enslaved Orsino and Orlando. Vere Cavendish, however, was not about to tell her so. After staring impassively at her legs, his eyes returned to her face.

'If you feel like a piece of meat in a shop window, Miss Leigh, it is because, at this stage of your career, that is precisely what you are. You have little or no experience, but you are decorative and we have established that you walk and move well.

'And if you enter the profession, you must have no illusions. I do hope that you have no visions of aristocratic admirers and champagne suppers. Life in the theatre is hard work. I expect my company at rehearsal at eleven o'clock sharp each morning until four in the afternoon. After the performance of the current play in the evening, I expect everyone – including attractive young ladies – to evade the attentions of the stage-door Johnnies and go home in order to study the play in rehearsal in readiness for the next day's work. Do you understand?'

'Yes.'

'And do you still wish to proceed?'

'Yes.'

'Yours is a raw talent, Miss Leigh – if talent is the right word – but I think we can make something out of you, if we work hard enough for long enough. And I would like to make it clear that I am taking you on because you have the voice, manners and appearance suitable for the so-called "drawing-room" pieces that are a feature of the Cavendish repertoire. Not for any other reason,' and he stared straight into her eyes.

He means Lord Melton, Marion thought, and her whole body seemed to blush with the humiliation.

'Read *Richard II* and report here at eleven on Monday morning,' he said, rising from his seat. 'Mr Ramsey, my business manager, will confirm the terms and conditions of your employment.'

And he was gone, leaving Marion to stumble off the stage and drift home in a daze.

Chapter Seven

Five guineas a week. Marion had hoped for more, but she reminded herself that she was new to the profession and must work her way up the ladder. At least she would be paid for rehearsals, her costumes would be provided and, should the size and importance of her roles increase, her salary would be reviewed later in the season.

Richard II was a disappointment, too. It was just her luck, she declared bitterly, to start with a play containing only four speaking parts for women, none of which amounted to a hill of beans. Even the queen had precious little to say, though she did have the touching and poetic farewell scene in which she kissed the king, *twice*. Marion sighed but knew that her chances of playing his consort were nil.

She was one of the first to arrive at the theatre on Monday morning, finding a vantage point on the stage from which she could watch the members of the company as they gathered in huddles of twos and threes, the buzz of conversation ceasing as the white-haired man and the clipboard man from the audition walked in. The older man introduced himself as Albert Harding, the stage manager, and Marion soon learned that he was Cavendish's deputy in matters relating to the production, in addition to

controlling all the production staff. The man with the clipboard was William Tucker, the prompter, whose
additional duties included assisting the stage manager and
acting as super master. The third member of the
Cavendish team was Richard Ramsey, the business manager, who kept the accounts, looked after advertising and
printing, and was in charge of the box office and all the
front-of-house staff.

After the introductions, the actors helped to set up rows
of chairs in a semicircle on the stage and even carried
tables to the back, on which some of the younger men
perched. Marion, who had secured a chair at the end of
the back row, noticed that Bert Harding and Will Tucker
were seated facing the company, with a vacant seat
between them, and that another empty chair was placed
prominently in the centre of the company's front row. For
the leading lady? And in she swept, in a rustle of silk and
self-importance, acknowledging the bows of the men, who
stood up as she entered, and sitting down in a flurry of
flounces. Brassy-blonde, with a poor complexion and hard
eyes, she began fanning herself ostentatiously, talking
loudly to the good-looking young man on her right, who
looked rather pleasant – a bit Edward Druce-ish, Marion
decided – whereas Arlene Sidley looked quite the opposite.

Bert Harding looked at his watch and walked into the
wings, reappearing minutes later with Vere Cavendish,
whom he conducted to his seat with all the dignity of
some ancient ritual. Such were the deference and air of
ceremony that Marion believed Cavendish to be already in
character as King Richard but she would learn that
rehearsals at The Cavendish were always like this.
Immaculately dressed in a three-piece suit and white shirt
with starched collar, so that beside him all the men on the
stage appeared crumpled and shabby, he stopped to kiss

Arlene Sidley's hand and exchanged an intimate smile and a whispered word with her before sitting down, but no one else was singled out for special recognition.

'You have all had an opportunity to read *Richard*,' he began without preamble, 'so I shall not keep you in suspense about the allocation of parts. After that we will do one read-through at sight and then you will go home to study. I want you word-perfect, starting tomorrow.'

A ripple of nervous laughter ran through the company. By no means everyone thought he was joking.

'Naturally Miss Sidley will be my queen,' and he treated her to the full battery of his most charming smile. 'Arlene, my dear, I am sorry that the part is so small, but you will be so busy for the rest of the season that you will bless me for this little respite, I assure you.'

Evidently Arlene had resigned herself to the situation because she merely smiled and regally inclined her head.

Cavendish began by allocating the male roles, Will Tucker handing out crimson-covered folders to each actor in turn. 'Now we come to the women,' he said. 'Unfortunately Shakespeare did not do you proud in this play. Apart from the queen, we have the Duchess of Gloucester and the Duchess of York,' and two folders were handed to the ladies in question, 'and the only other lady who has anything to say is an attendant to the queen. Miss Leigh, you will be that attendant.'

There was a stir of surprise among the company. 'Miss Leigh? Who the hell is she?' Arlene Sidley was heard to hiss at her companion.

'Perhaps, Miss Leigh, you will be good enough to stand so that everyone's curiosity can be satisfied and we can proceed with the job in hand,' Cavendish drawled.

As Marion stood up, Arlene's head swivelled round and Marion saw the cold eyes narrow as they assessed the competition. Then, just as the Sidley looked away, Cavendish said softly: 'And Miss Leigh will also understudy the queen,' and immediately the eyes snapped back to Marion and this time there was no disguising that venomous glance of animosity.

Marion sat down again, shaking, and took the proffered crimson folder. She had a speaking part. True, it was only six lines, but it was a start.

There followed weeks of numbing, unrelenting hard work. Vere Cavendish's original warning had erred on the side of caution; with no evening performance to be staged, rehearsals lasted all day, Sundays included. There was no break for luncheon, people snatching a bite if and when they could, or going without. The manager was on the stage throughout: in a chair stage left, or standing in the centre, or acting out the movements of his own or other parts. Every now and again he interrupted a speaker, with a 'No, my dear, that is not quite what I want' if the offender was female, or a 'Good God, is that the best you can do?' to a man, and he would illustrate how the words were to be spoken and how the accompanying action should be performed. There was little levity and nothing slipshod during Cavendish rehearsals; the Chief was a martinet, a perfectionist and a hard taskmaster, and he had a tongue that could make even the most seasoned professional flinch. Marion spent half the time longing to be noticed by him, and the other half scared stiff that she would be noticed.

It seemed that he was an organised man. Whenever an alteration was made or a new idea came to him, he immediately wrote rapid notes on a pile of papers that rested on a small table beside his chair. Amid the chaos – of carpenters measuring onstage and hammering off, of actors with questions (some of which were more sensible than others), of plaintive requests from the musical director for 'just ten minutes of your precious time, for God's sake', of the logistics of moving the supers around the stage without blocking the audience's view of the principals – Cavendish remained in control: sharp, sarcastic, withering, relentless in his pursuit of perfection but never flustered or panicked. And if he worked his company hard, he worked himself even harder. Aware that he stayed on at the theatre after the company was dismissed, Marion hid in the wings one night and watched as, from a seat in the stalls, he took a scenic and lighting rehearsal, directing the position of the great gas battens, the use of coloured gauzes and the clear, clean focus of the lime-light. And he was in the theatre before rehearsals started, working in the office that he shared with Bert Harding and Dick Ramsey.

Yet he seemed to thrive on it because, although sometimes he looked tired, he exuded an energy and a magnetism that invigorated and uplifted the entire company. He was more stage manager, or director as it would become called, than actor at this juncture, and only rarely did King Richard participate in the rehearsals, Cavendish doing just enough to cue the next speech. Marion could understand why he conserved time and energy in this way but found herself longing to hear that magnificent voice speaking those lovely lines.

Apart from the musical director and the chief scenic painter, who was not a Cavendish employee but a free-lance artist, the only person allowed any licence with Cavendish was Arlene Sidley. She rehearsed with exaggerated intensity, as though her scenes were the linchpin of the entire production, and a quite disproportionate amount of time was spent on them. This suited Marion in her role as understudy but clearly irritated everyone else, except Cavendish, who exercised unusual patience with her. Arlene would repeat her speeches over and over again, experimenting with emphasis and intonation, or she would constantly try out new manoeuvres in order to ensure that the audience would see her profile, or her eyes, or her graceful walk to full advantage. Marion assumed that Cavendish accorded her the courtesy due to a leading lady, but an incident occurred that threw new light on the situation.

Arlene had decided to emphasise her superiority to the new *ingénue* by totally ignoring her; it was just as if Marion did not exist. Naturally an exception had to be made for the small scene that was Marion's big moment in the play, when the lady attendant tried to cheer up the queen by suggesting various pastimes that would entertain her, but even then Arlene managed subtly to convey her contempt. Disheartened and depressed after one particularly uncomfortable rehearsal, Marion collapsed into a chair in the greenroom but, to her surprise, she was joined by the good-looking young man who had sat next to Arlene on the first day, his position in the company underlined by his role as Henry Bolingbroke.

'Don't let the Sidley get you down,' he said kindly, speaking softly so that no one else could hear. 'You are doing fine. If you weren't, the Chief would have made it very clear and probably replaced you – believe me, it has happened.'

'I keep thinking that it must be my fault.' When he shook his head, Marion went on: 'Why does she hate me? What have I done?'

'Your only crime is to have been born fifteen years later than her and to have had Aphrodite, or Venus if you prefer, wave a very special wand over your cradle.' He laughed at her embarrassment and added: 'And if you are wondering why the Chief puts up with it, come with me.'

He led her out into the wings. On the stage Bert Harding was talking to the head carpenter, and several groups of actors were rehearsing little scenes and interchanges of their own. Cavendish was standing beside his chair, the chair into which Marion had seen him throw himself a thousand times in attitudes of exhaustion, irritation or despair, reading a sheaf of notes. Behind the chair was a folding screen, and behind the screen stood Arlene.

'Step out so that she can see you,' Marion's companion murmured, 'and watch.'

Puzzled, Marion did as he said. Arlene turned, saw her and their eyes met. With an almost triumphant air, she leaned round the screen and, taking the papers playfully from Cavendish's hand and placing them on the table, she pulled him round the screen and into her arms. And then Arlene Sidley kissed him, at length and extremely thoroughly.

Marion backed away. 'How could she do that,' she said, in a bewildered voice, 'when she knew I was watching?'

'She did it *because* you were watching. That was a demonstration of her power. She is the Chief's current mistress and she wanted you to know it.'

Marion flinched and turned away so that he would not witness her reaction. This was the theatre and she must become accustomed to such straight talk, but she also wanted Vere Cavendish and could not bear that want to be expressed in such crude terms.

'Will he marry her?' she asked. 'They do marry their leading ladies, don't they, the great actor-managers? It's one of the secrets of their success – two talents combined, and all so very respectable.'

Her companion smiled grimly. 'He won't marry her, not if he has a grain of sense. She is over the hill, fading fast, and needs him much more than he needs her. Oh no, unless I am very much mistaken, the Chief has set his sights a whole lot higher than the Sidley.'

'Then why does he have her as his leading lady?'

'She has a following and he needed to put bums on seats.' And he roared with laughter at Marion's discomfiture. 'Also, there is a frightful shortage of first-class leading ladies at the moment and I dare say he couldn't sign up a better proposition.'

'It is very kind of you to be so reassuring.'

He smiled and raised her hand to his lips. 'Perhaps I recognise the future when I see it.'

Appearances were important to Vere Cavendish, judging by the inordinate time he spent on silent rehearsals when he arranged the cast in pleasing patterns, and by the gorgeousness of the costumes. Marion had only one dress, but it was far more sumptuous and splendid than she had imagined: a tight-fitting bodice and full skirt of black velvet slashed with panels of silver tissue, the bodice boned to thrust up her breasts, and cut so low that she had to assume that modesty was not a feature of Richard's court. How she would dare to wear it, let alone walk out each night before a thousand pairs of prying eyes, she could not imagine. Because she was too tall and slim to wear Arlene's dresses, the wardrobe mistress made a separate train that clipped to the back of the skirt and a mantle of silver tissue that floated from the shoulders, just in case Marion had to step into the queen's shoes. A waste of time, in Marion's opinion, because nothing short of the bubonic plague would keep the Sidley from the theatre.

It was the custom at The Cavendish to have two dress

rehearsals, the first being a dress parade in front of the Chief, followed by a silent walk-through of the full play in order to remedy any deficiencies in the costumes. In the dressing room she shared with the Duchess of York and the Duchess of Gloucester, Marion found the atmosphere friendlier than at any other time. With the wardrobe staff and dressers hurrying in and out, trying to be in half-a-dozen places at once, the two older women helped Marion to dress and showed her how to make up her face with Leichner greasepaints. When her thick dark hair was coiled over her ears and anchored by a net sewn with black beads, the other women were satisfied with her appearance and waved aside her gratitude for their assistance. 'Think nothing of it. The only reward we want is to be there when the Sidley claps eyes on you,' and they made her wait in the dressing room until they were certain that everyone else had gathered on the stage and then they orchestrated her entrance, one on either side of her as they led her out.

Cavendish was talking to Bert Harding and had his back towards them but, at the audible gasp from the cast, he turned round and looked at her: looked at the gleaming ebony hair, at the perfect oval of her pale face dominated by the immense blue eyes, at the curve of her pink-rouged lips and at the expanse of creamy shoulders and half-exposed breasts. Taken unawares, for a brief moment he allowed his amazement and his undoubted admiration to show in his face, but then abruptly he turned his back on her again, leaving Marion to enjoy the blazing fury in the Sidley's eyes.

He watched most of the run-through from the stalls, with Harding and the wardrobe mistress, occasionally holding up proceedings while he hurried on to the stage through the side door connecting the auditorium with his

office. In Marion's scene with the queen, she followed
Arlene on to the stage as usual and was concentrating on
coping with the unaccustomed weight of the velvet and
the tightness of the silver band across her forehead when
Arlene stopped suddenly, forcing Marion to veer sharply
to the left in order to avoid cannoning into her and causing Marion to trip, whether over the hem of the dress or
her own feet she was not sure. All she knew for certain
was that she looked a fool and she was convinced that
Arlene had done it on purpose.

'Step forward, Miss Leigh,' came the inexorable voice
from the stalls. 'Yes, the effect is charming, but I believe
the dress is a fraction too long. Shorten it by an inch or
so – I am sure the audience will appreciate the glimpse of
a pretty ankle.'

As Marion resumed her place, she saw that Arlene's
lips were set in a grim line of defeat. She had made
Marion trip on purpose, and Cavendish knew it and
had retaliated – no leading lady, however indispensable,
was allowed to spoil his production. Marion would
have no further trouble from Arlene during working
hours.

By eleven o'clock that night, many of the cast had been
sent home but although Marion looked optimistically at
Will Tucker each time he entered the greenroom, he only
shook his head and gave her a smile of encouragement. At
last she was alone in the room and, too tired to find out
what was happening elsewhere, leaned back and closed
her eyes. Suddenly a hand touched her bare shoulder and
she started into consciousness, her heart lurching as she
looked into the deep midnight eyes of Vere Cavendish
and realised that it was his hand that still lingered on her
bare flesh.

'Wait for me in your dressing room,' he whispered and

was gone, his voice sounding out on the stage only seconds later, as if he had never left it.

In the dressing room, vacated long ago by the duchesses, Marion sat down on the stool in front of the mirror and stared sightlessly at her reflection. He hates me, she thought, he intends to dismiss me. I am pretty, but not pretty enough to compensate for my many deficiencies. Or, and if anything this was more terrifying, he likes me, he wants to make love to me, and if he did, what the hell was she to do? Fear mixed with longing and confusion, so that when he walked in, closing the door behind him, she simply sat rooted to the spot.

He stood behind her, resting his hands on her bare shoulders so that she trembled, his eyes locked with hers in the mirror. Slowly and very deliberately he moved his hands lightly and caressingly over her shoulders, inching down to the white mounds of her breasts, which thrust so provocatively from her dress, sliding his long sensitive fingers expertly inside the bodice, freeing her breasts so that they spilled into his hands. Then, and only then, did his eyes wrench themselves from hers as he looked down at her nakedness, at the erect rosy pink tips, and bent his head and pressed his cool, hard lips against her flesh. Marion had not known desire before but now she recognised it, as if an old friend had suddenly become a lover, and recognised, too, the sharp intake of his breath and the shudder of longing that ran through him. Inhaling the smell and the very essence of him, she felt the nearness of him for the first time and wanted to be even nearer.

Then he straightened up and drew the bodice back over her chest. Again he looked at her in the mirror. 'You are very beautiful, Marion Leigh, the audience will love you and I am pleased with you. That is all you must remember. Dismiss the jealousy and carping of your rivals from your mind and don't look at the notices in the newspapers unless I tell you to. In this production your beauty will carry you through, but for more demanding roles we need to put in a certain amount of work, *here* . . .' and he pressed his hand against her diaphragm, but now his touch was no longer sexual. 'All that beauty and height and presence, but such a little voice. We will work on it together, Marion, when *Richard* is in full flow.'

She opened her mouth to thank him but no sound came.

'I know you are tired,' he went on, 'and what I am about to ask is unreasonable and inconsiderate, but we have never rehearsed your understudy of the queen. Come,' and he held out his hand and led her through the passages to the darkened and deserted stage.

Letting go of her, he went to the gas table and lit a flare, giving just enough illumination for them to see each other.

'You know the words, of course,' and he guided her through a silent reproduction of Act V, Scene I, the king's farewell to his queen. It was like a ballet, she in her flowing sensual dress and he in shirtsleeves, his collar open, so that when he touched her she could feel the muscular strength of his arms and discern in the dim light the pulse beating at his throat. And then he spoke and she took up the lines and they played it out together until they came to:

'One kiss shall stop our mouths, and dumbly part;
Thus give I mine, and thus take I thy heart.'

Alone in the theatre, they stared at each other, and his head bent towards her and his lips pressed against hers.

'Give me mine own again,' she said, ' 'twere no good part
To take on me to keep and kill thy heart.'

And he kissed her again, still the same kiss, his lips firm and fresh against hers, but unyielding and strangely impassive.

Then his hands gripped her shoulders and he held her away from him, his face taut and beautiful in the shadowy light. 'That is how we kiss on the stage, Marion, but this,' and he drew her within the circle of his arms, 'is how I really feel,' and the sensual curve of his lips found hers again. Startled, she stood quiet and unresisting as his tongue brushed against her lips, gently probing until he eased them open and slid his tongue into her mouth. At first his exploration was soft, persuasive, seductive, but then his arms tightened around her, pressing her against the hardness of his body, and his kiss deepened into a hungry search for greater fulfilment.

When finally he let her go, Marion was bewildered and confused, overwhelmed by sensations she had never before experienced, and yet filled with a strange ache, a disappointment at the withdrawal of his touch.

'You do not relax, Marion,' he said softly, tilting her chin towards him. 'You do not let yourself go. All your passion is pent-up inside you and you will not be an actress until you can release it on the stage. But first you must learn to achieve that release and relaxation in your personal life, and I think that is another area we can work on together.'

Guiding her back to the dressing room, he swiftly and efficiently unbuttoned her dress and left her to change. When she was ready, he escorted her into the street and saw her into a cab with the distant courtesy and aloofness of the old Vere Cavendish. It was as if nothing had happened between them. In the days that followed, when he failed to single her out from the crowd by word or glance or gesture, Marion decided that she had dreamed the entire episode.

The idea that Marion might have touched Vere Cavendish, let alone kissed him, never entered Charley's head. So far above her, so godlike, did he seem that even the possibility of touching the hem of his regal robe on The Cavendish stage took a dizzying leap of her imagination.

When the management gave Marion two free tickets for the opening night of *Richard*, Charley had no difficulty in persuading her sister that she should be allowed to attend. The difficulty arose in finding a companion for her, because Frances flatly refused to cross the threshold of that supposed den of iniquity. Charley would have been perfectly happy on her own but knew better than to suggest it, and in the end it was an inspired, and impassioned, plea to her Uncle John that solved the problem. Sitting beside him in the auditorium, wearing the same green dress that she had worn to *Masks and Faces* that terrible night, she had a weird sense of *déjà vu*. Uncle John looked so like her father that she could almost believe she was with him again, and she realised just how the two identities had merged into one in him and just how close she felt to her uncle. She had nearly shaken off her sudden fit of depression, but this real sense of love and companionship lifted the last vestiges of her loneliness and she turned to him with a beaming smile.

'Thank you *so* much for coming, and please thank Auntie for lending you to me. Did she mind awfully being left at home?'

'I have every hope and expectation that your aunt is bearing up tolerably well under the pain of my absence,' John replied gravely.

'Was she dreadfully disappointed that there wasn't a ticket for her?'

John shook his head. 'Your aunt has not quite decided where she stands on Marion's choice of career.'

'She disapproves, like Frances,' Charley exclaimed in dismay.

'If Marion languishes in obscurity, your aunt is unlikely to broadcast their relationship to her friends. Should Marion become the next Ellen Terry, I think I can safely predict that she will be elevated to the status of favourite niece.'

'And what about you, how do *you* feel about it?'

'Marion will never be my favourite niece. That position is already filled.'

Charley laughed and squeezed his hand, the raising of the safety curtain preventing her from exploring the subject further. She had come a long way since that first visit to the theatre and on this occasion had done her homework, familiarising herself with the Shakespeare text and even swotting up the historical details of Richard's reign, but even so she was still so excited that she could barely breathe.

At the interval her normally pale face was faintly flushed with pink and her eyes were dazed and shining.

'I must say that Marion looks very well, very well indeed,' John pronounced, in what he knew was a classic understatement. In fact, he was stunned by the beauty of his niece on the stage, her loveliness gleaming under the lights.

'I wish I looked like that,' Charley said wistfully.

'You are equally lovely in your own way.'

'No, I'm not.' She seemed about to say something else but that dazed look in her eyes deepened and instead she went on: 'But, Uncle John, isn't *he* the most wonderful actor in the world?'

Indeed, Richard was always to be one of Cavendish's finest roles, a part in which he was *supposed* to luxuriate in the language, where his talent for verse-speaking was fully aired, and where his personal beauty was intrinsic to the character.

Charley did not wait for her uncle's reply. 'And he has staged the play so well,' she rushed on, 'and cast it perfectly. Except for the queen, who is ghastly. She is much too old. Surely Mr Cavendish knows that Richard's queen was only a child?'

John looked at her thoughtfully. 'You know a bit about this sort of thing, don't you?'

'I have a lot to learn,' Charley said gravely, 'but I want to know everything there is to know about the theatre.'

'A modest ambition indeed!' John smiled, but the smile did not quite reach his eyes. 'Do I gather that you want to follow in Marion's footsteps?'

'Please don't tell anyone,' she begged. 'It's a secret. They'll have a fit if they find out.'

'If things turn out the way you want, they are bound to find out.'

'Yes, but by then it will be too late to stop me.'

They were sitting at the back of the stalls, the orchestra playing loud enough to ensure that their conversation was not overheard.

'At the moment I cannot get away,' she said miserably, 'and after the audition last week it looks as if I never will.'

'*Audition!*' John sat bolt upright in his seat and stared at her in horror. 'You have tried to get into the theatre already?'

'Yes, but they wouldn't have me. It was the most humiliating moment of my entire life,' Charley wailed, gazing at him with tragic eyes. 'They said I was too tall. Uncle John, if they had said I was too old or too young, I could have borne it. If they had said I was not good enough for the part, I would have understood and done something about it. But there is absolutely nothing I can do about being too tall!'

'It was very rude of them to say so.'

'They didn't say it to my face, but the acoustics in that theatre were perfect. A damn sight too perfect,' she added balefully.

'Charley,' and John took hold of her hand, 'are you absolutely set on such a step? For some time I have been intending to talk to you about the printshop and to offer you a permanent position in the company. None of my own children shows any interest in the business and, although I love them dearly, I am forced to admit that none of them is as intelligent as you. Please, won't you . . .'

But Charley was squeezing his hand and shaking her head. 'I'm sorry, really I am. I'm very flattered and I'm very grateful, but the theatre is where I want to be. The theatre is what I want to do with my life. The theatre *is* my life.'

She was so young, John thought sadly, yet somehow he knew that she knew her own mind and would not change it. He sighed deeply.

'I cannot say that I approve of such a course and I cannot actively encourage you. But I will say this: forget that nonsense about being too tall, and forget any other personal slights that may come your way. You are a very remarkable young lady, Charley. You are bright and beautiful, capable and courageous, and I believe that you can and will succeed at *anything* you set out to do.'

Charley smiled at him through a mist of tears. 'Thank you. Darling Uncle John, when the time comes for me to leave, I won't miss the others but I will miss you.'

'Just don't go away without telling me.'

Promising to keep him fully informed, Charley returned
her attention to the stage and blissfully allowed herself to
fall again under Cavendish's spell. If she'd had any doubts
about the future, this evening would have banished them
for good. The sight and sound of his King Richard only
made her more determined than ever to stand on a stage
beside him one day. If Marion can do it, so can you, she
told herself firmly.

Chapter Eight

For the first few weeks of *Richard*'s run, Vere ignored Marion, but then the call-boy delivered a note to her dressing room. 'The manager presents his compliments to Miss Leigh and will be pleased if she will present herself in his office before the performance tomorrow evening.'

The formality, and coolness of tone, made Marion blanch. She had been flattered and encouraged by a deluge of flowers and, in order to avoid her admirers, was finding it necessary to take a cab from the stage door to her home every night. However, she was keenly aware that Vere had not told her she could read the notices and she therefore concluded that the critics had been unkind. Doubtless their judgement had been 'pretty but inexperienced', or words to that effect, and she had been trying to take Vere's silence as approval of her performance and Arlene Sidley's stony-faced disdain as proof of her popularity with the audience.

It was after a very uncomfortable twenty-four hours that she knocked nervously on the office door and found herself alone with Vere. He did not ask her to sit down.

'Are you prepared to put in some extra hours this week?' he asked abruptly.

'Of course.'

'Be here at eleven tomorrow morning and brace yourself for some very hard work. You and I have to find out if we can make a silk purse out of a sow's ear,' and he nodded his head in dismissal.

An apprehensive Marion arrived early and hung around the greenroom and the wings, waiting to be called. She had expected a hush to hang over a deserted theatre, but instead the stage staff were cranking the machinery high on the gridiron and fly galleries, and the peripatetic presence of Richard Ramsey indicated that the front-of-house staff were busy about their duties. When Vere did appear, he was deep in conference with Bert Harding but, seeing Marion, he beckoned her on to the stage.

'We are going to work on that little voice of yours,' he said, 'until it can be heard at the back of the gallery.'

As he placed a hand firmly on her diaphragm and began explaining breathing techniques and voice projection, Marion glanced self-consciously at the carpenters and stagehands around her.

'They are not taking any notice of you,' he said crisply, 'so ignore them. I want all your attention and concentration focused on your work.'

Every morning for a week he drilled her, giving her exercises to practise at home as well as tuition in the theatre, and at the end of that time he seemed satisfied with her progress.

'You must keep practising,' he commanded, 'but we have established that you can do it.'

'It is very kind of you to go to so much trouble,' and Marion's hesitant voice contained an unspoken question.

But he did not explain why he had devoted valuable time to her theatrical education, and not once during that week was his attitude towards her anything other than that of manager and mentor.

Only when the company was called for the first rehearsal of the new production did things become clear. Tom Robertson's *Birth* required a smaller cast than *Richard*, there being only eight speaking parts for men and two for women. Marion was not familiar with the work but presumed that she must be wanted for a servant girl or something similar, because she noticed that not everyone involved in *Richard* had been called. Vere would play the Earl of Eagleclyffe, Marion's friend who played Bolingbroke would be Paul Hewitt, and the actor who played John of Gaunt was Jack Randall. After the five minor male roles had been allocated, Vere announced that Arlene Sidley would play Sarah Hewitt and that Marion was to be the Lady Adeliza.

She sat in a daze of happiness, leafing through the script in its crimson folder, finding that the Lady Adeliza was by far the smallest of the five principal parts, but not caring because it was such a massive step up from her present role.

'I cannot imagine why he chose me,' she confessed to Bolingbroke/Hewitt, after the initial read-through.

'It is quite simple: you are building a following. Already you have heaps of admirers who will come to the theatre merely to see you. Doesn't much matter to them what the play is about, as long as you are in view a lot of the time. Behind his more actor-ish flourishes, the Chief is a sharp enough businessman to use that to his advantage.'

Marion had mixed feelings about that assessment, because she would have preferred to be chosen for her talent rather than her looks, and she was rather disappointed that Vere played her brother, not her lover, in the play. Still, they had several scenes together and, as rehearsals got under way, he began taking infinite pains with her performance. So much so that people noticed.

Dressed in a soft-brimmed black hat and a long dark coat that ended only inches from the floor, he was at her side constantly, taking her through her paces and making suggestions that would enhance the characterisation. He sat with her in the greenroom and on several occasions, when the clamour and clatter of the carpenters became too intrusive, took her down to his dressing room for extra coaching. There was no suggestion of impropriety – the door of the room was left wide open, so that they could be seen by anyone who cared to look, but Marion felt it was no coincidence that the most frequent passer-by was Arlene Sidley. Coolly, because Marion was enjoying her revenge, she gave the leading lady several opportunities to retaliate, standing in the wings while Arlene was with Vere by the screen, but when Arlene laid a coaxing hand on his arm, he merely shook it off and moved away.

The affair was over, Marion was sure of it, and she was gripped by a cold, sick excitement.

'I am surprised you are not playing Jack Randall,' she said timidly to him, 'it being the biggest part.'

'My following would never accept me in such a role, not yet at any rate. To please the public I must play the lover, but perhaps I may mature into Jack one of these days,' and he smiled at her in a heart-stoppingly intimate way.

'It is a wonderful play,' she said fervently, flattering him for selecting it for his repertoire.

'No, it is workmanlike but little else,' he replied bluntly, 'as was *Progress*, which I staged last season. Robertson's best works are the preserve of the Bancrofts and, until they drop off the twig – the management twig, I hasten to add – no one else can touch them.'

'You were with the Bancrofts, I believe?' Marion

prompted, trying to coax him into talking about himself because she knew so little about him.

They were sitting in his dressing room, which was plainly furnished with the essentials: a dressing-table, littered with greasepaints and combs, and a large triple mirror; two chairs, one in front of the dressing-table and one for visitors, a closet for clothes and costumes; a sofa bed along the right-hand wall; and a full-length mirror on the left. Vere leaned back in his chair, gazing into the middle distance, displaying to the full his broad-shouldered, long-limbed figure and his brooding, magnetic attraction.

'I was with the Bancrofts for six seasons,' he said, 'when they were at the Prince of Wales. I met them when I was in *Much Ado* at the Olympic in '74 and that year I toured with them before joining them permanently in the autumn.'

'What was the best season you had with them?'

'Oh, '75 to '76,' he replied promptly. 'Ellen Terry joined us, and to have her and Marie Bancroft in the company was magical. We did *The Merchant* – my God, you should have seen Nelly's Portia . . . Well, perhaps you have, she's since done it with Irving at the Lyceum.'

'I have never been to the theatre as a member of the audience,' Marion said shyly. 'It was not the sort of thing my family did, and anyway it would have been too expensive.'

Vere stared at her in silence for a few moments, but whether his expression denoted astonishment or understanding she could not tell.

'The rest of the repertoire was *Money* – we must do that here; and *Masks and Faces* – Ellen played Mabel Vane, which you could do; and *Ours* . . . Lord, I *live* for the day when I can do *Ours* at The Cavendish, and *School*, and

Society and *Caste* . . . Damn it, I know them inside-out and they are so right for me!' His face darkened, but in a moment he was himself again. 'The Bancrofts are reviving *Society* this season and I believe *Ours* is scheduled for next year, so I must be patient.'

Marion wanted to continue the conversation but did not know how. Sometimes she had the feeling that it was better not to speak to him at all than to say something less than brilliant.

'It must have been hard to make the decision to leave them,' she ventured.

'They taught me everything, or nearly everything, I know, but branching out on my own was inevitable. I calculated,' and he leaned towards her, 'that the Bancrofts were making five hundred pounds a week clear profit at the stuffy old Prince of Wales. God knows how much they are pocketing now at the Haymarket. I promise you that Squire and Marie Bancroft could retire tomorrow and live in luxury for the rest of their days.'

Marion's eyes had widened at the size of the sum he mentioned. 'Is that why you took up management,' she asked innocently, 'to make that sort of money?'

Vere looked shocked. 'Money is always a secondary consideration to one's artistic integrity,' he protested vehemently, 'but there is the advantage of choosing one's own parts and I make no apology for casting myself to advantage.'

She could understand that becoming a star, *ipso facto*, was a compelling motive for shouldering the burden of management but, she suggested, did not the anxieties and duties of the position handicap his own performance?

'Management is a step that any ambitious actor must take,' he said, 'for it is either that or soldiering on in mediocre roles for the rest of one's days. But no, I do not find it a handicap and,' and he shrugged eloquently, 'the day might come when one has had enough of strutting the stage and when management is an end in itself.'

Marion had the oddest feeling that this conversation was telling her something about Vere Cavendish, that somehow it held the key to his character, but for the life of her she could not tell what it was.

He was staring past her again. 'I wonder what their profit at the Haymarket was last season,' he murmured. 'Their lease is five thousand pounds a year, and there are the conversion costs to take into account, but most of their productions are revivals . . .' He picked up a pencil and began doing rapid calculations on a piece of paper. 'Good God,' he exclaimed under his breath, 'if they aren't clearing twenty thousand a year, I'm a Dutchman!'

As far as Marion was concerned, £20,000 a year was fantasy-land but, judging from the look of intense concentration on Vere's face, it was very real to him.

'And you know the most amazing thing of all?' He looked at her and smiled cynically. 'Robertson handed the Bancrofts their success on a plate! Not only did he write the plays, but he conducted the rehearsals. Very well, I admit I was a beneficiary – not directly, because he died before I joined the company, but his legacy lingered on. What wouldn't I give for his advice on *Birth* right now! It is much more melodramatic than the works with which I am familiar and sometimes I can see why Squire and Marie did not do it.'

Concerned at the frustration in his tone, Marion reached out and gripped his hand, and he smiled at her in that wild, beautiful, Byronic way.

'There is more to Robertson than meets the eye,' he went on. 'People put him down as domestic and commonplace, but in that domesticity is a freshness, a humour and sincerity that strike an immediate chord with our primarily middle-class audience.'

'Class,' murmured Marion, 'always class.'

'Of course.' Vere gripped her hand hard. 'In *Caste*, D'Alroy says; "Caste is a good thing if it's not carried too far. It shuts the door on the pretentious and the vulgar; but it should open the door very wide for exceptional merit. Let brains break through its barriers, and what brains can break through love may leap over."'

Again Marion felt that he was telling her something about himself, and possibly about herself.

'*Birth* deals with these aspects of ambition and achievement even more convincingly,' Vere continued, as if this explained everything.

'It is going to be a huge success,' Marion maintained stoutly.

He entwined his fingers with hers, caressing them softly. 'I believe you are right, and a large part of that success will be down to you. You are my lucky charm,' and he began kissing her fingers, lifting them to his lips and gently biting them. 'And with my lucky charm *and* my beautiful mistress, how can I fail?'

She jerked free, glaring at him indignantly.

Vere smiled and reclaimed her hand. 'Do you really think that I would insult you by referring to another woman? The *theatre* is my beautiful mistress . . .'

By Christmas, when *Birth* opened to rave notices, the greenroom gossip about Vere and his new favourite had reached the Lyceum, where Edward Druce had a small part in *Two Roses*. Edward wanted to defend Marion's honour but, in all honesty, not knowing the nature of her relationship with Cavendish, did not feel he could do so. Thinking about it and imagining them together, painful as it was, he could believe the truth of the allegations and insinuations only too well.

Besides, it explained something.

He had caught a matinée of *Richard* one day and went backstage to see Marion after the performance. Congratulating her effusively, he exclaimed: 'Wouldn't it be wonderful if we could appear on the same stage together one day!'

'Wonderful,' Marion agreed.

'I hereby stake my claim to a starring role beside you. After all, I virtually discovered you!'

Edward was sincere, but in a lighthearted way, and it was unfortunate that he struck the wrong chord in Marion. She was only too aware of what she owed to him, of the start he had given her in the profession, and was still old-fashioned enough to be haunted by the fact that she had borrowed money from him. Marion hated being under an obligation.

'If you are not doing anything on Sunday,' Edward continued sunnily, 'please come to luncheon with my people. They are quite reconciled to the theatre now, you know – thank God for Irving, it's he who has made the difference! Do say yes!'

Good God, was he actually considering *marriage*? Because that was the obvious conclusion to be drawn from such an invitation. Marion gazed at him in horror and embarrassment. She was not ready to settle down, and in any case did not wish to settle down with Edward Druce. She was head-over-heels in love with someone else. Far from linking herself with a 'leading juvenile', as the old stock companies would have described Druce, she aspired to the heady heights of an actor-manager. Now, for Marion, only Vere Cavendish would do.

'I am afraid that I am not free on Sunday,' she said lamely.

'Another day, perhaps?'

'I do not think so, Mr Druce.'

His face, that very handsome face, tautened and he glanced at the banks of flowers in her dressing room.

'Forgive me, Miss Leigh,' and he bowed stiffly. 'I expect you receive more invitations than you know what to do with.'

Edward was very much in love with her and took her rejection hard. Now he thought he knew why she had rebuffed him, and all he could do was hope that the stories about Vere Cavendish, about his way with women and his treatment of his myriad conquests, were untrue and that he would be kind to Marion.

Certainly he could not interfere. She would not believe him if he told her about Cavendish's reputation and, in truth, was that reputation so much worse than many another man's? It was just that Edward had seen Cavendish as Squire Thornhill in *Olivia* and he had been that part to the life: like Thornhill, Cavendish was exactly the handsome, reckless, unworthy creature that good women are fools enough to love.

For her part, Marion was sorry to lose his friendship but did not see what else she could have done or said in the circumstances. And she was genuinely unavailable on Sundays. If she was not working, it was her duty, to Frances and to the twins, to spend that day at home. She did so uncomplainingly, but occasionally did feel a pang of regret at the loss of the outings and parties she was forced to forego. Sometimes the younger members of the company gathered together for a convivial lunch and at first Marion had been included in the general invitation, but lately, after several refusals, they had stopped asking her. The company began to consider her standoffish, opined that she gave herself airs unbecoming to a young, unknown 'juvenile', and concluded that all the admiration was going to her head.

Druce did not repine for long, but another of Marion's admirers found her notoriety harder to bear. No gossip linking her name with Cavendish had reached Peter Frith-Tempest, but he was sufficiently a man of the world to suspect that Marion's spectacular rise was due to more than her undoubted, but as yet modest, talent.

Like many men, Peter was a mixture of impulse and reflection, but the more he thought about something, the more he tended to decide it was a bad thing. Accordingly the more he analysed Marion's connection with the theatre, the more he despised it and despised her. Which was all very well when contemplated in the privacy of his rooms, but in a seat at The Cavendish, squirming with desire for her, the reality was rather different.

But which was the illusion and which the reality? Peter Frith-Tempest was an ambitious man who intended to reach the top of his profession. In the course of his work he was eager, vigilant and conscientious; he was also suspicious, selfish and ruthless. These traits he considered acceptable and normal, while he knew that he was considered an all-round good fellow, because his rise had not been marred by ungenerous acts or the jealousy of his peers. Always he bore in mind that the perfection of this life must be marred, that one day a worm would wriggle out of the formerly unblemished surface; yet it had never occurred to him that he might be the cause of his own downfall and that the canker might be a direct result of his love for the theatre.

He had controlled it so well, kept it in its place. Damn it, he could pinpoint the peccadilloes of dozens of his friends and acquaintances, whose private infatuations were far less admissible than his own. Be that as it may, it remained intolerable that so respected an observer of the London stage should fall in love with an actress. And it was bad enough for a barrister to consort with a *coquine*, but suppose he submitted to pressure and followed his father into the Foreign Office?

He knew that he did not have the moral courage to take the risk and, hating himself for this weakness, rationed his visits to The Cavendish Theatre. However, in February Vere Cavendish was among the sixteen actors commanded to dine with the Prince of Wales at Marlborough House, a Royal gesture that signalled a new status for the male members of the profession. The occasion resulted in an avalanche of invitations from Vere's society friends, who wanted to hear the inside story of that gathering, and Peter again found himself sharing the Meltons' hospitality with the man.

Moodily crossing the hall after dinner, he stopped suddenly as he heard a muffled sob. Glancing up, he saw young Celia sitting at the top of the stairs, her hair wound up in curling papers and her eyes red.

'What's all this?' Peter ran up the stairs and sat down beside her. 'And why aren't you in bed? Oh, I get it – you wanted to see the great actor himself and you are upset because he did not bow to you.'

'Of course he bowed to me, *beautifully*, but he prefers Eleanor to me,' she wailed.

'I am sure Mr Cavendish has no personal preference.'

'Yes, he does. And he has an assignation with her.'

'Now you really are talking nonsense, dear child.'

'I heard him,' Celia insisted. 'He sneaked out to meet her while you were scoffing the port.'

Come to think of it, Cavendish had excused himself

from the table for a few moments after the ladies had withdrawn.

'Eleanor dawdled in the conservatory – I haven't a clue what excuse she gave Mama but evidently she thought of something. Oh, she's sly and horrible and I hate her!'

'Did Mr Cavendish join Eleanor in the conservatory?'

'I'll say so! And I sneaked in and listened.'

'Are you sure that he didn't see you?' Because surely either Cavendish had been playing a joke on the child or she had misconstrued his meaning.

Celia gave him a withering look. 'I was ready for bed. Do you seriously think that I would let him see me looking like this?'

'You are letting *me* see you looking like this.'

'You don't count. I promise you that Eleanor said: "I will be in the park at eleven on Saturday morning." And he replied: "In that case, Miss Melton, I might just happen to be passing that way myself."' And Celia burst into tears again.

'I would not call that an assignation exactly,' Peter said doubtfully.

'Oh, men are so stupid! It's obvious that he has succumbed to her wiles,' Celia proclaimed wildly. 'She has had a mash on him for ages, although what he sees in her is beyond me. Do you realise,' and her voice began to rise, 'that I might have to treat him as a *brother*!'

'Celia, I do assure you, I promise you, that such a notion is absolutely out of the question.'

'Well, I am not going to sit idly by and watch it happen.' Celia blew her nose loudly and looked at Peter defiantly, an infinitely comic little figure in her curling papers, but with tragedy in her eyes. 'Eleanor will not be in the park on Saturday because I'm going to tell Mama about the whole thing.'

'No,' Peter said hastily. 'Honestly, darling, that is not a good idea.' He thought rapidly. 'We must be subtle about this and catch them in the act. I will go to the park on Saturday and look out for them.'

'Spy on them, you mean?' Celia's eyes gleamed.

'I suppose so. Oh dear . . .'

So on Saturday Peter saddled his hack and trotted into the park, trying to look inconspicuous but not furtive. He spotted Eleanor soon enough, remarkably trim and elegant in a dark-green velvet habit, trotting sedately on one of Melton's high-class chestnuts, but by fifteen minutes past eleven o'clock there was still no sign of Cavendish. Peter began to feel easier. Probably the child had dreamed the whole thing.

But suddenly there he was, acknowledging the greetings of London society as if born to it – which perhaps he was, for no one knew. What's more, and Peter was ashamed to admit that he was disappointed, the man sat his black mare superbly and looked the part, too, immaculately turned out in tight trousers, a Savile Row coat and glossy top hat. Peter realised that he should not have been surprised. Had Cavendish not looked good on a horse, he would not have been here. If he was not born into high society, he would not have ventured through its portals before learning how to dress and dance and talk, thoroughly familiarising himself with that society's manners and mores.

He was riding directly towards Eleanor and, ah, now they saw each other and reined in, with elaborate exclamations of surprise. Peter ground his teeth; Cavendish was a consummate actor, but Eleanor must have been practising for weeks. Cavendish wheeled his horse in a showy 180-degree turn and proceeded down the Avenue, back the way he had come, stirrup-to-stirrup with Eleanor.

Was Cavendish paying serious court to Melton's eldest daughter?

'They did not meet in the park,' he told Celia.

'You're lying. I saw her face when she came back.'

'Then Eleanor is reading more into a casual meeting than Cavendish intended,' he said firmly. 'Forget about it, Celia. He won't marry Eleanor. Your father would never allow it.'

'They might elope,' Celia maintained obstinately.

'Nonsense. Mr Cavendish would never alienate your father. They are business partners and Mr Cavendish needs him.'

Visiting his father later the same day, Peter asked casually: 'Vere Cavendish . . . is he sound, do you think?'

Sir Charles glanced up from *The Times*. 'Why do you ask?'

'No reason. Merely that he has several thousand pounds of your money and I was wondering what we really knew about him.'

'I think that I can say with confidence that I know everything about him.'

'Oh, come on, Father. You don't know everything about me, let alone Cavendish!'

'I mean that I know everything I need to know,' Sir Charles said stiffly. 'Meyer and Melton are good enough recommendations for me.'

'Let's concentrate on Meyer. Keeps a close eye on the business, does he?'

Sir Charles smiled. 'If Cavendish had a wife, she could not know as much about him as Meyer does. Very well, so Cavendish used to have a reputation . . .'

'With women?' interrupted Peter.

'Probably, but I was referring to his gambling habit.'

'Gambling!' Peter nearly choked on his whisky.

'He had a bit of an addiction when he was a young man, at the Prince of Wales with the Bancrofts. Living above his means by all accounts but, then, who doesn't at that age?' And Sir Charles gave a benevolent shrug.

'I didn't, and when I tried to, your attitude was rather different.'

'Point is, Vere Cavendish learned his lesson – gambling doesn't pay and he doesn't do it any more. Works the clock round – Meyer checked. Pops into the Garrick occasionally, but usually Cavendish goes home to a solitary supper and mugs up his words, and presumably mugs up what the minions must do, for the next day.'

'You make Meyer sound like the secret police.'

Sir Charles laughed and returned to his paper, but Peter continued to wrestle with the problem. He instinctively felt that Vere Cavendish was not born a gentleman and that, even off the stage, he was putting up a façade. So if he was serious about Eleanor Melton, he must be naive enough to believe Robertson's twaddle – he had acted in plays such as *Caste* and *Birth* so often that he believed ability would gain him acceptance in the highest social circles and that, if an obstacle to elevation remained, love would overcome it. In which case, both Cavendish and Eleanor were due for a mighty disappointment.

On the other hand, Cavendish might be more likely to seduce Marion.

Frankly, Peter could not decide which was the lesser of the two evils.

One evening at the end of March, shortly before Holy Week and with the opening of *Masks and Faces* only a fortnight away, the crowd of Marion's admirers at the stage door was unusually rowdy. A group of young men – students, she decided in retrospect – jostled and pushed her, demanding her autograph on their programmes. It was customary for the Cavendish company to respond only to written requests for autographs, but so overpowering was the insistence of the youths and so impenetrable the wall of bodies between her and the waiting cab that Marion had no choice but to start signing her name. The crush carried her, slowly but inexorably, along the street, with the bodies of the men pressing against hers so closely that she could smell the drink on their breath. Then she stumbled and fell against the man nearest to her, and only the mass of packed bodies prevented her from falling to the ground. Angry and afraid, she kicked out sharply and used her elbows to fend off the strong arms that suddenly gripped her waist.

'I beg your pardon, Miss Leigh,' said the sarcastic voice of Vere Cavendish. 'Perhaps you do not wish to be rescued. Perhaps sprawling and brawling in the street is your idea of fun.'

Marion sagged as if the stuffing had gone out of her, and felt herself being lifted to an upright position as the crowd melted away. Aware that her clothes were rumpled and her hair awry, she thanked Vere for his intervention and walked shakily back to the cab. To her astonishment, and at that moment not entirely to her pleasure, he climbed in beside her.

'Go via the Garrick Club,' Vere shouted at the driver, and banged his cane on the roof as a signal to start. 'Do you live with your family?'

'My sisters.'

'Tell me about them.'

'Frances is very musical and teaches singing and piano. I keep telling her that, with her voice, she ought to perform, but I'm afraid that she considers the theatre to be the path to ruin.' Marion smiled wryly as Vere laughed.

'Charley works in our uncle's printing company, and the twins are at school. I would like to send them to a really good academy, with boarding facilities, where they could complete their education but, of course, that is out of the question.'

'A seminary for young ladies.' His voice was mocking but perhaps the tone was not intentional. 'I take it we are not paying you enough to allow for that.'

'I didn't mean it to sound that way.'

'Of course you didn't.' He took her hand, patted it comfortingly and then realised that she was trembling violently. 'Those oafs upset you?'

'I really do apologise for that awful scene!'

'Why on earth should you apologise?'

'When you hired me, you said that I must have nothing to do with stage-door Johnnies.'

'You silly goose!' And in the dim light of the cab she saw the flash of his white teeth, and the outline of that classic profile beneath the shiny top hat. 'I meant that you ought not to make assignations with the fellows. What happened tonight was not your fault, and in future I shall ensure that you are escorted to your cab after each performance.'

'Thank you.' Marion began to feel better and dared to clasp his hand more tightly. 'I do feel that I am being very feeble, but I suppose men are better than women at shouldering their way through crowds of followers.'

'If only it was as easy as that,' he groaned ruefully. 'You would be amazed, Miss Leigh, at the lengths to which we must go in order to placate, amuse or generally keep at arm's length the ladies whom we dare not offend.'

'Lady Melton,' Marion hazarded.

'Worse – her daughters! And they aren't the only ones. Believe me, if I had a pound for every dance I have danced, for every ride in the park I have endured, for every tête-à-tête I have suffered in the cause of keeping my public and my backers happy, I would be as wealthy as Bancroft and Irving combined.'

She laughed, the sparkle returning to her eyes and spirits as she revelled in being alone with him. Something of her mood must have conveyed itself to Vere, because he let go of her hand and slipped an arm around her, drawing her close against his shoulder.

'Marion,' he murmured, 'darling Marion . . .' And the warmth of his voice, the intimacy of the moment, his use of her name, all these things raised Marion's face and tilted her lips towards his. 'Will you have supper with me tomorrow night?' he murmured, after they had drawn, breathlessly, apart, 'and perhaps we can continue this conversation where we left off . . .'

Chapter Nine

It being the Saturday before the Easter break, no matinée was scheduled, so Marion washed her hair and took a long bath and afterwards, alone in her room, she stared at her naked body in the mirror.

Would he like it? Would she please him? Because, in accepting his invitation, Marion knew – or hoped she knew – what she was agreeing to do. Each time she thought about it, that same sensation of sick excitement twisted her stomach so that it was impossible to eat or drink, impossible to think of anything or anyone else, impossible that Frances could not know what was in her mind.

Dressing for the theatre, she put on the old gown of violet silk, recently refashioned yet again, with the bodice cut lower and the skirt draped more stylishly.

'I may be a little late this evening,' she told Frances casually as she flung on her mother's old black velvet cloak. 'There is a party after the show . . .'

'At least have the decency not to wake me when you do finally come home,' her sister snapped.

Marion felt guilty but also absurdly happy and, struggling to reconcile the two warring emotions, realised that she was reacting like an unfaithful husband to the strictures of a jealous wife. 'Let's be friends,' she begged, hugging Frances impulsively. 'I cannot bear it when you are so cold and distant.'

'And of course your feelings are the only ones that matter.'

Her sister's body was as stiff and unresponsive as her words, and reluctantly Marion released her. For a moment she stared into those icy blue eyes, remembering the days when they had shared everything and knew everything about each other. Tonight she did not even know whether or not Frances was fully acquainted with the facts of life, let alone dare confide in her what she intended to do.

Richard was on tonight's bill, so she was spared any contact with Vere during the performance. After the curtain she took her time changing her clothes and creaming off the greasepaint, but still she was ready before any message arrived from him and, sitting nervously in the dressing room, she began to feel that this assignation, and her behaviour, was cheap and tawdry and that she should not go through with it. Then she remembered that it was 1 April and wondered if this was Vere's idea of a joke. She was just deciding to creep off home by herself when a knock sounded firmly at the door.

'I will see you to your cab, Miss Leigh,' Vere said loudly. 'We don't want a repetition of last night, do we?'

He was in full evening dress – white tie, black top hat and black cloak – and looked so outrageously handsome that Marion felt a surge of pride that, for this evening anyway, he was hers.

The cab headed west, twisting and turning through a web of narrow, unfamiliar streets, and stopped outside an impressive porticoed entrance in a discreet cul-de-sac. As Marion started up the steps, the door opened and, unsure whether this was a restaurant or an hotel, and whether her guide down the long passage was doorman, butler or *maître*, she followed him into an opulent reception area. There a very fat old woman greeted Vere like an old friend and directed him up a curving staircase to an upper landing and into a small but elegant room, the centrepiece of which was a table laid with two places.

Marion's first reaction was one of fierce disappointment. She had been looking forward to taking her seat in a public place, where heads would turn at their entrance, where the men would admire her and where the women would envy her possession of Vere Cavendish. She ought to have known better. A woman of good character could not be seen dining out with a man who was not a relative, and equally he could not invite her to his rooms, so a private dining room was the only solution.

'This is very charming,' she said, and indeed the room was pretty, its pale-green furnishings and Louis XV gilt so like a stage set that she felt at her ease. 'What is this place exactly – part of an hotel or restaurant?'

'A club,' Vere said smoothly, 'a gentleman's dining club.'

Marion had heard of gentlemen's clubs and the old-fashioned stuffy atmosphere of St James's and Pall Mall, and she stifled another stab of disappointment. She had mistaken his motives for seeking her company, but she would try to be a charming colleague and business associate.

'I wonder if we will be celebrating two weeks from now,' she remarked. 'Having enjoyed two successes this season, is it greedy to want three?'

'*Masks and Faces* will please the public but not the critics,' Vere prophesied, handing her a glass of champagne. 'I took the liberty of ordering dinner in advance, by the way – a bit of fish, and then some chicken, and an ice.

Only a light supper, but I find it more than enough after the theatre.'

'Thank you . . . But why won't the critics like *Masks*? Mind you, I don't think that the part of Ernest Vane does you justice.'

'Spoken like a loyal wife,' and he raised his glass to toast her and, although she knew he referred to her role as his stage wife in *Masks*, Marion's heart lurched. 'I only agreed to do the piece because Arlene wanted it, and because there is such a paucity of choice. I find it maddening – London is bursting with dramatic talent, but where are the playwrights to provide the material?'

'I suppose *Masks* is a trifle old-fashioned,' Marion said as a waiter wheeled in a trolley and began serving the fish.

'It was first produced thirty years ago,' Vere said feelingly. 'There are some classics which stand the test of time, but I am desperate to find a good, new writer.'

'The Shakespeare has been your triumph this season.'

'Ah,' and his eyes gleamed. 'That is one reason I wanted to talk to you tonight, away from the theatre.'

Delicately Marion speared a piece of fish, considered putting it into her mouth, but knew she could not swallow it. Instead she laid down her fork, picked up her champagne glass and smiled at him encouragingly. So this was a business meeting, nothing more, nothing less.

'I thought you and I might tackle *Romeo and Juliet* next season.'

She choked on her wine and, after regaining her breath, gaped at him in utter astonishment. 'But I'm new,' she said at last, 'and the Lyceum is doing it. They open at the beginning of May.'

'And the word is that the production is terrible.' He leaned forward urgently. 'No, that's wrong, doubtless the *production* will be wonderful. It always is at the Lyceum and I am sure that Ellen Terry will give her all. But Irving as Romeo? No, no, never in a million years – as Hamlet or Macbeth, as Othello or Iago or Shylock, yes, but not as Romeo, not as a young and ardent lover. He has the voice but not the looks.'

Vere had the looks and the voice. Looking at him, so near and yet so far away across the table, Marion knew that any woman would believe in him, and welcome him, as a lover. But her, as Juliet?

'I don't think I could do it. I am not ready . . .'

'But that is the joy of it – Juliet was so young and so vulnerable. Have you read the fiery-footed steeds, Phoebus's lodging speech, Act III, Scene II? Very poetic, but in fact Juliet is absolutely panting to be in bed with Romeo. You could do that, Marion, with that amazing beauty of yours. You could portray that blend of innocence and lust.'

Marion gave up pretending to eat the fish and pushed the plate aside.

'The Lyceum production can work to our advantage,' Vere went on. 'You and I can show them how it ought to be done.'

'What will Arlene say?'

'Arlene will be leaving The Cavendish at the end of the season. I am not renewing her contract.'

Marion remained silent as the remnants of the fish were removed and replaced by chicken. She did not protest when her glass was recharged.

'I will help you every inch of the way,' Vere said softly, 'and as my leading lady next season, I will more than double your salary. Would twenty guineas a week enable you to send your little sisters to boarding school?'

'I think so.'

'And could we persuade your musical sister to join the company? If there are no singing or piano parts in the programme, we will insert some specially.'

Marion, ignoring the food but sipping the champagne, sensed the room starting to swim. Frances, at The Cavendish! She began to laugh. 'I told you, she thinks the theatre is the road to ruin and if she could see me now, alone with you in a private dining room, she would consider her opinion entirely justified.'

'Are you afraid of me, Marion?'

'Yes. Of course I am.'

'Do you want me to take you home? I will, this minute, if that is your wish.'

She hesitated, her mind telling her to leave now, her body sending a very different message.

'Or may I persuade you to stay?' He rose, walked round the table and pulled her to her feet and into his arms.

Involuntarily her lips parted for his kiss, but nothing she had experienced before prepared her for this. His lips were hard, bruising and demanding; his tongue invaded and possessed her, leaving her melting and wanting more. When at last he released her, his expression, the light in his eyes and the lines of that beautiful mouth, contained a challenge, not the softness of seduction. Innocent virgin that she was, Marion knew full well that this was the vital moment: she could go or she could stay but, if she stayed, she knew what to expect.

'You are not hungry,' he said, 'and neither am I. Shall I tell them to clear away the food, bring some more champagne, and leave us alone?'

Mutely she nodded and drained her glass, sitting sedately on the sofa until they were alone again.

'I have wanted you from the first moment I set eyes on you,' he murmured, sitting down beside her, his eyes devouring every curve and seeming to discern every intimate crevice beneath the folds of violet silk.

She felt his hard fingers fumbling with the buttons at the back of her bodice and then she was naked to the waist, her heavy breasts spilling into his grasp and, cupping them, he lowered that wonderful dark head to take one rose-pink nipple in his mouth. Licking, suckling, biting gently with tongue, lips and teeth, he aroused first one nipple and then the other to taut points of aching awareness, as his hands lifted and crushed her breasts together. The pleasure was intense but Marion's excitement was tempered by embarrassment as his fingers moved to her back and trickled tantalisingly down her spine, venturing to push inside her drawers to caress the curve of her buttocks.

Then he pushed her back against the cushions and those wandering hands lifted her skirt, sliding up her stockinged legs to linger on the bare, silken flesh of her inner thigh. Marion tensed, frozen with suspense as to what his next move would be, her whole consciousness riveted on the pulsating heat that burned through her underwear. He placed the flat of his hand, hard, between her legs and, after an agonising pause, moved it back and forth massaging her slowly through the thin material of her drawers until a strangled gasp escaped her.

'Yes,' he said roughly, his voice almost unrecognisable, 'yes, good girl, you *can* do it. Close your eyes and just feel. Don't think, *feel* . . .'

She obeyed, or tried to. At that moment he could have told her to jump off Westminster Bridge and she would have done his bidding. Those sensitive fingertips worked their way beneath her drawers and slipped expertly into the most secret crevice of all, exploring with devastating intimacy, as his mouth devoured hers again. When his fingers withdrew, she felt a stab of empty disappointment but immediately he pulled her to her feet, the violet silk cascading to the floor and, as he crushed her against him, she felt the hardness of his arousal pressing into her body through the flimsy folds of her petticoat. Releasing her for a split second, he threw off his jacket.

'Undo my shirt,' he commanded and together they took off his tie and then his shirt. His broad chest was covered in dark, curling hair, which tapered down to the waistband of his trousers and, her full, creamy blue-veined breasts thrusting against him as he clasped her close, she discovered that his skin was smooth as satin, but that when he moved there was a dizzying sensation of controlled muscle power rippling beneath the surface.

He lifted her, carrying her through a door she had hardly noticed and laying her on a bed she had not guessed at. By the light of a single lamp, he pulled the pins from her hair, releasing the ebony cascade to tumble down the white curves of her back. Then somehow – because Marion's eyes were still closed – she was naked and his hand gripped hers and guided it to his groin. Hesitantly she groped at the hard bulge in his trousers, hearing the sharp intake of his breath before he kissed her again, more urgently and deeply than before, and when his clothes were discarded she was aware – was *only* aware – of his erection throbbing against her thigh. His fingers slid back into the crevice, beginning a gentle but persistent massage, until he judged the time was right.

'You haven't done this before,' he whispered, 'so I must hurt you, but only for a moment, I promise . . .'

Easing her legs apart, Vere positioned himself between them and lifted her to meet him. Slowly he entered her, sending a shaft of pain shuddering through her so that she gasped and went rigid. He paused, allowing her body to accept his, and then began to move with deep, slow strokes. It felt wonderful, but Marion lay motionless, not knowing what to do, sure somehow that she was waiting for something to happen. Gradually he increased the tempo, driving into her relentlessly until, after what seemed an interminable time, he moved yet more quickly and then, with a groan, lay still.

But almost immediately he raised himself so that he could look down at her face, and although she felt him shrink slightly, he remained inside her. Gazing at her, kissing her, Vere began to move again, slowly at first but, as before, the pace gradually gathered momentum as he grew larger within her. The dark, brooding face looked down at her, intense, concentrated, and Marion knew nothing but glorious swirls of sensation, waves that lifted her but never broke.

'Marion, Marion,' he murmured, still thrusting into her so that she wanted to cry out: No more, enough, are you never going to stop – because what she was waiting for never came. 'Come with me, come with me, darling, *please*,' but she couldn't, she couldn't . . .

Marion was sure that everyone must know what had happened, that she must look different in some way, or behave differently. So she was astonished that Frances said nothing the next morning and that, when she arrived at the theatre for an all-day rehearsal, none of the company noticed anything amiss. She was certain that her face flamed scarlet when Vere walked into the greenroom, but no one looked at her, not even Vere, and as the day wore on his attitude towards her was the same as always. By late in the evening she was convinced that she had disappointed him the night before and that she would not be alone with him again.

She was standing in the wings, watching him scribble notes by his chair when he looked up and beckoned her over. Pretending to make a point concerning her role, he said quietly: 'I will dismiss you in a few minutes. Wait for me in my dressing room.'

It was a long wait but when he did arrive, Vere caught her in his arms with a series of short, sweet, stabbing kisses. 'I have been wanting to do this all day,' he groaned, and ravenously his tongue prised open her lips and plunged into her mouth.

Marion loved his kisses, loved that closeness and reassurance, and really was happy to leave it there, held by him and kissed by him. Yet when he released her and turned away, she again feared that he did not want her any more.

'I cannot stay – the gasmen and the limelight master are waiting for me. Marion, darling, I must exercise superhuman control and keep my hands off you until opening night. All our passion and energy must go into the play, don't you agree?'

Marion nodded mechanically.

'But on the Saturday after opening night, please have supper with me again,' and he smiled down at her with the light of romance in his eyes.

Marion nodded again and then he was gone, and she realised that she had not spoken a single word. She was standing there, cringing at the episode, when suddenly he reappeared.

'Have you money for a cab?' he asked solicitously. 'Here,' and he pressed some coins into her palm before disappearing for a second time.

Doubtless he intended to be kind but, to Marion, this was not how things were meant to be. She wanted dignity and respectability, not a furtive kiss and the fare home.

She loved him. She loved him to distraction. Already, in her mind, they were Mr and Mrs Vere Cavendish, the most successful partnership on the English stage. So she allowed him to set the pace and make the rules, a passivity that would have astonished those who knew her. But then, what her sisters never did realise was that all bossy Marion, surrogate-mother Marion, really wanted was to be loved and looked after, as she believed she loved and looked after the rest of the family.

After the opening of *Masks*, Vere suggested that she read the notices. As he had prophesied, the critics were bored by 'a tired old favourite', but they conceded that 'not often has it been performed better than by the current cast at The Cavendish'. While Arlene's portrayal of Peg Woffington captured most attention, several papers singled out Marion for special mention: 'a rising talent . . .', 'the lovely Miss Leigh brought a touching fragility to Mabel Vane', 'such admirable diction has not been heard on the popular stage for many years'.

Thus encouraged, Marion told Vere that she would attempt Juliet.

'I never doubted it for a moment.' Sitting opposite her at table in the green boudoir at his 'club', Vere shot her an amused glance. 'Designs are already being drawn up for the sets and costumes, and you and I begin private rehearsals next week.'

'What do you mean by private?'

'Just the two of us together, working on our scenes. The rest of the cast can pick up their parts easily enough in the usual rehearsal time, but in this production everything rides on *us*. You and I have to carry the entire performance.'

'Is it too late to change my mind!'

'This production is a gamble, but that is what makes it so exciting,' and his eyes shone.

'It seems positively suicidal for me to try to compete with Ellen Terry,' Marion said feelingly.

'Not if we play to your strengths – your youth, your beauty and your voice, which is improving in richness and flexibility every day – and, after all, every reading of a part is different. Just do exactly what I tell you and you will be fine.'

He sounded so confident that he transmitted that sureness to Marion. No one had ever told her what to do. All her life she seemed to have been making the decisions and carrying the responsibilities and, instead of resenting his dominance, she welcomed it, feeling a lightness and release as if a great burden had been lifted from her shoulders.

'I was thinking about what you said the other day,' she remarked nervously, 'about new playwrights, and I was wondering if anyone had adapted any of Wilkie Collins's books for the stage.'

'There have been stage versions of some of his novels and he has also written works specifically for the theatre. Fechter did several of his plays, and the Bancrofts did *Man and Wife*, before my time unfortunately.'

'*The Woman in White* would be my suggestion.'

'Yes, I know the work,' Vere said thoughtfully. 'They did it at the Olympic in '71, although I was out of town at the time and did not see it.'

To Marion his knowledge of the London theatre was encyclopaedic 'One character, Marian Halcombe, is a woman of such spirit and determination that she fills me with the utmost admiration. How Walter Hartright can love the lovely but utterly feeble Laura is beyond my comprehension.'

'If you are about to make out a case for playing Marian, instead of Laura, in this as yet hypothetical production, forget it.' His tone, and his expression, held the unmistakable ring of authority. 'For your entire career you will play the "good" women, the sentimental, noble-hearted, sometimes helpless creatures who wait for three acts to claim the hero. The real Marion Leigh may despise them, but her public wants to see her in such roles. And what her public wants is what Marion Leigh, and her manager, will provide.'

He paused, watching her, and then went on: 'However, Marion Leigh's real problem, if such one can call it, is her beauty. To use *The Woman in White* as an example, Walter Hartright loves Laura because she is beautiful, albeit less than scintillating company. The description of Marian, on the other hand, specifically denies any aspiration to good looks. It is a role that, as long as your looks last, you can never play.'

'In that case, my beauty is my curse,' she declared melodramatically.

'Without that beauty, you would not be sitting here now.'

His words, sharp and surely intentionally cruel, were like a slap in the face. Marion sat frozen, knowing that she ought to retaliate, but emotionally and verbally paralysed. As her silence extended, seemingly for ever, a look of disappointment crossed Vere's face.

'On one level I am trying to indicate that, if you were not as beautiful as you are, you would not have achieved your current place in The Cavendish company,' he said. 'On another level, your appeal to your public is this: that beneath the innocence and naivety of your performance, and the characters you portray, lurks a passion which the touch of the right man can release. And on another, and far more basic level,' and here Vere's voice took on a low, resonant growl, 'to enable you to release that passion on the stage, on cue and as required, I will provoke you into releasing it off the stage, whether you want to or not.'

He stood up and rang the bell. 'While the meal is being cleared away, perhaps you would care to change into something more comfortable,' and it was clear that this was not a question but a command.

In the bedroom Marion picked up the nightgown that was lying on the bed. Low-cut and sleeveless, it had hardly any bodice to speak of and, although the skirt was long and full, the filmy silk was virtually transparent. After she had put it on, she could not bring herself to move. He expected her to walk into the other room in this . . . this whore's gown? It would have been easier to walk on to The Cavendish stage in it than face him alone, but if she did not do it, some other woman would and then Vere would marry that woman instead of her. Act, Marion said to herself, act . . .

So she entered the room with her head held high and did feel a rush of pleasure at the look on his face when he saw her, at the way his eyes darkened and his mouth tightened and a muscle twitched in his cheek. Rather to her alarm, although what else she had expected she did not know, he had changed into a heavy silk dressing-gown of dark blue, wrapped over and loosely belted, which ended just below the knee so that she could see his long, well-shaped legs. She had a strong suspicion that he was not wearing anything underneath.

'The old saying goes that anticipation is better than realisation,' he said slowly, 'and it is true most of the time. However, what is *always* true is that anticipation is at least half the fun. Only under extreme circumstances should a man grab a woman and take her by surprise. The

most long-lasting and exquisite pleasure needs the tease of
anticipation, the knowledge that soon the act will take
place; it needs that edge of excitement, that sitting-on-
the-edge-of-your-seat tingle of desire. Have you felt that
tonight, Marion?'

'Yes, of course,' she said quickly, but knew that her
response was too much that of a pupil agreeing with her
master, and that it lacked sincerity. Judging by his slight
sigh, Vere knew it, too.

'You ought to sit like this,' and, as if on a stage set, he
posed her against the sofa cushions, arranging her skirt to
reveal white thigh and black triangle through the thin silk.
As a final touch, he eased the bodice open so that the
material ruched round her naked breasts. All this done
without a caress but with the eye of an artist. 'I wonder,
shall we make a courtesan of you, Marion?'

'I don't want to be a courtesan,' she said, startled. 'I
want to be a . . .' and she stopped.

'A wife,' he supplied for her. 'The two do not have to be
mutually exclusive, you know! Come here and kneel
down in front of me,' and to her horror he untied his belt
and opened the robe, revealing his nakedness.

Somehow, the last time, she had managed not to look at
his body, but now there was no avoiding it. How ugly it
was! It reared up at her from a nest of dark hair, repulsing
her, amazing her that something so huge had entered her
own narrow, fragile passage. Sitting forward and spreading his legs, Vere positioned himself so that the thing
nestled between her breasts.

'Hold me,' he whispered, pressing his lips to her forehead but, even as her hand hovered uncertainly over him,
he took her head in his hands and guided her lips down
and on to him. 'Kiss me, Marion. Take me into your
mouth and kiss me.'

She tried, she really tried, brushing her lips against it. 'Use your tongue,' he whispered and she did that, too, but then the thing twitched and suddenly it was in her mouth and halfway down her throat, or so it seemed, and involuntarily she gagged.

Again she felt, rather than heard, Vere's soft sigh.

Without a word he picked her up in his arms, carried her to the bed, removed her gown and his robe, and lay down beside her.

The light was on. It seemed even more intrusive now than it had last time and Marion wished that she dared ask him to switch it off.

That beautiful mouth was kissing her breasts lightly, brushing them like the wings of a moth, fluttering down her stomach and resting a while on the softness of her inner thigh. Then a finger probed between her legs and located the pulse of her clitoris, enabling his tongue to begin its work, and a surge of pleasure spread through her, a sensation of wanting to open and engulf him. But instead her eyes would persist in opening and, seeing him there, the awful ugliness of her secret parts pressed against his face, Marion was too embarrassed to relax, her awareness of the indignity of her position making her more and more tense. If it were dark she was sure she could sink into the sensations and lose control. But not with the light on.

When Vere moved on top of her, even Marion could not hold back a gasp of pleasure as he entered her with a long, delicious slide and began a slow, controlled thrusting. The pleasure was exquisite, but Marion knew that it ought to be building to a peak and that to make it happen she must participate, but she could only lie inert and wait with helpless longing for a fulfilment that never came. However, overriding these sensations was her total awareness of what was happening, and her dominant desire was to please, to please Vere and be what he wanted her to be. So, with an instinct as old as time, Marion closed her eyes and moaned and gasped, as he was gasping, and when, after what seemed an eternity, he cried out and shuddered and came, she clasped him close.

'Marion,' he said in the cab as he took her home, 'our destinies are linked at The Cavendish for the foreseeable future. But if you lie in the bedroom, and I mean lie in both senses of the word, you must do so with more conviction.'

Charley had widened her reading to include *The Era* and *The Entr'acte* as well as *The Stage*, a financial outlay that was proving detrimental to her modest savings. But only in early May did she see another advertisement that seemed worth answering, her chief criterion being that the notice said 'urgent' twice, thus raising the hope that haste might outweigh other considerations.

Interviews were to be conducted at an office in Garrick Street, so Charley took an omnibus to Trafalgar Square and walked from there. She had sneaked into Marion's room and borrowed a silk petticoat, which rustled and swished in the most satisfying way, not only giving a girl added confidence but, in Charley's case, also making her feel much more grown-up. But as she entered the agent's waiting room, most of her courage evaporated and her heart sank. The room was crowded with theatricals of all shapes, sizes and ages, male and female, all wearing a carefully posed expression of relaxed nonchalance, which grew stiffer and more artificial as the morning wore on and it became apparent that the agent had not arrived. At lunchtime the room emptied as most people abandoned the wait and strolled off for a cup of tea, but Charley was determined to sit there for ever if need be.

Her patience was rewarded when, at about two o'clock, the door opened and a small, balding man sprinted across the room towards the far door, evading the outstretched hands and imploring looks of those who remained. Clearly the great man had arrived and a bored youth, sitting at a desk in the corner, called out a name, sending a shabbily dressed middle-aged man rushing eagerly into the office. Obviously he was not a rival for her position, the advertisement having stated both 'young' and 'woman', but Charley tried to guess how many other people were candidates for the same job and, with the room filling again after the lunch hour, her heart and her courage sank into her boots.

It was impossible to read anything into the faces of those who preceded her into the office, because they preserved their aplomb at least as far as the street, and so, when Charley's name was called, she did not know if the vacancy still existed.

'You're new,' the agent said, staring at her keenly.

Humbly Charley admitted that this was her first foray into the world of the professional theatre.

'What engagement are you after?'

'The position with The Pastoral Players, the touring company which . . .'

'What experience do you have?'

'I have appeared in amateur productions,' Charley lied airily. 'Alicia in *Lady Audley*, Mabel Vane in *Masks*, that sort of thing. I have learned a terrific amount from my sister – Marion Leigh, she's at The Cavendish, perhaps you have heard of her.'

The agent's expression changed imperceptibly and he looked at, and listened to, Charley with more attention than before.

'How old are you?'

Charley was seventeen years old. 'Twenty.'

'Stand up and read this,' and he handed her a script.

Not for nothing had Charley substituted for Marion, reading to the family in the evenings and giving elocution lessons to the twins. She knew that she was not as good as Marion but still she read with a blend of panache and sensitivity, prowling around the room with a swish of the silk petticoat.

The agent watched and listened. A competent reading, but nothing to set the world on fire. He had heard better – in this office this afternoon he had heard better. But Charlotte Leigh had something. Beneath that tight cuirass bodice of red-brown velvet, the white blouse with the high collar, jabot and frilled cuffs, and the chocolate-brown flounced skirt, there moved a long, lean, lissom body, small-breasted and narrow-hipped. And her height! Not to everyone's taste, but he liked it. Legs up to the armpits, he thought, his pulse quickening. What a Viola, what a Rosalind! But most striking of all was her colouring, that tawny, flaming mane of russet hair that escaped in tumbling tendrils around her face, and those blue-green eyes alert with intelligence. Her vivacity burned into one's consciousness. Put Charlotte Leigh on a stage and she would not merely stand out from the crowd, she would outshine the limelight.

'The Pastorals are paying two pounds a week and, apart from period pieces, you find your own costumes.'

'I'll take it.'

He wrote down a name and address and a brief note of introduction. 'Report here tomorrow, and don't let me down.'

Charley took the note, but still she hesitated.

'You do not owe me commission,' he said kindly. 'In this instance The Pastorals employed me. But you pay your own train fare, and find lodgings when you reach Bristol.'

'Bristol.' John Leigh stared at her dully. 'Oh, Charley . . .'

'I know. I've been looking forward to this day for ages and yet suddenly I feel terribly sad.'

'I'll not stand in your way or try to stop you. Just remember that I'm here if you need me and that there will always be a job here for you if the theatre turns out badly.'

She hugged him fiercely. 'And you won't tell the others where I am, will you? I couldn't bear it if Frances turned up and made a scene.'

'I will keep your secret, Charley, if only because I am so glad that you confided in me.'

'Well, I had to tell you what was happening,' and she grinned at him with a touch of her old humour. 'I can't leave without my wages.'

'Minx!' And when he went to the safe to fetch the money, John was reminded sharply of all the times she had come to ask for the 'rent money' and he had the sensation of a wheel coming full circle. Whatever happened, it was the end of an era.

After another hug and a final admonition that she must keep in touch, he escorted her out of the building and, unknown to Charley, stood watching her until the bright flame of her hair was lost to view.

At home Charley ruthlessly pillaged the house for anything that might be useful for the roles she would be expected to play: one of her mother's few remaining silks; a pair of white gloves that Frances cherished – a bit tight for Charley, but they would do; a fan and a belt from a drawer in the twins' room. Then she packed her own clothes. And she kept Marion's silk petticoat.

Next morning she wrote a note, saying simply: 'I have

gone to be an actress. Don't try to find me,' and left it on the kitchen table. After lugging her case as far as Euston, she called a cab.

'Paddington Station,' she said and, as the cab headed west, Charley did not look back.

'Uncle John says that he knows no more than we do,' a distraught Marion reported.

'Then we must waste no time in alerting the police,' Frances asserted.

'We might do better to make our own inquiries through the managements and agents,' Marion suggested, distractedly running her fingers through her hair.

'But Charley does not want you to find her,' Arabella said quietly.

Frances glared at her. 'What Charley wants, and what Charley will get, are two very different things.'

'I wonder . . .' Marion sat down and made a conscious effort to calm herself. 'Perhaps Arabella is right. Uncle John said that we should leave her be and let her make her own way in the world. Of course . . .' and she stopped.

'Go on,' Frances prompted grimly.

'I am afraid that he did express his concern about Charley having chosen the theatre as a profession. Frances,' and Marion forced herself to meet her sister's eye, 'please do not say anything. I am feeling dreadfully guilty as it is.'

'So we just let Charley go?'

Marion, perhaps for the first time, was trying to put herself in Charley's place, trying to project herself into her sister's feelings, emotions and desires, and suddenly she was certain that Charley's love for the theatre ought not to be thwarted. After all, *she* had fought hard enough for the right to pursue her own career on the stage.

'Yes,' she said simply, 'and now that there are only four of us, and we will not have Charley's contribution to our finances, we must move.'

Frances began reconnoitring various districts and properties, but could not find a house that was both suitable and affordable. With more time at her disposal before rehearsals began for the next season's productions, Marion made a few inquiries of her own.

'After the school fees have been paid, we cannot afford a house,' she decided, 'so we must settle for rooms. Good rooms, of course,' she added hastily, seeing the shocked expression on her sister's face, 'a positive *suite* of rooms.'

'*Lodgings!*' breathed Frances in a 'that it should come to this' tone of voice.

'It need not be that bad,' Marion said encouragingly. 'We could start by looking near the Tottenham Court Road. You would be close to your friend, the Scarlatti woman.'

At that Frances looked more thoughtful and, when they found rooms in Gower Street, with permission to install some of their own furniture and, most importantly, the piano, she became almost reconciled to the idea. Bloomsbury, she decided, might be a rich source of pupils and, being more centrally situated, she might consider taking on a few theatricals for singing lessons and voice coaching.

'I suppose if it suits you, the rest of us will have to put up with it,' she told Marion, with a martyred air, 'and of course your journey time to the theatre will be more than halved.'

Arabella and Imogen were glad to be leaving the house and its associated memories, and put themselves out to be co-operative. When the time came to pack their belongings, Arabella helped Frances to clear the attic, while Imogen sorted through the few items that Charley had left behind. She found a couple of crumpled theatre programmes and stared at them for a moment, puzzled, before throwing them on the pile of rubbish for burning. And then, from the back of the same drawer, she pulled out the photograph of Vere Cavendish.

Sitting back on her heels, Imogen stared at the picture, and its simple caption, for a long time. So this was Vere Cavendish. She had not realised how very handsome he was. And Imogen, young as she was, sensed the threat that so handsome a man could pose but only interpreted that threat in its most simple form, knowing that she did not want Arabella to see him.

So Imogen tore the photograph into small, and yet smaller, pieces and crumpled them in her fist. She went downstairs and threw the scraps on to the kitchen fire, and stood watching them shrivel and blacken and die.

Chapter Ten

Frances had sworn never to set foot in the theatre yet here she was, standing in the wings, staring with dull resentment at the empty stage. The Cavendish, closed for the summer break, was at its most unglamorous, the auditorium shrouded in dustcovers; and Frances had been unprepared for the silence and the gloom, the crypt-like cold and the intricate loops and lines of the ropes, weights and pulleys high above her. And the smell! Retreating to the greenroom, where Marion had told her to wait, Frances found her nostrils wrinkling with dainty distaste at the pervading odour of grease, gas, human bodies and, not to put too fine a point on it, the sanitation or, in this instance, the lack of it.

The greenroom, however, passed muster. The chairs were comfortable and, on days when a fire burned in the grate, it would be quite cosy. Unfortunately an awful fate drew her to the window, which opened on to a yard covered by a canvas awning under which old scenery was stored. As Frances idly tried to discern the design on the big flat nearest to her, something grey and furry darted across it and disappeared into a corner. Frances froze. She must be mistaken, but no, there it was again or, more likely, another one. Probably the yard was swarming with rats and, shuddering, Frances moved as far away from the window as possible, involuntarily raising her skirts slightly and glancing nervously round the room.

She ought never to have come. She had known it from the start and she should have had the courage of her convictions. But without Charley's wages, the sisters needed extra money and, because the twins were away at boarding school, Frances had the time and the freedom to take on new work. In the end it had not been the pleas of Marion that had persuaded her but the reasoned arguments of Maria Scarlatti. Much to Frances's surprise, Maria not only spoke well of The Cavendish's reputation, but felt that the position of singing coach to the company would be a sound career move, while occasional singing roles could only enhance Frances's professional reputation. So here she was, kicking her heels while Marion – who ate, slept and dreamed Juliet these day – ironed out a few problems with Vere Cavendish.

She was curious to meet him, this Mr Cavendish, whose name dropped constantly from Marion's lips and, hearing sounds of activity outside, Frances ventured again into the wings.

On the stage the lights were brightening; two men were pushing a piano into a central position, and her sister was talking to a very tall man who had his back to where Frances was standing. Frances's lip curled disdainfully. Just as she had expected – a very rackety type indeed, in a dark overcoat that ended a mere foot from the floor and a dark, wide-brimmed hat. That decided it; Frances was leaving, *now*. But at that moment Marion beckoned and Vere Cavendish, because obviously it had to be he, turned round. He removed his hat, but his only other acknowledgment of her presence, as Marion effected the introductions, was a grave bow of his head. Then he ran an infinitely practised eye over her and Frances became angrily aware that he had assessed every detail of her person.

'I will see you first, Miss Leigh, because I have a busy musical day ahead. We are taking full advantage of the blessed hush – believe me, we are enjoying the week of the carpenters' holidays as much as the carpenters themselves.' He smiled, but Frances remained resolutely hostile. 'When you are ready,' and, with Bert Harding, he made his way to the stalls. Marion hovered in the wings.

'Where the hell is that piano player?' came Vere's bored voice from the auditorium and a young man hurried on to the stage, clutching a sheaf of sheet music. Frances regarded him with contempt. As she did not want this job, she was not in the least nervous but she had no intention of giving a mediocre performance. She had brought her own music and, a touch haughtily, discussed the sequence of songs with the accompanist. After a little lady-like cough, she began to sing.

To Marion's intense relief, it was glorious. She had been concerned that Frances's voice might be lost in the vastness of the l,000-seater auditorium, but the notes rang out with a clarity and carrying power that would not have disgraced the nearby opera house, soaring with a strength and sureness that demonstrated her sister's complete confidence in her ability. Only at the end of the second song was there a slight wobble, a point at which voice and piano did not quite coincide.

'We will do the Mendelssohn next,' Frances hissed at the accompanist, 'and this time do you think you could get the tempo right?'

Marion grimaced, knowing that Vere would have heard the remark and, sure enough, when Frances finished the song, that beloved voice drawled: 'As apparently you are a more skilled exponent of the piano than our resident musicians, Miss Leigh, perhaps you would care to dazzle us with a piece from your vast repertoire?' And Marion withdrew further into the wings, wincing, because Vere and Frances were not getting off to a good start. One of them was going to regret this challenge, and that person would not be her sister.

An expression of smug satisfaction settled on Frances's face. With a swish of her skirts, she settled on the piano stool, ostentatiously tossed the sheet music to the floor and without hesitation launched into a brilliant burst of Chopin – flashy, sparkling and showy. This was followed, and the transition in itself displayed a fluid mastery, by a slow and dreamy extract from a Beethoven concerto, which was brief but ravishing in its beauty. Barely had she begun the third piece, a work by Bach for the left hand alone, when a dry expressionless voice from the stalls said: 'That is more than enough, Miss Leigh. Kindly continue with the audition.'

Will Tucker handed Frances the script of *The Ticket-of-Leave-Man* and here Frances faltered. She was no actress. Her speaking voice was thin and hard, rather like her face, and she altogether lacked spontaneity, so that her reading of any part was stiff, unnatural and unconvincing. Yet her physical resemblance to Marion was striking and undoubtedly the reason why Vere called both sisters simultaneously to the front of the stage. When he ordered them to turn so that he could see their back views, Marion's memory of her own audition flashed into her mind with such clarity that she threw him a swift glance of appeal: please, she prayed, don't let him ask Frances to unpin her hair, and as for ordering her to show her legs . . .

A smile stole across Vere's face. 'Take off your hats,' he

called out, in that same expressionless voice. 'I want to see your hair.'

'Just do as he says,' Marion begged an outraged Frances. 'Mr Cavendish has his reasons for everything,' and, she muttered to herself, this one had better be good.

'Walk up-stage, Miss Leigh – no, not you, Marion. Lord, this is going to be confusing. Miss *Frances*, walk to the back of the stage . . . that's far enough.' Vere was out of his seat and, motioning Bert Harding to accompany him, walked forward to the orchestra pit, close enough for Marion to overhear their conversation. 'The drawing room scene in *The Woman in White* . . . When Marion moves to the piano, she goes past a screen, through a gauze curtain and sits down to play. Except that behind the screen Frances, with an identical dress and hairstyle, changes places with Marion and becomes Laura while she is at the piano, playing behind a romantic filmy gauze.'

Still talking, Vere began walking towards the door linking the auditorium with his office. 'See Mr Ramsey about your contract, Miss Frances,' he said over his shoulder.

Frances found herself sitting in the office with Dick Ramsey and listening to the terms and conditions of her proposed employment, being offered a sum of money that made her gasp and which she knew she could not refuse. Almost before she knew what she was doing, she had agreed.

Settling quickly into a routine at The Cavendish, Frances was surprised by the amount of care that went into the visual and sound effects of each production. She soon developed respect for the musical director, not only because of the quality of the musical content of the plays but also because of the excellence of the entertainment provided during the intervals. When the season got under way, she noted that some members of the audience did not drift away to the bars during the intermissions but stayed in their seats, listening to the orchestra. Reluctantly, she had to hand it to Vere Cavendish: for him, only the best would do.

She was kept busy. Her chief task was to coach Marion and another actress in a number of songs required for *The Ticket-of-Leave-Man*, but Vere had decided that Frances's talent should be displayed, behind another film of gauze, in the usually offstage concert hall. He placed her in *Romeo and Juliet*, singing a lively Italian folk song with a lute and wearing a blonde wig so that no one would confuse her with Marion; and she 'walked on' several times in *The Woman in White* as part of the substitution plot, as well as playing the piano. Sometimes Will Tucker asked her to assist him in drilling the supers, particularly if the sequence had a musical background, and he always treated her with a discreet deference, placing her on a professional level apart, and slightly above, the company. With the acting staff, she was not popular; there was too much disapproval in her demeanour and too obvious a curl to her lip. She complained, loudly and constantly, about conditions backstage and blamed the drains for every sore throat, loss of voice or rheumatic pain suffered by the cast.

'I would not have believed that even a theatre would expect its staff to manage with so few lavatories,' she said indignantly to Marion in the greenroom. 'And the state of them – ugh!' and her nose wrinkled and she refused a cup of tea with the meaningful look of one who is watching her intake of liquids for obvious reasons. 'Someone will become seriously ill in this theatre one day,' she predicted, 'and then your precious Mr Cavendish will have some explaining to do.'

'Nonsense,' Marion protested, her mind less on the

sanitary arrangements than hoping Frances would not discover just how precious Mr Cavendish was to her, not just
yet anyway.

To many of the company Miss Frances also had a disconcerting habit of popping up suddenly when least
expected, her sharp nose poking into other people's business and her bright eyes missing nothing. Indeed, she
overheard conversations that made her hair stand on end
and her face flame. The gaps in her sexual education,
except for the practical aspect, were soon filled and she
was picking up a vocabulary that would have shocked
her only a short time ago, and to some extent still did.
Only with Marion did she have a blind spot, remaining in
ignorance of her sister's relationship with the manager,
probably because the possibility of such a relationship
simply did not occur to her. Frances never questioned the
fact that she was dismissed from a rehearsal earlier than
her sister, or that from time to time Marion went out to
supper after a performance while Frances went home
alone. She was sensible enough not to expect her sister's
life to change merely because she, Frances, had joined the
company.

As for Vere, Frances was far more objective about him
than Marion had ever been. She judged him to be in his
mid-thirties and in this was correct, Vere being thirty-four
years old at the time. His good looks and elegance of
manner were so obvious as to be overly intrusive in any
assessment, however cool, and much against her will
Frances found that she could not remain totally immune
to his sophistication. She had never seen, let alone met,
anyone quite like him before. The fathers of her pupils, for
instance, represented a wide range of professions and
backgrounds, but none possessed that almost indefinable
air of being completely at ease, and completely in control,

in any situation. There was a remoteness about him, an aloof quality, that was inhibiting, almost frightening. Outspoken though Frances might be in her comments and complaints about The Cavendish, she made sure that the manager was never within earshot; and she noticed that no one, within her hearing, made any adverse remark about him. Watching Vere covertly whenever the opportunity arose, she saw him perpetually criticise the performances of his actors, but she was professional enough in her own sphere to recognise that in fact he was provoking them into giving their best. The perfectionist in him, the element of the teacher that she saw in him, struck a chord that she had not expected and which at first made her resentful – Frances did not want to like or respect him – and then forged what she thought of as a personal bond between them. She alone, she decided, discerned his finer points and really understood him.

Yet the whole of London was at his feet, during this season of 1882–3, and it was Marion who stood beside him. This was one of the most glittering seasons ever staged at The Cavendish, a time when Vere Cavendish and Marion Leigh were a golden couple who could do no wrong in the eyes of their adoring public, whose *Romeo and Juliet* touched such a chord that Henry Irving never attempted it again. And, in the midst of the euphoria and energy that pervaded The Cavendish, only Frances stood aside and watched, as if from the outside, deeply lonely and unhappy. She suffered no lack of personal success, her musical talent being recognised and applauded at every performance, but she felt out of place, unfulfilled, and demeaned by what she saw as exhibiting herself to the masses.

The only occasions that made Frances happy were the days, usually Sundays, when they were invited to the homes of Marion's artistic friends and admirers. Often a mere three miles from Piccadilly, but with grounds worthy of a country house, these gracious establishments provided an environment that Frances felt to be worthy of her presence and of her aspirations. Here, she thought, as she sat on sweeping green lawns under lilac and chestnut trees, was where she belonged. This, she told herself, as she learned to play croquet, and played it rather well, was the world in which she had been intended to shine. She even had the satisfaction of believing that *she* had made possible this entrée into a higher social circle.

'You never received such invitations before I joined The Cavendish,' she remarked to Marion as, dressed in big hats and soft chiffon dresses with trailing skirts, they sauntered through a crowd at a garden party.

'You are forgetting that the twins were at home in those days,' Marion replied coldly. 'I had to refuse such invitations on account of my domestic responsibilities.'

'Of course you were not as well-known then as you are now,' Frances conceded, 'but I still maintain that from the start people recognised me as a lady.'

'More likely they recognised you as a suitable chaperone for me,' Marion muttered waspishly.

They made a charming picture, Marion in pale mauve and Frances in forget-me-not blue, and attracted a flattering amount of attention. Although Frances could not help but notice that Marion received the most admiration, fortunately she was unaware that people took her for the older sister.

'Of course,' Frances went on, 'in some ways it is a pity that these gatherings are attended by so many theatrical types, but one cannot have everything.'

'We are privileged to meet a great many important people,' Marion exclaimed, 'who can make a valuable contribution to our careers – critics and writers, painters and poets, and musicians. If you listened to what they were saying, and cultivated their acquaintance instead of that insufferably superior expression on your face, you might learn something. At times I get the impression that you would prefer all the people to vanish and leave you alone in the house.'

Wistfully Frances looked at the lovely old mansion, with its wide verandah, French windows and green-shuttered bedrooms and then she surveyed the crowd milling about on the lawns, and she sighed. To enjoy this place in peace and solitude was exactly what she would have liked to do. Instead of which, she had to endure these uncongenial people and go home to her shabby lodgings.

'We ought to count our blessings, I suppose,' she said, 'because at least we do not have to endure Mr Cavendish on these occasions. What does he do with himself on Sundays?'

'I have not the slightest idea,' and a blush tinged Marion's cheeks. 'However, I am afraid you are to be disappointed this afternoon, because Mr Cavendish is here.'

'Where?'

Marion indicated a secluded corner of the garden that had been marked out for tennis and where four of the younger men had made up a set. Watching them from the sidelines, in conventional morning coat and top hat, was Vere Cavendish.

At that moment Marion was commandeered by a group of admirers, but Frances excused herself and, after a moment's thoughtful hesitation, set off across the grass towards the tennis match.

'Such energy and enthusiasm,' she said languidly, after manoeuvring herself into a position next to Vere and exchanging greetings. 'These games are all very well for the young, I suppose, but just watching them makes me feel hot and bothered.'

Two of the men had given their racquets to the two teenage daughters of the house who, dressed in ankle-length flannel skirts and long-sleeved blouses, wide leather belts and stiff-brimmed boaters, took their places on the roughly marked court.

'I am sure that nothing could disturb your equilibrium, Miss Frances,' Vere said gravely and then continued with elaborate gallantry, 'and, besides, surely you cannot be more than a year or two older than those young ladies?'

Frances positively bridled with pleasure. 'We do not usually have the honour of meeting you at our Sunday gatherings,' she gushed, as if she was the hostess and chatelaine of the house. 'I do hope that you don't spend the day cooped up in the theatre.'

'All too often that is exactly what I do. Oh, good shot,' and he applauded as one of the girls sent a ball skimming out of her opponent's reach. The girl looked round and saw him and, child though she still was, blushed and sent him a charmingly flirtatious smile.

Firmly Frances grasped Vere's arm, her touch feminine and decorous, yet determined and not to be denied. 'The afternoon is very warm. Do you think that we could find something cool to drink?' And she guided him away.

'Is your sister here?' Vere inquired off-handedly.

'Oh, she's around somewhere, busy as usual.'

Vere nodded and, apparently resigned to his fate, found the refreshment tables and brought Frances a glass of lemonade.

'Isn't this better than that stuffy old theatre? You ought to get out into the fresh air more often.'

'I manage a day off from time to time, and very occasionally I even go into the country for a weekend. For instance . . .' And Vere described several social engagements with peers of the realm and leading entrepreneurs, which caused Frances's eyes to widen, her expression to change from arch to thoughtful, and her mind to consider the possibilities that suddenly opened in front of her.

She saw Vere Cavendish in an entirely different light. The attraction that he held for her at the theatre, to which she could never admit because it was inextricably linked with that theatre, now became not only acceptable but blindingly obvious and designed by fate. Here, on these gracious lawns and against the backdrop of this house, he looked so absolutely right and so thoroughly at home that one could forget he was an actor. What's more, these aristocratic connections enlightened her about his pedigree.

'Do you see much of your family?' she inquired.

He looked taken aback. 'Not as much as I would like,' he replied guardedly.

'Of course the long journey to Derbyshire must be difficult to fit into your crowded schedule.' When Vere still looked puzzled, Frances went on: 'Chatsworth . . . the home of the Dukes of Devonshire. The family name is Cavendish, isn't it?'

'I am not often in touch with that side of the family,' he said, after a long pause.

'Do they disapprove of your theatrical career? Surely that cannot have come as a surprise to you, Mr Cavendish, and only makes your entry into such an environment all the more puzzling.'

'One must make a living.'

Frances nodded, believing that she understood: he came from an impoverished branch of the family, she decided, and was endeavouring to acquire the financial means and the social standing to which his breeding entitled him. Her own social aspirations and conformism enabled

Frances to recognise Vere Cavendish's overwhelming ambition, even if she drew the wrong conclusions about his background and the demons that drove him.

'So I and my sisters have found,' she conceded, 'and we share your reason for entering the theatre. However, I have a more cynical view of the welcome accorded us than does Marion. She continues to bask in the glow of her popularity but, on an occasion such as this,' and Frances gestured at the party going on around them, 'I am aware that only artistic people are present, because they will accept actresses into their midst. True society, respectable society, is not represented here.'

Vere inclined his head in reluctant agreement.

'Therefore the question I have to ask myself is this: will it be possible for me – and my sisters, of course – to make the transition into that respectable society one day, when our personal circumstances permit?'

'I cannot give you a categorical answer to that question, Miss Frances. Certainly I believe that we are entering a period when the talent of a classical actress will be taken seriously, but equally there are circles where old prejudices still flourish.'

'I knew it,' Frances said bitterly, 'but that fool of a sister of mine sees only the romance, the glossy surface of the applause and admiration, and does not look beyond to the humiliation that lies ahead.'

'But Marion loves the theatre,' Vere exclaimed, using her first name in his surprise and in his sincerity, 'and I doubt if leaving it is her ultimate objective. She shows every intention of taking her acting seriously, and striving to be among the very best in the profession.'

'Do you love the theatre, Mr Cavendish?'

He stared at her, aware of the incongruity of this con-versation, with her of all people, Marion's sister and yet a comparative stranger. There was a detachment between them, which one of them was trying to bridge, but her questions revealed a mind and a personality with which Vere could identify.

'I love the theatre more than anything,' he said quietly. 'It is the means of my livelihood and it has been good to me. However, one should not equate "the theatre" with acting. I feel that it is, or should be, perfectly possible for the theatre to be the means of providing an acceptable income without the necessity of strutting the stage oneself.'

Frances gazed at him with shining eyes. He had expressed his position perfectly. Now she knew that, to Vere Cavendish, the theatre was merely a means to an end; it was a route to fame and fortune. The Cavendish Theatre was only a springboard to a property such as the one surveyed today. She was sure that he held the same regard for social position and financial security that she did. From that moment Frances was convinced that she was the only person who understood him, the only woman who had cracked his veneer and probed beneath the surface, the only woman who could make him happy. Just as Marion envisaged herself as Mrs Vere Cavendish, one half of a successful actor-management team, so Frances saw herself as the wife of a socialite and successful businessman, whose days as an actor were but a distant memory.

If Vere and Marion had any plans for private conversation that afternoon, they were to be thwarted. Frances was impervious to any hint that she might circulate among the other guests, oblivious of any lack of enthusiasm for her company on Vere's part and of any glance or caress that he discreetly shared with Marion. When the majority of their fellow guests had departed, they were among the select group that stayed for supper, after which Marion gave a reading. Vere was prevailed on for a recitation, and Frances played the piano and sang. The large, elegant drawing room, a soft translucent light filtering through the chestnut trees in the summer dusk, was a world far removed from the tawdriness and garishness of the theatre; if the discussion still centred on the arts, the various views and sentiments were expressed in educated voices and in an intelligent fashion, unlike the crude and disgusting gossip of the greenroom. Buoyed up by happiness, Frances gave a particularly fine performance, which was received with exclamations of delight, and as she acknowledged the bravos it seemed incredible that no one else knew that tonight she had sung for Vere Cavendish and for him alone. Glancing at him, she was sure that his eyes met hers in an intimate fashion and that they shared a very private moment.

Returning to her seat next to him, she said: 'I much prefer singing in the drawing room to performing in the theatre, Mr Cavendish. Such a milieu is much more *me*.'

'Your voice would be utterly charming in any setting, Miss Frances, but you must not contemplate giving up the theatre. Truly, The Cavendish could not bear to part with you.'

'Really?' She glowed, believing that by his reference to The Cavendish, he meant himself.

'The part of the singing fairy in *A Midsummer Night's Dream* would be exactly right for you. Do say that you will stay with us next season.'

Vere had caught her at an opportune and vulnerable moment. At any other time and in any other place, Frances would have resisted the suggestion strongly. Now she smiled. 'If you insist,' she agreed coyly.

At the theatre next day she expected him to seek her out

for a special word and was puzzled by his failure to do so. When a week went by without any advance in their relationship, Frances began to grow anxious, until suddenly she saw the reason for his reticence. Of course he could not single her out in front of the entire company, and no opportunity had arisen for a private conversation. Therefore all she had to do was create the circumstances for an encounter and all would be well.

She began to hang around backstage, loitering in the wings during performances and lingering in the green-room long after she could have gone home. On several occasions she was alone when he passed by – no one within earshot, no one looking their way – but he did not stop to speak to her. Instead of pressing her to his manly chest and murmuring, 'Alone at last', which was Frances's vision of heroic behaviour, he walked past her or looked through her as if she were not there. In desperation her attempts to make her presence felt became less discreet, until one Saturday night she determined on a make-or-break confrontation.

Marion was dining with some aristocratic admirer after the performance so, instead of going home alone as usual, Frances changed into her best silk dress, the bodice revealing a modest V of pearly flesh and, on the pretext of waiting for Marion, hid in the dressing room until the chatter of voices faded away and quiet fell over the darkened rooms and passages. After extinguishing the light in her room, Frances cautiously opened the door and peered out. At the far end of the passage light streamed out under two doors, those to Vere's dressing room and to Marion's. Willing her sister to leave for her supper appointment before Vere departed from the theatre, Frances retreated into the darkened dressing room and, leaving the door ajar, listened for signs of activity. After a few minutes she heard a click, and a flood of light illumined the corridor. Someone knocked on a door.

'Vere.' It was Marion's voice, soft and urgent. 'I'm ready if you are.'

Another click and more light. 'Has everyone gone?' Vere.

'Ages ago.'

'Come here, into the light, where I can see you properly. You look gorgeous. A new dress?'

'For you.'

'For me to admire, or for me to unbutton? A ravishing dress, my darling, in every sense.'

The colour was draining from Frances's face, and she was feeling very cold. Very cold and very stupid. Slowly, flattening herself against the wall, she peered round the door.

Vere was kissing Marion, but it was a kiss such as Frances had never imagined, hard and rapacious, his body crushing her against the wall, his fingers unbuttoning the bodice of her dress.

'Later,' Marion gasped, surfacing for air. 'After supper . . .'

'I have waited all week,' Vere said roughly, 'and I want you now.'

Frances watched as he bared her sister's breasts and bent his head, kissing them, caressing them, while Marion leaned back against the wall, her eyes closed. Then they moved into his dressing room, stumbling, mouth stabbing hungrily at mouth, until they collapsed on the day-bed.

'Someone may see us,' Marion protested.

'I don't give a fuck what they see.'

'Please . . .'

He cursed but, as Frances turned her face away, he got up, and closed and locked the door. Inching down the passage, Frances listened and, with every sound, her very essence, her very reason for living, drained from her. She knew what they were doing. Those sounds, those groans, the slap of flesh on flesh, the creak of the bed, she had heard emanating from her parents' room, and although in those days she had had only an instinctive, vague understanding of what was taking place, theatre gossip and plain common sense had since enlightened her ignorance.

In a fog of misery, Frances regained the sanctuary of her dressing room and sagged to the floor, resting her head on the dressing-stool, clutching it for support and comfort. Fool, you silly, stupid *fool*! He never wanted you, he never noticed you, it was Marion he wanted, and Marion whom he had. Spurned, rejected, feeling so inferior that she did not know how to face the world again, Frances lay in taut, tearless misery until she heard Vere and Marion pass the door – he was laughing, damn it, *laughing*! Then she lit the gas, sat down and stared at herself in the mirror.

Her face was very white, but it was still Marion's face, such was the resemblance between them. But now Frances knew that she was but a pale imitation of her sister. Substituting for Marion on the stage, through a film of gauze, she was apparently an equally poor alternative in real life. But did she want to take Marion's place in real life? Did she wish that it was she, Frances, who lay helpless under the assault of Vere Cavendish on that bed tonight? Part of her screamed assent but another part, the larger and more dominant, was sickened by the idea.

Frances was always the sister most attuned to her circumstances, ever more likely to be bound by convention. Since coming to The Cavendish she had been struck by the contrast between the plushness of the auditorium and the squalor of the backstage facilities, and now she wondered if this reflected the true nature of Vere Cavendish himself:

was he all good looks and charm on the surface, but degradation and filth beneath?

Battling with her hurt and pain, she was ashamed of her passion for him, which must never be spoken of, never admitted, to anyone. But as Frances looked into the reflection of her stricken eyes, she was seized by an irrational desire to strike back – only at that moment she did not know whether she wanted to kill him or kill herself.

Chapter Eleven

Nothing had been said but Marion was aware that her sister was holding back, struggling to dam a pent-up torrent of words which, if released, could fatally damage their relationship. No doubt about it, Frances had found out about her affair with Vere and in a strange way her silence on the subject was more disturbing than a full-scale row would have been.

However, Marion was even more concerned about her relationship with Vere. He had not proposed marriage and, while she assured herself that it was only a matter of time until he did, she knew moments of sheer panic when she sensed a slackening of his interest in her and envisaged a future without him.

Add to these concerns the proposals for the new season's programme, allocating Marion roles that were far less challenging than her current repertoire, and it was little wonder that she was irritable and unsettled, as if this golden season could never be re-enacted and a prize beyond price was slipping through her fingers.

One Sunday morning she woke early and lay quietly in the bed next to Frances, feeling distinctly underwhelmed at the prospect of spending the day alone with her sister, when suddenly she was overcome by nausea. She managed to make it to the kitchen, where she was sick into a bowl, and had cleared up the mess by the time Frances, limping ostentatiously, appeared in the room.

'Frances, you are a fraud. There is nothing whatever the matter with your foot.'

Due to the complicated special effects he wanted to stage, Vere had started early rehearsals for *A Midsummer Night's Dream*, which was to be the centrepiece of the new season's repertoire. Evidently trying to rival Irving in the role of pageant-master, he was saturating the production with gimmicks, of which 'flying fairies' were only the start. Scenery was flying as well, while chariots and clouds descended from the heavens, and traps catapulted Puck into the centre of the action. However, they were going through a phase where everything that could go wrong did, from a badly balanced weighting system in a fly-gallery which sent a piece of scenery tumbling to the stage, narrowly missing a fairy's vulnerable limbs, to a faulty gas jet that threatened to set fire to another fairy's hair. Unfortunately, in the second instance, the victim was Frances who, much to her regret, had felt unable to renege on her promise to play the part of the singing fairy in the production. She was still smarting from this incident, the smell of singeing locks acrid in her nostrils, when a more serious accident occurred.

At one point Frances had to make a dramatic entrance by means of a trap, and from the start she disliked the entire procedure. It necessitated descending to the mezzanine floor underneath the stage, a narrow cramped area that was a veritable forest of posts and mechanical devices with mysterious names such as bridges, sliders, tackle and sloats, and in which a host of men scurried like sailors in the between-decks area of a ship. The particular trap that hoisted Frances to the stage was a simple affair, a small platform set within a wooden frame, operated by stage-hands hauling on ropes, while small hinged flaps in the stage floor opened as she passed through and closed instantly behind her, leaving no visible opening. But during one rehearsal, instead of delivering her smoothly to stage level, the platform jerked, sending Frances stumbling to her knees on the stage while the flaps of the trap door imprisoned her foot. Her shriek, remarked Marion afterwards, was enough to frighten the horses in the Strand.

'I could have been killed,' Frances said balefully in the Gower Street kitchen. Her sister, she noticed unsympathetically, was looking like death.

'Minor cuts and bruises,' Marion scoffed, 'and I do not think you should have made so much fuss.'

'I am not going on that thing again, and that's final. As a matter of fact, I concede that the incident could be a blessing in disguise; the manoeuvre was highly undignified. I am a singer, not a pantomime fairy.'

'You caused trouble for the stagehands,' Marion reproved. 'They could have lost their jobs.'

'But I said, several times and with increasing volume, that they were not to blame. Human error, it was not. That trap has had its day – it is antiquated, worn out and past its prime. It ought to be replaced but, oh no, your precious Mr Cavendish prefers to lavish his money on artistic advertising posters, pretty programmes and on commissioning an original musical score when there are plenty of good tunes already.'

'I thought you approved of Vere's attention to detail and of his emphasis on the musical contribution to his productions.'

'I did, I *do*, but it is a matter of priorities, isn't it!'

The kettle boiled and Marion made the tea, hoping that

she could drink a cup without vomiting it up again. What had she eaten last night to bring on such an attack?

'Sooner or later someone will be hurt in that theatre.' Frances could not let it drop. 'To be realistic, I doubt if The Cavendish is that much worse than many other establishments, but one does wonder what the Metropolitan Board of Works, whoever they are, look for during their safety inspections.'

'Frances, I simply cannot take responsibility for matters outside my control. It takes me all my time to study my own lines and act my own roles – the rest I leave to those better qualified than me to deal with such matters. I take my money and am grateful for it, aren't you?'

'Have you noticed that Mr Cavendish doesn't put *them* on the traps or wires?'

'Who do you mean by *them*?'

'You haven't noticed, have you!' Frances glanced at her incredulously. 'Oh well, there is none so blind as those who do not want to see.'

'Stop talking in riddles and tell me who *they* are.'

'The society girls who have walk-on parts in the *Dream*.'

'What about them? I thought it was encouraging that society was allowing its daughters into the theatre.'

Frances sighed, her expression pitying yet exasperated. 'You do not watch them rehearse – when the supers are called, you go off with your nose in the air. But I often help with those rehearsals, and next time you ought to join me so that I can explain a few things.'

'I do not need your explanations. I have forgotten more about the theatre than you will ever know!'

'No, Marion, it is your morals that you have forgotten. Or perhaps you abandoned them willingly, along with your dignity, your virginity, your future prospects and your common sense.' Frances could contain herself no longer. 'You fool,' she shrieked. 'I told you what would happen if you got involved with the theatre and I was right! Don't you realise how totally selfish you have been, because the stain on your character will rub off on mine, and on Imogen and your darling Arabella, while God alone knows what cesspit Charley is lying in.'

The last vestiges of colour draining from her already ashen face, Marion fought back. 'There is no disgrace in being Mrs Vere Cavendish.'

'But you are not that woman, and I am not sure you ever will be. And if he discards you, what then? What man will want damaged goods like you?'

'Vere will not discard me. We are to be married.'

'He's asked you to marry him, has he?'

'Not in so many words,' Marion admitted, 'but it is clearly understood.'

'I do hope that it is as clearly understood by him as it is by you,' Frances said in an ominously quiet voice.

Marion flinched and turned her face away. This was dangerous ground, the conversation was coming too close to her own deepest fears. 'He loves me,' she maintained stubbornly, 'and that he *has* expressed in so many words, and on many, many occasions.' But had he? When she came to think about it, he had expressed his desire for her time and again, but love . . . ? Had he ever actually mentioned *love*? No, she thought bleakly, he hadn't . . .

'What do you know about him? Have you met his mother? Does he *have* a mother – living, that is? Come on, tell me about this husband-to-be of yours.'

'He doesn't talk about himself much.'

'How odd. Most of the men I meet at the theatre, and at other functions, talk *only* about themselves. Couldn't be that your darling Vere has anything to hide, could it?'

Marion struggled to find a suitable reply, but of more immediate concern was the struggle to retain the contents of her stomach. Realising that she was losing the battle, she jumped to her feet and rushed back to the bowl, vomiting copiously into it while Frances watched in shocked silence.

'A tummy-upset,' Marion explained weakly. 'Something I've eaten . . . or a touch of flu, perhaps.'

Oh no, Frances was thinking, *no* . . .

A few days later, helping Will Tucker with the supers, as the supernumeraries or extras were called, Frances noted that Marion was watching from the wings. They were working on a scene involving Theseus and Hippolyta, and among the young ladies in the train of Hippolyta were half-a-dozen of the fashionable amateurs to whom Frances had referred. The Cavendish rules regarding these newcomers were that the girls did not speak to professional actresses, that they were positioned at the very front of the stage, and that under no circumstances was any discipline to be imposed on them. Their presence was strongly resented by authentic members of the profession, who depended on such work for their livelihood, and their frivolous approach sorely tried the patience of the bona fide members of the company.

'Why do they do it?' Frances asked Will Tucker. 'They cannot need the money.'

'They are not receiving much money, which is one reason why the Chief has them here. As for why they are doing it, I understand that ladies only work for charity and suddenly this work has become the smart thing to do.'

'So we are expected to endure the insolence of these girls in order to save Mr Cavendish the inconvenience of paying a proper salary?'

'That's only part of it; point number one, should we say. Point number two, bearing in mind that supers have to provide their own costumes, the society girls can afford to dress better than your average actress *and* can provide some pretty fancy jewellery, gloves, stockings and shoes to go with their couture gowns.

'Point number three,' and Will was ticking them off on his fingers, 'all the friends and relatives of Lady This or the Honourable That will come to see the show and, as these girls know everyone who is anyone, each of them is good for a block of stalls, or two or three boxes, most nights of the week.'

'Very well, I concede that they are good for business, if nothing else, but I am not sure that explains why Mr Cavendish is so nice to them.'

Will shrugged. 'We are supposed to feel flattered that they choose to honour The Cavendish with their presence. It was the Lyceum that started the trend, and by no means every theatre in London is considered respectable enough to shelter these delicate flowers beneath its roof.'

'I cannot see the problem,' Marion insisted when Frances took a break from the rehearsal and joined her in the wings. 'Even if they are giving you a hard time in rehearsal, they will not be here for long – they are hardly likely to allow any commitment to the theatre to interfere with their social lives.'

Frances sighed. 'For a moderately intelligent woman, you can be remarkably stupid at times. Watch Vere now, with that girl, the one with the chestnut hair and . . . let's be kind and call it a *healthy* complexion.'

'Frances, I never knew you could be such a cat! I happen to know that girl: Eleanor, Lord Melton's eldest. And Lord Melton is not only good for a regular box but happens to be one of Vere's principal backers, so of course Vere will put himself out to be pleasant to her.'

'Watch,' Frances said stubbornly.

Vere ended the rehearsal and walked off, studying a page of notes and passing the sisters in the wings without seeing them.

'Now,' murmured Frances.

With an air of casual innocence, Eleanor Melton detached herself from the group of her peers and followed Vere at a safe distance. To Marion's horror, Frances set off in pursuit.

'Oh God, this is simply awful,' Marion groaned as, a step or two behind her sister, she crept along the dark corridor towards the dressing rooms. 'You have done this before, haven't you? My God, that is how you found out about Vere and me – you saw us . . . It is *too* ghastly and I think I am going to be sick.'

'You have been sick once today already, and do shut up or they'll hear us.'

'Good, because I think we ought to stop this nonsense before it goes any further.' But Marion followed her sister into the adjacent dressing room and strained her ears in order to catch Vere's conversation.'

'Miss Melton . . . Eleanor . . . you really are very naughty. You must know that this simply will not do.'

'I don't care what people think. I want to be with you, and I don't care who knows it.'

'It is terribly flattering and you are very sweet. But our worlds are far apart, and that is the way they must stay.'

'But I love your world – it's much more fun than mine! And I . . .' She could not say 'I love you', because her upbringing had been too rigorous for that, but she could try to say it in a roundabout way. 'I don't mind being poor. I'll do anything and go anywhere. I'll go on the stage – I could be just as good, if not better, than Marion Leigh.'

Marion drew in her breath sharply. 'Bloody cheek,' she muttered.

'My dear Eleanor . . .'

Marion knew that tone of voice, and knew the gesture that accompanied it, and indeed in the next room Vere was stroking Eleanor's hair in an infinitely gentle, almost paternal, way.

'. . . you are so young and, believe me, this hurts me more than it hurts you. But it can never be. We must part, and one day you will thank me for being cruel in order to be kind.'

Marion nudged Frances. 'You must admit he's a class act,' she whispered.

'I will die if we cannot be together,' sobbed Eleanor.

'No, you will marry that disgustingly wealthy and horribly handsome young Beauchamp boy, of whom I am so jealous that the thought of him is like a knife in my heart . . .'

Marion choked and had to stuff the hem of her skirt into her mouth in order to stifle her giggles.

'. . . and you will have three, no, four children and live happily ever after.'

'Do you really think that I ought to marry Gerry Beauchamp?'

'Reluctantly, I have to say that he would be the perfect match for you, curse him!'

'Mama and Papa are terribly keen on the idea. Years ago they wanted me to marry Peter Frith-Tempest, but neither of us felt it was right. Actually, I think he feels the same about Marion Leigh as I do about you – he goes all pink when her name is mentioned and he thinks that no one has noticed.'

In the darkness Marion smiled and preened a little. Dear Peter . . .

'We will stay friends, won't we, Eleanor? And now goodbye, my dear, and be happy.'

'I cannot be happy without you.'

'You must try. It is our tragedy to have been born too soon, for I sense that in a year or two things may be different, but,' and he checked himself hastily, 'you must not wait for that time to come. I could be wrong, and the beautiful bloom of your youth must not be wasted.'

'By then I suppose Celia will be falling in love,' Eleanor sniffed, 'and she will make an even bigger mess of it than I have.'

'Ah, Celia,' and propelling Eleanor gently to the door, Vere smiled a very secret smile and a faint light shone in his eyes, 'little Celia . . .'

After Eleanor's footsteps had faded, Marion looked triumphantly at her sister. 'You and your suspicious mind,' she mocked.

'He is up to something,' Frances insisted, 'I am sure of it.'

Laughing, Marion walked into Vere's dressing room and threw her arms around him. 'I would not have eavesdropped for the world,' she assured him, 'but I could not help overhearing. Darling, you were *wonderful* – that poor girl . . .'

Vere kissed her and then collapsed theatrically into a chair. 'I'm exhausted,' he complained, wiping imaginary sweat from his brow with a melodramatic gesture. 'Acting the part, and writing your own script as you go along, is no joke.'

'I thought it was hilarious.'

'You must not mock the lady, Marion. You, too, were young once.'

'I'm not exactly a withered old crone now.'

'No, you are absolutely lovely. God, I need a drink.' Vere reached into a cupboard for a whisky bottle and poured himself a tot, an unprecedented action on his part at this time of day. 'Now do you believe that handling unwanted admiration can be as difficult for a man as for a woman?'

Not only did Marion believe him but she experienced a rush of love, confidence and happiness that was the closest she had ever come to ecstasy.

'The Leigh sisters have been a great success.' Ernest Meyer was not referring to the plaudits of the audience but to the box-office receipts.

'Miss Frances is a highly talented musician while Miss Marion is a beautiful, elegant and accomplished actress,' Vere observed.

With the shrewdness of one accustomed to reading between the lines, Meyer prompted: '*But* . . .'

'Marion Leigh has her limitations,' Vere replied guardedly, 'which, in all fairness, must be offset against her assets.'

Meyer smiled, appreciating the language of the balance sheet, but Lord Melton laughed loudly.

'Those assets, especially two magnificent breasts, surely outweigh any minor limitations.'

'Marion's beauty gave her a head-start, providing her with untold opportunities, but it exerts its own tyranny, in that it demands roles which display it to advantage.'

'So her beauty is both an asset and a disadvantage?' Melton shook his head in bewilderment. 'Seems bloody peculiar to me.'

'The lady wants to be taken seriously. She dearly wants to be a great actress. Now, a great actress could gain an entrée to the profession through her looks, but her talent would take her to the top despite the early limitations imposed on her.' Vere frowned in his earnest wish to explain. 'Marion Leigh has talent: she can move well and has a pleasing stage presence; she can portray a muted, passive suffering and deliver comedy lines with a pleasing lightness of touch and instinctive good timing. But,' and he looked at Ernest Meyer as he gave an honest answer to the man's original question, 'she is bound and gagged by a suffocating, inhibiting self-consciousness.'

'Don't talk about binding and gagging her, old boy,' groaned Melton. 'The imagination boggles . . .'

Fortunately Melton was looking the other way when Vere's glance lighted upon him, otherwise the noble lord's involvement in The Cavendish might have ended there and then. For a split second Vere's face registered a total repugnance of such sentiments, and an even greater disillusion with the company he kept, but almost immediately the smooth, suave veneer reflected his return to the real world.

'There is something missing,' he said slowly. 'Heaven knows I have tried to press the right button in order to find it, but she never lets go. She seems incapable of being carried away by emotion; she cannot realise the full force of the power within her and therefore cannot lift an audience to that peak of experience. In the end Marion Leigh is only an entertainer. She has become – my God, I have *made* her – a professional; she can give a reliable performance, but never can Marion Leigh "tear a passion to tatters". Those huge blue eyes can blaze in anger or sparkle with amusement, but those eyes, and that beautiful body, are incapable of burning with passion.'

'Needs a good rogering,' growled Melton. 'That'd teach her a thing or two.'

'I would not bet money on that,' Vere said with considerable conviction.

'Stands to reason,' Melton went on, as they rose from the table prior to rejoining the ladies and Meyer left the room. 'And my God, Cavendish, I'm getting bloody tired of waiting.'

'You have my every sympathy,' Vere replied evenly, 'but I cannot force Marion into your bed, however much you or I might wish it.'

'No, but you could be a damn sight more helpful than you have been so far! If you had not constantly assured me otherwise, I might even think you'd kept her for yourself. Come on, man, you know the girl. What should I do?'

'Well . . .' Vere hesitated. 'Have you considered paying court to Frances?'

'Yes,' Melton replied bluntly, 'but she's too thin. No, it's Marion I want. Look, every time I ask her out, she has a million excuses. Tell me honestly, is she involved with someone else?'

Vere hesitated again. 'No,' he said, after a long silence. 'She has been seeing someone,' he went on slowly, 'but I believe the relationship is over, and anyway it never amounted to much.'

'So what do you advise?'

'Press your suit again, Melton, openly and honestly. If that fails, and I fear that at first it might, you must bring pressure to bear.'

'What sort of pressure?'

Vere told him and then added: 'And, Melton, may I ask a favour? Go easy on the girl. I don't want her hurt or upset. Both Marion and Frances Leigh have become an integral part of The Cavendish and are essential to our future success. In fact, I have become quite superstitious about them!'

In the drawing room Vere rejoined Lady Melton, flirting dangerously with a citadel he had no intention, or desire, to storm, but which he knew must be kept sweet.

He was not a bad man, and it was not his fault, or so he believed, if his mistresses expected more from a relationship than he was prepared to give. Vere Cavendish had his own agenda and was pursuing a plan that had been carefully thought out and, so far, just as carefully executed. Until now, the possibility that someone could get hurt along the way had never crossed his mind, which was surprising because he could be caring, kind and sensitive. No, Vere Cavendish was not a bad man, merely a very ambitious man, who was extraordinarily single-minded and obsessive in pursuit of that ambition.

A week after the Eleanor Melton episode, Marion was sick again. She had been sick nearly every morning for two weeks and, with other signs also in evidence, knew that she had to face up to the truth. Frances found her sitting in the kitchen, staring blankly into space.

'Do you have something to tell me?' Frances asked, in a slightly sarcastic tone.

'Yes, I rather think so.'

'You *think* so? I'm practically one hundred per cent certain myself.'

Rather relieved that she did not need to spell it out for her sister's benefit, Marion sighed. 'I didn't realise it was that obvious.'

'It will be obvious to everyone soon. So, what are you going to do?'

'Do? Marry Vere, of course.'

'See him as a family man, do you?' Frances said caustically. 'Patter of little feet around the theatre, founding of a dramatic dynasty, baby Cavendish making its first entrance as a babe-in-arms in – Lord, I don't know – some god-awful play that calls for a babe-in-arms.'

'Yes,' Marion said defiantly, 'yes, I do actually. That is exactly what I see.'

'More fool you.'

'Vere will be pleased about the baby, and I think that you might show a little more enthusiasm.'

'Me? Oh, I'm absolutely thrilled for all three of you,' and Frances stalked out of the room.

Marion stayed where she was, but the exchange with Frances had done her good. It had strengthened her determination to ensure that this pregnancy had a happy ending, if only to prove her sister wrong. And she really began to believe that Vere would be pleased about the baby and that he would marry her gladly. In fact, the baby was an absolute blessing, because now Vere would *have* to marry her . . .

Chapter Twelve

When Vere did not invite her for supper on Saturday evening, Marion was forced to corner him in his dressing room after the performance. It was not an auspicious start, she thought wretchedly, because she had wanted to raise the subject subtly, lead up to it in an indirect way, and for this she needed more time and a more romantic setting.

Still, he smiled and offered her a seat as he poured himself a glass of whisky. She had been preparing for this all day but, now that the moment had arrived, she was overcome by nervousness. Looking at him, she was struck again by how little she actually knew about him and she made the mistake of saying so.

'You know as much as you need to know. Why is it that, for a woman, that is never enough?' Vere pushed back his chair slightly, increasing the physical distance between them by a few inches, but she could sense that mentally his withdrawal was infinitely greater.

'You've never mentioned your family. Considering how close we are to each other, such an omission seems very strange.'

'Perhaps I do not talk to you about my family for the

same reason that I do not talk to my family about you.'

Marion pounced. 'So you have a family!'

He paused for a generous gulp of whisky, his eyes alert and wary. 'There are many components to my life: my family, my friends, my business associates, my lovers *and* my theatre. It seems clear to me that not all these components can meet and be in harmony. Some, perhaps most, of them flourish best in isolation.'

She had not realised before that he was such an immensely compartmentalised man. 'Could you envisage a set of circumstances in which your family, your lover and your theatre met in harmony?' she asked after a long, and very tense, silence.

'Say what you have to say, Marion, and get it over with,' he said harshly.

She sank to her knees in front of him, gazing up into his face. 'I'm having a baby,' she said, trying to smile, 'and I want you to be as happy about it as I am. I want you to marry me out of inclination, not obligation.'

In another of the long silences that punctuated their discussion, Vere sighed and, leaning down, put his arms around her and laid his cheek against her hair. 'I was afraid that was what you were going to say,' he said sadly. 'Marion, I am very fond of you but I never promised marriage.'

A wave of pain engulfed her, but Marion was not surprised. Secretly, deep inside, she had known. She had always known. But that did not mean that she would give up trying.

'But you love me. The very existence of our child proves that you love me!'

'I have loved you, in my fashion.' He kissed her forehead and hugged her a little closer. 'I have desired you, and admired you, and respected your dedication and your talent, and your sense of responsibility towards your sisters.'

'Yet that is not enough to make you want to marry me?' Marion was incredulous and she wanted to cry.

'Marriage must either be expedient, or it must be the result of blind, overwhelming, irresistible love. You and I fit neither scenario.'

'Speak for yourself,' she said bitterly.

He chose not to hear her. 'I do not place much faith in the notion of that overwhelming passion – I am thirty-four years old and haven't found it yet! But expediency has its merits, and for me that means marrying money and social status. Which is exactly what you should do.'

'Just how do you expect me to explain away the baby?'

'The baby . . .' Unseen by Marion, Vere winced, the muscles of his jaw tightening as he controlled his response. 'Do you want it?'

'Of course I want it.' And suddenly Marion knew how true that was. She had been too concerned with Vere's reaction to analyse her own, but now she was flooded with the being of her child, completely taken over by it, utterly certain that without it she would be bereft. Until now she had not thought about having children of her own, but somehow they had always been there, an essential part of her life-plan, and without them she would never be complete.

'In that case,' Vere said quietly, 'you may rely on me for adequate financial support. If, on the other hand, you decide that you cannot go through with it, I will put you in touch with someone who can take care of it. At my expense, of course.'

An abortion. He was suggesting that she get rid of it, flush it out of her, one of life's little mistakes . . . *no*.

'No,' she said shrilly.

'It is your choice,' he said gently, 'and I will do everything I can to help.'

'Everything except marry me. And doubtless your offer of financial help is dependent on my keeping my mouth shut.' She pulled away from him, tears pouring uncontrollably down her face. 'You really know the ropes, don't you! How many times have you acted out this little scene?'

'Never before,' and he stared at her steadily, 'never, in my life, I promise you.'

'You can keep your money.' Marion scrambled to her feet and picked up her cloak. 'I want this child, even if you don't. I intend to have it, and love it, and bring it up, just as if . . .'

'. . . it was one of your sisters,' Vere said drily.

'Just as if it had a father,' and Marion slammed the door behind her.

She cried all the next day while Frances watched with a look of resignation, a look of 'I told you so' on her face. Marion cried for lost love, for the knowledge that he had never loved her, and out of sheer desperation and blind panic over what the future might hold. And she cried out of anger at herself, cursing herself for a weak and foolish woman who ought to have known better, a barrage of self-abuse made more poignant because she knew that Frances agreed with every word.

Eventually Marion cried herself to sleep and awoke on Monday morning feeling calmer. 'It was my fault,' she announced. 'I handled the matter extremely badly and getting hysterical won't help. No, one must keep things in perspective and I'm sure that now Vere has had time to think it over, he will see the situation differently.'

So she spoke to Vere again that night.

'You must have thought about it all yesterday and, now

that you've had time to get used to the idea, you have changed your mind, haven't you!'

She looked very beautiful, still in her costume and make-up, her eyes sparkling with a determined confidence. Vere looked at her sadly and did not reply.

'Our marriage would be an excellent thing for The Cavendish,' she exclaimed. 'The public would be pleased and our popularity would soar. Of course we'll have to tie the knot quickly, or everyone will start doing sums on their fingers when the baby is born . . . Well, they'll do that anyway, I suppose! It doesn't matter. What matters is that you and I can be a great partnership, and we'll have a family to follow in our footsteps.'

'No, Marion.' His voice was so low that it was little more than a whisper.

She continued as if she had not heard. 'I can carry on working until the end of the season. I feel ghastly first thing in the morning, but fortunately I'm fine later on. With any luck, I'll be able to continue right up until the last moment which, by my reckoning, should be . . .'

'*No*, Marion.' His voice was stronger and he gripped her by the shoulders. 'You are right – I *did* think about it on Sunday, but I'm afraid that I did not change my mind. I cannot marry you. You must accept that.'

'I won't accept it! I *cannot* accept it!' She stared up at him wildly. 'You *must* marry me. I'll make you marry me. If you don't, I'll tell the whole world whose baby I am carrying and . . .'

'That is your prerogative, but I would advise caution. Instead of the world's opprobrium falling on me, as you hope, I fear that you would be the one in disgrace. Unfair, I know, but such is the way of this world. More importantly, do you want to continue working in the theatre?'

'Of course.'

'Then I urge you to be circumspect. Other theatre managements are unlikely to welcome you with open arms if such a reputation precedes you.'

'But you *must* marry me!' she cried despairingly. 'What else am I to do?'

'I repeat what I said on Saturday: I will support the child financially or I will arrange an abortion. The choice is yours.'

'And I say again that you can keep your goddam money because, if that's all you have to offer, I don't want it.'

'I have thought for a long time that you were stupid, but it is clear that you have gone completely mad.' Frances had just learned that Marion had refused Vere's help and that she intended to keep the child. 'No one keeps an illegitimate child, absolutely no one, not even the little sluts in the slums.'

'What do they do about it? Surely not everyone has an abortion!'

'According to the gossip at the theatre, most do. Alternatively, there seem to be some singularly unpleasant baby-farms to which the unfortunate child is despatched, or the infants are abandoned and taken into the care of the parish.'

Marion went white. 'I couldn't possibly do that.'

'You cannot keep it,' Frances reiterated. 'Apart from the disgrace, who would look after the child while you worked? And you could not continue at the theatre, because no reputable company would employ you.'

'I cannot give up the theatre. It's my living, and it has become my life – the theatre . . . and him . . .'

Frances seized her opportunity. Rather a sister who was an actress than a sister who was an unmarried mother. 'Of course you must not give up the theatre, therefore you must get rid of the child.'

'I suppose you are right,' Marion said desolately.

'Thank heavens you are seeing sense at last! Now, if you won't ask Mr Cavendish for the money and the name of a doctor, I will.'

'No.' Marion was determined to remain adamant on this point. 'I will take nothing from him. Please try to understand, Frances, that I must keep a fraction of my self-respect. I have to go on working with him. I have to face him every night, on stage and off, and enact intimate scenes with him on that stage.'

'Surely you cannot continue at The Cavendish!'

'I am a professional,' Marion said obstinately, 'and I will prove to him just how professional I can be. Apart from which, I cannot hope to command the same fees in another company.'

The financial argument seemed sound. 'In that case I must find out the name of someone who can do the operation,' Frances said briskly. 'One of the girls at the theatre will know.'

'Don't let anyone suspect why we need it,' Marion cried in alarm.

Frances gave her a withering look and next morning went to see Maria Scarlatti. Taking her friend into her confidence, she asked Maria to visit her at the theatre before the evening performance and to say that her maid was pregnant. As Frances expected, help was forthcoming and several girls came up with the same name.

'A woman called Susan, in Brodlove Lane. It's somewhere in the East End between the Commercial Road and,' Frances consulted the piece of paper in her hand, 'the Highway.'

'It sounds a bit off the beaten track,' Marion said with a brave attempt at lightness.

'You could say that,' Frances said drily. 'I suggest we walk to St Paul's and take a cab from there.'

'*We . . .*'

Frances looked at her in genuine surprise. 'You don't imagine that I would let you go alone?'

They went on Saturday night, their logic being that Marion would have Sunday in which to recover from the ordeal and she could be back at the theatre on Monday, with no one any the wiser. In Marion's dressing room they put on their shabbiest skirts, over which they threw a couple of old hooded cloaks purloined from the theatre wardrobe, and then walked east along the Strand, skirting St Paul's before they felt sufficiently anonymous to hail a cab. But the driver's reaction was unexpected.

'Yer want me to go *where*? Come off it, ladies, yer've got to be jokin'!'

'Why, what's wrong?' Frances demanded.

'You may want to risk life and limb down in the docks but I'm damned if I do, and what's more, there ain't nothing that'll persuade me.'

'We will pay extra,' Frances said desperately.

' 'ow much extra, and why d'yer want to go to that bleedin' place anyway? Don't sound as if you belong in that neck of the woods.'

'Never mind that, will you take us or not? We will pay double the fare.'

'That'll be five shillin'.'

Frances was sure he had inflated the price, but the sight of Marion's white face beneath her hood proved a stronger incentive than money. 'Very well, five shillings it is, but no more.'

'I'll take yer to the Commercial Road,' the driver said, 'but no further.'

'Give us directions to Brodlove Lane from where you leave us,' bargained Frances.

They did not look out of the cab during the drive, neither of them wishing to see or remember more of this episode than was entirely necessary, so the shock when they alighted in the Commercial Road was all the greater. It was as if they had stepped into a different world, a country far from their comparatively genteel upbringing, and a million miles from the society of the West End. Here, as they set off tentatively down the road in the direction that the cab driver indicated, was a darkness impenetrable yet alive. The narrow street was deserted, yet the sisters sensed that people were about, concealed in doorways and behind corners, watching them from the shadows. Marion and Frances linked arms and hurried on, heads down under their hoods, ready for any confrontation, but when a figure materialised suddenly in their path they both gasped.

It was a woman, young and thin, in a misshapen bonnet and woollen shawl. On this occasion, Marion's reactions were the quickest.

'We're lookin' for Susan in Brodlove Lane,' she said harshly, in the Cockney accent of the most humble supers at the theatre. 'Are we on the right road?'

'That'd be tellin',' the girl said slyly.

' 'ere's a tanner fer yer trouble, but I ain't got no more to spare. Please, dear, it's urgent.'

In the darkness they could just make out the expression that flitted across the girl's face, greed and indecision vanquished by sympathy.

'It ain't far,' she replied grudgingly. 'Cross Cable Street and a little to yer left. Susan's is the fifth 'ouse,' and she took the sixpence and melted into the shadows.

One advantage of travelling so late was that the public houses were closed. They passed one now, dark and shuttered, yet the stench of beer, tobacco and vomit still lingered in the gutters. The night was clear and to their right they could make out the vague outline of the huge dock warehouses, while ahead there gleamed the silvery sheen of the river. Coming towards them on the other side of the street, a man strode purposefully and swiftly. Pressing themselves against the dingy walls of the adjacent hovels, the sisters would have been more confident had he been drunk, swaying and lurching along the alley, but he did not lift his head and, after waiting for his footsteps to fade, they pressed on. One, two, three . . . They counted the doors along the lane and gripped each other tightly before knocking on the door of the fifth. Suppose this was not the right house? It might not even be the correct street. *Anyone* could be on the other side of that door. With memories of every Gothic thriller they had ever read, of every villain in every book and play, Marion raised her hand and pounded on the door three times and then, after a short interval, knocked another three times. Feeling frightened and faintly ridiculous, they tensed at the rattle of bolts and chains on the other side of the door, which then opened a crack.

'Susan?' Marion's voice was hoarse.

' 'oo wants 'er?'

'I need your help. I've been told that you can . . . can take care of things.'

The door opened wider and a woman's head peered out, a pair of bright eyes assessing the unexpected visitors and ensuring that the women were alone.

'It's a bit bleedin' late, ain't it?'

'I had to be at the theatre this evening.'

At that Susan seemed satisfied and she beckoned them inside, closing the door and then pushing past them to lead the way into the back room. The only light came from the fading embers of a fire in the grate, but Susan fiddled awkwardly with an ancient oil lamp and soon it glowed into life, casting flickering shadows on the walls and enabling Susan and her visitors to look at each other for the first time.

Marion and Frances were not sure how they had expected the abortionist to look and were surprised at how much she resembled their washerwoman: the same scrawny body, haggard face and straggly grey hair pulled back into an untidy bun, and the same bright-as-a-button eyes alert with an animal cunning. Only Susan was dirtier and shabbier, when she spoke she showed bare gums and a few blackened teeth and her breath reeked of gin.

'Both of yer, is it?' she asked and, when she had ascertained that Marion was the patient, she nodded and eyed the sisters eagerly, divining 'quality' beneath the shabby cloaks. 'It'll be extra,' she said, 'it bein' so late.'

After her experience with the cab driver, Frances had expected nothing less. 'How much?' she asked wearily.

'Three pahnd,' Susan said and then grinned. 'No, guineas,' she amended, attempting a refined accent. 'In advance.'

'Half now and half afterwards.'

Susan grudgingly agreed, holding out her hand for the first payment. 'Yer'll 'ave to wait a sec while I pop out for a few pennorth of gin. Make yerselves at 'ome, ladies.'

They did not feel like sitting down so stood uneasily, glancing round the little room. They had lived in some humble lodgings themselves at various times, but here the cracked ceiling, the damp-stained walls, the rickety table and the armchair with its stuffing spilling out, the broken sofa and threadbare square of carpet reeked of a poverty beyond their imaginings and yet always feared. The all-pervading smell was a stench of rotten food, damp and booze, the filth making it obvious that hygiene was not Susan's strong point.

'You don't have to go through with it,' Frances said suddenly. 'It might not be safe, she doesn't seem . . .' Her voice trailed away.

But at that moment Marion was more afraid of a downward slide into the slums, which she felt could so easily happen if she lost her place at The Cavendish, than she was of the operation. 'I must take the risk. We have come too far to turn back and, besides, if I don't go through with it, I could end up living in a place like this.' She gagged slightly, the smell making her feel sick. 'Why does she want the gin?'

'I rather think that gin is Susan's only anaesthetic.'

'Oh God.' Marion closed her eyes and swallowed hard, gagging again. 'But the public houses are shut. Where will she find alcohol at this hour?'

'I expect Susan has a ready source of supply.'

Sure enough, when Susan returned, she was staggering under the weight of a big jar of raw gin, some of which, judging by the colour in her cheeks, she had sampled *en route*.

'Take off yer cloak and yer drawers and sit on the sofa,' she commanded Marion, pouring gin liberally into a cup, 'and get this down yer.'

Marion obeyed, grimacing horribly at her first taste of the spirit, but swallowing the cupful. And the next, and the next . . . while Frances stood, silently watching her beautiful, elegant, capable sister subside into a drunken stupor.

'I reckon she's ready,' and Susan arranged Marion on

the sofa, spreading her legs wide. 'You could 'old 'er legs up a bit,' she told Frances, 'but shut yer eyes if yer don't like the sight of blood, 'cos I don't want two of yer on me 'ands.'

Frances complied and gratefully shut her eyes, but not before she had seen Susan produce an appalling piece of bent wire, apparently her sole surgical instrument.

'I hope that thing is clean,' she said faintly.

'Course it's clean,' Susan said indignantly 'Washes it regular, don't I!'

Frances did not feel equal to inquiring further. Eyes tightly shut, she held Marion's legs and was aware of a sudden convulsion in her sister's body as the wire penetrated. Her drunken snores were broken by a scream, and then Marion's body sagged, but whether into a deeper sleep or into a faint Frances did not know.

It seemed to take for ever. Frances was stiff and uncomfortable. Occasionally she opened her eyes but carefully ensured that she looked away from the bloody mess that had been Marion's groin and white thighs. But at last, at long last, Susan's voice said: 'That's it. All done.'

Frances dared to look directly at her sister, but was horrified by the amount of blood still seeping from her vagina.

'We'll give 'er a wash and bind that up with a bit of rag and then everythink in the garden will be luvverly,' Susan said cheerfully.

Was that flow usual in the circumstances? Susan seemed unperturbed and presumably she knew about these things. Frances helped to wash the blood from Marion's legs and, disliking the look of the dirty cloth proffered by the abortionist, tore strips from her own petticoat for a pad to wedge between the thighs. Then she waited for her sister to wake from the gin-induced sleep but, while Susan dozed in the armchair, Frances's brain was busy. Marion could not possibly walk back to the Commercial Road and, even if they did manage to get that far, there was no certainty of finding a cab. When Marion began to stir, Frances shook Susan awake and explained the problem.

'There's a bloke with a cart usually goes up Covent Garden way,' Susan offered. 'I'll speak to 'im but . . .'

'We will pay him for his trouble.' Frances said wearily. 'Offer him half-a-crown to take us to the nearest cab rank.'

The summer morning was sunny and light when they ventured out into the street, the driver helping to lift a faint and virtually comatose Marion on to the open cart. Not a very dignified form of transport, Frances thought grimly, pulling the hood closer around her face as they trundled through the East End, but then the entire episode had been humiliating. When finally they reached Gower Street, she had to half-carry, half-drag Marion up the stairs to their rooms, where she undressed her and put her to bed. Marion lapsed again into unconsciousness, leaving Frances unsure whether it was a healthy sleep or a more sinister condition. Worn out, but too worried to rest, Frances made a pot of tea and settled down to watch over her sister.

By early afternoon the flow of blood was still heavy and, changing the pad for the umpteenth time, Frances saw that Marion's skin had a greyish tint, a pallor and a sheen that were beyond Frances's experience, but which she instinctively knew did not bode well. It was as if the life blood were seeping from Marion's suddenly frail form while Marion herself lay quiet, too lethargic and drained to confront death and make a fight of it.

At four o'clock Frances made her decision. Whatever

needed to be done, she must do. Even though procuring an abortion was as illegal as performing one, she must fetch help. Disgrace, even jail, was preferable to the death of her sister. Giving Marion a last kiss and a despairing look, Frances ran into the street and hailed a cab. 'The Cavendish Theatre,' she said, 'and hurry.' Please God, she prayed, let Vere Cavendish be working this afternoon or, if not, please let the doorman know where to find him.

Hurrying into the theatre, her spirits rose. The lights were on, the sound of voices and hammering resounded through the empty auditorium, and to her overwhelming relief she saw the tall figure of Vere on the stage.

He listened to her in silence and, propelling her along beside him, shouted at Bert Harding: 'Something's come up – I may not be back tonight' and together he and Frances hurried to the cab that was waiting outside.

'Why didn't she come to me?' Vere's face was white and strained. 'I *told* her I would do anything . . . If she had only come to me, this need never have happened.'

Frances did not reply. Her anxiety had not decreased, yet now it was mingled with an extraordinary feeling of relief, that she was not alone, that someone else was making the decisions and would know the right thing to do.

In the lodgings Vere took one look at Marion and scooped her up into his arms, carrying her down the stairs and out to the cab. 'Bart's Hospital,' he rasped, and sat back, holding Marion in his arms, looking down at her grey and increasingly lifeless face. 'Marion, Marion,' he murmured, 'you and your foolish pride. I should have known that you could not accept my help. I should have found another way . . .'

'What will we tell the doctors when we reach the

hospital?' Frances asked. 'They are bound to know what we have done, and it is against the law . . .'

'I know someone there, a doctor who does what he can to help in such situations and who will not report the matter. Oh, I dare say some people would call him a disgrace to his profession and, yes, he does line his own pocket to some extent. On the other hand, he is a realist who knows that if he does not perform such operations, the girl will go to a back-street abortionist, who will botch the job and the girl will end up like Marion.'

'You would have sent her to this doctor in the first place?'

Vere nodded. 'He would have performed the operation in a private clinic, with proper anaesthetics and in fully sterile conditions. Damn you, Marion,' and he hugged her more tightly to him, 'don't die. Whatever you do, don't die!'

'But he is not in a private clinic now.'

'I'll slip him a suitable fee. Even in the hospital he can take care of the matter and keep his mouth, and a few other mouths, shut. Don't worry, Frances. Your only concern is Marion.'

He had addressed her as Frances for the first time. And when they reached the hospital, he was still holding Marion and so he asked Frances to find the money in his coat pocket and pay the fare. Hesitantly she plunged her hand into his jacket – in his haste at the theatre he had not stopped for his coat and hat – and fumbled for the cash. She had never touched him before, except for holding his arm, and was acutely aware of the warmth and strength of his body. As she withdrew her hand, she took a long look at Marion's limp form and admitted to herself that, given the chance, she would have gone to bed with Vere Cavendish. There, but for the grace of God . . .

In the hospital they waited, Frances and Vere, an uncomfortable alliance. They had nothing to say to each other but both tensed at the same moments, both watched the passage of doctors and nurses in the same hope of news, and both prayed the same prayer for Marion's recovery. Eventually the doctor called Vere and took him aside, apparently preferring to explain the details to him, and when Vere returned he so far forgot himself as to take Frances's hand.

'Marion will be all right,' he said, a slight tremor in his voice, 'but it was a damned close-run thing. That bloody abortionist nearly killed her!'

Frances clung to his hand. 'Will she have to stay here?'

'For a few days.'

'The theatre . . . She will worry terribly about the theatre.'

He smiled wanly. 'What are understudies for? I am very much afraid that Marion will have more than that to worry about when she wakes.'

'What do you mean? Is she permanently injured in some way?'

He hesitated, a flicker of embarrassment on his face. 'Miss Frances, this is not a topic that normally I could, or should, discuss with you, but I think it best that you know the truth. In order to save Marion's life, the surgeon had to remove her womb. Marion will never be able to have children.'

Frances stared at him, too shocked to be embarrassed.

'Will she be upset by this?' Vere asked quietly.

'Upset? She will be devastated.'

'I doubt very much if I will ever have the opportunity to raise the matter with her and so . . .' Vere paused, released Frances's hand and searched for the right words. 'Please tell her that I am sorry. Please tell her that I grieve for her and for our child. I think . . . I think that I would even have married her if it would have saved her from this.'

Frances watched as he rose and walked out of the hospital. In the last twenty-four hours she had made every effort for Marion; she had made decisions and sacrifices of which she had not known she was capable, but there was one thing that she knew she would not, and could not, do: she would not convey that message to Marion. Until her dying day, her sister would remain in ignorance of the full extent of Vere's remorse.

When Marion returned to Gower Street and began her fight back to full health, she refused to talk about her sterility. The sense of deprivation cut so deep, and the hurt was so intense, that it was too painful to discuss. Frances did feel obliged to mention Vere's contribution to her recovery, and indeed Marion had a hazy recollection of his face close to hers, and of the sound of his beloved voice.

'Perhaps I should thank him,' she said uncertainly. 'I ought to speak to him, it would be only courteous.'

'Ignore it,' Frances said quickly. 'Trust me, Marion, you would only embarrass him. After all, he only did what anyone would do.'

'I suppose so.' A shadow passed over Marion's pale, thin face and her eyes lingered longingly on the fresh flowers that had arrived, with Vere's card, that morning. 'Very well, when I see him I will pretend that nothing has happened. It is you, Frances, to whom I owe all my gratitude.'

'You would have done the same for me.'

'Probably,' Marion agreed, 'but, even so, I owe you a lot. In return, one of these days, you must ask a favour from me.'

*

Convalescence gave Marion time for thought. The twins came home for the summer holiday, full of health and spirits, and it was a comfort to Marion to know that she need not worry about them. But she did worry about Frances. The odd thing about her sister was that she looked and sounded utterly lovely on the stage but, at closer quarters, the vision faded. Frances had the bone structure, the hair, the eyes and the figure, but it was as if something was eating away inside her, destroying the beautiful blossom before it could burst into full bloom, leaving a shell that was hard, thin and brittle. Frances was unhappy and, in her present weakened state, Marion took the blame on herself.

However, lying awake in the night, racked with guilt and unhappiness, Frances was the least of Marion's problems. Eventually the two sisters took a cab to the City, to John Leigh's printshop.

'Uncle John, Charley was very fond of you,' Marion said steadily. 'We cannot believe that she would not get in touch with you after so long an absence.'

'She hasn't written to you then?' John prevaricated.

'Uncle John, please.' Marion, still looking pale and ill, gazed at him wearily. 'We realise that Charley has probably sworn you to secrecy and we are not asking you to break her confidence. But we are desperately anxious about her and need to know that she is well . . . that she is *alive* and well.'

John leaned back in his chair and stared thoughtfully at them. He was not sure that he trusted Frances, but Marion seemed sincere in her concern.

'I have received several notes from her,' he admitted reluctantly, 'the last only three weeks ago, so I can assure you that Charley was very much alive and well then.'

'Thank God,' Marion said fervently, closing her eyes

with relief. 'Where is she, what is she doing, will she be coming home . . . ?'

'Hey, slow down. I cannot tell you much. Charley has been with a touring company and, before you ask, I do *not* have a return address and cannot write back.'

'She must have hated us very much, to run away like that and send no message to us.' Marion lifted her eyes and looked at him. 'If you do get the opportunity, please tell her that we are sorry, and that we love her and want her to come home.'

John shifted his gaze to Frances.

'Yes, indeed,' Frances agreed stiffly. 'And I am sure that you would like her to resume her old duties here.'

'Most of all I want Charley to be happy. But, yes, I will convey those sentiments to her if I can.'

'Thank you.' Marion stood up and pulled on her gloves. 'And thank you for putting our fears at rest.'

'Marion, I have never mentioned this before but I would like to tell you how much I admire the way in which you have kept the family afloat since your father died. You, too, of course, Frances,' he added hastily. 'Initially I was unhappy about your connection with the theatre, but in fact The Cavendish has an excellent reputation and Mr Cavendish seems to have looked after you very well.'

Marion burst into tears and fled from the room.

'She has been ill,' Frances said hastily, 'and is not herself.' And thanking him again for the news of Charley, she retreated.

Chapter Thirteen

Marion returned to The Cavendish at the start of the new season, virtually unchanged except for a becoming pallor and slight weight loss. It was gratifying to know that she had been missed: Dick Ramsey assured her that box-office receipts had been down during her absence and he sincerely hoped that she would remain in robust good health for the foreseeable future.

Apparently Vere acceded to her unspoken wish for the matter to be forgotten, because he did not mention it, bar the customary inquiries after her well-being that any manager would make. However, at times Marion would look up to find him watching her and he was also careful to dismiss her from rehearsals before she tired. His consideration was unobtrusive, but it was there and Marion tried not to think about it because, if she did, tears had a disconcerting tendency to sting at the back of her eyes.

At the party after the première of the *Dream*, Lord Melton promptly loomed alongside, dabbing perspiration from his brow. 'My word, but you were on top form tonight. Divine, my dear, utterly divine.'

'I was hoping that you would be pleased.'

'You were? You were actually thinking of me?' he asked eagerly.

'Your opinion is of the utmost importance to all of us at The Cavendish.'

'And especially important to you,' he suggested optimistically.

'As the leading lady of the company, I am very aware of my responsibility to Mr Cavendish and his business associates,' she replied cautiously.

'Has Cavendish been speaking to you about me, and about my influence in the theatre?' Damn, Melton thought, shouldn't have said that, but Marion was only shaking her head and looking puzzled.

'I ought to mention that your floral tributes did much to raise my spirits and help me on the road back to health,' she said quickly, in order to fill the silence.

'Jolly good. Nothing like a few flowers to cheer up a girl,' he beamed. 'And the fruit – you did receive the fruit?'

'I enjoyed it very much. Indeed, there were days when nothing else tempted my appetite,' she assured him hastily. 'I do apologise for not sending you a formal note of thanks but I was not sure . . . a gift to an actress . . . perhaps *Lady* Melton was not . . . ?'

'Quite, quite,' and he coughed. 'Absolutely, understood, my dear. Oh, Miss Leigh, *Marion*, if you knew how much I long to be alone with you . . .' And his eyes travelled lasciviously over her body, still scantily clad in Titania's bewitchingly beautiful white gown.

Out of the corner of her eye, Marion saw that Vere was watching them, and he was frowning. Could he possibly be jealous? Well, she would show him that other men wanted her, and found her beautiful, even if he didn't.

She pretended to be shocked. 'Why, my lord, what

could you possibly have in mind? No,' and she closed her fan and laid it softly and flirtatiously against his lips, 'don't tell me, or you will regret it in the morning.'

'My dear, it is *years* since I did anything that I regretted the next morning,' Melton said with great feeling.

'Then I would not wish to be a bad influence on you,' Marion rejoined, 'by being the cause of your straying from the straight and narrow.'

'I think that, as a gentleman, that is supposed to be my line,' he said with a twinkle.

He wasn't so bad, Marion decided. In fact, once he stopped leering at you, he was rather sweet. It was just the thought of being touched by that quivering mountain of flesh that was off-putting.

'Dare one inquire if you are sufficiently recovered from your illness to accept a supper invitation?'

'I dare say that such an invitation might be considered, as long as it was clearly understood that supper was the only item on the menu.'

Despite this stipulation, Melton brightened. 'You will be cosseted and pampered as never before,' he promised, 'and you will forget that you were ever unwell.'

Vere was still watching. Marion smiled, tapped Melton's cheek with her fan and backed away. 'I will think about it.'

Next day a package was delivered to her dressing room and, after opening it, she allowed the diamonds to cascade and ripple through her fingers. No need to wonder if the stones were genuine; this particular suitor would not have sent paste. 'While you are thinking about it,' the card read, 'please wear this.' Dressed in Titania's décolleté gown, Marion clasped the diamonds around her neck and admired the effect. There was no doubt about it: diamonds suited her.

Not only would she accept the necklace, but she would wear it during the performance that night. That would send a message winging its way to Lord Melton, who would certainly be occupying his box. But, where Lord Melton was concerned, Marion knew exactly what she was doing.

Equally, or even more, important, the diamonds would give Vere a message, too. Marion was certain that he could distinguish the genuine article from the fake and, indeed, when he met her on the stage, she had the satisfaction of seeing him do an entirely unrehearsed and *de trop* double-take when he saw the necklace. In response she could not resist directing at him a defiant glance and the disdainful twitch of an eyebrow.

After the performance Marion created a precedent by granting Lord Melton a private interview in her dressing room. She thanked him for the gift and agreed to dine with him on the forthcoming Saturday.

Then she removed the necklace and replaced it in the box. For several minutes she sat and gazed at it, but she was not admiring the ice-fire of its stones – to Marion, the necklace represented the first instalment of a pension plan. Badly frightened by her glimpse of London's slums, she had decided, with cold calculation, to give Lord Melton what he wanted – or, perhaps, to *sell* Lord Melton what he wanted, would be a more accurate term – in return for financial security.

Having changed and dismissed her dresser, Marion was gathering up her personal possessions prior to leaving when she heard the click of Vere's door. She froze, her heart thudding uncomfortably. Every evening until tonight she had made sure that she left the theatre before him, so that there was no possibility of any personal contact, but now he would see the light under her door and would know that she was still here and that in all probability she would be alone.

Marion held her breath and listened. Several footsteps in the corridor and then a long pause, as Vere hesitated outside her door. Knowing that nothing could come of it, knowing that it could change nothing, yet still half-hoping for a miracle – it was not too late, they could put the past behind them – Marion willed him to knock. Instead all she heard was the footsteps resuming their passage to the street, walking quickly and purposefully, virtually fleeing. And Marion's breath exhaled in a long, sobbing sigh as slowly she picked up the diamonds and thrust them into her bag.

Lord Melton – 'call me Reggie' – took her to supper at an establishment similar to that patronised by Vere but, thankfully, not the same one. She was wearing the diamond necklace and, in order to give Melton his money's worth, accompanied it with her most daring dress – Vere's 'ravishing dress', the bodice of which barely covered her breasts. The instant she divested herself of her cloak, she noted the direction of her host's gaze and noted, too, that it returned there and lingered there constantly all evening. Reggie was excited by her breasts; he wanted to touch and kiss them nearly as much as he wanted to have sex with her. Very well; in that case he would not touch them this evening. They were worth another, and very expensive, gift.

So, at the dinner table, Marion leaned forward in order to expose her cleavage and turned her upper body in such a way that her breasts kept moving and threatening to fall out of her dress. And when, supper being over, they sat on the sofa, she swished her skirt deftly and crossed her legs so that a pretty ankle was displayed. Surprisingly, Melton was not the bore she had imagined but rather an amusing conversationalist, telling her stories about his society friends and relatives and making some interesting comments about the theatre. All in all, the evening passed pleasantly and only once did Marion feel a familiar pang of hurt.

Reggie was describing the chaos at his home, due to the forthcoming marriage of his daughter Eleanor.

'I thought I had not seen her at the theatre lately,' Marion said slowly. 'Is she marrying young Beauchamp?'

'Why, yes. How on earth did you know that?'

'I heard a rumour to that effect,' she said with difficulty as the pain stabbed her, not pain at the recollection of Vere's conversation with Eleanor but at the memory of her own fierce, exultant happiness afterwards. Marion felt that she would never be that happy again, that she could never love like that again; that part of her life was over.

'Am I allowed a kiss?' Reggie asked wistfully when she rose to take her leave, and Marion presented him with a flawless cheek to which he pressed his lips, wet and rubbery, and then she permitted him to wrap her cloak around her and to stand close as he did so, breathing in the scent of her skin and hair. 'Next week?' he urged.

But Marion only slid him an enigmatic glance from beneath hooded lids as she made her exit.

Reggie got the message. On Monday evening another package was delivered: earrings to match the necklace.

And so the game began, as Melton laid siege to Marion and she lowered one defence at a time, while week-by-week and month-by-month her store of goodies grew. Her increasingly elegant and expensive wardrobe she flaunted to the world, but she made no ostentatious display of the diamonds and other precious stones, wearing the pieces only for him.

When she wore the earrings, she allowed him to kiss and nuzzle her ear, thrusting wetly with his tongue, and the later gift of a bracelet gave him access to the white slenderness of her arm. The ring, he said indignantly when he saw it on her finger, was cheating and so Marion promised a kiss, a proper kiss, when they said good night, thus leaving her suitor in an agony of anticipation and arousal for the entire evening. Another bracelet arrived – did he believe that her other arm would prove the route to her bosom? It would not close over her ankle, but she secured it by the judicious use of a garter. By now the placement of the piece had become Melton's chief concern and he could hardly wait to get Marion alone, so that he could discover its whereabouts and savour the delights to come. His puzzlement at the apparent absence of the bracelet was comic to see, and for a while Marion pretended not to understand his frantic signals, but eventually she vouchsafed him a brief flash of the garter on her silk-clad leg and smiled at the expression on his face. Vere Cavendish, she thought with commendable detachment, remembering his little lecture on anticipation, would be proud of his pupil. After dinner Melton loosened the garter with trembling fingers and removed the bracelet. Slowly, reverently, he caressed her slender foot and ankle, sliding his hands over the silken stockings, up calf, knee and thigh before lingering on the even silkier texture of the smooth whiteness above the stocking-top.

At that point Marion playfully rapped his knuckles with the fan that had become an indispensable part of her flirtation, and Melton stopped immediately. He really was rather sweet, Marion decided again, staring down at the balding grey head and perspiring puce forehead of her admirer. Give him his due: Reggie played the game and never went further than she allowed. Her motive being financial gain, she might not have broken off the relationship even if he had forced himself on her, but that little touch of respect, that inescapable reminder that he was an English gentleman, made the relationship bearable, made the difference between an ordeal and a passably enjoyable game.

In the sixth week, the package contained a rope of graduated pearls, but instead of a single drop as the focal point, there were two. Melton was influencing the progress of the game, or trying to, and wryly Marion conceded that the piece had wit and that he had paid his dues. That Saturday night she appeared before him barenecked but with the rope of pearls stuffed into her cleavage, so arranged that the two immense tear-drop pearls protruded artistically in the perilously deep V of the richly embroidered cream silk gown. With a muffled groan Melton pressed her hand to his lips and throughout the meal, which he barely touched, watched the calm rise and fall of her bosom and waited in a barely controlled fever of impatience. When at last he unbuttoned the bodice and buried his head and hands into the mounds of her white breasts, Marion felt nothing. She was neither aroused nor repulsed by his touch, but simply suffered it.

After that, it was onward and downward to his ultimate goal. The gift of a brooch was pinned to her drawers and located after much fumbling and heavy breathing, during which he was allowed a quick grope into forbidden territory beneath the garments. And then the *pièce de résistance* arrived: an incredibly ugly but fabulously valuable stomacher, a heart-shaped ornament of antique gold, studded with diamonds. The final hurdle required all Marion's ingenuity; after much thought and a bit of practice she embedded the jewel in the triangle of thick dark hair at her crotch, and over it she tightly wound a long white gauze scarf, passing the material several times between her legs and around her body. The hard edges of the gold mount pressed into her flesh, but it was secure enough to allow her to negotiate the short distance from the cab.

Over dinner she led the conversation round to The Cavendish and expressed dissatisfaction with the roles allocated to her during the current season.

'Lady Teazle is fun but I am detesting the rest,' she said, with some exaggeration. 'I was wondering, Reggie, if you have any influence with Mr Cavendish over the content of the repertoire.'

'I might.' After his discussion with Vere, Melton had been anticipating such a development. 'What parts would you like to play next season?'

'Mr Cavendish has mentioned two plays: Bulwer Lytton's *Money* and Robertson's *Society* – apparently the Bancrofts will not be using it again – and I am content with my roles in them, even though they are milk-soppish as usual. But I don't think he has decided on the Shakespeare.' She leaned towards him, her lovely eyes glowing. 'I am tired of doing the same old thing over and over again – different name, different lines, different costume, but essentially the same part. I want to do something bold and wicked – I could be wicked, couldn't I?'

Melton sucked in his breath sharply. 'God, Marion, you and I both know you could!'

'*Antony and Cleopatra*,' she announced. 'I believe I could look the part and the costumes would be stunning. To give him his due, I think Mr Cavendish would show to advantage as Antony, so I doubt he could raise any objections.'

'I will speak to him at the first opportunity.'

'Promise.'

'I promise and now, Marion, *please* . . .'

She pushed back her chair from the table, walked across the room and, for the first time, opened the door to the bedroom. Preceding him to the bed, she sat down and patted the space beside her. 'First,' she murmured, 'a kiss on the cheek, then my ear, and then my arm . . .' and so on, reliving every step of his chase until the penultimate one, at which stage she lay back on the bed and pulled off her dress, revealing the gauzy cloth as her sole undergarment. Indicating that he should unravel the scarf, she helped with the twitch of a hip and the raising of a leg, until she lay naked before him, the jewelled ornament lying in her lap like a shield protecting her private parts. While he tore off his clothes she removed the jewel, placing it carefully on the bedside table where she could see it, and parted her legs for him, helping him inside her with a deftness that she hoped was not too obvious. However, his haste was so great that she doubted he was aware of anything but his own instant gratification, and instant was the word, because after a few frantic thrusts it was all over. Painless, thought Marion, but guessed that he would get his second wind and have another go, and that would take longer. It did, but not much longer, and for Marion there was scarcely a vestige of sensation.

Smiling at him and sipping champagne, she slowly came to terms with the path she had chosen. Thus far she had been a passive participant in this game but from now on he would expect, and had the right to expect, a more active response from her. The fact that she felt so little when he was inside her could be due to the loss of the child and the subsequent operation, or to the absence of any emotion for him, other than affection. But she was afraid that there was more to it than that and she had to fight against the realisation of just what a wonderful lover Vere had been. Her tragedy was to have found the best first, but to have been too inexperienced and innocent to know that he was the best.

'Cleopatra!' In that single exclamation Vere conveyed astonishment, horror and trepidation. 'She isn't up to it, honestly she isn't.'

'My dear chap, she will look wonderful.'

'Yes, but my problem is that there is rather more to Cleopatra than merely looking seductive in revealing costumes.'

'Look, old chap, I don't want to have to insist but . . . yes, actually I do insist.'

They were sitting in Vere's office at the theatre and accordingly the atmosphere was less relaxed and cordial than when they sat over the port at Melton's table. As Vere got over his surprise and rationalised the situation, he looked keenly at the cheerful countenance of the noble lord and drew his own conclusions.

'Lord Melton,' he said delicately, 'do I take it that congratulations are in order?' and he watched to see if he had overstepped the mark with a man who could be friendly with his social inferiors on some days and, well, less friendly on others.

However, the beatific smile that irradiated the plump, ruddy features of his companion contained reassurance on that point, but a more disturbing implication on another.

'She is mine,' Lord Melton said, with a simplicity born of sincerity and a limited romantic vocabulary. 'On Saturday, at long last, she was mine. She led me a merry dance, I can tell you, but it was worth it.'

'I am glad for you.' Vere's voice was carefully controlled.

'Yes, she was worth the wait. What a woman! Which is why I think you are wrong about Cleopatra. Now that I am releasing the secret passion within her, the scope of Marion's theatrical performances will be greatly enhanced.'

Vere's jaw tightened imperceptibly. If Melton had been talking about anyone else, it would have been funny but, as it was, a very unpleasant sensation lodged itself firmly in the pit of his stomach. He stared at Melton, unable to escape the mental picture of Marion lying underneath that mountain of flesh, and his skin crawled. His hand shook slightly as, after offering the case to his guest, he lit a cigarette and then leaned back in his chair with his customary suave smile. He could not afford to alienate his chief backer and did not wish his dependence on the man to be emphasised.

'In that case, of course *Antony and Cleopatra* will be in next season's repertoire. I shall rely on you to release the passion off the stage while I concentrate on assisting Miss Leigh with her performance on the stage,' and he exchanged a man-to-man smile with his associate.

Melton was still beaming, anticipating passing on the good news to Marion, the only cloud on his horizon being the seemingly interminable wait for Saturday night. 'I wanted to set her up in a little nest,' he confessed to Vere, 'up St John's Wood way, but she won't have it. Cannot leave her sisters. Devoted to them, damn it.'

'Admirable, in its way.'

'Maybe, but Barbara is beginning to look askance at my absence every Saturday night. I try not to leave it too late, to join Babs at whatever do she's at, but despite my best efforts, suspicion is rearing its ugly head. For instance, this coming Saturday she has decided to give a bash at our place. I cannot wriggle out of it altogether, but I absolutely must sneak off for a couple of hours.' Melton paused and looked at Vere with hope in his eyes. 'You couldn't cover for me, I suppose?'

'How do you mean?'

'Go to the party. Hold Bab's hand – metaphorically speaking. No, damn it, hold it physically if it'll do the trick. Take her mind off me. She likes you.'

'Most gratifying. May I inquire if your daughters will be present?'

'The bride-to-be will be taking the plaudits of the crowd. You know, until now I never realised what a fishing expedition the marriage market is, how the congratulations are heaped on the bride for landing the poor fish, while he stands around with a glassy stare and his mouth hanging open.'

'And little Celia?'

'Being launched on an unsuspecting world, even though she has not made her official début. Excited about being a bridesmaid and refusing to keep a low profile. Little Celia ain't so little any more.'

Vere smiled politely.

'Do yourself a favour, Cavendish. If and when you marry, don't have daughters. All you will get is constant worry and enormous expense. I used to think that daughters would be a comfort to me in my old age, but it turns out that they are like all women – driving me relentlessly to an early grave.'

'I wonder if Marion Leigh's father thought that.'

'Eh? Oh him, ghastly chap. Frankly, I prefer to believe that the gorgeous girl was a changeling and nothing whatever to do with him.'

'Do you realise that she has four sisters? Just imagine, Melton, five little Leigh girls.'

Melton gave that deep, sighing groan of longing that escaped him at moments of high arousal. 'Oh God, *five* of them, all in plaits and pinafores. Where does Marion come in this pantheon of pulchritude?'

'I'm not sure but, as she has referred to two sisters at school, she must be at the middle or upper end of the line-up.'

'Whatever the case, I'm damn sure she's the prettiest,' Melton declared fervently.

'Hear, hear,' Vere agreed. 'No bunch of flowers could contain a more beautiful bloom than Marion.'

Arabella and Imogen did not see eye-to-eye over the theatre. While Arabella complained about Marion's refusal to allow them to see her performing, Imogen did not add her voice to the argument. Imogen had not forgotten the photograph of Vere Cavendish and she had no intention of reneging on her vow to keep Arabella away from him, and away from men like him.

During school holidays, on nights when Frances was needed at the theatre, an elderly neighbour was paid to keep an eye on the twins. It was a routine deeply resented by them. A baby-sitter at their age! Watching the old lady doze by the fire, it seemed to Arabella and Imogen that they should be taking care of her, not the other way round. Several times Arabella jingled the coins in her pocket and suggested sneaking out to the theatre: they could see most of the play and, leaving before the final curtain, could be home long before Marion and Frances. If the old lady woke and missed them, she would not dare say so – she needed the money too much. But on each occasion Imogen vetoed the idea, and each time Arabella gave way with surprising subservience.

But at Christmas 1884, a year after the start of her liaison with Melton and when the twins were fifteen years old, Marion announced that they could attend a performance of *Society*. The old Robertson favourite was playing to packed houses, alternating with *Money* in a bill that was taking the West End by storm.

'Lord Melton has kindly offered his box for the evening,' Marion told them, 'so behave yourselves. During the interval sit well back so that no one can see you and don't, on any account, leave the box unless you have the most urgent call of nature. You can have some chocolates as a treat and I will arrange for ice cream to be sent in to you.'

'I don't mind fetching the ice cream,' Arabella said immediately.

But Marion was adamant and, to Arabella's annoyance, when the day came Imogen seemed intent on obeying the instructions to the letter. She ensured that they sat at the very back of the box and sedately studied the programme. Meanwhile, Arabella inched forward and peered out at the rapidly filling auditorium.

'Come back here,' hissed Imogen. 'Someone will see you.'

'If no one is to see us, why were we told to wear our best frocks?' Arabella asked, with irrefutable logic. 'Anyway, I don't want people to see me but I do want to see them, and I must have a good look at the auditorium.' Yet after only a few minutes, she pushed back her chair and sat quietly waiting for the curtain to rise.

'You don't seem very thrilled,' Imogen remarked. 'Having got inside a theatre at last, I expected you to be leaping up and down with excitement.'

'It is exactly as I envisaged it,' Arabella said calmly,

'the people in evening dress, the red and gold of the seats and decorations, and the buzz of the crowd. I have thought about it so often that it feels familiar.'

No one knew Arabella better than her twin, yet even Imogen could be surprised by her sister from time to time. Arabella possessed perfect aplomb, an air of self-containment, of utter certainty and confidence, which could be highly disconcerting.

'I wonder if Charley felt like that when she came here,' Imogen murmured, thinking about the theatre programmes she had found in Charley's room.

But Arabella remembered that Charley had been allowed to see Marion's début in *Richard*. 'She must have liked it, otherwise she would not have run away to join the theatre. I do wish she would come back and tell us about it.'

'I don't. I don't see why we should bother with her, because she has not bothered with us.'

'I cannot think of any reason why she should,' Arabella replied. 'We did not let her join in things when she was at home, did we? She was always by herself.'

'Except when *he* . . .' Imogen's voice faltered as the memory of their father rose before them, as vivid and disturbing as the ghost in *Hamlet*.

Arabella immediately reached out and squeezed her hand, and then moved her chair closer. 'You can have first pick of the chocolates – there are some of your favourites. And we'll stay at the back of the box during the play as well as during the intervals, if that is what you want.'

However, Imogen decided that this was not necessary and, as the curtain rose on Sidney Daryl's chambers, they moved forward and rested their elbows on the plush-covered ledge. Nervously, Imogen waited for the first entrance of Vere Cavendish, sitting impatiently through the first thirty or forty lines of dialogue, telling herself that the photograph flattered him and that in the flesh he would be a big disappointment. But then he walked on to the stage, Sidney Daryl in his morning jacket, greeted by applause from the audience, and even more impossibly handsome than Imogen had remembered and feared. When he began to speak, the deep musicality of his voice delivering the lines with charm and wit, Imogen glanced at Arabella and, indeed, as the play progressed she spent nearly as much time surreptitiously watching her twin as she did watching the stage. But Arabella's expression was no window to her thoughts. She looked alert and interested, and she smiled at the jokes, but Imogen could not detect any greater interest in Vere Cavendish than in any other member of the cast. Even Marion was observed with that same oddly critical eye and curiously adult air of detachment, as if Arabella had seen it all before and was comparing these performances with a thousand others.

'Did you think Mr Cavendish handsome?' Imogen asked at the end of Act I.

'Of course, didn't you?'

'I've seen better.'

Arabella considered this statement. 'That's silly. Men really do not come any better-looking than that.'

'So you like him?'

'I neither like nor dislike him,' Arabella replied patiently, 'as I do not know him. I *do* think he is terribly good as Sidney Daryl. In fact, he acts the pants off everyone else, including Marion, although don't tell her I said so.'

Imogen looked at her reproachfully, considering this last stricture redundant and an insult to her loyalty and intelligence. 'I wonder if Lord Melton is good-looking.'

'He is so rich that it doesn't matter what he looks like.'

'It would have to matter, wouldn't it? To do . . . to do what he and Marion do.'

'We don't *know* they do it.'

'He doesn't give her presents for nothing,' Imogen maintained, 'and Frances looks so disapproving.'

'Frances can easily look disapproving about nothing. But, yes, I concede that most likely they are doing it and, if so, Marion goes up in my estimation. She has the courage to make the most of what she's got while the going's good.' Seeing Imogen's inquiring look, Arabella elaborated: 'Marion is frightfully pretty, but she will lose her looks as she gets older. We all will.'

'You do say some peculiar things sometimes.' Imogen paused. 'You won't lose your looks,' she said earnestly.

'Yes, I will. At least I hope I will. Look, aren't we supposed to get some ice cream?'

'During the next interval. Have another chocolate. No, not that one, you pig . . .'

But during the second interval no ice cream appeared and Arabella grew impatient. 'I'm going to look for it.'

'We promised Marion . . .'

'Stop being so stuffy, Ginny, anyone would think that you had aged into Marion's elder sister. I won't go far, just into the corridor, in case they have forgotten the number of the box.'

The crimson carpeted corridor was deserted, although the buzz of conversation wafted through the open doors of adjacent boxes. A liveried footman appeared, carrying a tray of drinks and, seeing Arabella, paused and smiled before entering the neighbouring box. Solemn-faced, Arabella stared back and did not return his smile.

Then suddenly Sidney Daryl was walking down the passage towards her. Having changed his costume, and taking advantage of a long monologue by another character at the beginning of Act III, Vere had switched from actor to manager and was paying his respects to the minor royalty occupying one of The Cavendish boxes. Rounding the curve in the corridor, he pulled up short. There before him was the most exquisite creature he had ever seen, young but tall for her age, and slender in her demure dark-blue velvet dress, ash-blonde hair combed back from a heart-shaped face and her huge sapphire eyes fixed on him unblinkingly. For a split second they stared at each other, but then a third figure stepped between them. Imogen, shorter and stockier than her sister in an identical blue velvet frock, with raven hair framing her pugnacious little face, stood in front of Arabella, blocking her from Vere's view. She stared at Vere in silence, eyes blazing with anger beneath the beetling heaviness of her dark brows.

'Go away,' she said, and pulled Arabella back into the box.

Arabella, peering round Vere's tall figure, saw a waitress approaching with a tray of ice cream and allowed herself to be hauled back into obscurity.

Vere did not recover so quickly. He was accustomed to having an effect on little girls – indeed, on girls of all ages, shapes and sizes – but this incident was outside his experience. For a brief moment he stood, seeing and yet not seeing the waitress pass him and enter the box, the only image before him those two faces: one so angelic, the other so malevolent. Their effect on him was quite out of proportion to the episode. What importance could they possibly have, those two young girls? And yet Vere was shaken, as if he had been vouchsafed a glimpse of the future and it boded ill.

'I don't know who is occupying Melton's box tonight,'

he remarked to Richard Ramsey, 'but I should steer well clear, if I were you. Among the party is an angel and a devil, and I have the very strong impression that if you give the angel a single glance, let alone the brush of a fingertip, the devil will stab you in the back, the heart *and*, for good measure, the jugular.'

Chapter Fourteen

'Are we allowed to say that we saw the play?' Arabella asked while the porter loaded the luggage aboard the train.

Marion nodded. 'You may stress the fact that you occupied Lord Melton's private box at his express invitation.'

'Honestly, Marion, you are such a snob,' Arabella exclaimed.

'But on no account do you mention that we were in the play,' Frances emphasised. 'The nature of our work is a forbidden subject, is that clearly understood?'

'Yes, Frances,' the twins chorused and nudged each other. Frances said the same thing at the start of every school term, so if it was not understood by now it never would be.

'Have you got everything?' Marion asked vaguely, not being too sure these days about school requirements.

'Of course, they have. I double-checked the list myself,' Frances replied irritably.

'Do we *have* to go?' Imogen burst out.

'What's all this? I thought you liked school,' Marion said in surprise.

'I don't. I hate it.'

'Arabella?'

But Arabella merely shrugged and did not answer.

'Of course you must go,' Marion went on with a forced heartiness. 'I never heard anything so silly. You are very lucky to go to such a good school. When I think what Frances and I would have given to have all the advantages you enjoy . . .'

'Yes, Marion,' Arabella said politely, but Imogen scowled.

Marion and Frances stood on the platform, waving until the train was out of sight, before returning to the cab. Settling down in a scented flurry of velvet and furs, Marion frowned.

'We ought to send them by carriage,' she fretted. 'Travelling by train is not smart, and it might not be safe.'

'For heaven's sake, we are not made of money,' Frances expostulated, 'and the school sends someone to meet the train.'

'I suppose you are right.' Marion's mind began to wander again, back to the vexed matter of the *Cleopatra* rehearsals. 'Those twins,' she said suddenly. 'I will never understand them. I used to believe they would grow out of it but the older they get, the odder they get.'

The journey into Surrey was soon accomplished and, dismounting from the cart that had brought them from the station, the twins sedately mounted the staircase to their dormitory, followed by the school porter and his boy with the luggage. Four beds were arranged in the room, each covered with an identical blue quilt and with its own small bedside cupboard and tall clothes closet. However, on the cupboard beside the bed usually occupied by Arabella stood a vase filled with exotic flowers and greenery.

'Do you like them?' said a voice from the doorway. 'I brought them from Mama's conservatory – she's frightfully proud of having fresh flowers all year round. Oh, never mind the flowers, how *are* you? I've missed you so dreadfully!' And the girl came into the room and threw her arms round Arabella.

The newcomer was petite with thick tawny-gold hair pulled back into a loose plait, an oval face that was attractive rather than beautiful, and big grey eyes that were anxious, as Lady Sarah Vale waited for Arabella's approval.

'The flowers are lovely. Thank you,' and Arabella allowed Sarah to kiss her cheek.

'I've just been to see the puppies and they are absolutely adorable. Do come and look, now, before you take off your coat.'

'Very well,' and Arabella moved to the door. 'Coming, Ginny?'

'No,' and Imogen turned her back on them, pretending to fiddle with the straps on the luggage but, after they were gone, she walked to the window and watched the two fair-haired girls cross the courtyard in the direction of the stables.

Lady Sarah was the reason for Imogen's sudden dislike of school. She had arrived last term and, although Imogen was accustomed to the hero-worship afforded Arabella by many other girls, from the start this one was different. Why, fumed Imogen, did Sarah need to be at school, any school, let alone this one? She was already nauseatingly adept at everything. Having been educated at home by the best governesses, teachers and tutors that money could buy, her grasp of academic subjects was well up to standard, while her fluency in French, Italian and German was unrivalled. Her dancing was graceful, her music and drawing remarkably fine, and she rode like Diana. Most galling of all, she had dared to tutor Arabella on horseback and, under this guidance, Arabella began to ride with the grace and confidence of one who had been brought up with horses from her earliest days.

And it was not only the riding. Arabella made a point of speaking French and the other continental languages while in Sarah's company, querying her pronunciation here and adding an idiom to her vocabulary there. Imogen noticed that her sister watched how Sarah walked, as well as listened to her talk, and that she quietly copied many of the girl's mannerisms. Imogen was no fool. She was quite capable of working out that part of Arabella's interest in Sarah Vale sprang from her position in society and that Arabella was modelling her behaviour on that of a real-life high-born lady. But never before had Imogen felt quite so shut out.

Then, just before the Christmas holidays, Imogen had overheard Arabella and Sarah talking at the stables.

'I'm dreading the holidays,' Sarah groaned. 'All those parties, it is so *boring*.'

'Poor old you.' Arabella sounded solicitous.

'Bella, couldn't you come to stay? We could have so much fun and everyone would simply adore you.'

A spurt of anger gripped Imogen. Of course everyone would adore Arabella but, *merde*, how they would detest Imogen – except that Imogen would not be invited. With anger sliding into cold fear, she waited to find out what Arabella would say.

'That's awfully sweet of you, Sal, but I'm afraid that I cannot get away these hols. Family, you know . . . yuk!'

And they had not been back in the place for five minutes before the whole thing started up again. Did this stupid Sarah whatshername not realise that Arabella belonged to *her*?

For a while Imogen bided her time, determined not to alienate Arabella by showing any jealousy and working hard in those studies at which she excelled, so that

Arabella could be proud of her. For every subject in which Sarah came top of the class, Imogen matched her in another, while Arabella, seemingly without trying, was an easy winner in the rest. Somehow a certain equilibrium in the relationships was achieved and maintained.

Or so it was until the day that Sarah's parents visited the school. Families were not encouraged to call during term time, but naturally an exception was made for an earl and countess. Weekending with friends nearby, they were accompanied by one of Sarah's brothers, who travelled in his own smart equipage like a Regency Corinthian. When the worst of the grovelling was over, the countess said to Arabella: 'I am so glad that Sarah has found such a good friend. She was becoming too isolated at home, being the youngest in a family of boys, and we thought that school might bring her out of her shell.'

Arabella dropped a courteous and graceful curtsy and smiled, fully aware of her effect on the aristocratic party and on the dashing young Lord Henry in particular.

'This is Arabella's sister,' Sarah said grudgingly.

'Really? Good heavens, and you are twins if my memory serves me correctly. Well, you are certainly not identical, are you! Never mind,' and the countess smiled kindly, 'I expect you are the clever one.'

And Arabella is the pretty one, thought Imogen, ten-out-of-ten for observation. But she smiled and curtsied and looked suitably humble.

'Want to drive the chestnuts, Sal?' Henry challenged his sister. 'You talked of little else in the Christmas holidays. Only Miss Arabella rivalled my chestnuts for your attention.'

'Not in front of everyone,' Sarah whispered shyly.

'Coward! How about you, Miss Arabella? Could you fancy a turn in my chariot?'

'You will have to show me how to hold the reins – I haven't done this before.'

'My pleasure,' Henry said, with feeling, and helped her up.

'Henry, be careful,' the countess said anxiously.

But Arabella was not afraid, either of having an accident or of making a fool of herself in front of the entire school. With complete composure and concentration, she listened to Henry's instructions, ignoring the pressure of his hands on hers and the warmth of his body as he sat close beside her.

The school was housed in a large country mansion set amid rolling lawns and herbaceous borders, and boasted an imposing circular front drive, which enclosed a lawn and a large fountain. The chestnuts set off at a smart trot but Henry, keen to show off to his audience and even more to his passenger, soon had them going full tilt. There was never any danger; as they rounded each curve, sending up a spray of gravel, his hands were clamped over Arabella's on the reins and he was in full control. Indeed, sitting with Arabella clasped within the circle of his arms, he was more in control of the horses than he was of himself.

But Arabella felt that she was driving and loved the wild freedom of it, throwing back her head and laughing until her hair came loose and blew in the wind. Stepping down reluctantly, she turned and smiled at Henry, an unrestrained smile full of gaiety and love of life, which made his knees go weak and his heart do the flip-flopping somersaults of the hopelessly lovelorn.

'Oh, Sal,' she said, hugging her friend, 'I must do that again or *die*!'

At that moment Imogen knew that she must act.

The fourth bed in their dormitory was occupied by a

He had arrived at the end of Marion's first week of illness, with flowers and a bottle of brandy, and Marion's pay packet. He did not need to do that. Many West End managements still declined to pay actors for absence due to sickness. But not Vere Cavendish. And when Frances opened the envelope, Marion's wages had been supplemented by twenty pounds, doubtless out of Vere's own pocket. Damn the man, why must he always do the right thing! It would be so much easier to hate him, to really hate him, if he behaved badly.

The delirium passed and Marion lay very still. 'She is sinking,' the doctor said, 'and may not last the night.'

She looked so like their mother, the white pinched face and dull dark hair against the pillow, and Frances was frightened. What would they do, she and the twins, if Marion died? 'We need you,' she sobbed, grasping Marion's shoulders and giving her a little shake. 'You cannot die. What will happen to us if you die?' To her astonishment, Marion's eyes opened and, Frances believed, looked at her with recognition, as if hearing her sister's plea. Pouring a substantial dose of brandy from the bottle that Vere had brought, Frances held the glass to her sister's lips and Marion swallowed it obediently; and then she gave a little smile and the ghost of a sigh, and slept. For days she slept and slept, and slept her way back to full consciousness and, if not to full health, then to the highest degree of health that her abortion-scarred body could hope to attain.

By the beginning of Holy Week the two sisters were resting by the sea on the south coast, taking short walks along the promenade at Bournemouth while Marion regained her strength. Naturally the twins knew their whereabouts but the arrival of Arabella and Imogen, before the end of the school term, was unexpected.

'We have been expelled,' Arabella said calmly. 'They do not want "our sort" at their school.'

'But why . . . ?' Marion stared at them with a weakness and weariness that were the legacy of her illness.

'They found out that our sisters were actresses.'

Marion buried her face in her hands. Staring out at the horizon over the sparkling sea, Frances asked, in a tight, tense voice: 'How did they find out?'

Arabella executed that calm, supremely elegant shrug that she had perfected in the years since their father died. 'We did not tell them, if that's what you are thinking.'

'So, *how* . . . ?'

'News circulates. Things get around. Perhaps someone saw you at the theatre and made inquiries. Does it matter?'

'No, I don't suppose so.' Marion leaned back in the garden chair and stared out to sea, as Frances took the twins indoors in order to bespeak a room for them. 'How young they look,' she said when Frances returned. 'How fresh, and untouched . . .'

'But they are not untouched. The tentacles of your reputation, or lack of it, reach out and coil around us all!'

'Yes,' Marion said quietly. 'I thought you would say that.'

'They were doing so well at that school. Arabella was like *this*,' and Frances crossed her fingers, 'with that girl, the earl's daughter, and who knows where such a friendship might have led? Arabella was on the way to becoming all you hoped and planned she would be, whereas now . . . All because you had to go into the theatre. And where has it got you, might I ask? Just look at you!'

'I would rather not, if you don't mind. My hair is still falling out.' Marion removed her hat and ran tentative fingers through her fever-thinned and shorn locks. 'I suppose I can wear a wig if I go completely bald. Would anyone notice the difference, do you think?'

'Only your lover, if you took it off in bed, and he is so bald himself that he would have no right to criticise.'

Marion winced. 'Is there anything else you want to say? We might as well get it over with.'

'I am calling in the favour that you owe me. I am asking you to give up the theatre and help me found a school. The twins could come, and we could search for Charley. There was a house . . . Well, that house is unlikely to be available now, but I could look for something similar. If we could afford it, of course.'

Marion was still weak from her illness, hardly able to bear the sight of herself in the mirror because of the ugliness of her balding head. The prospect of facing an audience terrified her. The prospect of facing that audience in *Antony and Cleopatra* made her break out in a cold sweat. Vere knew I could not do it, she thought, he knew that I was not up to it, but Reggie made him try . . . And he never shouted at me or lost his temper . . . Oh, Vere, *Vere* . . . You were right when you said that for my entire career I would play good little women, but if that is all I am fit for, I am not sure that I want to go back to the theatre.

And Reggie, what about him? He had managed without her during her illness, so he could go on managing, Marion reasoned. As for her 'pension plan', probably she had milked him for as much as she could reasonably expect.

'Why don't you answer?' Frances implored. 'Are you thinking about Vere Cavendish, even after all the harm he has done? For God's sake, Marion, he was even the cause of the typhoid. I said from the start that The Cavendish

Theatre was an unsanitary health hazard, mainly because Mr Vere bloody Cavendish only spends money on painting over the surface, in order to hide the rotten wood beneath.'

Marion did not blame Vere for her fever, believing that the backstage facilities at The Cavendish were no worse than those at any other theatre. But the loss of her child, and all the other children who might have been conceived . . . Ah, that was another matter. The days when she had dreamed of herself and Vere as the golden couple of the English theatre, up there with the great husband-and-wife teams such as the Kendals and the Bancrofts, seemed to belong to a past existence and to a different woman. Sometimes she thought his rejection of her would have been easier to bear had he loved another; at least there would have been a logic to that, however hurtful. But, as far as anyone could see, Vere was not close to another woman; even Reggie remarked on the other man's total immersion in his work and lack of a private life. Vere was living like a monk and surely he could not be happy? What a waste, it was all such a terrible waste . . .

'You told me that I was to call in that favour one day,' Frances reminded her.

Tears were spilling down Marion's face. Everything had come together at once, conspiring to create a set of inescapable circumstances: her illness and loss of looks; *Antony and Cleopatra* and her fear that she would never rise to great heights in the theatre; the expulsion of the twins and the reminder of her lost reputation. And Vere . . . ? Vere would be with her, wherever she went and whatever she did.

'The school,' Frances persisted. 'Could we afford it?'

The jewellery boxes were lying in the bank, their secrets known only to Marion and their donor. She had not told

Frances of the full extent of Reggie's generosity and she would not tell her now. Some of those boxes would stay where they were, but she could dispose of a few and give the proceeds to Frances. Surely it was a small price to pay, a small gesture to the sister who had saved her life.

'Yes, we can afford it,' Marion said.

By August, Marion and Frances were working in the house that they had acquired for the school, making preparations to open the establishment in mid-September, when Charley walked through the open front door and into the kitchen.

Glowing, vivid and beautifully dressed, she made a marked contrast to her untidy, flushed sisters in their old working clothes and pinafores.

'You will never guess where I am going for my next engagement,' Charley announced cheerfully, after the hugs and kisses and exclamations were over. 'The Cavendish! Isn't it splendid that we can keep it in the family!'

Marion burst into tears and ran out of the room, while a look of absolute horror registered on Frances's face.

'You must cancel your engagement at The Cavendish! Marion survived hers, but only just. Vere Cavendish is dangerous and he will be the death of someone – perhaps one of us – sooner or later.'

'More likely that one of the Leigh sisters will be the death of him,' Charley joked.

'Laugh if you like, Charley, but The Cavendish is a death trap.'

Part Three

Chapter Fifteen

Charley had turned her back on the old and looked ahead to the new with the enthusiasm and fearlessness of the very young, and when she arrived at the Bristol address provided by the theatrical agent, she was breathless from carrying her luggage but unfazed by having her entire worldly possessions contained in two small bags.

Her inquiry for Mr Daniel Crisp was met with the information that this gentleman was working and Charley's subsequent request that the landlady, as her informant proved to be, direct her to the theatre was met with a pitying smile. The Theatre Royal was but a short walk from the lodgings, she was told, but Mr Crisp was not to be found there; Mr Crisp was at the Clifton Zoo. The Pastoral Players, it appeared, performed in the open air.

Learning that Charley was not only new to the Players but that she had never set foot in Bristol before, the landlady summoned her son to act as guide and escort. Seizing one of Charley's bags, the youth set off at a brisk pace and in complete silence. It was a long walk and the afternoon was hot. Feeling guilty at putting the youth to so much trouble, Charley worried about whether or not she ought to offer him a tip, but when in sight of the Zoo he merely pointed, thrust the bag into her hand and turned, leaving Charley to travel the final few yards alone.

She found the company resting beneath a tree, still in costume after the afternoon performance, and made her way towards the burly, blond-haired figure of Dan Crisp. Introducing herself, she was fixed by a pair of piercing blue eyes, eyes that, she would learn, could twinkle with amusement, blaze with anger, turn hard with displeasure, cool with sardonic impatience, and icy with contempt. Now their expression was welcoming and, as their glance assessed Charley's physical attributes, approving.

'Best if you watch from the wings tonight,' he said, with a lordly gesture at the 'stage', as if the green grass and the well-worn props were equal to the boards of the Lyceum, Covent Garden and Drury Lane. 'We're doing *Twelfth Night* and I'll only want you to walk on in this piece, but watch Olivia carefully and commit as much to memory as you can. Then, when you go on as one of her attendants, you'll be less likely to bump into her. Now, let me think . . . *Lily*,' he bellowed suddenly.

A young woman scrambled to her feet and hurried towards them, her plain dark dress giving Charley no clue as to her role in the play, her faded blonde hair and highly rouged cheeks oddly familiar.

'Lily, this is Miss Leigh who is joining our little band . . .' At which point Lily shot Charley a startled glance before frowning, as if trying to remember something, or someone. 'Look after her for me, my dear, and show her what's what. We'll organise her properly tomorrow when we reach Weston-super-Mare.'

Left alone, the two women smiled at each other, the one shyly and the other appraisingly.

'Weston-super-Mare?' queried Charley. 'Aren't we staying in Bristol?'

'Never stay anywhere for long,' Lily replied. 'A night here, two nights there, it can be as many as five towns a week. What's your name again?'

'Charlotte, but everyone calls me Charley.'

'Leigh, did Dan say? Look, I'm sure we have met somewhere.'

'Peg Woffington,' Charley burst out excitedly. 'You were in *Masks and Faces* with my sister, Marion. Oh, Miss Palmer, you were wonderful, absolutely wonderful!'

The obvious sincerity of this outburst, and the shining admiration in the girl's eyes, quite won over the other woman. 'Call me Lily,' she said graciously, 'and yes, now I remember, at the party after the last performance, with . . .' Discreetly she did not complete the sentence.

'With my father.' Charley's cheeks reddened. 'He died,' she said miserably.

'I am sorry . . . And your sister – what theatrical extravaganza is she gracing with her presence?'

'Marion is at The Cavendish – only a small part, but she does have a few lines to say.'

Lily digested this in silence and it was obvious from her expression that the news did not meet with her undiluted approval. 'There is no justice,' she muttered at last.

'The thing is,' Charley ventured, 'that Marion does not exactly know where I am, that I'm here, that is . . . Lily, you won't tell her that we have met, will you, please?'

A glimmer of a smile returned to Lily's face. 'Not on your life,' she returned robustly. 'She may be your sister, Charley, but Marion Leigh is no friend of mine and I don't owe her nothing.'

'Neither do I,' Charley agreed fervently, 'and she is not my friend either. What part are you playing in *Twelfth Night*?'

'Maria,' Lily said with satisfaction.

'I bet you are marvellous.'

'Yes, I am rather . . . Look, Charley,' and Lily led her further away from the group of actors to a spot where they could sit on the grass together, 'basically there are two types of person in a touring company like ours: there's the sort who gives themselves airs, and thinks that they're the bee's-knees and God's gift to the the-ay-ter; and then there's the sort who's honest and upfront, and who mucks in and helps out. Now, I'm one who trusts my first impressions and I reckon that you are one of the latter sort.'

'I should jolly well hope so,' Charley said indignantly. 'I leave the airs and graces to my sisters.'

Lily laughed and nodded approvingly. 'I could tell you a whole host of stories about how I come to be here, but I'm going to tell you the truth, because you are just starting out in the profession and only the truth will help you on your way. I am here, playing Maria in a respectable touring company, because I couldn't get a decent job in London. You see, in the profession only London counts, and it is the ultimate ambition of every member of the profession to take the great capital by storm.'

'But you were in London,' protested Charley.

'Resting, most of the time, and walking on if I was lucky. Too dependent on my looks and when they faded, so did I; when they disappeared, so did the engagements. I did *Masks* with those amateurs because they paid me well, and they were gents, treated me with courtesy and respect, which is more than can be said for your sister, but that's by-the-by. Then this job came up and I grabbed it. Out-of-town, yes, but it is a living *and* parts like Maria.' Lily smiled but her eyes were sad. 'I have accepted the fact that now I will never play Maria, or any parts of such importance, in the West End where it matters.'

'Then I have made a mistake,' Charley gasped, 'I ought to have stayed in London.'

'No, no, you did absolutely the right thing. Here, with us, you can learn all you need to know, and play parts that you'd never get a sniff at in London, and it's right for you because you are at the beginning of your career. Too many of us are struggling, like me, or at the end of their careers, like old George,' and Lily indicated an elderly, greying man dressed as a sea captain. 'Now, come and meet the girls. Have you had anything to eat today?'

Charley confessed that she had been too excited to eat.

'We'll find you something – must keep your strength up.' Lily rose and threaded her way through the recumbent figures of the company to a group of lively young ladies whom she introduced as Ada, Estelle and Irene respectively. Bread, cheese and slices of cold beef were produced from a basket, and ale was sloshed into a mug. Charley sipped it cautiously, not having drunk beer before, but found it very much to her taste.

'I really must pay you for this,' she began but was promptly shushed by her new-found friends.

'With us, it's share and share alike,' Ada said firmly. 'The time will come when you can do us a good turn.'

'Have you a place to stay tonight?' Estelle wanted to know.

Charley looked worried. 'I came straight here from the station, via Mr Crisp's lodgings. I suppose I ought to have made inquiries with his landlady, but I didn't think of it at the time.'

'You can shake down with us for the night,' Lily offered, 'can't she, girls? We'll squeeze you in somehow. It is only for one night and old Mrs B, our landlady, won't mind when she hears that you're new. You can pay her a bob for breakfast.'

Charley was beginning to feel that she was running up a debt of gratitude that she could never repay, but again the girls brushed aside her thanks and chattered on about the company, pointing out people and things of interest. The beautiful dark-haired woman in a white gown and a cap studded with seed pearls was Florence Weston, the company's leading lady, in her Olivia costume. Sitting with her, in doublet and hose, was a vivacious young actress who, according to Charley's informants, had joined the Players for the summer tour, playing Viola, Rosalind and Helena, but who was returning to London in the autumn.

A sudden chill of fear gripped Charley's heart. 'What happens in the winter?' she asked anxiously. 'The agent who hired me didn't say . . . I mean, he never mentioned that the company played out-of-doors, or that the engagement might be so short.'

'We carry on through the winter,' Irene said, straight-faced. 'It can get a bit chilly by December, of course. Poor old Ada got frostbite last year, didn't you, love? And if it snows, one of us has to follow the principals around, holding an umbrella over them.'

Doubtfully Charley regarded her with wide-eyed concern, unsure whether to believe her, but her dilemma was solved when the girls broke into gales of laughter.

'She's having you on,' Lily reassured her. 'In the autumn we become the Crispin Comedy Company and tour a different repertoire around the provincial theatres. I expect that the agent signed you up for both tours but, even if he didn't, you tell Dan Crisp that he did.'

Engulfed with relief, Charley joined in the laughter at her expense. 'Even in the summer there must be cold, wet days.'

'Mr Crisp usually manages to find an alternative venue,

even if he pitches a marquee.' Lily paused, following the direction of Charley's gaze and locating the object on which it was transfixed. 'I see you have discovered our leading man.'

An exquisite young man was seated on a chair, his long legs elegantly crossed. With his noble profile, dark eyes and brown hair curling tightly over his well-shaped head, he had a youthful beauty that contrasted with the more mature, sardonic good looks of a Vere Cavendish. His Orsino costume and his air of languid grace gave him the appearance of a gilded Elizabethan in a painted miniature, needing only a pomander and a carpet of flowers to complete the illusion.

'Gosh,' was all Charley managed to gasp, choking on a chunk of cheese. 'What is his name?' she asked when she got her breath back.

'Benet Darcy,' Lily said drily, 'or so he would have us believe. Don't worry, Benet Darcy is merely a phase you must go through. He is a rite of passage for every female joining the company, but it doesn't last long.'

'The light that dazzles eventually illuminates,' Estelle proclaimed cryptically.

'Talking of which, time to prepare the lamps,' and Irene stood up and stretched. The hot afternoon was softening into the gold of evening and Irene cast an approving eye at the cloudless sky. 'There'll be a good moon tonight,' she predicted.

Behind a row of canvas flats, which screened the off-stage area from the audience, the junior members of the company began preparing for the evening performance while the principals lolled idly in lordly splendour. Eager to help, Charley primed the oil lamps and learned where to place them to best advantage in order to illumine the Players as dusk fell. Props were checked, instruments tuned, costumes straightened and make-up freshened and, peering cautiously round a screen, Charley saw that the audience was drifting to its places. A lion roared, setting off a reaction from other zoo animals and adding an odd, eerie dimension to Charley's experience of the evening. And then the play began, and from the moment Benet Darcy strode out on to the grassy sward and proclaimed: 'If music be the food of love, play on,' Charley was engrossed in it, enraptured by the privilege of seeing it from the wings, dodging out of the way as the actors made their exits and entrances. Always alert and intelligent, she monitored the movements of Olivia and her attendants as she had been instructed to do, and was happily confident of coping with the less-than-challenging role allocated to her. Who knows, she thought with a surge of excitement, this time tomorrow I might be out there myself!

At the end of a scene in the third act, Olivia came off the stage and began tugging forcefully at the folds of her dress. 'Blasted hem has sagged. I noticed it the moment I went on and I have endured *agonies*. Will someone please bring me a needle and thread?' Without hesitation Charley hurried to the props table where, earlier, she had seen a sewing kit and swiftly threaded a needle with white cotton. Instead of handing the needle to Olivia, she kneeled down and began repairing the hem of the dress. Needlework was not Charley's forte, nor was it her favourite occupation by any means, but no girl could have lived in the Leigh household with its essential make-and-mend philosophy without becoming proficient in any aspect of repairing and altering clothes. Charley's long, slender fingers worked swiftly, the needle flying, her russet head bent to her task, and she was finishing the job when Dan Crisp, as Sir Toby Belch, left the stage and paused beside them.

'You are?' Florence Weston, as Olivia, inquired graciously.

'Charley Leigh, Miss Weston.'

'Thank you, Charley, you have been most helpful.' Miss Weston inspected the work closely and found it satisfactory. She walked away with Dan Crisp. 'That girl,' Charley heard her say, 'will be very useful.'

Charley's reaction to the 'emergency' had been instinctive, not calculated to win praise, but nonetheless she glowed with pleasure. However, perhaps the happiest moment of her entire day came late at night when she and the girls tumbled into their lodgings and, staggering with tiredness and giggling under their breath, mounted the stairs to the two first-floor bedrooms that they shared. All five congregated in Lily's and Ada's room and, after much massaging of sore feet and aching necks, it was decided that Charley should doss down there for the night.

'I'll sleep on the floor,' Charley insisted. 'I'm too tall to fit into someone else's bed. I don't mind. I can sleep anywhere.'

'Keen, ain't she,' said Estelle laconically.

'She'll learn,' agreed Irene with a yawn. 'See you in the morning, girls.'

Make-up was removed, clothes tossed carelessly into a heap in the corner, to be sorted out the next morning, and Lily and Ada subsided into bed.

'Are you sure you'll be comfortable, Charley?' asked Lily sleepily.

'I'm fine, thank you.'

And she was. Charley could not have rested more comfortably and contentedly in the finest four-poster with swan's-down pillows, goosefeather mattress and silk sheets than she did on that floor, cushioned by Ada's pillow and Lily's quilt. For Charley, shut in her lonely attic for so long, the greatest luxury in the world was the sound of the steady breathing of her companions and the warmth of their friendliness. Less than twenty-four hours had elapsed since she left home, but already the great adventure was living up to every expectation. Already Charley knew that the theatre was friend, family and home and she suspected that it always would be.

From Weston-super-Mare the Players travelled to Taunton, Exeter, Plymouth, Paignton and Torquay; then on to Yeovil, Sherborne, Southampton, Salisbury and Winchester before appearing at Merton College, Oxford. Cheltenham, Gloucester, Worcester, Birmingham . . . to the zoos and botanical gardens, parks and pavilions, piers, playing-fields and recreation grounds, jolting in third-class railway carriages, coping with inadequate changing facilities, staying in poor hotels and shabby lodging houses which, with board, swallowed all Charley's meagre pay.

But nothing lowered Charley's spirits or sapped her vitality. Her 'usefulness' was proved time and time again, not only by the ease and grace she brought to her humble stage roles but by her willingness to work behind the scenes. No task was too tedious or too lowly for her. She sewed her costumes, and helped others with theirs; she mended or embellished props; she took on the entire responsibility for lamps; and she ran errands for anyone who cared to ask. Starved of love and affection at home, Charley was like an eager puppy who rushed about, tail wagging, saying 'please like me', and lazy members of the company took shameless advantage of her good nature. The principals were the worst offenders, Benet Darcy making it abundantly clear that although Charley was granted the privilege of cleaning his shoes, her place was on her knees in an attitude of worship while she was doing it.

Gradually Dan Crisp developed an unconscious and involuntary reliance on her, utilising her services for personal requirements as well as jobs relating to the company. '*Charley* . . .' From Weston to Worcester, the bellow became familiar. 'Drat the girl, where is she?' But often she was out of earshot because she was busy about the very task that he was contemplating for her. Charley did not need to be asked; she had the invaluable gift of anticipating the next job, of working it out logically, or remembering what had been done on previous occasions, and not needing to be told twice. And if there was no obvious work to be done, she would find a job such as cleaning the stage jewellery or lovingly repainting a throne. Charley could not stay still. Hers was a restless spirit, inherited from her father, galvanised by his nervous energy, love of enterprise and speculation, and fuelled by his stamina, optimism and courage.

For friends she had the stalwart group of girls, and several of the younger men would travel in their railway carriage and eat with them. Meals were irregular and unpretentious: sandwiches and buns on the train, bread, cold meat and ale at the railway stations, pies in the taverns. Charley liked the taverns best, loving the warmth and the crush and the conversation, pushing in with her friends while the principals removed themselves to a private room, and old George Allen settled down with his pint and a pipe by the fire. If I were not an actress, Charley thought, as she watched the buxom barmaids, I would have worked in a pub.

One day she was sitting closer than usual to old George when she heard a rumbling, ruminating noise as he cleared his throat and then that massive bass voice, trained to reach the farthest corner of a 2,000-seater auditorium, boomed: 'When I was a boy, I saw Kean.' Charley turned to see who he was talking to, but he was alone, staring into the fire.

'Oh Lord, George is off.' Lily picked up her mug of ale and crept to a table by the door, followed by the rest of the group.

'Come on, Charley,' hissed Estelle. 'Once old George has started reminiscing, there's no stopping him.'

But Charley, mug in hand, hesitated and then slowly gravitated towards George. Drawing up a stool, she said in awe: 'Mr Allen, did you really see Edmund Kean?'

His eyes were closed but, opening one, he established the identity of his listener and nodded. 'Not only that,' he said impressively, 'but I met a man who saw Garrick.'

Charley had been conscious of old George only as an irritant. When any of her friends grumbled about something, he could be relied on to rumble: 'You young 'uns don't know you're born; now, when I was your age . . .' But no one stayed to hear the rest and Charley had been guilty of melting away with the others. Now, in this simple figure of an actor of the old school, she recognised a living link with the great theatrical past, a participant in the heritage of the English theatre.

'Was Garrick the greatest actor of all?' Charley breathed.

'They say that takes too narrow a view. He was more than that – Garrick was a truly great man as well as a great actor.'

'What was it about him that made him so much better than anyone else?'

'As an actor his imagination was so powerful that he could transform himself into the character; his own personality vanished so completely that men swore he could change his very features. As a man, Garrick was a scholar, a diplomat and a shrewd financier, a man of means and good breeding, who rose to the top of his profession with comparative ease, unlike poor, flawed Kean.' George took a long swig from his jar and leaned back contentedly. It was not often that he had an audience for his memories, let alone one as attentive as this. 'I was eleven years old when I saw Kean. He was Shylock that night and it was towards the end of his life, when the drink and the dissipation were taking their toll, but I'll never forget it.'

'What was he like?' Charley asked, knowing that the question, and any answer, was inadequate.

'Thunder and lightning,' George said simply, 'wild and extravagant, and often incorrect. But, as Samuel Phelps said, he lifted you off your feet.'

'I wish that I could lift people off their feet,' Charley said wistfully.

'Perhaps you will, it's early days yet, but genius is granted to very few.'

She left him then and returned to her friends, and a barrage of teasing, but she sought him out again and again and they became a familiar sight, the heavily built, grey-haired old man and the lissom, russet-haired young girl who sat at his feet and absorbed everything he knew about the theatre.

From him Charley learned the history of her profession and, alone of her sisters, she entered into the fabric of the theatre. Mention Macready to Marion and she would have looked blank, but Charley wanted to know everything and wanted to be one of that great company. She listened to age-old stories about Garrick, Sarah Siddons and her brother John Kemble, Kean, Macready and the Vestris-Mathews partnership, all artists who had died or reached their peak too early for George to have known them, but she also pumped him for every detail of his own career. From his first job, touring the northern circuits in the days when actors were 'rogues and vagabonds', George went to a stock company in Manchester, where learning 500 lines a day was normal and where, over a period of as little as three years, an actor could play 400 roles. It was as if his progress mirrored that of the theatre itself, because when he left the stock company in 1850 in order to join Phelps at Sadler's Wells, he was unconsciously gravitating to one of the two actors who could take advantage of the new theatrical reforms. And when, in 1856, he moved to the Princess's, where Charles Kean was mounting plays with lavish scenery and costumes of meticulous historical accuracy, he transferred to the other.

Then George went to Buckstone at the Haymarket, where Sothern was star of the company, and in 1865 he was at the Olympic with Henry Neville, Kate Terry and Lydia Foote.

'And then?' Charley asked.

But at this point George was less forthcoming, and only gradually did Charley learn that while at the Olympic he had started drinking too much. He became unreliable and was out of work for a long time, until he sobered up sufficiently to land a berth on a provincial tour.

'What is the most important lesson you have learned?' she asked. 'I don't mean not forgetting your lines or not bumping into people, but something really important, about the theatre itself.'

'I believe that only an actor can restore or advance the prestige of the theatre, and that only an actor can win success for an individual production.'

'That is unfair on the other participants,' Charley argued. 'An actor needs back-up; he needs good management and good material. It could be said that an actor is only as good as his material.'

'I disagree. The actor is king. Without a great actor, even the best efforts of management and playwright can appear shallow and dull. They need him more than he needs them because, when the chips are down, the great actor can rise above the shortcomings of the production and wring a reaction from the audience.'

It was an argument that would return to haunt Charley during the sleepless nights and dark days that lay ahead.

The winter tour of the Crispin Comedy Company extended Charley's experience in several ways. First, she discovered that her fascination with all aspects of the theatre included the backstage machinery. Setting up in one provincial theatre after another, she was enthralled by the drums, shafts, windlasses and pulleys and by the complex web of ropes on gridiron and fly-galleries. She climbed high above the stage in order to learn how scenery was put into place, how the noise of wind or thunder or rain was made, and how the lights were operated. As the pantomime season approached, she watched the stage staff working on the wires for the flying fairies and she descended under the stage in theatre after theatre, familiarising herself with traps and bridges.

Too tall to be a flying fairy, Charley resigned herself to yet another minor role in *Cinderella*, but on one never-to-be-forgotten day, a large hamper arrived from London containing the costumes for the pantomime. Florence Weston, who was playing Cinderella, was entranced by her ballgown and was soon happily making minor adjustments to her 'rags' or, rather, she summoned Charley to make the alterations for her. Kneeling down with a mouthful of pins, rather like Cinderella helping others to prepare for the ball, Charley nearly swallowed the pins as a wrathful shriek drowned Miss Weston's remarks.

Turning, she saw the actress cast as Prince Charming advancing to centre-stage, holding a jacket and a pair of tights in one hand and with an expression on her face that suggested there was a very nasty smell under her nose.

'If you think,' she snarled at Dan Crisp, 'that I am walking on to the stage in *this*, you are very much mistaken. Nor am I singing that very silly song you have compelled me to rehearse this week. I have said from the start that I am a serious actress and that pantomime is an insult to my integrity and my intelligence.'

Dan Crisp had used up all his arguments and persuasiveness with this particular lady and wisely sought an alternative solution. Looking round the stage, his eye alighted on Charley. He beckoned. Taken aback, Charley pointed a finger at herself and mouthed 'Me?' before rising to her feet, apologising politely to a displeased Cinderella, and advancing to centre-stage.

'Can you sing?' Dan demanded.

'A bit. I'm not as good as my sister Frances, just as I cannot act as well as my sister Marion, but . . .'

'Very well,' he said impatiently. 'What about that costume – would it fit you?'

Dubiously Charley took the garments and inspected them. 'Too small,' she said, 'particularly the tights.'

'*Bob* . . .' bellowed Dan, summoning a young man from the wings. 'You are about the same height as Charley. Have you a pair of white tights that would fit her? The jacket, I think, may do, but she'll need boots . . . Take her away, for God's sake, and bring her back dressed.'

Bewildered, Charley put on the London costumier's jacket with borrowed tights and boots and, feeling self-conscious beyond belief, returned to the stage. She braced herself, staring sightlessly into the middle distance, feeling all those eyes boring into her legs – legs never before exposed like this, legs usually concealed beneath comforting petticoats and skirts.

Strewth! Dan Crisp saw what the theatrical agent had seen straight away. Those endless legs. What a natural for breeches parts.

'Take over as Prince Charming,' Dan said huskily. 'I want you word-perfect by the end of the week.'

Charley was word-perfect that same evening but did not boast about it. In a daze, she heard Dan say that her wages would be raised to three pounds a week, but she did not really care about the money: if given bed and board, she would have worked for nothing. She was so happy, she could burst. Pantomime was not beneath Charley's dignity, pantomime was fun, and her enjoyment of it was infectious. The audience sensed it and responded accordingly. Charley, long legs posing, russet hair tossing, entered into the spirit of pantomime and sparkled, slapping her thigh with zest and making love to Cinderella with an ardour that caused a few twitching eyebrows and nudging elbows.

'She isn't one of *those*, is she?' whispered Estelle.

'I don't think so.' Lily shook her head and refused to believe it. 'But, judging by the look on Benet Darcy's face, we are about to find out for certain.'

The company was in Leeds, with *The School for Scandal*, *The Rivals*, *She Stoops to Conquer*, *The Belle's Stratagem* and *Adrienne Lecouvreur* in its repertoire as well as the pantomime, but the day after Lily noticed that appraising look in Darcy's eye, they moved on to Bradford. Disembarking from the train, the girls saw Darcy crook his forefinger and beckon to Charley.

'Bloody cheek,' exclaimed Irene. 'Who the hell does he think he is!'

'Ignore him, Charley,' Estelle advised.

But Charley was already bounding towards her hero with an eager smile and adoration shining in her eyes. To her surprise he thrust a small parcel into her arms.

'Tomorrow morning,' he said without preamble, 'you will bring this to the Victoria Hotel. Do not inquire for me at the desk – I will tell you at the theatre tonight what room I am in. If anyone at the hotel asks any awkward questions, say that I left this packet on the train and you are delivering it to me.'

He walked away and Charley returned to her friends who, seeing the parcel, gave a collective groan.

'Oh no, he never did, not the parcel routine.' Lily prodded the packet angrily. 'You do know what this means, don't you?'

'I'm not sure,' Charley admitted.

'In that case, when you and I have settled into our humble lodgings – because the Victoria Hotel, where Darcy stays, is way out of our league – you and I had best have a little chat.'

The 'chat', when it did come, was more serious than any conversation she had shared with Lily since joining the company. 'If you want to go to Darcy's room, then go – I'll not try to persuade you otherwise,' Lily said bluntly. 'All I want is for your eyes to be as wide open before you go as your legs will be when you get there.'

Charley's face reddened. 'You don't have to worry. I know what he wants, and it is what I want too.'

'You do realise that you are not the first to be handed that parcel?' When Charley nodded, Lily sighed but went on: 'I know that you think you are in love with him, but . . .'

'I don't just *think*,' Charley broke in hotly.

'. . . *but*, as I was about to say, do you think that he is in love with you?' Charley's hesitation was an answer in itself and Lily nodded grimly. 'Well, that's something, I suppose. Next question: do you know how to stop a baby happening? Because, by all accounts – and this is hearsay, because I succeeded in cultivating an immunity to his charms – your Mr Darcy does not favour the use of a French letter.' Seeing Charley's blank look, Lily explained that some men were willing to wear a rubber sheath during intercourse. 'There's withdrawal, but I doubt if Darcy is the sort to put your welfare before his own self-ish pleasure, and anyhow it's dangerous. So, as he ain't no gentleman, it's down to you, and to vaginal sponges and the "safe period". When did you last have a bleed?'

Charley told her and Lily said that, in that case, she ought to be safe. 'It ain't scientific or anything like that,' she told Charley, 'but, as old wives' tales go, this one has common sense on its side and a lot of experience to back it up. We'll fix you up with a sponge as well, of course.'

None of this was quite how Charley had envisaged her deflowering. In her imagination, Benet had wooed her with sweet words and flowers, before seducing her beau-tifully in the moonlight. Oddly, Charley's fantasies had not included a wedding – the theatre, and some basic instinct in herself, had made her more realistic than that. Too young and inexperienced in love to realise how appalling was Darcy's treatment of her, or to see the funny side of the situation, Charley earnestly thanked Lily for her help and advice.

The next morning, pale with nervousness and lack of sleep, she set off for the hotel clutching the parcel like a talisman and repeating Benet's room number over and over again, as if it were the password that would open the door to a secret world of exotic delights. Boldly she walked through the lobby and up the stairs, trying to look as though she had every right to be there, and knocked on the door. Glancing anxiously to left and right for inquisitive chambermaids, Charley fairly hurtled through the door when it opened.

'I don't think anyone saw me,' she gasped. 'Oh, I say, what a gorgeous room!'

In fact, the accommodation was modest by the hotel's standards but to Charley, accustomed to poverty, it seemed the height of luxury. Her interest in the furnishings was genuine, but her minute inspection of the same also enabled her to avoid looking at her host, if that was the right word, who was in a disturbing state of undress. When he came inescapably close, her suspicions were confirmed: Benet Darcy was wearing a crimson silk robe and nothing else.

He was an exceptionally beautiful young man, and he knew it. This morning the brown curls were becomingly tousled, the brown eyes smiled lazily, and the robe revealed a matted chest and his long, well-shaped legs, which looked even better in the flesh than they did in the costumes with which Benet graced the stage. And then he touched her for the first time, pulling Charley to him so that her back was against his chest and running his hands over her body, first cupping her breasts and then sliding over the curves of waist and hips before pressing into her groin and, through her clothes, rubbing between her legs.

The most extraordinary feeling came over her. From the dryness in her throat, a melting sensation flowed down and centred, with throbbing sweetness, in the cleft where his fingers were probing through the folds of skirt, petticoat and drawers. Pressing herself against him, Charley arched her neck and closed her eyes as his mouth burned cheek, neck and throat.

'Take off your clothes.'

Turning to face him, she saw it: his robe had parted and this thing was poking out at her.

'I have never done this before,' said Charley, eyes riveted and, as ever, the willing pupil. 'Will you show me what to do?'

At that, the thing seemed to grow bigger and more purple, rearing up at her, fascinating and hypnotic, and Benet seized her by the shoulders, forcing her mouth open with his tongue and thrusting it halfway down her throat. They fell back on to the bed as he pulled her skirt up and her drawers off, and clumsily he lay on top of her and rammed the thing into her. A moment of searing pain and then he was moving inside her and it was lovely; then it began to be wonderful, and Charley was just starting to respond to his rhythm when he shuddered and shouted, and stopped. Charley felt the thing slither out of her and lie limp against her thigh.

The emptiness, the disappointment at the lack of fulfilment, was intense but Charley was made of strong stuff. Alert, intelligent and inquisitive, she was also that rare and almost mythical being, the original passionate redhead, with a flame in her that burned as brightly as her hair. While Benet slumped back on the pillow Charley raised herself on one elbow and looked at him, and knew that she did not love him. She felt warm and close to him despite the emptiness inside her, but she did not love him. However, she admired his beautiful body and, pulling the robe over his unresisting arms, she investigated it with eyes, fingers and mouth, exploring and nuzzling every curve and crevice. Lingering longest over the thing, Charley subjected it to a lengthy and intense inspection, peering at it with the thoroughness of an anatomist, before flicking the tip with her thumb and forefinger to see if it would bounce back. Poor little thing, so limp and defeated, but Benet lay there with such uncaring, selfish satisfaction that Charley's aching void demanded fulfilment and revenge. Stripping off the last of her clothes, she lay down naked beside him.

'Benet,' she said, kissing his ear, 'could we do that again? I seem to have started something that I cannot finish.'

Opening his eyes, he saw the long white translucence of her nakedness and reached for her, and Charley, responding to his kiss, felt the resurgence of the thing as it blossomed and bloomed hard against her. Her only problem was that she was too aware of him and of their naked bodies. Part of her was participating, and sensing and feeling, but another part of her was up there on the ceiling watching, analysing, cringing and self-conscious. The trick, Charley decided, was to merge the two parts.

He had taken hold of her hand and guided it to the thing, indicating that she should stroke it, up and down, in and out. Charley complied, feeling it grow stronger and harder but most of all she wanted it close to her and, manoeuvring herself under him, she stroked it along the moistness of the cleft between her legs. By accident it touched a spot that she had not known existed until now, a small hard knob which, when touched, sent a shaft of desire spiralling through her.

'Oh,' groaned Charley, 'oh yes,' and she rubbed the tip of the thing against her until she could bear it no longer and guided him inside her, crying out again with the pleasure of that sensual slide. Moving with him, straining to take him deeper and deeper inside her, Charley felt the delicious spiral climbing and she gripped him hard, wrapping arms and legs fiercely round him. If it stopped, if he stopped, she would surely die. She strained again, tightening muscles she did not know she had, and suddenly it was happening. Effortlessly, involuntarily, she was convulsing, shrieking and shuddering, exploding like a shooting star that reaches a peak and then falls to the ground.

In the ensuing peace, she was engulfed by a flood of goodwill towards him. She would not call it love, not any more, but in its place was the affection of shared experience and gratitude for a gift that was so beautiful. The two Charleys, the one on the ceiling and the one on the bed, were not yet fully merged – she was still conscious of being here, actually in his bed, lying naked next to the theatrical star over whom a thousand women swooned – but slowly they were relaxing into one woman, who knew exactly who she was and what she wanted.

It took more than a year for her to come to terms completely with this new self, by which time Benet Darcy had left the company and Charley was playing good roles and understudying Viola, Rosalind and Helena. At last her prayers were answered when at Torquay the season's Viola went down with a sore throat and heavy cold caused by performing out-of-doors in all weathers. Fortunately, Charley's pale slenderness disguised a robust constitution and she was able to take over the part with maximum enthusiasm and minimum nerves.

In the early hours of the next morning, unable to sleep as memories of the occasion and the euphoria of the applause whirled inside her head, Charley crept out of bed, slipped on a dress and wandered down to the seafront. A grey dawn was silvering the sea, which stretched like silk to the horizon until, in the lovely stillness, the sun bathed a mackerel sky in rose-pink light, and gentle ripples left mother-of-pearl scallops on the shore. Charley's hair, flaming against the pallor of her finely chiselled face, stirred in the faint breeze.

This morning, walking alone by the sea, she felt different. Something entered her soul and stayed there, like a rod of steel inserted in her spine, supporting her and bringing with it a deep-seated sense of security. Suddenly she realised that all the strength she needed lay within herself, and that she was complete within herself and needed no one. The old Charley – the Charley alone in the attic or the one up on the ceiling – merged painlessly with the new, reborn Charley. Personally and professionally, she had achieved self-reliance.

Chapter Sixteen

Eighteen months after Charley joined the Pastoral Players, a note was delivered to Dan Crisp at the Winchester theatre. It was mid-September and, due to wet weather and repeated illnesses, Dan had arranged for the company to change to the winter repertoire two weeks earlier than usual. They were setting up *The School for Scandal* and Dan was not surprised to find that the note requested a box for that evening's performance. What did surprise him was that the request came from Vere Cavendish.

It was flattering when West End managers took an interest in one's productions – and Dan maintained stoutly that he could compete with any of them for excellence of acting and delivery – but there were drawbacks. For a start, the cast would become over-excited and this volatility would have dire effects on the standard of performance. But, as Cavendish had generously offered to order supper for the company after the show, they could not be kept in ignorance of his presence. Anyway, someone would spot Cavendish, who tended to stand out in a crowd, and inevitably word would spread. Dan sighed, knowing that the main reason for the company's excitement would be each individual's hope of attracting the favourable attention of the great man. Of course, everyone was under contract but could he, in all conscience, refuse a fellow member of the profession such a golden opportunity, should it arise? Well, yes, in one case he most definitely could, and if need be, he would.

At a small table in a corner of the office, Charley was working on the accounts. Her assistance with the bookkeeping had come about in the natural unpretentious fashion that most things came about with Charley.

'That cannot be right,' she had heard Dan mutter vehemently one day as he toiled over the books. 'At least, I bloody well hope it isn't right or we're sunk!'

'Having trouble with the accounts?' Charley peered over his shoulder. 'I always found it a most satisfying job. I liked making the entries and filing the dockets neatly, and leaving everything tidy at the end.'

'You know how to do book-keeping?'

'I used to do it for my uncle.' And Charley explained about John Leigh's printing firm and her work there. 'Would you like me to do it for you? The principle has to be the same surely, whatever the nature of the business. Let me see, your income will be box-office receipts and your outgoings will vary somewhat from summer to winter. Do you pay for the gas separately or is it included in the rent of the theatre? And I expect that you want to know which productions are the most popular, so you list the takings for each play. And that means that you keep a note of the production costs for each play . . .'

'Charley, is there anything that you cannot do?' he said reverently.

'No,' Charley said promptly, and laughed. 'I am perfect in every way, Mr Crisp, didn't you know that?'

'Many a true word is spoken in jest,' he murmured. 'I'll give you an extra pound a week.'

'Done,' and they shook hands on it.

In addition to these talents, and despite the problem of her height, which made it difficult to find men tall enough to play opposite her, Charley was developing into a quick-witted, intelligent and adaptable player. Therefore, no, he could not spare Charley but he could take comfort from the fact that she did not show to best advantage in *The School for Scandal*; she was playing Maria, the leading juvenile part, and doing so charmingly, but the costume did not flatter her. Charley was too tall for elaborate frocks and powdered wigs, looking her best in breeches or in dresses with simple, flowing lines.

'Another box taken for tonight,' he said with studied casualness as he wrote a special note for the resident front-of-house staff. 'And you will never guess by whom.'

Charley glanced up politely.

'Vere Cavendish.' To Dan's astonishment, Charley's face flamed and then went deathly white. 'Do you know him?'

'I won't have to meet him, will I?'

'Possibly, at supper after the performance. Why?'

'If I tell you, you must promise not to say anything about it to him.' Having received Dan's reassurance, Charley went on: 'My sister Marion is at The Cavendish and I don't want her to find out where I am.'

'Why not?'

'It is too complicated to explain.'

'In that case, keep out of Cavendish's way, but if he asks to be introduced to you, I cannot refuse.'

As soon as she had finished her work in the office, Charley sought out George Allen and found him in the wings, watching the excited mill of players with a world-weary cynicism.

'I gather they have heard about Vere Cavendish,' Charley said.

'Not that it will get any of them anywhere,' George said sourly. 'The standard of the company is rather low this season.'

'Thanks a lot,' Charley replied indignantly. 'I suppose the low standard is why I get to play Maria?'

'Yes.' But George smiled and amended the brutal impact of that opinion by saying: 'But you are the only one whom Vere Cavendish is likely to notice.'

'But I don't think I want to be noticed,' Charley said miserably. 'I do and I don't, if you see what I mean. Oh George, what on earth will I do if he finds out I am Marion's sister? He is bound to tell her that he saw me with this company.'

'After all this time, would it matter if he did?'

'It is selfish, I know, but with things as they are I am *free*. I can do what I like, go anywhere with anyone, free of all the carping and back-biting and criticism . . .'

'Free of all family responsibility,' George suggested drily.

Charley's chin tilted defiantly. 'Yes, I admit it, but in my defence I reckon I had more than my fair share of it at one time. I owe them nothing, believe me!'

'Leigh is not an uncommon name,' George consoled her.

'And I do not look like Marion,' she said eagerly, 'so there is no reason why he should connect us.'

'Don't you want to go to The Cavendish and be a success like your sister?'

Charley groaned. The news of Marion's triumph in *Romeo and Juliet* and the other Cavendish productions last season had filtered through to her and she was not above feeling a strong surge of sibling jealousy. She had not forgotten her youthful crush on Vere Cavendish, and the idea of Marion starring with this figure of godlike proportions made her grind her teeth in envy and rage.

'That is why, in one way, I wish he *would* notice me,' she said despairingly. 'Of course I would go to The Cavendish like a shot if I had the opportunity, even if it did mean facing Marion and the others. But why are we even discussing it? Like everyone else, I have a contract with Dan Crisp.'

'If Cavendish wants something, he will get it. Always did, and I reckon he always will.'

'George,' Charley said slowly, 'do you *know* Vere Cavendish?'

'Met him when he was just starting out, best part of fifteen years ago – no, I tell a lie, more like fourteen. He joined a tour I was doing and stayed for a couple of years.'

'*George!*' Charley was nearly as impressed by this as she had been by his anecdotes of Garrick and Kean. 'Tell me everything!'

'We were doing the usual sort of stuff,' he said reflectively, 'much the same repertoire as we are doing now, plus *London Assurance*, *Two Roses*, *Lady of Lyons* and *Masks and Faces*. Cavendish was a gift to a company like that – good looks and upper-crust accent. Ideal for the juvenile lead, which, with almost indecent haste, he rapidly became.'

'That must have made him unpopular with the company.'

'No, he was well liked by everyone. He worked hard and played hard, as suave a man-about-town off the stage as he was on. Always smartly dressed and well groomed. Gave the impression of having pots of money and a host of rich connections, but I always had the sneaking suspicion that he hadn't got a shilling. Just as I always suspected that his beautiful diction was the product of the elocution class rather than family background. Charley, if his real name is Vere Cavendish, then I'm the Prince of Wales.'

'There is no disgrace in using a stage name, and Vere Cavendish sounds much better than Benet Darcy! Even Estelle admits that she changed her name.' But Charley did feel a brief pang of disappointment, as if Cavendish had let her down in some indefinable way. 'Did you find out what he was doing before he joined the tour?'

'He made no secret of the fact that he had been appearing in amateur productions while working in the City, but he was never specific about the nature of that work.'

'Where did he go when he left the tour?'

'He said he was going to the Lyceum and I have no reason to disbelieve him. I do know he went to the Olympic soon after that, and then to the Bancrofts. No one was surprised when he left – it was obvious that he was learning as much as he could, as quickly as he could, and that he was chafing to be off to the lights of London. No good knocking them dead in Doncaster for a couple of nights: Cavendish knew that he had to be a hit in a London hit.'

'I know the feeling.' Charley sighed. 'But come on, George, you've seen them all: tell me honestly, is Vere Cavendish any good?'

'Oh yes, no doubt about it. He was not merely good, he was *really* good – the best young juvenile I've seen in years. He has deserved his success, even if there are those who slight him by saying that he can only play undemanding roles and that in many ways he is only acting himself, or himself as he would like to be. And, same as you, Cavendish has a head on his shoulders and an above-average brain. He learned that, these days, shows are directed to the educated audience in the boxes and the stalls, and that an actor needs at least a veneer of education and sophistication.'

'Thank you for the compliment, George. It is very flattering to be bracketed intellectually with Vere Cavendish, but somehow I do not imagine I will achieve the dizzy heights of management. I will always be a humble player, like you.'

But the idea, as yet no more than a tiny spark, lingered at the back of Charley's mind. Other women had managed theatres – Lucia Vestris had done it and, according to George, so had Louisa Herbert, Elizabeth Yates and Louisa Nisbett, while Marie Wilton worked on her own before marrying Squire Bancroft. With these precedents, why shouldn't she aim for the very top of the tree? But first, and Charley's heart lurched in a most uncomfortable manner, she had to get through tonight's performance with the knowledge that Vere Cavendish would be watching every move she made.

As Dan had feared, the performance fell far below the usual standards of the Crispin Comedy Company. Under-rehearsed and over-excited, not only were lines forgotten and some good bits of business muffed, but the entire company, with the possible exception of Charley, was playing straight at Cavendish's box with a reckless disregard for the rest of the audience or for the muddle that was bound to ensue. It was the muddle that was Charley's undoing.

When Joseph Surface knelt at Maria's feet, he was so intent on giving Cavendish a good view of his best profile that he subsided to his knees in a different place from the one choreographed at rehearsal. Seconds later the entrance of Lady Teazle, also artfully taking up a favourable position, gave Charley her exit, by which time she was so

thoroughly fed up that she turned with an exaggerated
flounce in order to stalk off in high dudgeon.
Unfortunately she failed to notice that one of Joseph's
knees was firmly planted on the trailing hem of her skirt.
As she turned, a nasty tearing sound heralded disaster.
Jerked to a sudden standstill, Charley staggered and fell
sideways into one of Lady Sneerwell's chairs, which
promptly collapsed under the unexpected assault. Amid a
gale of laughter, Charley struggled to her feet and fled
the stage, wig askew and torn skirt flapping, miserably
conscious that although some of the audience would not
know whether the incident was accidental or intentional,
one notable onlooker would certainly be aware of the true
circumstances. Bloody Joseph, Charley fumed, and backstage that night there was a great deal of bickering over
who was to blame for the numerous gaffes.

Having seriously considered missing the party, but
deciding that she ought not to offend Dan Crisp and could
not afford to turn down a free meal, Charley crept into the
hotel, hoping to slide unobtrusively into a place at the
opposite end of the room from Vere Cavendish. To her
horror, the company was standing in vivacious groups –
the closer to Cavendish, the more noticeable the vivacity –
as drinks were served, and she realised that her late arrival
only served to make her more conspicuous. Hesitating in
the doorway of the supper room, looking for a suitable
group to join, Charley saw Vere Cavendish look straight
at her, glance at the programme that he was holding and
speak quietly to Dan. Then Dan's familiar boom rang out:
'Leigh, that's right. Charlotte Leigh.' Vere was still looking at her, and Charley could have sworn that his face
reflected a flash of recognition before an unmistakable
glint of amusement sparkled in his eye and his lips
twitched. Then he turned away.

Mortified, Charley huddled in a corner until she could sit down to supper but the free, and excellent, meal was wasted on her. She could think only of that gorgeous man, of the utter fool she had made of herself and of the humiliation of being passed over so pointedly. She was sure he had connected her with Marion, and her costume had not saved her from being recognised as Maria – damn her height and the red hair, which had escaped its confining pins when the wig fell off. And it was one thing to hope that she would not have to meet him, quite another not to be given the opportunity.

Then, during her fourth season with Dan Crisp, the Players were invited to perform at Melton House, the country seat of Lord Melton, set in a splendid park amid the rolling acres of Wiltshire. Rumours flew round the company with the speed and accuracy of Cupid's dart: the Prince of Wales would be there, someone swore it was true; the Earl and Countess of Pembroke would journey from Wilton with their house guests; according to the Pastoral Players, half of *Burke's Peerage* would watch them perform on a woodland stage.

They were invited to luncheon before the afternoon performance of *As You Like It* and to supper after the evening's rendition of *A Midsummer Night's Dream*. Charley, promoted to Rosalind and Helena, was quietly confident of making a good impression. Wearing a new silk dress in a favourite shade of soft dove-grey, she floated down the terrace steps to the wide lawns, where luncheon had been laid on tables beneath the trees, and was introduced to her first lord. Admittedly Lord Melton's appearance was not unduly prepossessing, but he was kind and courteous to a young actress, introducing Charley to Lady Melton, his daughter Eleanor and her husband, his younger daughter, Celia, and other members of the several local house parties that had gathered for the occasion. However, aristocratic courtesy to a band of strolling players went only so far, and Dan Crisp and his company were seated at a separate table for luncheon.

An open glade bordered by great spreading trees had been selected as the setting for the entertainment and, on a warm and sunny afternoon, the Players embarked on *As You Like It*. The audience was enlarged by the presence of household staff and estate workers, sitting at a discreet distance behind the gentry, and so Charley, concentrating on her performance, did not see a tall, dark figure slip inconspicuously into the back row.

That afternoon Charley played Rosalind with all the gaiety and sparkle and the woodland magic that epitomise Shakespeare's romantic comedies. Her speech was the music of a swiftly running river, effortlessly giving the verse its inflections, never failing to find the rhythm, yet always using that rhythm to elucidate the meaning. Into this melody she wove a fluency of movement, one gesture flowing into the next, with such grace and charm that the Rosalind she brought to that green glade that summer afternoon, the sun glinting on her russet hair, forever lingered in the memory of those who saw her.

Taking her bow, Charley's main thought was: 'It worked – this afternoon I got it right', and she felt a fierce exultation that all the training, the sacrifices and the hard work had paid off. Then she saw him, walking towards the front row, applauding, a look of sheer incredulity on his face; and Charley knew the leap of sheer joy, because for her this was a victory. She turned to face him and gave him an individual, almost mocking, curtsy and a triumphant smile. However, when confronted by him moments later, she was less sure of herself.

'A memorable performance, Miss Leigh. Thank you.'

She had not expected his gratitude and was caught off-balance. 'Thank you for attending our performance,' she returned. 'We did not realise you would be among Lord Melton's guests.'

'I arrived late, not entirely by accident. I find that many theatrical companies perform better if they do not know I am in the audience.' And he grinned at her with a wickedness that clearly conveyed his memory of their previous encounter.

To her intense annoyance, Charley felt the familiar flush staining her cheeks. 'That was the most awful evening of my entire life,' she said with feeling.

'You were not to blame and, if it is any comfort to you, the incident inspired a particularly successful bit of business in one of my productions. Besides, you were not happy in Sheridan, while this afternoon your joy was shared by everyone.'

'Rosalind is my favourite role.'

'Even though there are so many seminal performances with which you will be compared?'

'If one worried about that, one would never act at all, because there is a fearful dearth of new material.'

They were standing in the glade, virtually alone, as the guests returned to the house and the Players drifted away to the rooms set aside for them to rest and change. He asked a few questions about other roles in her repertoire, and drew an unexpected response.

'My height is a disadvantage. Dan says that it's a problem finding leading men tall enough to play opposite me, and I have to position myself very carefully on the stage so that I don't tower over them.'

'You wouldn't have that problem with me.'

Charley gazed at him blankly.

'Would you care for an engagement at The Cavendish

next season, to play Rosalind with me and do a Robertson revival?'

She looked up at him and oh, the heaven of looking *up* at a man who topped her by a good four inches. 'I have a contract with Dan Crisp for next season.'

'Leave Mr Crisp to me.'

'Please do not bother him. It is very kind of you and I do appreciate your offer, really I dó, but I couldn't possibly . . .'

'Is it money? I am sure that we could reach an agreement.'

There was nothing for it but to tell him. 'It isn't the money. It is my sister, Marion. And my other sisters, but particularly Marion.'

He looked at her in astonishment, the relationship evidently coming as a complete surprise to him. Then, wordlessly, he took her arm, guided her to a chair and sat her down. 'Obviously you have not heard that Marion is no longer with The Cavendish. She has retired from the stage.'

'I understood that she was doing so well!'

'Apart from a little trouble with Cleopatra, she was doing very well and will be much missed by her public.' His voice took on a neutral, oddly formal tone. 'Unfortunately she was ill, a bad attack of typhoid fever, although I am pleased to say she has made a full recovery.'

'What is she doing now?'

'I understand that she is to become a schoolteacher.'

'Frances!' exclaimed Charley. 'That bloody Frances. Sorry, I know that bad language is inexcusable, but Frances is enough to make a saint take the Lord's name in vain. She always wanted to be a teacher, and now she has forced Marion to do the same. I wonder how she managed it. Has Marion been having man trouble?'

'You would have to ask her about that. Miss Leigh,

won't you reconsider? My offer is impulsive – I did not know that I would see you this afternoon – but many of life's best decisions are taken on the spur of the moment.' He smiled at her, a smile so irresistible that Charley went weak. 'In fact, your relationship with Marion and Frances only makes me more convinced that this was intended to be. The public would simply love another Leigh sister at The Cavendish and I do think that we would be awfully good together, you and I.'

So did Charley, and not only on the stage. She held out her hand in that boyish gesture that suited her so well, even when she was not wearing breeches. 'It is a bargain, Mr Cavendish, as long as you can square Dan Crisp. He has been very kind to me and I would not want to let him down.'

'Trust me,' he said and, standing up himself, took both her hands and pulled her to her feet. Retaining her hands in his, he said quietly: 'Say nothing about this to anyone until after I have spoken to Crisp. I will try to have a moment alone with him after the *Dream*.'

'You do not seriously think that I can rejoin the company without giving a full – and I do mean *full* – account of our conversation!'

'Tell them we have been discussing Marion, a logical explanation and one that has the added advantage of being true.'

They walked towards the house in a silence that did not appear to affect him, but which made Charley feel gauche and awkward.

'Why me?' she asked suddenly.

He looked at her gravely. 'Why not? Can you think of anyone else – an actress who has appeared in this company in recent years, for example – who could fulfil my requirements better than you?'

Charley could not, but remained wary. 'I do not really know what your requirements are.'

'You will find out,' he said softly, 'very soon. Possibly too soon, and maybe the hard way. Perhaps you ought to have a word with Marion before you commit yourself.'

'Marion is the last person I would consult about anything,' Charley returned hotly. 'My sisters and I do not exactly see eye-to-eye. In fact, we have not even *set* eyes on each other for years.'

She could have been mistaken but she could have sworn that he looked relieved.

After answering the questions hurled at her by her envious colleagues, Charley sat down and tried to gather her thoughts and conjure up the image of his face, but she could not do so. Try as she might, the features had a fatal tendency to blur, leaving only a memory of those dark eyes and that mobile mouth, and the lingering sense of the magnetism of that powerful body. Too attractive for his own good, thought Charley, and certainly far too attractive for *her* good.

The evening performance of the *Dream*, in the woodland glade lit by lanterns and a full moon, was a magical merger of fantasy and reality, and Charley played Helena half in a trance, quite carried away by the perfection of setting, occasion and verse. Afterwards, at supper served on the terrace, because the night was so still and warm, and wearing her dove-grey dress, Charley found that word of her relationship with Marion Leigh of The Cavendish had spread.

Lord Melton was positively sentimental. 'My dear Miss Charlotte,' and his pudgy hand clutched hers. 'I had no idea . . . Knew she had sisters, of course. I did meet Miss Frances . . .'

'I bet that made your day.'

Her companion brightened. 'Miss Frances is absolutely charming, of course, but perhaps a trifle shy.'

'Shy!' scoffed Charley. 'Frances is so strait-laced that if you laced her any tighter you would cut off her blood supply.'

Lord Melton let out a guffaw of delight, attracting attention from other diners, including Vere, who frowned. 'You and I . . .' he began, but was interrupted by Charley.

'Did you know Marion well?' she asked, in all innocence. But even in the limited light on the terrace she could discern, and interpret, the flush that empurpled Melton's face. 'Lord Melton, you old rogue . . .'

'Fond of her, you understand,' and he clutched Charley's hand harder. 'I shall miss her terribly . . . Unless, of course, you and I . . .'

'Lord Melton . . .'

'Call me Reggie,' he whispered.

The idea of him and Marion in bed was so amazing that Charley was both fascinated and repulsed. 'Reggie, you are an absolute sweetie, but you must appreciate that there are some things that sisters simply do not share, and a man is one of them.'

'That is a terrible shame because I think you are terrific fun.'

'We can still have fun together – outside the bedroom.'

'I must have a word with Cavendish. He must bring you to London. You have wasted far too much time in the provinces already.'

Charley placed a finger to her lips and indicated to him that Vere was deep in conversation with Dan Crisp. With great dramatic effect, she crossed the fingers of both hands and smiled at her companion.

'You can have anyone else, Cavendish, but not her!'

'She was Rosalind this afternoon, and such a Rosalind as in my wildest dreams I never hoped to see, but her range is limited. She is too big, boyish and capable to take on some of the roles in your repertoire so, tell me, why are you so keen to keep her?'

Dan Crisp did not answer, having no wish to advertise Charley's other, and varied, talents.

'I have a girl in my company who could fill the gap,' Vere said persuasively, 'and she's good – I was considering her for my Rosalind.'

'Then why not use her?'

'Because my public would flock to see another Leigh sister. Come on, Crisp, that connection means nothing to you and your following, but I could make Charlotte Leigh a star, just as I made her sister a star. I will pay the girl's salary for a year, by the way.'

Dan glanced at Charley and saw the expression on Lord Melton's face and the curious radiance that seemed to emanate from the girl tonight. He could not hold on to her much longer, he knew that.

'Suppose the other girl brought a "dowry",' Vere suggested casually, 'a bit of backing for your new season – not that it would have to be repaid.'

Cavendish was bribing him to let Charley go. What the hell – she would not stay beyond next season anyway, not after this, so best take the money while the going was good. Dan nodded.

'You have met my little girl?' Lord Melton asked Charley as his younger daughter slid into the chair next to him.

Celia Melton was petite and slender with her mother's thick chestnut hair, large hazel eyes and the longest, softest fringe of eyelashes that Charley had ever seen. Probably by 'little' Lord Melton meant 'young' but, if

Charley was any judge, Celia was certainly old enough to know how to flutter those eyelashes and get exactly what she wanted. Rather like Vere Cavendish, as George Allen had said, and she glanced again at the two men discussing her future.

'Are you really Marion Leigh's sister?' Celia asked. 'You do not look like her at all.'

'We take after different sides of the family.'

'I did not think her Cleopatra was so very bad, but perhaps it was the contrast with Mr Cavendish's Antony that put people off. He was absolutely splendid, everyone said so.'

At that moment Vere Cavendish stood up and shook hands with Dan Crisp, and immediately Lord Melton went across to join him.

'But I think I liked him best as Alfred Evelyn in *Money*,' Celia continued dreamily. 'Such a noble character, and he made love to Clara so gallantly. Do you think that Clara is a prettier name than Celia, Miss Leigh?'

Lord Melton turned towards Charley and, with a beaming smile, gave her a thumbs-up sign.

'I think Celia is a beautiful name,' Charley replied, her smile lighting up her face and eyes, 'while Clara has little to recommend it, beyond the difficulty of shortening it to something even more ugly than the original.'

'What are you laughing at? Is Papa being silly again?' Celia screwed round in her chair and located her parent, still talking to Cavendish. 'You'll have to watch Papa, Miss Leigh, he has a tendency to be silly about actresses.'

'Doesn't Lady Melton mind – about the actresses?'

'She pushes it firmly to the back of her mind,' Celia said solemnly, 'and besides, she is in no position to criticise. She is sillier about Mr Cavendish than Papa has ever been about anyone.'

'You seem very well informed.'

'I am the youngest in the family, so I spent a lot of my childhood listening at doors and hanging over the banisters. You would be amazed at the things people do and say when they think they are unobserved. Perhaps I should put some of my knowledge to good use. I could do a jolly decent line in blackmail!'

'I think that any line in blackmail would be indecent,' said Charley, laughing, not entirely sure that Celia was joking.

Celia was beckoning to Vere Cavendish. 'I sat next to him at supper,' she told Charley.

Charley had noticed that Vere sat with the gentlemen and not the players. 'Lucky you.'

'Luck had nothing to do with it. I changed the place cards when no one was looking.' Celia patted the chair that her father had vacated and Vere sat down. 'You seem very pleased with yourself, Mr Cavendish.'

'I have every reason to be pleased. I have secured the services of Miss Charlotte Leigh for next season.'

Vere smiled at both young women and Charley smiled back, glowing with happiness, while Celia gave an excited yelp.

'Does that mean you will do *As You Like It*? Oh, you must, you will be perfect as Orlando.'

'I doubt that perfection is possible, Miss Celia,' Vere said gravely, 'but, yes, undoubtedly we will perform that play. And Robertson's *School* – are you familiar with it, Miss Leigh?'

'Do call me Charley, everyone in the Players does, and it will save a lot of confusion. And no, I don't know that play.'

'You are a natural Naomi,' Vere assured her, 'and in view of your, er, equally natural suitability for breeches parts I will look into the possibility of doing *The Wandering Heir*.'

'That is a Trollope adaptation, isn't it?'

But before Vere could answer, Celia chipped in: 'Mr Cavendish, you will give me a part in *School*, won't you? Just a teensy-weensy one?'

'My dear Miss Celia,' Vere began.

'I saw it at the Haymarket and I know for a fact that you need schoolgirls draping themselves over the stage and squealing girlishly. I am awfully good at girlish squeals, Mr Cavendish. Try me.'

'I am sure that there is no end to your talents but, as for displaying them at The Cavendish, you know as well as I do that you must ask your parents before you ask me.'

'I can handle Mama and Papa, no problem! And after all, they allowed Eleanor to go to The Cavendish, so it would be unfair to stop me.'

She was wriggling nearer to Vere with every sentence. If she comes any closer, Charley thought, she will be in his lap, and of course that is exactly what she wants and where she believes she belongs – in Vere's lap, purring like a kitten and looking cute. But there cannot be anything in it: she cannot be more than seventeen years old and he must be more than twice that.

'Someone is trying to attract your attention, Miss Melton,' she said.

'Peter,' said Celia, not bothering to look round and confirm the statement. 'Our respective parents think that he and I are a marriage made in heaven and are trying to pair us off with about as much subtlety as shoving a bull into a field with a cow on heat. Don't look so startled, Charley – I'm a country girl at heart. They are wasting their time, of course. Can you think of anything more ghastly than being pushed into the arms of your sister's cast-offs?'

'You and I may not agree on everything,' Charley said gravely, 'but there we are in entire accord.'

'I suppose I must go and be nice to him.' Celia rose reluctantly. 'Better keep on the right side of the old folk in the circumstances. Goodbye, Charley, and good night, Mr Cavendish,' and she extended her hand for him to kiss. 'I trust that we will see you again very soon.'

To Charley's disappointment, Vere Cavendish did not resume his seat. 'Be at The Cavendish by the last week in August at the latest,' he said with cold formality before he left.

Chapter Seventeen

After an emotional and happy reunion with Uncle John, Charley had set off in optimistic mood to visit her sisters. Having been assured that she would receive a warm welcome, Marion's tears and Frances's dire warnings came as something of a shock. But worse was to come.

Marion returned to the room, red-eyed, a clean white cap concealing the short uneven tufts of dark hair, and made stiff inquiries after Charley's health. Obviously she was trying to live up to her promise of receiving her sister back into the fold, but every mention of the theatre, and particularly of The Cavendish and its manager, caused her eyes to fill and her voice to choke. The twins were summoned to greet the prodigal but, after only a few minutes, while Charley was still gasping at the fresh impact of Arabella's beauty, they were ushered out again. It was left to Frances to voice the inevitable verdict.

'We are sincerely glad to see you, Charley, but you must understand that we cannot have any contact with the theatre. We have put our past behind us, and the parents of our prospective pupils are unaware of our artistic leanings.'

'Surely they will recognise you?' Charley asked, but then she looked at Marion and realised that the remark was tactless. No one would know Marion for the glowing Juliet of a few years ago.

'I shall be known as Mary Leigh here,' Marion informed her.

'Therefore,' Frances went on, 'you have a choice. There is room for you here, and a new life, if you wish it. However, if you choose to remain in the theatre, I am sorry to say that you are not welcome in this house.'

'But I cannot give up the theatre! Marion,' and Charley appealed to her sister, 'you understand!'

Marion was feeling guilty, as if she were reneging on a promise, and if Charley's engagement had been with another company she might have made a stand. But she simply could not bear the thought of her sister taking her place at The Cavendish. She knew that, at the moment anyway, she did not possess the generosity of spirit to listen with equanimity to talk of Cavendish rehearsals, Cavendish premières, The Cavendish company and . . . *him*. It was asking too much. Besides, her first loyalty now lay with Frances.

'I do understand, Charley,' Marion said, 'but I also understand what Frances is saying. We have too much at stake here, in this new enterprise of ours, to risk losing it because of a connection with the theatre.'

'In that case I will not trouble you again,' and Charley gathered up her gloves and stalked out of the house.

So much for fairy tales about prodigal sons, she thought bitterly; the instant a prodigal sister crossed the threshold she was thrown straight out again. Tears stung her eyes, and halfway down the drive she paused in order to blow her nose and glance back at the house. A handkerchief was waving at a window and Charley could make out the gleam of a beautiful blonde head. Arabella seemed an unlikely ally but Charley was comforted, and she waved and smiled before continuing more cheerfully on her way.

Accustomed to being alone, and secretly rather relieved at the licence to carry on with her own way of life, Charley soon settled into her new routine. News of her arrival in London had circulated, and The Cavendish was deluged with messages from friends made within the ranks of the Players over the years. Through them she found a room over a small shop in the Strand, only a short walk from the theatre, which boasted a private door from a side alley and its own narrow staircase to the first floor. The rent was rather more than she had wanted to pay, but for this privacy Charley was willing to make economies elsewhere in her budget.

She managed to pay a week's rent on the room in advance but it was a close-run thing. In all her years with the Players, Charley had not managed to save a single penny but, passing Coutts Bank in the Strand, she vowed to turn over a new leaf: now that she was a West End leading lady, she would save money and open a bank account towards the day when she became the greatest actress-manager in the country.

In fact, Charley began to be more aware of money generally, at the theatre and around her in the opulent venues and society of the West End. Money lay behind most of the initial differences that she noticed between The Cavendish Theatre and Dan Crisp's company. Entranced by the artistic excellence of The Cavendish bill posters, by the quality of the programmes, and by the music specially commissioned for *As You Like It*, Charley was astonished at the financial outlay on a single production. The time and money spent on each piece of scenery and every prop, however inconsequential, was a lesson in meticulous detail and unbridled extravagance.

The task before her was daunting, but Charley still danced her way to work each morning, dashing from the brilliance of the August day into the shadowy theatre, shouting a cheerful good morning to everyone – from humblest super to the Chief himself – tossing aside hat and gloves and leaping on to the stage, where a few dim work-lights picked out the rudiments of a forest or a palace room. For Charley there was nothing more invigorating than that unhealthy atmosphere, nothing more cheerful than that gloom, nothing more luminous than that darkness.

And for weeks there was nothing more important in her life than the sharp clap of Vere's hands as he stopped a rehearsal. Daily, Charley offered thanks to the benevolent deity who had arranged *As You Like It* as her first production at The Cavendish. She shuddered to think what might have happened if, stripped of her familiarity with the words or bereft of movement and gesture, which had become second nature to her, she had been pitchforked into a new part in a strange play.

'I used to think that Dan Crisp's rehearsals were models of thoroughness,' she commented to a young actor in the company called Edward Druce, 'but, compared with The Cavendish, they were slipshod and perfunctory.'

'I know the sort of thing – speeches cut to the first line and the last, just enough to give the cues.'

'And while the main rehearsal was taking place centre-stage, several minor ones were going on at left, right and back, particularly duels and quarrels.' Charley smiled at him – such a pleasant young man, and good-looking, too, with eyelashes as long and thick as Celia Melton's. 'Whenever I was struggling with an important scene, there was always a background noise of the clash of walking sticks and angry voices.'

'Here we do not rehearse a duel with walking sticks but with the genuine props. What's more, the Chief believes that hand props ought to weigh about the same as the real thing, so that the actor wields them with appropriate effort.'

'Even the script is fully printed out for everyone,' and Charley smoothed the embossed crimson folder. 'Dan Crisp did provide scripts – we didn't have to write them out ourselves, as happened not so long ago – but each actor was only given his own part, not the entire play.'

Restlessly she stood up and walked to the greenroom fire and back again, lighting one of the Egyptian cigarettes to which she had recently taken. People always stared at her, as if smoking was a truly shocking thing for a woman to do, and this pervading air of disapproval increased Charley's liking for the habit. She began to enjoy a mild flirtation with danger, and to appreciate that her position as leading lady gave additional scope for cultivating the occasional eccentricity. Her fellow players, Edward Druce among them, watched her admiringly.

'Everyone is awfully glad you've come to The Cavendish,' Edward said impetuously. 'Things will pick up again now.'

Charley looked at him inquiringly. 'Pick up?'

'I wasn't here, but I'm told that your sister's departure left a dent in the box office. Of course the Chief's following still came in droves, but Marion's understudies were not up to the job and her eventual replacement was a disaster.'

'So the company doesn't resent an interloper from the

provinces landing the best roles? It did occur to me that they might.'

'They like you, so do I, everyone does . . .' Edward floundered but was determined to press on. 'You're not the sort of leading lady who is standoffish, like Marion . . . Oh Lord, I'm sorry.'

'No need to apologise. Miss High-and-Mighty Marion was born that way. And thank you, Edward, for the charming compliment.'

'I was wondering if . . . if you would care for a bite of supper after rehearsal tonight,' he said desperately, but without much hope.

Charley smiled but shook her head. She felt that it would not do for the leading lady to consort with the leading juvenile, however pretty he might be, and anyway had decided to keep business and pleasure strictly apart. Of course there was one exception she was prepared to make to this rule and, although he showed no sign of reciprocating her passion, Charley lived in hope.

Edward sighed and tried to accept his rejection philosophically. Usually he fell in and out of love several times a season, but the Leigh sisters seemed to hold a special attraction for him. He had cared deeply for Marion and had been genuinely hurt when she made it clear that he was no longer good enough for her. Now he had decided that Charley had more personality and vivacity in her little finger than Marion possessed in the whole of her full-bosomed body, and he had the peculiar feeling that he was not going to recover from this attachment to the younger sister as easily as he had from his infatuation with the elder.

'Oh Lord, I'm called,' he groaned as Will Tucker shouted his name in the doorway. 'Wish me luck. The

Chief has more edge to his tongue than a rapier when he is in the mood. Do you know what he said to me yesterday? The lights were on and I had been giving the scene everything, so I was in a proper lather of perspiration. "Your skin has been acting at all events, my boy," he said. "What a pity that the rest of you did not see fit to follow its example."'

Charley laughed and followed him out of the green-room in order to view the rehearsal. Watching Vere working with the young man, she was reminded of one of George Allen's favourite hobbyhorses – that the demise of the stock company as a training ground had severely limited learning experience, and that there were now too many modish young West End or touring actors whose looks, manners, dress and social skills were their only qualifications for the job. Almost certainly Edward Druce had been hired for his suitability for the part of Lord Beaufoy in *School*, but if he paid as much attention to all his mentors as he did to the Chief, progress was by no means impossible.

Her respect for Cavendish grew with every passing day. She had seen little of his Orlando, because he rehearsed his own part seldom, but time and again she witnessed the way he brought another role to life for the benefit of its interpreter; simply a few words, a movement or a gesture, and there it was. However, he had left Charley's role untouched so far and she was worried about it, because although she knew Rosalind, she did not know his Orlando.

As if reading her mind, he suddenly stopped the rehearsal, walked to the chair and table beside the screen, picked up a sheaf of notes and beckoned to her. 'I need you to stay late tonight,' he said, not looking at her but turning the pages of the notes in search of a specific entry.

'We need to work through some of our scenes, so report to my dressing room at ten.'

At last something was about to happen, but was that something professional or personal, or both? Surely he did not need to keep her late only to rehearse their scenes? It must mean he wanted to be alone with her.

Her heart seemed to be thudding in her very throat when she knocked on his door at ten o'clock that night.

'Sit down,' and he indicated a chair. 'Drink? I only have whisky here, I'm afraid.'

'Thank you, yes.' She thought she discerned a flicker of surprise on his face, but he poured a slug of Scotch into a glass and handed it to her. 'Did Marion drink whisky?'

Pouring his own drink, his hand jerked slightly and a few drops spilled on the dressing-table. 'I have no idea,' he said after a moment's pause. 'She did not drink Scotch with me but, then, I never offered her any.'

Charley was pleased. There were too many occasions these days when she wondered if Marion had been here before her. 'So why did you offer it to me?' she asked.

'Because you are different from Marion,' he replied neutrally.

'Thank God you noticed – I have worked on that difference, ceaselessly and assiduously, for years!'

He smiled, or at least his mouth did; his eyes remained remote and strangely wary. 'I hope your family will not be worried because you are late home this evening.'

'I live alone,' she answered boldly, 'in a room only a short walk from here.'

'How very unusual, but you are, aren't you!' He took a long, deep drink of whisky, swallowed, and sighed. 'The arrangement must be very convenient – being so close to the theatre, I mean.'

'It is convenient, Mr Cavendish,' and her voice dropped to a low murmur, 'in all sorts of ways.'

His gaze met hers, and held it until she felt as if she were drowning in those dark depths. He is going to kiss me, she thought, and half-swayed towards him, but he only drained his glass and set it down on the dressing-table.

'I have been reluctant to tamper with the natural flow and spontaneity of your Rosalind, but . . .' and he began to explain what he wanted of her. Although neither of them moved from their former positions, the distance between them seemed to widen. By the time they reached the deserted and darkened stage, he had withdrawn so much into himself, and receded so far from her, that Charley was worried that she would not give of her best. Stepping out of her skirt and standing on the stage in the breeches and plain white shirt that she used for rehearsals, a self-consciousness came over her for the first time in years. She watched, one hand on her narrow hip, as he lit the stage and stripped down to his shirt-sleeves.

At the beginning sheer habit and professionalism carried her through, but slowly the tension inside her relaxed and she warmed to the task, and to him. Acting with Vere was easy and instinctive, and Charley had enough experience to know that it was he who made it so. He was always there in exactly the right place, with a gesture or an inflection to which she could respond, so that acting with him became almost like a dance in which their two bodies moved in perfect harmony. And at times it was a very erotic dance, because this Orlando, intelligent and mature, left one guessing whether or not he was totally deceived by Rosalind's disguise. After an hour or more of his voice, his touch and the nearness of him, for Charley the sexual magnetism was flowing between them stronger than ever before. Surely he must feel it, too! But he made no attempt to touch her unnecessarily and when at last he called a halt to the rehearsal, she sensed again that he was putting mental and physical distance between them.

Yet, crazily, her hopes were lifted again when he offered to walk her home and together they stepped out into the eerie quiet of the virtually deserted Strand.

'Homework?' Charley asked, indicating the books and folders he was carrying.

'I am afraid so. There never seem to be enough hours in the day, or night, in which to fit the essential work, let alone put the finishing touches to the jobs in hand.'

'So why do you do it?'

He glanced at her curiously, gauging her mood and the seriousness of the question and, seeing the frank sincerity on her face, answered her accordingly.

'There is no choice. These days, if an actor wants to succeed, to take his place in the front rank, he must take up management. But the workload can become a burden, especially if, like me, one happens to be a perfectionist. There are always details that cannot be delegated, no matter how much faith one has in one's subordinates.'

'And they say that a woman's work is never done,' said Charley with a grin, striding out beside him. 'Is it worth it?'

'Financially or personally?'

'Either. Both.'

'The Bancrofts are retiring this year and if they leave the Haymarket with less than two hundred thousand pounds in their pockets, I will be very surprised.' He smiled as Charley let out a sharp whistle of surprise. 'On a personal level, well, that is a bit more difficult. The work creates its own momentum and its own responsibilities. Sometimes it feels like a treadmill that one cannot get off or slow down. What money one makes is ploughed back into the business, and even if one were making money there is no time to enjoy it.'

'Until you are old enough to retire, and then you are too old to enjoy it.'

'Exactly. I admit that, as I watched the Bancrofts reviving one Robertson play after another, I thought it would be easier than this, but something inside me does not allow me to give up, or take the easy option.'

They reached Charley's door and stopped, but her eyes never left his face, entreating him to continue.

'As a manager, one develops a strange relationship with one's own theatre and its public,' he said slowly. 'That theatre becomes inextricably linked with oneself, and the public begins to see it and, in this case *me*, as an old friend. I have chosen the play, cast it, produced and directed it, and am appearing in it. The entire production gains an added vitality simply because of these circumstances. The audience looks on The Cavendish less as a public place than as the home of a friend, which they visit after a long absence. An air of excitement grips them as they take their seats. Has the old friend changed or will he conjure up his old magic?'

'Would you like to come in for a moment?' Charley gestured, hesitantly, at the door.

'I really must get home and soldier on with this work,' and Vere tipped his hat politely and walked away into the night.

Charley opened the door but watched Vere until he was out of sight. Then she went upstairs and sank into a chair, staring sadly and sightlessly at the empty grate.

Wanting this man was like a ride at a fun-fair, up one minute and down the next. She did not believe he was oblivious of the strong sexual attraction between them, so why did he pretend that it did not exist? Having observed him closely since she arrived in London, she was almost certain that there was not a woman in his life, not unless that woman was content with an hour snatched irregularly here and there. Her own instincts apart, the time element equally discounted boys. So why, Charley wondered, was he living like this? Why was Vere Cavendish devoted to all work and no play, and why had he never married?

Charley was not the only person wondering about Vere Cavendish's way of life and bachelor status. These matters were also burning questions in the Melton household, but both ladies concerned were convinced that they knew the answer.

One afternoon in early October, Barbara, Lady Melton, impatiently awaited his arrival for tea. On such occasions she still assumed the aesthetic look, wearing a low-necked dress with puffed 'Renaissance' sleeves, no waist seam and a loose, flowing skirt in a soft green-and-yellow Oriental silk. Her figure was still youthful enough to allow the absence of stays with such a gown, and with her chestnut curls gleaming and only the merest hint of a grey hair, Barbara was happily confident that her looks belied her forty-five years. She had arranged herself in a languidly elegant pose and, when Vere was announced, extended a hand for him to kiss. He did so punctiliously, only allowing his lips the briefest brush of her fingers, but smiling into her eyes with a warmth that never failed to flutter her heart.

'I was beginning to be afraid that you were not coming,' she said with a pout.

'Barbara,' like some of Lord Melton's close friends, Vere had been honoured with permission to call her by her first name when they were alone, 'you know that I would not miss seeing you for the world. And particularly today, because this is the last time I shall be allowed out in the afternoon for quite some time.'

'Not more rehearsals – you have only just finished the last lot!'

'That's how it goes, I'm afraid. *As You Like It* is running smoothly – touch wood – so we start rehearsing *School* on Monday.'

'The new Leigh girl is charming everyone, I hope?'

'Our Charley is a huge success, which is good news for her, me, the theatre *and* your husband. Accordingly, to my equally huge relief, I can look Ernest Meyer in the eye again.'

'He did get terribly stuffy about money, didn't he, at the end of last season. As if it was your fault that Marion Leigh went down with typhoid and started behaving so peculiarly. Of course, the trouble with that sort of person is that he has no feeling for the arts. He looks upon it purely as a business venture and tries to equate running a theatre with running a cotton mill, or something of the sort.'

'I must confess that, under his scrutiny, my fairly modest overdraft was beginning to take on the size and importance of the national debt,' Vere admitted.

'With all the stress and strain, you began to look most unwell. I was very worried about you, and I simply will not allow it to happen again.'

Vere reached across and took hold of her hand. 'I do not deserve such a good friend. You have been there for me right from the very start, through thick and thin, through all the highs and lows. I think that you must know more about The Cavendish, and its manager, than anyone!'

'Which is why I want you to work a little less and play a little more,' she said, gently squeezing his fingers. 'If you go on as you are, Jack will not merely be a dull boy but a dead one.'

'But I cannot stop working at this pace. I am faced with a constant dilemma, a Morton's Fork of impossible choice.' Vere released her hand and walked over to the fire, where he paused, one hand on the mantelpiece, staring into the flames before he turned to face her.

At the outset Vere's relationship with Barbara Melton had been that of an artist seeking a patron. Knowing the value of his good looks, he had conducted a decorous flirtation with her, because she was the route to Melton and to his purse. However, over the years he had become genuinely fond of her. There were times when she seemed silly and affected, but that was only to be expected of someone in her position and Vere found that he could talk to her, and confide in her, in a way that he could with no one else. He could reveal nothing of himself to another man – with men it was essential to appear totally in control; and with women there was usually a factor, or several factors, that prevented him from unbending. The scarcity of friendship only made him value Barbara the more so and he tried to explain, sincerely and genuinely, the nature of his dilemma.

'I work hard in order to establish a business on a sound financial footing, but there is a constant clash between time and money. If I take the time to enjoy the fruits of my labour, the business suffers and accordingly so does the inflow of finance. If I concentrate on making money, the constant attention to a thousand details takes up all my time. Do you understand?'

'Oh yes, and I thank God that Reggie and I do not have the same problem. Mind you, he spends most of his time out of the house so, as he does not need to make money, he must be making something else – or *someone* else!'

'I am sure you are mistaken,' Vere said hastily. 'The fortunate possessor of your hand would have no cause to look elsewhere.'

'Thank you, Vere, but do go on – how can your dilemma be resolved?'

'Only with time and money,' he said wryly. 'I have concluded that I must battle on for another couple of years, by which time I should be sufficiently established to give up acting and concentrate on management.'

'But you cannot stop acting,' she wailed. 'We all love you too much to miss your appearances. You are the main reason why people go to The Cavendish.'

He sat down beside her and looked soberly into her animated face. 'Yet, despite the best efforts of us all, acting is not . . .' But, even with Barbara, he could not go on. 'Despite my best efforts,' he said quickly, 'I cannot fulfil my obligations as both actor and manager, and enjoy life at the same time. The work consumes me, day and night, sapping my energy, my strength and vitality and, God help me, my sense of humour. I promise you, Barbara, that once upon a time I was the proud possessor of a sense of humour.' Leaning back on the sofa, he put his hands behind his head and laughed. 'Once upon a time, when I was young, I used to tell myself not to hurry and not to worry, because one is here for only a short visit so one must not forget to stop and smell the roses on the way.'

Barbara was not to know that Vere had not voiced his ultimate ambition, but she had followed his disconsolate meanderings with close attention. 'I want you to be happy, Vere. If there is anything I can do . . .'

'You do too much already.'

'No, no . . .' She stretched out her hand and stroked his face, a face hauntingly handsome, saturnine in its brooding cynicism and remoteness. Only she, she felt, could smooth away the unhappiness and restore life and well-being to this man, a man whom only she fully understood. 'You need someone to look after you . . .'

Vere clasped her hand in one of his, and made a non-committal, dismissive gesture with the other. He started playing with her fingers, caressing them, one by one.

'You must have met someone whom you want, or wanted, to marry,' Barbara went on, hating herself, half-terrified, knowing that she was pushing the situation, and their relationship, to the limits.

'Yes, I have.'

'So why are you a bachelor?'

'Because she was, and is, not available.'

Her heart leaping exultantly, Barbara smiled. She had always known it, but it was pure joy to have it confirmed. Vere Cavendish remained a bachelor because she, Barbara Melton, was married to another. Of course, he was too reticent to make open advances to a married lady of her standing in society, but she began to feel that she ought to give him more encouragement. She had been a faithful wife for twenty-five years and, frankly, virtue was beginning to pall. With Reggie playing away from home, and the children growing up, Barbara was inching – well, sprinting actually – to the conclusion that she deserved a life, and a little fun, of her own. Why should she lie in bed alone, masturbating as she fantasised about Vere Cavendish, when she could have the real thing? He had waited patiently, adoringly, respectfully, for years and now she was seriously considering giving him his reward.

'She might be more available than you realise,' she murmured.

'I have been allowed to hope that the lady is willing,' he replied, 'but certain social conventions do not permit a relationship of any kind at this time.'

'Social conventions were invented in order to add spice to the chase.'

Vere laughed, pulling her hand to his lips. 'You are incorrigible and utterly delightful.'

'And late for another appointment,' she grimaced as the drawing-room doors opened and the butler advanced towards them. 'Damn, damn, damn . . .'

'I am sorry, too. Barbara, have you and Lord Melton decided whether or not Celia can take part in *School*?'

'We decided that there was no decision! Celia will do what she wants to do. Vere, that is the most extraordinary child – so petite and innocent, but with the power of an express train, crushing all opposition. I don't understand her, or where she came from. Reggie swears she isn't his, and I would do the same if the evidence was not against me! No, take her into *School* by all means, and I only hope you can make more of her than we have.'

'May I speak to her now?'

'If I know Celia, she is drumming her heels in the garden even as we speak, and counting the hours to her first rehearsal.'

Vere bowed and said a respectful farewell, although his lips lingered longer on her slender hand than previously, and then went in search of Celia. He did not have far to look. The moment he set foot in the garden, a thunderbolt in rose-pink silk hit him square in the chest and wrapped its arms around his neck.

'Kitten, you must not *do* that,' he protested, disentangling himself and holding her hands tightly. 'You are not a child any more, and young ladies do not throw themselves into the arms of strange men.'

'You are not a strange man,' she objected. 'You are going to be my husband.'

'Yes, my darling, but no one knows that but you and me.'

'So, let's tell everyone – now!'

Holding her by the shoulders, Vere propelled her through the garden until they came to a bench beside a small pond, where a fountain played. The afternoon was very still and warm, an Indian summer afternoon when only the song of a blackbird disturbed the peace of this quiet London oasis.

'I cannot ask your father for your hand in marriage, not yet,' he insisted. 'For one thing, you are too young. Your parents would not consider that you know your own mind.'

'Phooey,' Celia scoffed. 'They know that when my mind is made up, nothing will change it.'

'When it comes to the colour of a dress or a choice between two coming-out parties, I dare say you are quite correct. However, when it comes to a choice of husbands, I think you will find that they have more influence than you care to admit.'

'You are making excuses because you do not really love me,' and her pout was an exact replica of her mother's.

'Of course I love you, kitten,' Vere said tenderly, 'but I want to make sure that everything is right. I want our marriage to be blessed, by your parents and by society, so that we do not become outcasts.'

'I would adore to be an outcast, as long as I was with you.' Celia wriggled closer to him and laid her head on his shoulder. 'Being an outcast would be terribly romantic.'

'On the contrary, it would be a terrible shock, a poverty-stricken, lonely shock, which would soon sound the death-knell of romance. No, if you and I marry, Celia, it must be with everyone's approval, and in order to achieve that I need time.'

'Time to do what?'

'Make my fortune. I cannot marry you without some money of my own. And that money must also buy me freedom to give up acting, because with all the best efforts of London's greatest actor-managers, acting is still not a gentleman's profession.'

That is what Vere had been unable to tell Barbara – that he had chosen Celia as his passport into society and to the good life that was part and parcel of it. He had selected her years ago, almost as soon as he set eyes on her, because of her youth – which gave him time to achieve the financial stability he wanted – because of her prettiness and charming ways, and because she adored him. Of course she was wilful and empty-headed, but Vere was not marrying her for her conversation. He was marrying her for reasons that made it essential that her parents' permission was obtained and the thing was done properly, and being close to both Lord and Lady Melton did not blind him to the fact that, as a son-in-law, he might not receive an unreserved welcome.

'I think you are making excuses,' Celia accused again. 'You have found someone else, another woman . . .'

'I have given up all of them for you.'

'So there were other women, before me?'

'My dear Celia, I received my first kiss before you were born!'

'Then I have a lot of catching up to do, so kiss me now.'

After a quick glance over his shoulder in order to ensure that they were not observed, Vere gently tilted her chin towards him and kissed her lightly on the lips.

'That was not a proper kiss,' she objected.

'It is all you are getting. Anyway, how do you know what is, or is not, a proper kiss?'

'I have watched people do it and I have been dying to try it. Please, Vere . . .'

She was adorable, with those big eyes looking up at him through the fringe of dark lashes, and those pink lips so temptingly close, but Vere resisted the temptation and in fact did not find it difficult to do so. He was not old enough to be her father, but there were times when he felt as if he was.

'You must accept, my child, that there are some things in life that you cannot have merely on demand.'

His firmness with her was one of the reasons why her girlish infatuation with him persisted. Secretly Celia liked a masterful manner. 'Very well, but to make up for not kissing me, you must be more sociable. I hardly ever see you, and don't tell me that I will see you at rehearsals, because that isn't the same thing at all. You can start by joining our party for dinner at my godmother's place next week.'

'Celia, I'm sorry but rehearsals . . .'

'If you cannot make the time, you must understand that I will find someone who will.'

Vere sighed, but he could see her point of view. A young girl wanted fun and excitement, and wanted attention from her admirer. She could not be expected to wait quietly at home while he worked. There was a real chance he could lose her.

'What day next week?'

In his heart he feared it was the thin end of the wedge,

that gradually but inexorably Celia would force open the door on his private and working life and demand more and more of his precious time and attention. And so busy was he contemplating this dilemma, that he failed to foresee that, when he obligingly began attending more of the Meltons' social functions, both Celia *and* Barbara would think that he did so for her sake.

Chapter Eighteen

It was Vere's rapid exit from the theatre after evening performances, dressed in top hat and white tie, that first attracted Charley's attention, but in addition there were some mornings when Bert Harding started rehearsals without him, an unprecedented state of affairs at The Cavendish. Among the company the consensus was that the Chief had a woman in his life. Charley tried not to take it personally and found some compensation in her success as Rosalind. Not only was the public acclaim gratifying, but for a few hours each evening Vere Cavendish was hers, that flame of mutual desire licking at their loins in front of a thousand pairs of eyes, working a chemistry between them that packed the house every night. What's more, *School* was tremendous fun. The girl she played, the heiress Naomi, was witty and outspoken and, although played entirely in skirts, asserted that 'I wish I was a man' and 'I wish I'd been born a boy'. Charley could emphathise with these sentiments to an uncanny degree, and she believed that Vere was sincere when he replied: 'I don't . . . you're so much nicer as you are.'

The trouble was that life might be imitating art, in Vere's pursuit of an heiress.

Day after day, week after week, she grew more certain

that he wanted her as much as she wanted him, but something was holding him back and there was nothing she could do about it. Outside the theatre their paths never crossed, because he moved in circles to which Charley could not aspire. As they never met socially, and late-night rehearsals had been curtailed, how could she get him on his own?

Then *School* opened to great acclaim and Vere said something that triggered a response in Charley's agile brain. 'You were wonderful, Charley, and I have only one regret: that Marion was not here to play Bella. Then it would have been perfect.' At the time Charley merely replied tersely: 'Over my dead body', but later she remembered what Edward Druce had told her: that The Cavendish had been in financial trouble after Marion left and that she, Charley, was expected to revive its fortunes. It would be interesting, and useful, to find out if she was succeeding.

Charley's easy-going, unpretentious manner had won her a popularity at The Cavendish that Marion had never achieved, but while her friendliness with her fellow players and the stage staff was simply part of her nature, there were some relationships that she cultivated with an astuteness beyond her years. The most important of these was with Vere's business manager, Richard Ramsey. Through him, Charley gained access to the office when Vere was busy elsewhere, and in the course of their conversations pumped him cleverly for financial information. It was easy to exclaim over the lavishness of the sets and costumes and to coax Ramsey into telling her how much they cost, but Charley wanted more than that: she wanted to see the accounts. Her opportunity came when Ramsey was called away during one of their tête-à-têtes.

'I'll wait here for you, if you don't mind,' she said.

'I could be gone for an hour or more,' he warned.

'It is quieter here than in the greenroom. I am not getting to grips with Philippa in *The Wandering Heir* and would appreciate some time on my own.'

The instant the door closed behind him, she hurried to the desk on which the current ledgers were stacked, while the books for previous years stood on the shelves behind. Her familiarity with the accounts of John Leigh and Dan Crisp enabled her to pick out the salient points unerringly and she began making rapid notes on a sheet of paper for future analysis, but soon realised that most of these notes were superfluous. The facts screamed at her from every page, to such an extent that for a moment she doubted herself. Surely she must be wrong in her interpretation of the figures, or why was not something being done about it?

Charley ploughed on, an ear cocked for every footstep in the passage outside, but she needed a second secret session at Ramsey's desk and an inspection of previous years' accounts before reaching a definite conclusion. She had been right from the start. The Cavendish was in deep financial trouble. They were playing to full houses, but box-office receipts, programme advertising and income from contracting-out catering, bar and the cloakroom facilities did not cover the outgoings.

She listed the areas in which overspending had occurred and in which economies could be made. Ignoring rent, gas, company salaries and other basics, her first point concerned the lavishness of The Cavendish productions. Simply, too much was spent on each one and, as Vere put on three, sometimes four, plays each season, the overspend on costumes, sets, special effects, supers' wages, advertising and music added up to an astronomical sum. Previous years' accounts showed that such expenditure was not unusual; however, it was growing, as if Vere's desire to impress his public was growing.

Entries recording the purchase of rights to new plays were more puzzling. To Charley's certain knowledge, none of them had been produced, although she could not judge how carefully they had been considered. And the names of the playwrights who were the fortunate recipients of Cavendish largesse were perplexing: surely Michael Samson was the influential theatre critic of one of London's foremost daily newspapers? Being an intelligent young woman, Charley could see a reason for the apparent anomaly, but she would like Vere Cavendish to spell it out to her.

Then there was the entertainment account, and here the increase in expenditure over previous years was so exceptional that even the subservient Ramsey must have been roused to incredulity and the occasional query. Clearly Vere was not only a guest at these top-hat and white-tie functions; he was hosting them as well, and presenting the bill to the company.

In her room above the Strand, Charley put down the sheets of notes and stubbed out her cigarette decisively. Spring was blossoming in London, and Charley knew what she must do.

The next day she played the role of the neglected, resentful leading lady. 'It's all sweetness and light when you want a girl to come to London,' she complained, 'but as soon as you get her here, it's goodbye Charley.'

'What do you want?' Vere asked wearily. 'More money? A say in the content of the repertoire? Ask and it shall be given!'

'I want a long talk about all those things, and a few other matters as well.'

'Fire away.'

'On Sunday.'

'I am busy on Sunday, but . . .'

'All day Sunday,' and as he opened his mouth to protest again, she went on, 'in order to discuss my contract for next season, *if* there is a next season.' On his desk was a letter in a rough, uneducated hand and, reading it upside-down, she could decipher that it began 'My dearest . . .' 'I think your leading lady deserves one bloody day of your time, don't you?' she snapped.

His lips tightened and he did not reply.

'I will make all the arrangements,' she said grimly. 'All you have to do is be there.'

When she had gone Vere let out a deep groan and buried his head in his hands. In doing so, he disturbed the letter, which could now be seen to be addressed to 'My dearest Harry' and was signed 'Mother'. *Women*. Vere groaned again. Either he must give them up for good or he must marry one of them soon, in the hope that it would rid him of the others.

Outside the door Charley heard the groan but remained unforgiving. This had gone beyond a matter of personal feelings. Frances had described The Cavendish as a death-trap but, as far as Charley could see, if something were not done soon, it was the theatre and its entire company that would die.

Sunday dawned bright and warm and, with the daffodils nodding and dancing in the sunshine, Charley dared to drive in her hired carriage with the hood down.

'You are a Spartan soul,' Vere remarked as he took his seat beside her.

'With the amount of time we spend in the theatre, there is nothing like a blast of fresh air to blow away the cobwebs. Be honest, Chief, when did you last spend a reasonable part of a day out-of-doors, away from the fug of cigarette smoke and gas fumes? I bet – what shall I bet, the bill for our luncheon? – that it was that day at Melton House last summer when you saw a performance by The Pastoral Players.'

'You are probably right.'

'And at this moment you are wishing you had never gone there and never seen me, and then you would not have to be here now.'

'I do not mean to be rude, but . . .'

'. . . it's hard to break the habit of a lifetime.'

'Time is my enemy, Charley. If you could double, or preferably triple, the length of each day, I would be delighted to spend every Sunday in your company. As it is, I juggle balls, and the balls are increasing in number so that it is getting harder and harder to keep them all in the air at once, and it is forever on my mind that if I drop one, I may drop them all.'

'And by keeping this appointment with me today, you dropped one?'

'No. I dropped three.'

'Oh.' Charley digested this information in silence for a few moments. 'Sorry.'

'As I am here, may I inquire where we are going?'

'Richmond. I have ordered luncheon at a local inn. Incidentally, anticipating that the atmosphere might be less than cordial, I told them that we are Mr and Mrs Leigh, so that any arguments can be passed off as domestic discord.'

A reluctant grin tugged at the corners of his mouth and he turned to look at her. Dressed in a tight-fitting, fur-trimmed cloth coat in a flaming reddish-orange, which ought to have clashed with her hair but didn't, and a tall-crowned black hat sporting an exotic feather, Charley cut a dashing figure whom any man would have been proud to acknowledge as his wife. Vere's smile became rueful as another complication began to form itself into a ball, but he jettisoned it quickly over the side of the carriage and smoothly turned the conversation to uncontroversial subjects until they arrived at the inn. Dismounting from the carriage, he stood rather awkwardly while Charley gave instructions to the driver. Accepting hospitality from society folk was one thing, but he was embarrassed at being beholden to a jobbing actress – and one of his staff at that.

'Feeling at a disadvantage?' Charley inquired. 'I do hope so. It's about time a man knew how it feels to sing for one's supper, as it were.'

'I would be much happier if you would allow me to take care of the bill.'

'No chance. I say, are we going to fight over "the reckoning", like Kit Marlowe?' Charley drew an invisible rapier, essayed a few flamboyant strokes and made to stab him through the eye, much to the delight of a mixed bicycling party whose members were entering the inn. 'Today is my treat, Mr Cavendish, though I am well aware that you do not view it as such. This way,' and she stalked into the inn and down a passage, before flinging open the door to a private room overlooking the river. 'Sit down. Would you like a drink before we eat? Oh, do loosen up a bit! Anyone would think that a woman had never entertained a man to luncheon before.'

'I have a very strong suspicion that we could be breaking new ground.'

'Balls, and I don't mean the sort that you juggle. No one is going to tell me that Lucia Vestris or Louisa Herbert never initiated a business meeting over lunch.'

'Doubtless those two redoubtable ladies did so, but I

venture to suggest that they did it in their own homes, not in a public house.'

'Ah, in which case the cost of the exercise was less obvious and intrusive. I would have been delighted to entertain you in my home, Mr Cavendish, if it boasted a kitchen or a dining room. Unfortunately,' and Charley shrugged off her coat, 'the bed takes up most of the available space.'

Temporarily lost for words, Vere sat down and accepted a glass of sherry.

'Of course, my current living conditions do not mean that I do not yearn for respectability,' Charley said in a tone that indicated the exact opposite.

Vere laughed, watching as she tossed her hat on to a spare chair and produced her cigarette case. 'You are much too "racy" and unconventional to be respectable – too many cigarettes and breeches parts.'

'I expect you are right,' Charley said cheerfully, 'but I do aspire to a decent flat and,' she paused pointedly, 'an entertainment account through which to channel some of my expenses.'

'Have you been prying into my private affairs,' he asked curtly, his face white with anger.

'Of course not,' she lied, 'but it does not take a genius to understand what is happening at The Cavendish. You need to economise, and by sheer coincidence I have one or two suggestions.'

'So this is why you organised a meeting here – to make it more difficult for me to walk out. You ought to stop now, Charley, before you take this impertinence too far.'

'And you ought to stop overspending on productions before your extravagance puts you out of business, and me and all the others out of a job.'

In addition to being angry, he was struggling to accept such criticism, particularly as it came from a woman. 'I refuse to lower the standards for which The Cavendish has become renowned,' he stated flatly.

'You have two alternatives. First, you could spend less on the usual number of productions – which need *not* entail lowering standards, because many sets and costumes could be adapted and re-used.'

'Not if these productions are to be revived at a later date.'

'Or,' Charley continued doggedly, 'you could stage one play – and stage it as lavishly as you wish – which has a long run.'

'Instead of having a long run, it could fail within weeks of opening, and then what would you suggest I do?'

The waiter brought in the soup and they moved to the table, but neither Vere nor Charley felt like eating.

'There is no need to be so patronising,' Charley exclaimed indignantly. 'I am perfectly capable of seeing the advantages of repertory, but it's about time you saw the disadvantages.'

'You are only concerned with the financial aspects of the theatre. Repertory presents a constant challenge. It never allows one to stand still.'

'Yes, but that is not the reason you are doing it. There is no challenge in your repertoire. The plays you present have been tried and tested over decades and, in some cases, centuries. There is no experimentation, no moving forward. You play safe, and why you do so is linked with that infamous entertainment account we mentioned earlier. It is becoming more important to you to join in, and pander to, the social rituals of the upper classes than it is to work in the theatre and on the plays.'

This chit of a girl was coming a damn sight too close to understanding Vere's dilemma and he was reaching the conclusion that he did not want to be understood. 'Like any actor-manager, I choose to produce plays that will please my following and – yes, I admit it – display me to advantage. Irving . . .'

'Irving must make a loss at the Lyceum,' Charley cut in swiftly, 'and balance his books through his American tours. Why don't you tour the United States? I'll tell you why you do not tour – in the States or in the provinces – because you cannot tear yourself away from society. Vere, you cannot serve two masters!'

She was voicing his own fears so lucidly that, for a moment, he hated her. Celia. He clung to the thought of Celia. As soon as he was married to her, his role would be redefined and this balancing act would be over.

'In order to achieve a long run, you need a new play-wright,' Charley was saying, 'a writer who will give you a voice and an identity. How hard are you looking for him?'

'I was expecting you to say that you had found him for me.' Vere pushed aside his plate with an irritated gesture. 'For heaven's sake, young lady, do me the courtesy of granting me at least a modicum of intelligence. Of course I am looking for a modern playwright, but so far I have been disappointed. Until I do find him – or her, I'm surprised you didn't make that point – I am stuck with old plays, adaptations of popular novels, or translations from the French, such as that ghastly old charlatan Sardou, the artificiality of whose plots are too terrible to contemplate. In the circumstances, I think we do pretty well at The Cavendish. Even our adaptations are good, and I happen to believe that only the great masters of the novel – Dickens, Trollope, Thackeray, Scott – provide characters and situations comparable with Shakespeare.'

'And where does Michael Samson fit into that collection of the great and the good?' Charley demanded. 'And why are you wasting money on that garbage he writes?'

'So you *are* prying into my private affairs!'

'I may have sneaked a little look at a few manuscripts one day when I had nothing better to do,' Charley conceded unblushingly. 'And I know why you buy that trash – it is because he is the drama critic of an important newspaper and, in return for your interest in his plays, you expect him to give your productions good notices. There is a very nasty word for that sort of thing – bribery!'

By now they were standing, facing each other across the table, Charley taunting, Vere white and thin-lipped with anger. He came towards her and gripped her arms so hard that it hurt.

'How dare you! You, who are nothing but a slightly above-average actress with a good pair of legs, who was working in obscurity before I brought you to London, how *dare* you sneak into my office, pry into my private papers and then have the unadulterated cheek to tell me how to run my business *and* accuse me of malpractice!'

'You are hurting me,' and, as he released her, Charley rubbed her upper arms and grimaced.

'Apart from my utter incredulity at your crass impertinence, I fail to see why you did it. Just what did you hope to achieve?'

'I thought that I could join you in managing the theatre,' Charley retorted. 'Your accounts need as much cleansing as the Augean stables.'

His jaw dropped and he stared at her in blank disbelief. After a long pause, during which he mastered his temper, he said: 'It ought not to surprise you that I find it possible to refuse your offer.'

'In that case, I may not be able to renew my contract with The Cavendish next season,' Charley threatened.

'To the best of my knowledge and belief, you have not been offered another contract,' was his swift retort.

'And even if you had, there is a very nasty word for such behaviour – blackmail!'

'You need me – a Leigh sister – to make the season a success.'

'Do you really believe that you are the only above-average actress with good legs?'

He was calling her bluff, and no one had ever done that before. Outside the family, Charley had always succeeded, always been told that she was wonderful. She glared at him in a fury of frustration.

'I still say it was bribery,' she said, scowling.

'For someone who thinks that she is ready for management, you have a poor knowledge of business practice,' he said cuttingly. 'I dare say that my interest in Samson's work does predispose him to a benevolent view of *my* work, but that is not why I do it. Every manager in the country buys the rights to plays he has no intention of producing, simply because his option on the items prevents anyone else producing them. Also, in the mountain of dross he accumulates, the manager feels certain that, one day, he will find a nugget of pure gold.'

Everything was going wrong. He had an answer to all her questions and accusations, and was effortlessly maintaining a position of superiority over her that was so galling that Charley wanted to scream. She was right about The Cavendish and the threat to its future, she was sure she was right, yet, despite her careful preparation for this meeting, she was being outmanoeuvred and outsmarted. Looking at Vere, so controlled and in command and so damnably attractive, Charley's frustration reached breaking point. It was a choice between shouting like a fishwife and getting out. Charley opened the door and ran along the passage, through the main entrance to the inn and out into the weak spring sunshine. *Sans* hat and coat, she shivered and was deciding to walk towards the river when she saw, leaning against a wall, the machines belonging to the bicycling party that was lunching within. Seizing the nearest cycle, Charley struggled into the saddle, furiously hitching up her voluminous skirt and showing a great deal of leg in the process.

Having followed her to the door, Vere watched, his expression softening as he did so.

Wobbling, because she was an enthusiastic but inexperienced cyclist, Charley careered across the grass and down to the towpath beside the river.

Ignoring the bicycles, Vere unhitched a horse from the railing, swung into the saddle and followed at a discreet distance.

The towpath was wide and flat, with a grass verge between it and the river on one side, and lawns fringed by woodland on the other. Charley, trying to work off her anger, pedalled faster, gaining confidence and balance as a feeling of familiarity with the machine returned. She was wearing a flame-coloured silk dress that matched her coat and the more speed she picked up, the more the light, floating material billowed out behind her; but it was a while before she became aware of the encumbrance, and possible danger, of her attire. When she did realise that the folds of her petticoats were swirling close to the rear wheel, she took her left hand off the handlebars and grabbed a swathe of skirt. So far so good, but she had to do the same on the other side.

Behind her, the smile faded from Vere's face as he saw the danger and how she was attempting to deal with it. 'Charley,' he shouted, riding a little faster, 'stop before you fall off . . .'

Hearing his voice, she glanced over her left shoulder and saw him. 'Stop,' she heard him shout. Like hell, was her immediate response and she pedalled even faster, while pondering how to prevent the other side of her skirt entangling itself in the bicycle wheel. Either she had to grab it with her left hand, which was already full, or she had to take her right hand off the handlebars. Deciding that to take both hands off simultaneously was to court disaster, Charley made a tentative pincer movement with her left thumb and forefinger towards a bunch of silk pleats at her right hip. At the second attempt, and while looking at her skirt instead of where she was going, she connected with the material and gave it a sharp tug.

But she had not realised that her skirt had become tightly wound around the pedal, and she failed to notice the large stone lying on the edge of the path. The sudden jerk on the pedal unbalanced the machine, which veered to the right, keeling over and hitting the stone as it did so, and tipping Charley out of the saddle. Entangled with pedal and handlebars, she went over the grass verge and into the river.

The shock of the icy water was so intense that the breath was knocked out of her but, surfacing and trying vainly to find a foothold, she was aware of the heavy weight of the bicycle dragging her down. Struggling violently, thrashing with arms and legs, she tried desperately to free her petticoats from the various protrusions of the bicycle on which they were caught. Thus handicapped and unable to swim, Charley managed a feeble cry for help before she sank beneath the surface for the second time.

Then she felt strong arms pulling her up and her head broke the surface and, gasping and coughing, she took in great gulps of air. Her rescuer was holding her with one arm and tugging at her skirts with his other hand, and suddenly she felt the weight fall off her feet and legs, and she was free. Opening her eyes, she looked at Vere and tried to thank him, but no sound would come out.

'Save your breath for the next bit,' he advised and she felt him tense as he gathered himself for the effort of hoisting her on to the river bank. Managing to get a purchase on the grass, Charley dragged herself forward so that only her legs were trailing in the water and lay limp with shock, cold and exhaustion. Beside her Vere pulled himself on to dry land and lifted her clear of the river before he, too, sank to the ground and fought for breath.

Before jumping in to save her, he had ripped off his jacket and now he picked it up and wrapped her in its welcoming warmth. Silently he helped Charley to her feet and across to the horse, which, being a good-natured animal, had stayed where Vere had abandoned it so precipitately. Climbing into the saddle, Vere reached down, pulled Charley up in front of him, and set the horse at a gentle walk back to the inn.

By this time the absence of horse and bicycle had been discovered and an excited crowd had gathered, the excitement turning to astonishment as the horse and its sodden burden came into view. Eager hands helped Charley to slide to the ground, but quickly Vere was at her side and guiding her back to the room where their interrupted meal still lay on the table. While Charley shivered by the fire, Vere gave crisp instructions to the landlord.

'My wife and I need towels, the loan of some clothes while ours dry and some brandy. Also,' and Vere burrowed into a pocket in the jacket that Charley was still wearing, producing a wallet from which he extracted a bundle of bank notes, 'give this to the owner of the bicycle and this to the owner of the horse and apologise on our behalf for the accident and any inconvenience.'

Feeling was returning, slowly, to Charley's frozen body

and even more frozen brain. Fright was being replaced by humiliation as she faced the moral and financial obligation she was under.

'How much did you give them?'

'I believe the price of a bicycle is about ten pounds, so I thought twelve pounds would cover the cost of replacing it, plus the inconvenience caused to its owner. As the horse was returned undamaged, I deemed five pounds appropriate.'

'Thank you. Naturally I will reimburse you as soon as possible.'

He seemed about to argue but thought better of it. 'As you wish.'

A girl brought in a pile of towels and dry clothes and was followed by the waiter with a bottle of brandy and two glasses.

Vere locked the door behind them. 'Right, get out of those wet things. Why, is that a problem?' as Charley looked at him wide-eyed. 'You are the one who told them we were married, not me.'

Charley looked at the inviting heap of dry towels. The number of times she had fantasised about undressing with this man, in the most romantic, seductive circumstances, and it had to happen like this. Why, Charley thought bitterly, did life never live up to expectations? He was closing the curtains, but some daylight filtered in and the fire cast a bright glow around the room. Backing into the darkest corner, Charley wriggled out of her ruined dress and petticoats and embarked on the delicate operation of trying to remove her underwear while holding a towel in front of her. Oh, to hell with this . . . She sneaked a quick glance into the opposite corner, where Vere was stripping off his wet clothes. He had his back towards her and she received an indelible impression of broad, muscled

shoulders tapering to a narrow waist, lean hips, tight buttocks and long, powerful legs, dappled by flickering
firelight. Oh God . . . Charley nearly groaned aloud as
fresh life returned to the most intimate parts of her body –
life that she owed to Vere in more ways than one.

Swiftly she wrapped a towel tightly under her arms,
leaving her gleaming shoulders and long legs bare, and sat
down in front of the fire. Raising her arms with conscious
grace, she unpinned her hair and shook free a mass of
tumbling Titian waves, which hung down her back in a
thick, damp mass surmounted by aureoles of bright flame
as the shorter hairs dried.

Clad only in a towel wrapped round his waist, Vere
pulled up a chair and sat down, gazing into the fire with
an intensity that could have been caused by anger or by a
determination not to look at Charley. She stretched out
those endless legs and the towel slipped slightly open to
one side, revealing several inches of white thigh, but Vere's
gaze did not deviate.

'What is the matter with you?' she whispered. 'You
know what has been happening between us, on the stage
and off, yet you pretend that those feelings do not exist.'

'Get dressed,' he said harshly. 'When I told you to take
off your wet things, I intended you to put on dry ones, not
to sit around half naked.'

'You are more naked than I am,' she flashed, 'or isn't
that supposed to matter? Why is it expected that a man
will be aroused by a female body, while a woman remains
impervious to his?'

'I never really thought about it,' he said, nonplussed.

'You are very beautiful,' she said quietly, 'but you know
that, don't you? You trade on it, use it, a dozen times a day.'

'If the sight of my bare chest has such an unsettling
effect on you, I will cover it forthwith,' he said drily, rising

to his feet. 'In return, perhaps you would do the same to your legs.'

In reply Charley raised one foot in the air so that the towel fell open and one long, glorious leg was exposed to the hip. Vere closed his eyes, as if in pain, and turned away.

'Why,' Charley whispered, '*why* . . . ?'

'Because I have seen what thoughtless, selfish love can do, and the hurt it gives to other people. I do not want to hurt anyone again, any more than I want to be hurt myself.'

'But I do not want your love. I only want . . . You know damn well what I want . . .'

'You are a very unusual woman, Charley, but in the end even you will want love.'

'And love is something you cannot give.'

'You overlook the possibility that I may have given it to someone else.'

Charley stood up and stared at the contours of that harshly handsome face. 'No,' she said slowly. 'I think that all your life women have thrown themselves at your feet and you have known only a succession of easy conquests. But one day you will meet a woman who does not want you, and then you will know the pain of love.'

'Such profundity from one so young,' and his tone was light and bantering, 'but, fortunately for me, way off the mark. I hope to be married soon and my intended bride gives every impression of loving me.'

'But do you love her?'

'That is none of your business.'

'So you don't,' Charley retorted triumphantly.

'Get dressed, Charley.'

'I meant what I said earlier,' she said defiantly. 'I cannot stay at The Cavendish.'

'Don't be silly. Of course you will stay. Next season you and I are going to do *The Taming of the Shrew* and you know perfectly well that you would not miss that for the world.'

And of course he was right . . .

Later, at home, Charley succumbed to a sudden fit of crying, but when she was quiet again she saw, on the mantelshelf, a card requesting her company that evening at the home of Peter Frith-Tempest. Charley knew that his father, who had died recently, had been one of The Cavendish's backers and she had a vague recollection of meeting the son at opening-night parties. She had refused the invitation, in the naive belief that she would be other-wise engaged this evening, but now she decided that, with the help of a fresh dress and curling tongs, she would go.

'I hope that you don't mind,' she said frankly, extending her hand to Peter Frith-Tempest, 'but I found that I was free after all.'

'I am so glad,' he said sincerely. 'Do come in,' and he led her into the house.

The focal point of the small, bachelor establishment was a large drawing room lit by gas battens placed outside the windows, so that the room was suffused with a soft light through gauzy pale-pink curtains. A huge fire burned in the wide fireplace, which was flanked by banks of flow-ers and ferns; exquisite Persian rugs carpeted the floor, fine pictures adorned the walls, and a piano was placed on a low platform near the window. Half-a-dozen comfort-able armchairs were occupied by elegantly dressed ladies, while other guests arranged themselves on upright gilt chairs or an array of sofa cushions in soft velveteen and Liberty silks scattered on the polished floor.

The company was a congenial, indeed a daring, mix of

the theatrical, professional and business worlds. Singers
from Covent Garden mingled with barristers and bankers,
and actresses were not ostracised.

'You are a brave man,' Charley told Peter when he left
the piano after accompanying one of the opera artistes.
'Your courage, and courtesy, in inviting an actress to your
home are much appreciated.'

'There are actresses and actresses,' he said, laughing.

'But dare I assume that your father's recent death, while
obviously much lamented, has left you free to follow your
own interests and inclinations?' Suddenly she shivered,
her face whitening and her flesh rising in goose-bumps.
'Nothing to worry about,' she assured him airily, 'merely
a brush with death this afternoon.'

To the delight of the gathering, she gave an impromptu
performance illustrating her dip in the river and her gal-
lant rescue by an unnamed hero. However, Peter discerned
that she was more affected by the incident than she let on.
'Don't go,' he murmured as the guests began to leave and
Charley's eyes acquiesced to all that he was suggesting.

While he was saying good night to the last guests, she
sat down in front of the fire and wished that she could
turn back the clock a few hours, to another fire in another
room with another man. Kneeling beside her, Peter gently
caressed her bare arms.

'You are so cold,' he said, 'despite the fire.'

'Then warm me,' she whispered and drew him to her
with a desperate urgency. Closing her eyes, she shut out
the fair hair, blue eyes and the plain decency of his face
and substituted the dark, satanic intensity of Vere
Cavendish. And in that wild, demanding coupling it was
Vere whom she took inside her and Vere who loved and
satisfied her.

When she had found some sort of peace, Charley raised

herself on one elbow and gazed down at Peter Frith-Tempest. He was, she decided, an awfully good thing. Her professional ambitions were by no means dampened because Vere had dismissed them so summarily. However, Charley conceded that she might have been precipitate. In order to achieve those ambitions she needed the right kind of friends, and the perfect example was here beside her.

'Darling Peter,' she murmured, snuggling up to him and wrapping those wonderful legs around him, 'did you inherit your father's interest in The Cavendish Theatre, financial and otherwise?'

'Mmm,' he acceded limply, worn out.

'I do want to learn all I can about theatre management. Won't you tell me how it works, from a backer's point of view, and then we could remind ourselves how a few other things work,' and her hand teasingly stroked his penis until, to his surprise, it stirred into new life. 'We have a great deal to offer each other, Peter, don't you agree?'

Chapter Nineteen

'Good God,' Vere exclaimed, 'how can the running costs of *The Wandering Heir* possibly have escalated to one hundred and fifty pounds per performance? It is not possible, you must have made a mistake.'

'No mistake, Chief,' Richard Ramsey assured him. 'Please, you really must go through the accounts in detail and see if you can find any areas that can be cut back.'

'I said exactly the same thing to you three months ago,' Vere said impatiently, 'and I went through the accounts then. Much good it did us.'

It was now high summer and indeed, the day after his talk with Charley at the inn, Vere had called for the accounts and spent valuable time scrutinising them. The only economy he had made was the supply to the green-room of a penny newspaper instead of one costing threepence.

'I detest quibbling over a penny here and a penny there, or the cost of providing the cleaners with tea and a slice of bread and jam,' Vere snapped, 'and I refuse point-blank to cut corners in the staging of our productions. I have my reputation to think of.'

'If you cannot reduce the outgoings, you must increase

the takings,' Ramsey reasoned, 'and as far as I can see there is only one way to do that: tour.'

Vere groaned. There had been an element of truth in Charley's assertion that The Cavendish did not tour because he could not tear himself away from society. More specifically, the way things stood at the moment he had no wish to be out of London, or out of range of the Meltons' country home, while his relationship with Celia was at such a delicate stage. In addition, Vere had never been over-enthusiastic about the actual business of *acting*, and the prospect of treading the boards night after night in the provinces with only The Cavendish staff and cast for company was distinctly unappealing.

'Too late to arrange a tour for this summer, surely?' he said with relief.

'Not necessarily.' Ramsey shuffled some papers and found a list of dates. 'We are due to close the season on Saturday, 31 July and re-open the third week of September. If we closed a week early – advance bookings are bad for the end of July anyway – and gave the cast two weeks' holiday, we could open a tour on 8 August. Then the new season would open late, say Saturday, 2 October . . .'

'With the existing repertoire.' Vere nodded, and tried to look as if he was seriously considering the possibility.

'That would give us, let me see,' and Ramsey counted the weeks on the calendar, 'an eight-week tour, minus a couple of days at the end for the company to settle in at home.'

'Any chance of letting out The Cavendish while we were away?'

'There is always someone who wants to try out a production, and we know ourselves that there is an audience for it in the summer. You could tour longer if you liked – carry on into November . . .'

'No, no,' Vere said hastily. 'I need to start rehearsals for the *Shrew* by September at the latest. Anyway, as I said at the outset, surely it is too late to make any provincial bookings?'

'Not if we started the tour that bit earlier than the others, and slotted in before them in the schedules. Do you want me to make some inquiries?'

'No,' Vere said again. 'I'll think it over.'

He had no intention of doing any such thing and put it straight out of his mind; and when the note arrived from Barbara Melton he read it with equanimity, never suspecting for a moment the awful chain of events that was about to unfold.

The Meltons had been invited to a ball at a house near Henley and, it being Royal Regatta week, were sleeping there on the Saturday of the party in order to watch the rowing finals on Sunday. They, and their hosts, would be charmed if Vere would join them on Saturday evening; they calculated that, if he hurried after his evening performance at the theatre, he would be able to catch the last train from Paddington to Maidenhead, where a carriage would meet him.

Vere had never been to the Henley Regatta and it was exactly the sort of society occasion that appealed to him. This year the Royal Regatta, next year Royal Ascot . . . He despatched an immediate acceptance of the invitation.

The ball was in full swing when he arrived and, after the butler had divested him of top hat, cloak and cane, and the footman had taken his bag upstairs, he entered the ballroom to find Barbara hovering near the door.

'Thank God, I could not have borne it, had you missed the train,' she exclaimed.

'It is very kind of you to be so concerned about me,' he replied with a smile.

'Having got this far, it would have been too cruel had fate conspired against us!'

'It would?'

'Come, I will introduce you to our hostess. She is my cousin, you know, which is why I could arrange everything. She and I are like sisters, so naturally I could confide in her. She knows all about *us*.'

'She does?' a bemused Vere said, wishing that he could be similarly enlightened.

It might have been his imagination, but he did think there was an extraordinary air of conspiracy about his introduction to Barbara's cousin. The eyes, the glances, of the two women seemed so knowing, yet for the life of him he could not imagine what it was about him that they knew and he did not. Feeling more and more as if he had stepped into a real-life melodrama, with a dash of Sheridan thrown in, he played along with them out of sheer politeness.

'I must pay my respects to Lord Melton,' he told Barbara when they were alone.

'But, Vere, he isn't here – that is the whole *point*!'

'Oh.' He consciously stopped himself saying: 'It is?' 'How very ungallant of him to have abandoned you for the evening.'

'Good heavens, man, it took me a week to persuade him that he had more important things to do. Mind you, he is probably off somewhere with an actress on his arm.'

'Not one of mine. My girls were all present and correct when I left the theatre.'

'Tonight I don't care what he does. He has my blessing. Tonight what is sauce for the goose is sauce for the gander.'

'Good.' He had no idea whether it was good or not, but it seemed the right thing to say. Glancing at her covertly, he wondered if she was feeling unwell. Barbara could be a trifle temperamental and affected on occasions, but usually she was the one person with whom he could communicate, which made the existing muddle all the more puzzling. 'But Celia is here?'

'Yes, but I did not tell her that you were coming, so her dance card is full. However, as you can see, I have been awaiting your arrival,' and she showed him a virtually blank card.

'In that case, shall we . . . ?' And he led her out on to the floor, grateful for an activity that would reduce the need for conversation and mask his perplexity.

Celia danced by in the arms of a perspiring young Lothario. Seeing Vere, she did a double-take of utter astonishment and then flashed him a huge smile, which he returned over Barbara's head. The girl was really very beautiful, he thought with a mixture of pride and tenderness. He did not love her, but he did like her. She would grow out of her youthful impetuosity and stubbornness but, if she did not do so, perhaps she would keep him young. Whatever the case, dancing in that elegant ballroom in the heart of an English shire, he suddenly felt sure that he and Celia had a good chance of happiness, perhaps even a better chance than most couples.

However, he seemed doomed to be kept at arm's length from her that evening. Apart from an occasional word between dances and the lingering exchange of glances on the dance floor, there was no contact between them. Vere was tantalised by that radiant little figure in an ethereal white gown dancing past him, clasped in the arms of one admirer after another. An excellent dancer, Vere executed the steps of each waltz or polka impeccably and smiled down into Barbara's adoring face but his mind and, briefly, his heart were elsewhere.

But what was that – Barbara's *adoring* face? Horrified, Vere looked again, more closely. Escorting her into the supper room, his worst fears were realised: her manner was positively proprietorial and, which was worse, seductive. She must have been quite something when she was younger – the way she raped one with her eyes while she placed a prawn in her mouth must have driven the boys wild. True, she was very well-preserved and old Lord Whatsisname at the next table was riveted by the performance but he, Vere, was embarrassed and appalled.

Yet again he realised that there was a price to be paid for everything. Here he was, at one of the most fashionable balls of the Season, mingling with the cream of society in a manner that fulfilled his wildest dreams, and yet he could not enjoy it. Suddenly his dancing expertise was negated because he was treading on eggshells, watching every word he said and every move he made. The mildest comment was fraught with danger and *double entendre*.

Courteously he fetched Barbara an ice, removed a cushion that she deemed *de trop*, and refilled her glass with champagne. 'Is there anything else I can do for you?' he asked, before sitting down.

'Oh yes,' she murmured, 'a little later. Isn't anticipation wonderful!'

'Haven't you danced enough?' he said, deliberately misunderstanding in an effort to defuse the situation. 'I never knew that you had such a passion for it.'

'You know perfectly well that you are very well acquainted with the object of my passion.'

He *liked* the woman, damn it. So he had cultivated her with one eye on her husband's wealth, but he had enjoyed her company and her conversation, and even at this critical moment felt aggrieved at the possibility of losing them, because he was terribly afraid that he would lose them if he did not fulfil her expectations. But he had never thought of her as a lover, and never would. It was the radiant youth of her daughter that he wanted, not the crow's-feet at her eyes or the wrinkles on her upper arms, or her décolletage. He did not want her as a lover, nor even as a mother-in-law, but as a friend and confidante and someone utterly unique in his life. Lovers he could have any day, any number of them, any time; friends were harder to find. Vere comprehended, too late, that for him Barbara had been part of a package, that he had succumbed to an irresistible combination of Lord Melton's wealth, Lady Melton's friendship, and their daughter's eligibility.

He danced on, holding Barbara close and smiling into her eyes, exchanging smouldering glances with Celia from a safe distance. Could he salvage the situation? He needed to sleep on it, he decided – everything would be clearer in the morning – and at last it was time for bed.

'Good night,' Barbara said loudly, before whispering: 'I am in the room next to yours. *Au revoir* . . .'

He had intended to engineer a private word with Celia before retiring but, as Barbara's meaning sank in, he hurriedly asked a footman to show him to his room. As he had expected, a door connected his chamber with its neighbour.

Swiftly Vere locked the connecting door and, for safe measure, pushed a chest of drawers hard against it, praying that Barbara would not hear the noise of the furniture scraping on the polished floor. Then he did the same with the outer door, so that he could not be outmanoeuvred on that flank, extinguished the lights and sat down on the bed.

The connecting door rattled as Barbara tried to open it;

she knocked, quietly at first and then louder, calling his name softly.

Vere did not move. At all costs, and for both their sakes, this encounter must be avoided. In the morning he would plead fatigue and sudden indisposition, and pretend that he had not heard her at his door. Thus Barbara could avoid feeling foolish and, if the gods were with him, he could retain a friend.

Someone was trying the handle of the outer door. Vere sat motionless, feeling oddly guilty and besieged, afraid that the slightest creak of the bed or the minutest movement of a muscle would give him away. Bloody stupid . . . He could see the farcical aspect of this melodrama but did not feel at all like laughing. The handle of the outer door rattled again and this time a girlish voice was whispering his name. Celia. Oh no . . . Vere lay down on the bed, folded his hands behind his head and stared at the ceiling.

He heard the outer door of the adjacent room open, and then a muffled shriek.

'Celia, what on earth . . . ?'

'I thought this was your room, Mama. I have a headache.'

There was a brief murmur of voices and movements in the next room, until the door closed again and everything went quiet. After an uneventful half-hour, Vere stood up and tried to locate his night things, which had been unpacked by the servants while he was downstairs. But he did not feel sleepy. Even if he placated Barbara, how would she feel when she heard that he wanted to marry Celia? How *did* a middle-aged woman react when she was rejected in favour of her daughter?

Vere was no psychiatrist but he was fairly certain that his marriage plans would receive short shrift. Time, he thought, Barbara will need time . . .

Listening at the connecting door, he could hear her crying, the most heart-rending sobs, the sobs of a woman weeping not only for a lost lover but for her lost youth.

He wanted to comfort her, but he could not give her the only thing she wanted; and, long after dawn had broken and the sobbing had ceased, Vere still sat in a chair by the window, gazing sightlessly over the terrace at the beautiful wooded park and the grazing herd of red deer.

Barbara did not appear for breakfast and when the house party assembled in the hall before church, she was pale and red-eyed. Aware that she was avoiding his eyes, Vere approached her immediately.

'I hope that you slept well,' he said, holding her hand.

She pulled her hand free and still did not look at him. Nor did she reply to his question.

'I certainly did,' he went on. 'I was suddenly overcome with fatigue and a blinding headache, so I took some medication and knew nothing more until the maid woke me.'

'You are an excellent actor, Mr Cavendish, but we always knew that, didn't we!' She turned away. Haggard with grief, humiliation and lack of sleep, she looked ten years older than the woman who had welcomed him to the ball. His heart sank. This was going to be even more difficult than he had feared.

Celia was descending the stairs, in a fresh summer frock and a pretty hat and, although she was commandeered instantly by her mother, she flashed Vere a brilliant smile. So all was well in that quarter, at any rate. However, his reprieve might be temporary. It was imperative that he keep Celia under control while time healed Barbara's wounds.

Somehow he got through the church service and kept up a genial conversation with his fellow guests during the drive to the river. The day was grey and overcast, although so far the rain had held off, and the heaviness in the atmosphere matched Vere's mood. Others were less affected by the weather and the Stewards' Enclosure was a mass of colour and high spirits, the dresses and hats of the ladies vying for attention with the blazers and boaters of the rowing fraternity. Picnics were spread on the grass, while on the water some spectators gained an excellent view of the races from flat-bottomed skiffs.

For Vere, the day was spoiled irretrievably. His sole concern was to have Celia to himself for five minutes and implore her to be discreet. He drank champagne, nibbled at a piece of salmon, was charming to his companions; but while he cheered the oarsmen, from the single scullers to the flashing oars of the eights, he saw only Barbara's stony stare and the misery on her face, in sharp contrast to the vivacity of her daughter.

And then he realised that he had been going about this in entirely the wrong way. Celia was far more adroit at this sort of thing than he was. All he had to do was wander off on his own and she would extricate herself effortlessly from the party and follow him. Excusing himself casually, he wandered along the river bank, pausing ostentatiously in order to light a cigarette before mingling with the crowd, relying on his unusual height and Celia's natural talents to enable her to find him. Sure enough, not ten minutes had elapsed before he saw her hurrying towards him and he turned away from the river, walking in the direction of a row of carriages that would screen them from curious eyes and, in particular, from pursuing parents.

'Are you sure that no one followed you?' he demanded as she ran the last few steps towards him.

'Positive, not that I care two hoots one way or another.

Darling Vere, I could have *died* last night when all my dances were booked. Poor you, condemned to steering my decrepit Mama around the floor all evening.'

'Your mother is a very charming woman, young lady, and don't you forget it. But, yes, I was terribly disappointed, too.'

'Why didn't you let me know you were coming?'

'I assumed that your mother had told you, but apparently it slipped her mind. Don't blame her, Celia, she is bound to have more important things to think about than me.'

'Hm, there's something fishy about it, but never mind – I have you all to myself now. I was very good last night, don't you think, and didn't make a fuss, so I definitely deserve a reward – a real, proper, naughty kiss while no one is looking.'

She had that kittenish look on her face again, and Vere knew that although it was charming, it was also deceptive. If he refused, the claws could come out with surprising speed and, in view of what he had to say to her, he deemed it wise to keep her in a good mood. Besides, after watching her dance last night, he wanted to kiss her.

Concealed behind the carriages, he drew her to him and, bending low because she was such a tiny little thing, gently parted her lips and slid his tongue into her mouth, kissing her with a passion that surprised him and took Celia's breath away. When he released her, Celia was trembling and Vere himself was shaken. He had been celibate since Marion and evidently abstention did not suit him.

'That was gorgeous,' Celia gasped, 'even more gorgeous than I imagined. Can we do it again, please?'

'Later . . . Celia, darling, I want you to be very sensible and listen carefully to what I say. First, you must believe that I love you and want to marry you. You do believe that, don't you?'

Celia nodded confidently.

'However, it is very important that you and I do not see each other for a while.'

'What sort of "while"?' Celia wanted to know, the smile fading from her face.

'Only a few months.' But her expression told him that a few months was a lifetime to her. Vere seized both her hands and held them tight, his voice low and urgent. 'Remember, darling, that it is very important that your parents approve of our marriage, and I have the strangest feeling – just a sixth sense, really – that your mother is aware of an attachment between us and that she doesn't like it.'

'I see.'

'You do?' Vere brightened at this unexpected tone and attitude of reason. 'Believe me, I shall miss you just as much as, probably more than, you miss me. I think the best plan is for me to leave London for a few months and, with luck, when I return we can carry on where we left off.'

'Which was here,' and Celia threw her arms around him, lifting her face for another kiss. When they drew apart, she was remarkably composed. 'I must go back. It would be best if you did a sort of circle and approached from the opposite direction.'

'Celia, you will wait for me, won't you!'

There was no mistaking the sincerity in his voice and briefly Celia raised a gloved hand and touched his cheek. 'I love you,' she said, and walked away.

Vere lit another cigarette and slowly strolled back towards the finish of the course. She had taken it awfully well, really surprisingly well; she was growing up fast. In fact, had he thought about it more carefully, and known Celia better, he ought to have known that she had taken it far *too* well.

From Paddington, Vere went straight to the theatre. It was near the end of the season and therefore no rehearsals were in progress, but backstage staff were working on minor repairs to the scenery and lighting effects. After despatching two men with notes for Bert Harding and Richard Ramsey, Vere settled down at his desk.

'There is a great deal to be done,' he said when Ramsey hurried into the office. 'I have decided that we will tour this summer after all.'

The preparations were frantic. While Ramsey telegraphed theatre managers all over the country and painstakingly put together an itinerary, Vere and Bert Harding auditioned replacements for those cast members who could not, or would not, tour and worked out arrangements for transporting scenery, costumes and props.

'The proper way to do this,' Charley heard Vere remark, 'is to hire a private train but, as it is, we must make do with a railway carriage for essential scenery and borrow the rest from each theatre as we go along.'

'I might be able to help,' Charley offered. 'I worked in masses of provincial theatres with Dan Crisp, and the scenery doesn't change much in most of them. Where are we going? Oh yes, no problem there . . .'

She sat down with Bert Harding and concentrated on recalling the scenery and props commandeered at various theatres by the Crispin Comedy Company, thanking a kind providence that had aroused her interest in backstage matters. In addition, the company had to help newcomers who were replacing the few who had dropped out, and Charley herself had to learn a new role in *Money*, which was being revived from the previous year. She was playing Georgina, not Clara – which had been Marion's part in the original production.

'It is the school holidays,' Vere murmured tentatively. 'I don't suppose that Marion would be willing . . .'

'If she tours, I don't,' Charley said flatly, and that was how the matter was left.

Ever restless and eager for new experiences, Charley was looking forward to the tour. Being parted from Peter Frith-Tempest, who continued to be a kind and considerate lover, was not the wrench he might have hoped, and it would be gratifying to revisit her old haunts and renew old acquaintances in her glamorous new guise as the leading lady of The Cavendish. In all the rush and excitement, she thought nothing more of a brief meeting with Celia Melton. Dashing out to the Strand for a bite of lunch one day, she heard someone call her name.

'Miss Melton, I haven't seen you since you dropped out of *School* for the Season. I hope that you are well.'

'Fine, thanks. Much rather be at the theatre than all those dreary parties. The venues are different, but otherwise they are all exactly the same – same people, same food, same music, the same *ghastly* men . . .'

'A fearful bore,' Charley agreed, straight-faced.

'Anyway, I am so glad to have bumped into you,' Celia gushed guilelessly, 'because you might be able to save me the trouble of going into The Cavendish and bothering Mr Ramsey. My father wants a note of the itinerary of the tour – where you will be on certain days and so on. Do you happen to have the information?'

Charley fumbled in her bag and produced a schedule of theatres and dates. She did not need it any more – she knew it by heart. 'Will this do? It's a bit creased and messy, I'm afraid. Perhaps you should ask Mr Ramsey for a clean copy for his lordship.'

'This will be fine,' Celia assured her, tucking it away.

'And I believe that arrangements have been finalised for an American actor to lease The Cavendish while we are away, so that is good news on the financial front,' Charley offered cheerfully. 'Mind you, I expect Lord Melton knows that already.'

'I will tell him anyway. Thank you *so* much. *So* nice to have seen you again,' and Celia waved and returned to the smart equipage that was waiting for her in the road.

Strange girl, that, thought Charley, but not bad for someone of her class. Had it not been for the difference in their stations in life, she felt that she might have got on well with Celia; the girl could, almost, have been like a little sister. And Charley wondered, not for the first time, how matters stood with her sisters. Was the school a success? Would Marion have welcomed a tour with The Cavendish? Did they need the money? But Charley could not bring herself to find out. She could not make the first approach, not again, not after they had thrown her out the last time. She could not explain why the idea of having Marion in the company was so impossible but it was, and that was that. The Cavendish had become her territory and she resented any intrusion upon it.

As The Cavendish company moved out of the theatre and another moved in, everyone was harassed and short-tempered, but none more so than Vere. His tension was almost tangible, wound up tight as a spring, his face taut and unsmiling, and this unapproachability and acerbity worsened when the tour was under way. It was obvious that he loathed the entire business, that even the best of the provincial theatres compared unfavourably with The Cavendish, and that he was deeply unhappy because the productions fell below the high standards he set. After one particularly accident-prone performance at the Theatre Royal, Nottingham, during which the scenery had wobbled, a new actor had 'dried', and the locally recruited supers had bumped into everyone and everything, he lost what little patience he had left. Shouting was not Vere's style, but in a few well-chosen words he ripped into the stage staff, pulverised the actor who had forgotten his lines, and reduced the female supers to tears. Watching and listening from the wings, Charley knew that, despite that dreadful day by the river, she was the only person who could challenge him. When he went to his dressing room, she thumped furiously on the door and stalked in. He was removing his make-up, and he looked very tired.

'Who the hell do you think you are?' hissed Charley. 'For God's sake, everyone is doing their best.'

A shuttered look came over his face. 'Then their best is not good enough.'

'You know as well as I do that, because this tour was arranged at the last minute, we could not bring all our own scenery with us and that provincial theatres do not have your sort of money to throw at painting sets and providing first-rate props. And Bob may have dried tonight, but he was hired at short notice and has been absolutely brilliant until this evening. We can all have a bad day, you know, even you! And,' Charley paused for breath, 'Bert and Will were up all night drilling those supers, who are the best you will get here or anywhere else, outside London.'

'At least you may concede that I had my reasons, and not the reasons you suggested, for not wishing to tour.'

'I suggest that you expect perfection, all the time, every day and in every aspect of the production, and that no such thing exists. None of us is perfect, and that includes you!'

He drank from a glass of whisky, ready-poured on the dressing-table, and said wearily: 'If you've got all the vitriol out of your system, I suggest you go home. And if home means London, that is fine by me.'

'And leave you to vent your spleen – revolting phrase, but admirably accurate in this instance – on my under-study? Oh, *please* . . .'

'People pay good money to see us perform – money that they may struggle to find, money that they can ill afford, and it is incumbent on me to provide an enter-tainment that is worthy of them and that lives up to their expectations. They deserve the best, whether they live in Mayfair or Manchester.'

Charley stared at him in astonishment, at a face bare of make-up, tired and lined in the unforgiving light of the dressing room. 'You are a very peculiar person,' she said slowly. 'One minute you are cultivating high society and the next you are defending the rights of the common man. Where do you belong – East End or West End?'

'Some people fall between two stools, and I dare to sug-gest that the Leighs are among them.'

She acknowledged the thrust with a brief nod, no more. 'Chief, half the audience noticed nothing amiss tonight, and the half that did notice could not have cared less – they were too busy admiring your physique and noble profile, and my legs.'

Vere leaned back in his chair and laughed, running his fingers through his hair. 'Don't go to London, Charley. There are times, and this is one of them, when I think that you might be quite good for my morale.'

'Remember that it is no one's fault but your own that this tour is hurried and makeshift. You could have decided sooner, but presumably your private life dictated otherwise.' Their eyes met in the mirror and it was Vere who looked away first. 'Look on the bright side – houses are excellent and you are pocketing rent for The Cavendish into the bargain. As your private life cannot pursue you into the provinces, why not relax and enjoy the pleasure you are bringing to other people's lives?'

But Vere's guarded response proved prescient, and only a week elapsed before Charley was forced to eat her words. Vere's private life could pursue him into the provinces, and it did.

That night in Sheffield he did not hurry to leave his dressing room. One of the many uncongenial aspects of this tour was that he was thrown too much on to his own resources, that despite the hectic schedule he had time to think, and that a bottle of whisky was becoming his only companion. He sat at the dressing-table, drinking, making a few notes on that evening's performance, and even opened his copy of the *Shrew*, thinking that he might begin a little forward planning, but it was no good . . . His eyes insisted on returning to his reflection in the mirror, against the background of the shabby little room, and, deeply depressed, he had that 'what am I doing *here*?' feeling. He had worked so hard and for what – to spend the summer in hovels like this in the hope of paying off his debts?

Picking up the half-full whisky bottle and the Shakespeare, he turned out the lights and walked to the stage door. They were playing at the theatre again the next day, so the stage staff, even Bert Harding, had gone to their lodgings. Only the doorkeeper remained on the premises and he was snoring loudly, a jar of ale on the table beside him, when Vere passed. After a moment's hesitation, he decided not to call a cab but to walk back to his hotel, in the belief that the stroll and the night air might clear his head and enable him to put in a good hour's work before he slept. When he arrived at the hotel, the reception clerk was not at his post so Vere leaned across the desk, intending to take his door key from its hook. But the key was missing. Vere frowned, checked that it had not been placed on the wrong hook by mistake and then, with a shrug, assuming that he must have forgotten to bring it down, walked rapidly up the stairs and along the passage to his room. Sure enough, the door opened readily and he went in.

But the lights were on, the bed was turned down and there, sitting in an armchair by the fire, was Celia . . . Celia who, as Vere's horrified gaze confirmed, was barefoot, clad in a flimsy nightgown, and with her hair hanging loose around her shoulders.

Chapter Twenty

'What the bloody hell are you doing here?'

'Surprise!' Celia ran towards him, throwing herself into his arms, and she felt warm and scented. Roughly, Vere disentangled himself and held her at arm's length.

'How did you get into my room?'

'I told them that I was your wife. It's only a little lie, isn't it! A mere technicality.'

'Techni . . .' Panic was rising in him and the whisky he had consumed was no aid to clarity of thought. What in God's name was he to do with her?

'The bed is not very comfortable,' Celia confided, 'so I told them to light a fire. After they had brought me something to eat, of course.'

'So your arrival did not exactly pass unnoticed.' His tone was characteristically dry, but inwardly he was panicking. In complete contrast with Celia's arrival at the hotel, he was uncomfortably aware that no one had seen him since the end of the performance. For all anyone knew, he could have been in this room with Celia for more than two hours. As he looked at the bed, he seemed to see the imprint of her body where she had lain down.

'Get dressed,' he said in his most authoritative voice,

'because you cannot possibly stay here. No, on second thoughts, I will move to another room.' But whose? Suddenly he turned on his heel and hurried down the corridor to Charley's door and knocked insistently. When there was no response, he tried the handle and, as the door opened, he went in and shook Charley awake.

'I didn't know you cared,' she said sleepily. 'Or is it a fire?'

'Come with me.' And, taking her by the hand, he pulled her down the passage and into his room. As during his initial meeting with Celia, he left the door open.

Charley and Celia stared at each other, Celia smiling sunnily, Charley noticeably less enthusiastic about the reunion.

'She was waiting here when I got back from the theatre a few minutes ago. I want you, Charley, to sleep here with her while I use your room.'

'Why should I help you out of the shit?' Charley demanded. 'You got yourself into this mess, you get yourself out.'

'It isn't a mess,' Celia said indignantly. 'I worked out a plan and executed it perfectly. No one has the least idea where I am, and we can be married before they find me.'

As one, Vere and Charley looked at the pile of luggage stacked in the corner of the room.

'You took a cab to St Pancras,' Vere inquired wearily, 'and a porter helped you put the luggage on the train?' Celia nodded. 'Then another porter helped you to find a cab at Sheffield and you asked him at which hotel I was likely to be staying?'

When Celia nodded again, Vere and Charley exchanged a glance.

'They will be here first thing in the morning,' Charley affirmed cheerfully, 'but that is your problem. I'm going back to bed.'

'Please, Charley, don't leave me alone with her! Surely you can see how it looks . . .'

Charley looked at Celia in her nightgown, and then at herself in hers and at Vere still in his cloak, and dissolved into giggles.

'Celia is Lord Melton's daughter,' Vere reminded her coldly. 'You won't find the situation so amusing if he withdraws his backing for next season.'

Charley sobered immediately. Despite the late hour, she did not doubt for a moment that he had only just returned to the hotel and that Celia's presence came as a total surprise and shock to him. Even if she had been unsure, one glance at the whisky bottle and Shakespeare script would have been enough to convince her that he had not expected company.

'Do you mind not talking about me as if I wasn't here,' Celia complained.

'Don't worry, we are not in the least likely to forget that you are here,' Charley assured her, helping herself to a swig of whisky and passing the bottle to Vere.

'I have told you a thousand times, Vere darling, that I can fix Mama and Papa.'

'If you are referring to your brilliant idea of enlightening each of your parents about the peccadilloes of the other, then forget it,' Vere said flatly. 'For one thing, your parents are better informed on that subject than anyone else. For another, your mother's supposed *tendresse* for me is hardly likely to be much help in the circumstances. Quite the contrary, in fact.'

'Does Lady Melton have a *tendresse* for you?' Charley asked in an awed voice. Vere gave her a weary look, before tossing back a generous slug of neat whisky. Charley let out a long, low whistle. 'I compared your accounts to the Augean stables, but the shit you are in now would fill them ten times over.'

'Celia, why did you do it?' Vere asked quietly.

'I wanted to be with you, of course, and I thought you wanted to be with me. That's what being engaged means, doesn't it?'

'But I thought you understood when I asked you to stay away from me for a while.'

'Now I won't have to stay away. Now that I am here with you, they will have to let me marry you, otherwise there will be a terrible scandal.'

'My dear girl,' and gently Vere took her by the shoulders, 'it doesn't work like that. I am very much afraid that you and I will never see each other again.'

Celia began to sob, and for a few moments Vere held her and let her cry against his shoulder. Feeling embarrassed, Charley turned her back on them and busied herself pouring whisky into the solitary glass.

'Very well,' she said loudly, 'I will stay here with Celia tonight – I won't say "sleep here", because I doubt if any of us will do that. You go to my room and take this with you,' and she handed Vere the whisky bottle, 'and try to think up a bloody good story to feed to the aristocracy when it comes hammering on your door in the morning.'

Incredibly, after another burst of crying Celia fell sound asleep and it was Charley who sat up in bed, trying to eke out one glass of whisky and concoct a reason for Celia's presence in Vere's room in a Sheffield hotel. A fertile brain could manufacture a score of stories but each and every one would be a complete waste of time, because Celia would hole them on the water-line at the outset. Whatever fiction Charley and Vere dreamed up, Celia would confront her parents with the basic truth plus, probably, a little exaggeration and elaboration on how, where and

with whom she had passed the night. The bloody fool –
and Charley did not mean Celia. How had he got himself
into this, what did he see in the stupid bitch? But, no,
that was not fair: Charley could see perfectly well what
had happened and how his mind had worked, and the
only fault she could really find was his choice of girl.
Anyone with an ounce of sense could have seen that Celia
was not the discreet type, but apparently sense was not a
commodity that men possessed by the bucketful, or even
by the teaspoonful.

As the hotel began to stir into life, she left the slumber-
ing Celia and crept back to her own room where, as she
expected, Vere was wide awake. 'Just collecting my
clothes,' she said, but she paused before leaving. 'Without
Celia's co-operation, there isn't a thing we can do.'

'Yes,' he said. 'I came to that conclusion myself.'

He looked terrible, but a glance in the mirror confirmed
that she did not look that wonderful herself.

'I will help as much as I can,' she said, closing the door
behind her.

She dressed quickly and roused Celia. From the mountain of luggage she selected the most decorous
high-necked, long-sleeved frock that she could find and
insisted that Celia put it on, even though the hour was
early. It was imperative that the outraged parents found a
fully dressed and demurely coiffed daughter, not a girl in
a nightgown lounging in bed. Deliberately Charley
scraped her own hair into a severe chignon and tried to
look like a real dragon of a duenna mounting guard over
her charge.

Celia wanted breakfast. How could she eat at a time
like this, Charley wondered as she ordered the food to be
sent up and watched the girl tuck in? Was it youth or
breeding that enabled her to shrug off the exigencies of her

position? A bit of both, Charley decided, with all the experience of her twenty-one years, as she forced down a cup of tea and tried to remember what time the first train from St Pancras pulled into Sheffield station.

'Celia, you will be sensible, won't you,' she coaxed. 'I am sure that you do not wish Mr Cavendish to get into trouble over this business.'

The girl smiled non-committally and poured herself another cup of tea.

'I can get you out of this mess,' Charley promised. 'All you have to do is agree with everything I say, and your parents will be utterly convinced and pacified and you can go back to London with them as if nothing had happened.'

'But something did happen.'

'Like what?'

'That would be telling.' Celia lifted the lids of several platters, inspected the contents and speared a kidney with a fork. She bit into it with her small white teeth, her eyes fixed on Charley. 'You can tell them what you like, but I shall tell them any story that will force them to let me marry Vere.'

After that the morning seemed to drag endlessly until at last, sitting in a virtually stupefied state by the fire, Charley was roused by the sound of angry voices in the corridor. Fists were beating loudly on the door, which Charley had locked in order to prevent Celia from slipping away in search of Vere. Opening it, Charley was confronted by the hotel manager and the Meltons. She stood back until the exclamations and embraces of reunion were over and waited for the storm to break.

'Where is he?' Lord Melton demanded. 'If he has run away, he won't get far – I'll find him and, when I do, I'll kill him!'

'If you are referring to Mr Cavendish, doubtless he is either in his room or at the theatre,' Charley said pleasantly.

'This is his room,' the hotel manager objected.

Charley shook her head. 'As I found my accommodation uncongenial, Mr Cavendish kindly offered to change places with me. This is *my* room, where I found Miss Melton waiting when I returned from the theatre last night. Apparently she has a romantic notion of becoming an actress. Needless to say, I have spent the best part of the night endeavouring to dissuade and disillusion her.'

Vere entered the room as the hotel manager left and stood silently behind her. Lord Melton went even more purple in the face, let out a strangled gasp and made a lunge towards him, but was restrained by an ice-cool Lady Melton.

'She is making that up,' Celia said indignantly. 'This is Vere's room and I spent the night here.'

'With me,' Charley cut in quickly.

'I was alone with Vere for hours – in my nightdress,' Celia added reflectively. 'So you will have to let me marry him.'

'*Marry* . . . !' Lord Melton seemed on the point of apoplexy.

'Be quiet, Reggie. Let me handle this.' Lady Melton looked at Vere. 'Have you nothing to say for yourself?' she demanded.

Quietly and succinctly, Vere gave a truthful account of exactly what had happened the previous evening. When he admitted that this was his room, Lady Melton cast a scathing glance at Charley.

'So we have three different versions of events, and as one version comes from a daughter who has never given any cause for doubt, and two versions come from highly devious members of an extremely dubious profession, we all know who to believe.'

'Hey, wait a minute, that isn't fair,' Charley protested. 'And he never laid a finger on her, I'll swear to that on my life.'

'Your veracity has already been put to the test today, Miss Leigh, and has failed miserably.'

'Leave it, Charley,' Vere said quietly. 'They will believe what they want to believe. Besides, it doesn't matter any more.'

'Was marriage in your mind, Mr Cavendish, when you lured my daughter into this abominable plan?' Barbara Melton inquired icily.

'I did not lure her into anything but, yes, I did – do – wish to marry Celia.'

'For how long have you entertained this ridiculous notion?'

Vere met her eyes steadily. 'I proposed marriage to Celia a year ago, but I have wanted to marry her for a lot longer than that.'

Barbara flinched, thinking of all the meetings and flirtations conducted during that period, while all the time he had wanted to marry her daughter. 'And you consider yourself a good match, I suppose, yet the most assiduous search of Debrett or Burke has failed to reveal your antecedents. Perhaps you would care to enlighten us on that point?'

'No, Lady Melton, I would not. And, no, I do not consider myself a good match, not even good enough to kiss her fingers.' The heavy sarcasm in his voice, and the slight emphasis on fingers, conveyed its own message to Barbara, who had wanted him to kiss so much more than that.

'I will marry him,' Celia said defiantly. 'You can't stop me.'

'You are under age,' Barbara snapped, with the first indication that Vere might not be the sole object of her wrath, 'and will do as you are told.'

'You are just jealous because he wanted me, not you. I thought there was something fishy about you not telling me he was coming to Henley, so when we got back from the river I went into the room Vere had slept in. Guess what, Papa – there was a door connecting it with Mama's room. Only Vere wouldn't let you in, would he, Mama? Don't try to deny it – I can read you like a book!'

'You are developing a very nasty mind, Celia,' Barbara said coldly. 'It must be the company you are keeping these days, and the sooner you are removed from it, the better.'

'I agree,' Vere said with the same unflustered courtesy he had maintained throughout. 'I can only apologise for any misunderstanding and assure you yet again that no harm has come to your daughter. Doubtless, Lord Melton, I will be hearing from your solicitor regarding the return of the finance provided for the forthcoming season?'

'Too bloody right, you will. In fact, I will be seeking legal advice regarding the possibility of charges of abduction, attempted – or successful – rape, and . . .'

'Do shut up, Reggie,' Barbara said, tight-lipped. 'Quite obviously this dreadful business must be hushed up or Celia will be seen as damaged goods, whether she is or she isn't. Sever your business connections with The Cavendish, of course, but for the rest, however galling it seems, we must hold our tongues.'

'I wish you luck in persuading your daughter to hold her tongue,' said Charley waspishly. 'You could try cutting it out, of course. Would you like me to do it for you? It would be an absolute pleasure.'

Vere seized her by the shoulders and propelled her along the corridor and into her own room.

'Sorry, sorry,' Charley apologised. 'I know I wasn't helping, but honestly, that family! As for Celia, how you could encourage that brainless ninny is beyond me!'

'Theoretically she was the ideal wife. I do concede that the reality is rather different.'

'No fool like an ambitious fool, eh? A pity about the finance for the theatre, but all in all you've had a lucky escape.'

Vere did not reply, feeling no inclination or obligation to explain to anyone just what a setback to his plans this fiasco had been.

The sound of Melton voices carried along the corridor.

'You will behave yourself, Celia, and say what I tell you to say. As soon as we return to London, we will make plans for an immediate visit to the Continent – Paris, Florence, Rome . . .'

'I do not *want* to leave London. I don't want to leave Vere.'

'Pull yourself together this instant. Surely even you could not be so stupid as to have imagined that you would be allowed to marry a common actor, whose only passport out of the gutter were the passable good looks that God chose to give him.'

Vere's jaw tightened and his lips set in a thin, angry line. Charley made a very rude two-fingered gesture in the general direction of the speaker before shutting the door.

'Stay here until they've gone,' she advised him, 'and don't worry – my family is not in the least likely to hammer on the door, shouting rape.'

A wry smile tugged at the corners of his mouth and Vere gave a brief, appreciative shake of the head. However, he said nothing until the sound of voices and the tramp of feet along the passage had ceased, and the Meltons had gone.

'So there you have it, young Charley,' he said cynically. 'However hard one works and however much one abides by their rules, in the end it is always "them and us". What you have witnessed today is another triumph for the British class system.'

'It looked more like a victory of prejudice and ignorance over common sense and courtesy to me, but have it your own way. You usually do – have it your own way, I mean. It won't do you any harm to fail, just this once.'

'Except that this step, this marriage, this acceptance into that world, was the ultimate goal at which all the other successes were aimed.'

'Why?' Charley asked curiously. 'Why is it so important to you?'

But Vere could not find the words to explain what it meant to him. He could not convey to Charley, a young woman from a lower middle-class background, the extraordinary allure of that glittering, exclusive world he had glimpsed. She might, probably would, understand the attraction of its wealth and glamour, of the palaces and mansions, of the jewels and silks, of the caviare and iced champagne, and the exquisitely staged events through which that society moved like participants in a constantly changing, yet curiously stable, pageant. But he could not describe the intoxicating scent of *power* that permeated every drawing room and dinner party. In these days when the British ruled the world, moving within the highly exclusive inner circles of London society brought with it a delicious sense of being at the very heart of things. Even if the conversation centred on the theatre or the arts or was merely gossip, there was always that underlying sense of importance, of being with the people who mattered, at the centre of great events. That had been the stage Vere wanted to inhabit, that had been the proper showplace for his talents, and without it, without even the prospect of it, his life seemed meaningless.

Charley watched his face and interpreted his silence more accurately than he knew. 'Try again,' she advised. 'There are other girls, for heaven's sake. Choose one a bit older, and a lot plainer, and who knows?'

'Barbara Melton's vow of silence is unlikely to withstand my first handshake with such a girl, let alone an engagement announcement. She would be round to the girl's family with a highly embellished account of Celia's narrow escape before you could say *Love's Labour's Lost.*'

Conceding the point, Charley felt a pang of concern for Vere. Silly, really, to be worried about the future of this handsome, talented, capable man, but he was such a larger-than-life figure that she could not imagine how he would adapt to a lesser existence or cope with the limitations imposed on him.

Chapter Twenty-One

After Sheffield, Charley's relationship with Vere changed subtly. At the theatre he treated her with more equality and respect, but off the stage he seemed to avoid her intentionally, as if afraid that she might mention the Melton affair. She knew that he must be desperate for money. The tour and the letting of the theatre had helped, but large sums were needed to mount the lavish spectacles he planned for this, the 1886–7 season. If only he knew, she thought as he raised his hat to her and hurried past on his way to another meeting or to the Garrick Club, that, but for her, Peter Frith-Tempest would also have jumped ship.

'You received my letter?' Charley had asked him.

That letter had been uppermost in her mind since she and Peter were reunited and had fallen into bed. Indeed, it had been on her mind constantly since she despatched it from Sheffield weeks ago. They were now in her room above the Strand, having made love in a comfortable and satisfying way, rather like an old married couple. There was no eroticism or sexual tension between them, but neither were there any recriminations or acrimony. Drinking wine that Peter had brought with him and dining on game pie and potatoes delivered, piping hot, from a nearby hostelry, Charley felt that this was the right time to broach the subject of the letter and its contents.

'Good stuff, this,' enthused Peter, helping himself to another generous slice of pie. 'Reminds me of my childhood. The nursery food was appalling, but a kind housemaid used to slip me a portion of whatever they had in the servants' hall. To me, that good, plain grub was a damn sight more tasty than anything my parents put on their own dining table.'

'Must be nice to have the choice,' Charley said with some asperity. 'Most of us have to eat plain food or nothing at all.'

'Sorry, no offence meant.'

'So did you get my letter and, if so, did you understand it?'

'I received it all right but it was bloody cryptic, especially given your usual forthright approach.'

'Have you spoken to Lord Melton recently?'

'Funny you should mention that because, no, he and Aunt Babs have done a vanishing act. Shaken the dust of London off their feet and taken Celia with them.'

'So you are not aware that your Uncle Reggie has withdrawn his backing from The Cavendish?'

'Good God, has he? Are you sure? So that is why you said in the letter that I must not change my position *vis-à-vis* The Cavendish without consulting you.'

'Can you keep a secret? Silly question – of course you will *say* that you can, but I promise you, Peter, if a word of this leaks out, I will cut off your most vital appendage with the bluntest instrument I can find.'

Peter obliged with a suitably exaggerated shudder. 'Discretion is my middle name – correction, first name. Go on, please, I cannot stand the suspense.'

'Celia Melton decided that she wanted to marry Vere

Cavendish and ran away from home, turning up in Vere's hotel room in Sheffield.' Talking quickly, as an expression of horror settled on Peter's face, she went on: 'Naturally he called me and I spent the night with Celia, but the wretched girl did everything but shout rape when the irate parents arrived next morning. Being unimpressed by the truth, well, you can imagine how your Uncle Reggie and Aunt Babs reacted, particularly as Aunt Babs has been trying to unbutton Vere's trousers for years.'

'Charley!'

'It's true. Don't be so naive, Peter. Even silly Celia managed to work that one out. Mind you, for one apparently brain-damaged at birth, she shows a certain native cunning from time to time.'

'Steady on, she's sort of a cousin of mine.'

'Sorry,' Charley said sweetly, 'no offence meant.'

'Celia would not run away from home and inveigle her way into a man's bedroom,' Peter expostulated.

'Yes, she would, if that man was Vere Cavendish. You know her better than most people – have you never suspected she had a crush on him?'

Peter remembered the business of Eleanor's ride in the park, and grimaced. Yes, it was entirely feasible that Celia's childish infatuation had persisted.

'He never touched her, Peter, you have my word on it. She was in her nightdress and hair down to her waist – talk about Miss Seduction of 1886 – but he was fully dressed and, when he called me, had just come in from the theatre. It was not his fault. The entire fiasco was the result of Celia's romantic imagination.'

'That is difficult to believe and even more difficult to prove,' said Peter, his lawyer's brain at work. 'I can well understand why Uncle Reggie is severing all ties, and I am more than half-convinced that I should do the same.'

'Please don't,' Charley begged. 'I repeat that Vere was not to blame and, if you withdraw your support, the whole company will suffer. Why should a hundred or more people lose their jobs because one silly spoiled girl indulges in melodrama!'

He pushed aside his plateful of pie, having lost his appetite, and said nothing. Eventually he heaved a deep sigh. 'If you put it like that.' But his tone revealed deep reservations.

'I do, and I hope that you will put it like that if Uncle Reggie brings pressure to bear. Please, Peter, don't close The Cavendish, and don't let on that you know about Celia's escapade – because an escapade is all it was, I promise. Come on, my darling, would I lie to you?'

'I think you are capable of anything,' he said, laughing.

'Even capable of managing my own theatre one day?'

'I will be first in the queue to provide the required finance. Give me a preview of your prospectus. What will be your main objective?'

'Lavatories,' Charley replied promptly. 'Good, clean, hygienic backstage lavatories, and enough of them to serve the needs of all the cast and stage staff.'

Peter shook his head and, laughing, surveyed her over the rim of his wine glass. 'You are incorrigible, and I hope that you always will be. *But . . .*'

At his hesitation, Charley flaunted a brave smile. 'It isn't that I want anything personal. I would find another job, somewhere, some time, but others in the company might not be so lucky.'

'*But,*' Peter emphasised again, 'I am by no means convinced that Vere Cavendish is entirely blameless and, although I will not withdraw my backing at the present time, he remains on probation.'

So Peter – and Ernest Meyer, although Charley could

not claim the credit for that – remained on board, yet the season did not start well. The box office was at its lowest ebb since Marion's illness eighteen months before. Perhaps the Meltons were exerting an insidious influence from Italy, or was the public bored with the existing repertoire? After the success of the tour, a faint feeling of ennui began to seep into the warp and weft of The Cavendish and into its company, and the source of this disillusion could be traced to, and the blame laid fairly and squarely on the shoulders of, Vere Cavendish.

Charley knew that he was drinking. She could see the whisky bottle in his dressing room and smell the liquor on his breath, giving her an odd but insistent impression of her father. However, it did not seem to affect his work. Rehearsing the *Shrew* by day and playing the repertoire by night was a tough schedule, for Vere especially, but he showed no discernible signs of stress. It was merely that somewhere a spark was missing, from his personality and from his artistry and inventiveness.

Sensing that he was only going through the motions on the stage every night, Charley tried to give more. With that extra ounce of her own sparkle, she coaxed, cajoled and challenged him into a response, using her energy to fan the flame inside him until it began to burn more brightly once again. As it did so, and rehearsals for the *Shrew* were invigorated at the same time, a familiar sensation revived and stirred within her. She wanted him again. The old sexual chemistry reawakened, glazing her eyes but not blinding her to his faults.

They were ideally matched in the *Shrew*, the short, fast exchanges between Petruchio and Katharina rattling between them like gunfire. Against Charley's fiery intransigence, Vere was a charming suitor who became utterly convincing, almost frightening, in Petruchio's pretence of being an ill-tempered despot in his own home. Yet when Petruchio appeared to be the victor in the fight for supremacy, Charley managed to convey the impression that she was not cowed into submission but, having fallen in love with the man, was allowing him to believe he had won. There was an indefinable tongue-in-cheek element in her acquiescence, and particularly in her rendition of Katharina's final speech.

As the sparks began to fly between Vere and Charley on the stage, the spirits of the entire company lifted and optimism about the success of the season grew. The only weak spot in the preparations for the new production was the casting of Bianca, the young actress being pretty enough in a vacuous sort of way but strangely two-dimensional. Unresponsive to advice and impervious to insult, while Vere's sarcasm passed clean over her head, she was a problem not only because of her shortcomings in this role but because Vere feared she would be equally unsatisfactory in the other parts planned for her later in the season.

'I must have been mad to hire her in the first place,' he fumed to Bert Harding. 'Was I blind drunk when I auditioned her and, if I was, why didn't you stop me?'

'She does a very nice audition,' Bert replied equably. 'The trouble is, that is all she does nicely.'

'She'll have to go. We must replace her. But Bert, Bert, where do I find a new Bianca and a new Esther Eccles for *Caste*?'

Bert looked across to where Charley was talking to Edward Druce, who was making an excellent job of Bianca's suitor Lucentio. 'Marion Leigh could be a bit difficult at times,' he said slowly, 'too much on her dignity and too quick to climb on her high horse and ride off in a huff. But by God, Chief, the combination of

Marion and Charley would be a marriage made in heaven.'

'My thoughts exactly. I raised the possibility of Marion joining the tour, but mentioning Marion to Charley is like showing a red rag to a bull. Don't ask me why – I thought sisters were usually thick as thieves, loyal to the last and all that.' Vere sighed, with a blend of thoughtfulness and irritation. 'Does anyone ever hear from Marion?' he asked suddenly, 'because it would be interesting to know how her school is prospering.'

'Not that I am aware,' Bert said doubtfully. 'If it is not tactful to approach Charley, young Druce might be able to help. I seem to recall him mentioning that he was close to Marion at one time.'

'Really? Thanks, Bert . . .'

Later the same day Vere summoned Edward Druce to a conference, but it was not the professional elucidation of Lucentio that Edward expected.

'In the strictest confidence, Druce, I want to know if you retain any contact with Marion Leigh.'

'I tried to renew our friendship. When she and Frances set up the school, I went to see them, but Marion – well, it was more Frances really – showed me the door, in no uncertain manner. I don't think it was anything personal. It was the theatrical connection that they were determined to break.'

'Where is this school?' Vere asked casually and made a mental note of the address that Druce gave him. 'Is it doing well?'

'You seem very interested.'

'My interest is purely in a former colleague who left the company in unfortunate circumstances. Naturally I am concerned for her welfare.'

'That's frightfully decent of you.' Edward was genuinely

impressed. 'I have not dared to go back, but I can tell you who is up-to-date with the situation – Peter Frith-Tempest. Unlike us poor players, he was not banished to the wilderness. On the contrary, he has probably been cultivated as a source of prestige and a conduit to suitable pupils.'

'I might have a word next time I see him,' Vere said off-handedly, 'yet I don't want to push in where I am not wanted. It merely occurred to me to let Marion know that she is always welcome to return to The Cavendish, if playing schoolma'am is not living up to expectations.'

'If there is anything I can do to help achieve that, just let me know,' Edward said fervently. 'To have Marion as Bianca instead of this stick – sorry, Chief, but she is – would be fantastic. And before you ask, don't worry, I will not say a word to Charley.'

'Did Marion or Frances mention why the theatrical connection is anathema?'

'I gathered that the youngest sisters, the twins, were expelled from school because the authorities there were informed of the family's theatrical activities.'

'Such pig-ignorance is really appalling,' but Vere's expression was more thoughtful than indignant.

Despite his busy schedule, Vere drove out to the school and sat in the cab opposite the gates watching the comings and goings. He was in position early enough to see the pupils arriving, some on foot accompanied by mothers or maids, some delivered by carriage, and some in carriages that bore a coat of arms on the door. Vere was not sufficiently versed in heraldry to recognise any of the insignia, but he was well able to recognise that the school was doing well and that, bearing in mind that a proportion of the pupils were boarders, the Leigh sisters must be making a fair-to-middling living from the venture.

During the drive back to the Strand, Vere's gaze was blank and unfocused, his expression more sober and grim than ever before. He knew exactly how he could coerce Marion back to The Cavendish and even how to persuade Charley to accept her sister's presence, but the means of achieving this miracle was foul, not fair, and he hesitated to do it. Yet he wanted Marion back so badly that the plan continued to dominate his thoughts. A long time ago he had described Marion as his 'lucky charm' and, although he considered himself more pragmatic and less superstitious than most, he had come to believe that those days had indeed been charmed and that, with Marion and Charley together on his stage, the good times would return.

With his conscience putting up a spirited resistance, Vere might not have put his plan into operation, had not fate intervened by throwing into his path, as he stepped out of the cab in the Strand, the person of Peter Frith-Tempest. Having breakfasted with Charley, Peter was escorting her to the theatre for the day's rehearsals. Vere, ignorant of their personal lives and not really seeing Charley at all at that precise moment, fixed Peter with such an odd look that the other man faltered in his stride and returned the look quizzically.

'Anything wrong, old man?' he inquired.

'Wrong? No, no, nothing at all. My mind was a million miles away. Come in for a moment, if you can spare the time.'

With his usual good humour, Peter complied and, after bidding a discreet farewell to Charley, sat down in Vere's office.

'I hesitate to ask Charley about her sisters as there seems to be some ill-feeling between them,' Vere explained again, 'but I believe you keep in touch with Marion.'

'Strictly between ourselves,' Peter said confidentially.

'She would not want you or Charley to know about it.'

'She was on my mind, because I happened to pass the school this morning and I was pleased to see so many pupils converging on the place.'

'Happily I was able to help a little in that direction. Governesses are becoming a trifle *déclassé* in certain circles, particularly for older girls, and the notion of sending daughters to a genteel seminary where they could learn everything from English and elocution to piano, painting and posture proved a winner.'

'That would explain the carriage traffic,' Vere said with an effortlessly casual smile.

'You probably saw my young cousins, the Mannering girls. Then there are the daughters of Lord Rochford, and the Courtenay-Hardys . . .'

'Good heavens, it seems that Marion will be responsible for an entire generation of débutantes. I take it that she has recovered fully from the fever?'

'One hundred per cent,' Peter assured him. 'Her hair has not yet grown back to its former length, but it is as thick and black and glossy as before, and altogether she is in fine form.'

As yet another piece of information fell into his lap, and his slight unease over Marion's physical fitness and appearance was allayed, Vere seemed to be propelled along a path by forces outside his own control. He did not go out of his way to invite the Mannerings and the Courtenay-Hardys to the opening-night party for the *Shrew*, but his eyes were drawn to their names on Ramsey's list as if by a magnet. At the party he found himself gravitating towards them entirely naturally and without conscious effort.

'You are too kind,' he said, accepting their congratulations on his performance, 'but much of our success tonight is due to my leading lady. You really must meet Miss Leigh. You will be enchanted by her.'

'She seems remarkably talented for one so young,' Mrs Mannering observed.

'Perhaps it's in the blood – she comes from a theatrical family. A most interesting story, which she will be delighted to relate to you,' and, moving away, he beckoned Charley. 'The Mannerings have asked, most particularly, to meet you, so do be nice to them. They are cousins of Frith-Tempest and I don't want any more crises over finance.'

'Right-oh,' Charley said cheerfully and went across to do her duty. Almost immediately Mrs Mannering raised the matter of the theatrical family background. 'I would not go so far as to say that,' Charley replied. 'Apart from myself, only my two elder sisters have been in the theatre.'

'I remember a Marion Leigh,' Mrs Mannering exclaimed. 'Where is she appearing now? Not in London, surely, or I would have seen her.'

'She gave up the stage and became a schoolmistress,' Charley said innocently, having completely forgotten the implications of such a remark.

There was a moment's silence as the Mannerings, who had been joined by their friends, the Courtenay-Hardys, exchanged horrified looks.

'Where is this school exactly?' Mrs Mannering asked slowly.

Charley told them and, puzzled, watched the colour drain from several faces and rise to puce in others.

'But I interviewed Miss Leigh,' Mrs Mannering was squeaking, 'and she didn't look or behave like an actress.'

'It was Miss Frances who met the parents,' Mrs Courtenay-Hardy said stonily, 'and I was positive she reminded me of someone.'

'This is Peter's doing. Where the hell is he?' Mr Courtenay-Hardy wanted to know.

'Do you realise, Sarah,' Mrs Courtenay-Hardy was saying to Mrs Mannering, 'that our daughters are being educated by a pair of *actresses*.'

'Our girls are not setting foot in the place again. Heaven alone knows what sort of habits they have been picking up, and we can only hope that we have rescued them before irreparable damage has been done.'

'Now hang on a minute, what are you implying?' Charley began heatedly, but was interrupted by the arrival of an unsuspecting Peter Frith-Tempest.

'You recommended that school to us,' Mr Mannering accused. 'You said that the Miss Leighs were known to you, and not unnaturally we assumed them to be ladies. How dare you introduce . . .'

Charley was not listening to the rest of the tirade. She was staring incredulously at Peter. Stepping forward and interrupting Mr Mannering in full flow, she jabbed a finger hard into Peter's chest. 'You know Marion? You actually tout for business for that blasted school . . . Does that mean you have seen her recently?'

'Not that recently. Not for several weeks, as a matter of fact.'

'Weeks!' Charley's voice rivalled that of Mrs Mannering in its shrillness. 'I will see you in my dressing room *now*,' and she stalked off the stage.

But Peter was not permitted to follow her immediately. By the time he did reach her dressing room, he knew that the Leigh sisters' enterprise was irretrievably damaged. Not every parent would be appalled by the theatrical connection, but a majority would be, and the minority would feel obliged to be *seen* to be appalled.

By the time he left Charley, he was certain that their

relationship was irretrievably damaged as well. On his way out of the theatre he passed the open door of Vere's office and was called inside.

'I blame myself,' Peter groaned, sinking into a chair and accepting a whisky. 'I ought not to have encouraged my frightful relatives to attend the première tonight.'

'No, I am at fault for inviting them to the party,' Vere said unhappily, 'but they were on Ramsey's list and I thought . . . Well, I ought to have foreseen that Charley would speak to them.'

'No, I ought to have pre-empted the meeting.' Peter shook his head in despair. 'Marion and her school were my responsibility, not yours.'

'If Marion had not caught typhoid in my theatre, there might not have been a school. Look, mutual recriminations are not going to save Marion and her sisters. What we ought to be doing is working out how we can help.'

'Right now, I seem devoid of ideas.'

'I am not feeling inspired myself – it has been a rather exhausting day – but funnily enough something that was said to me earlier could prove prescient. I know, you know, everyone knows that Bianca is a disaster. What you need, this chap said to me, is Marion Leigh in the role.'

Peter jerked upright in his chair and his face brightened. 'Who says you are not inspired. That is a brilliant idea!'

'Would she come back to the theatre?'

'I think so,' Peter said slowly, 'but Frances would never allow it and, believe me, Frances rules that roost with the proverbial rod of iron.'

'After tonight Frances is not in a strong bargaining position,' Vere pointed out. 'Even Frances needs a roof over her head and, unless there is something that you and I do not know, Marion's return to the stage may be the sisters' only means of survival.'

'I could sound her out, go round to sympathise, explain and apologise . . .'

'No,' Vere said sharply. 'Never explain or apologise. Just tell Marion that a most unfortunate set of circumstances caused the Mannerings to connect them with the Leighs of The Cavendish. Whatever you do, don't tell her about Charley's part in this or she will never agree to appear here with her sister.'

'And if I manage to persuade Marion, who will coax Charley into co-operating? Don't look at me, Cavendish – I'll take care of Marion, but at the moment I am Charley's least favourite person in the world and have no influence whatsoever in that direction.'

'Leave Charley to me.'

Vere smiled confidently at his companion and raised his glass in salute. Everything was working out splendidly. As he had hoped, Frith-Tempest had offered of his own volition to intervene with Marion - Vere knew that if he, Vere, asked her to return to The Cavendish, she would refuse out of sheer pride and principle. As for Charley, he gathered that there had been a relationship of sorts between her and Frith-Tempest and its abrupt end played right into his hands. He thought that he could handle Charley, in fact it would be a pleasure. It was really wonderful how the expediency of the situation coincided so exactly with his own wishes. This conjunction of motives made him feel that what he was doing was destined for success. Vere really did believe that he was doing this for everyone's good.

After Peter had left, he went to his dressing room and, seeing the light streaming beneath Charley's door, paused and knocked.

'Come,' a muffled voice said.

She was sitting at the dressing-table, obviously close to tears.

'Why so sad? You were wonderful this evening,' and he stood behind her, his hands on her shoulders, smiling at her in the mirror.

'That bastard! He was making love to me, while all the time he was sneaking off to Marion behind my back!'

'You don't mean that he is Marion's lover?' For a moment, even Vere was disconcerted.

'He says not. He *says* they have never been lovers, that they are only friends. But in a way the actual extent of the relationship is not as important as the fact that he was seeing Marion without telling me, and that he was Marion's friend long before he was mine.'

'Why should the past bother you so much?'

'Wherever I go, Marion was there. Whatever I do, Marion did before me. All the time I feel I am being compared with her, unfavourably, that people are saying that she is prettier than me, and cleverer than me, and more talented than me. I just want to be myself, not a bloody Leigh sister! This drama tonight would not have happened, had someone not asked me about my blasted family. I ought never to have come to London – I ought to have stayed with Dan Crisp, where no one gave a damn about my sisters and where I could go on being myself.'

Vere let her talk, in the hope that she was talking it out of her system, and then he leaned down so that his face was level with hers in the mirror. She was still wearing her Katharina costume and, with infinite gentleness, his fingers caressed the smooth skin of her bare shoulders. He laid his cheek against hers, holding her gaze in the mirror.

'You will always be yourself,' he said, sincerely, 'to me

and to everyone else. If you think that anyone, in this company or beyond, sees you as a pale imitation of Marion, then you are very much mistaken. You possess your own personality and you display it – I might almost say *flaunt* it – to great effect.' He pressed his lips into the curve of her neck and felt her tremble. 'I did not know that Frith-Tempest meant so much to you. I am sorry if you are upset, if love . . .'

'Who said anything about love?' Charley burst out indignantly. 'I was not in love with him, or he with me. I doubt very much if he is *in love* with Marion. No, what he has betrayed is friendship and loyalty, and I will never forgive him.'

'I hope that you will, for both your sakes. Life is too short to harbour grudges.'

'Especially if it is a grudge against one of your business associates.'

He smiled appreciatively. 'I know that I have said this before, but you are delightful and I adore you.'

'You have never said that you adored me.'

'Most remiss of me. Consider it emphasised over and over again,' and his lips crept slowly and sensuously up her neck towards her cheek. 'It's happening again, isn't it . . . Those feelings between us . . .'

'I have my feelings under perfect control, thank you.' Charley tried to pull away but he was holding her too tightly against him. 'We have trodden this road before, remember, and it ended in tears. So if you think that I will fall into your arms merely because you have a vacancy, think again.'

'You have a vacancy, too,' he reminded her, 'and do remember, darling girl, that when we trod this road before I was engaged to be married.' He kissed her cheek and stood up. 'I am not engaged to be married now.'

And, with that tantalising reminder of his availability, he left her.

The next performance of the *Shrew* was torture for Charley, as the sexual tension flexed and stretched between them. The look in his eyes, the sound of his voice, the special note that voice seemed to hold just for her . . . He was doing it on purpose, teasing her, seducing her in front of a full house. She fought against him more fiercely than Katharina ever resisted Petruchio; damn it, she was not a pushover, an easy lay who would come running when the great lover crooked his little finger!

But he was so irresistibly attractive, so ideally suited to costume pieces. They were splendidly matched, both far above average height, Charley with her flaming hair and sumptuous brocaded gowns of russet and rich autumnal hues, Vere in Petruchio's flamboyant velvets. Yet it was his plainest costume that moved her most – the white shirt open nearly to the waist with full sleeves gathered at the cuff, the tight black trousers, wide leather belt and high polished boots; not historically accurate, perhaps, but the attire that suited him best and which thousands of women paid good money to see him wear. For Charley, standing close to him, touching him and touched by him, seeing the perspiration dampening his chest hair, the sight and sound and *smell* of him in that simple costume were almost too much to bear.

But bear it she did. Summoning her dresser and refusing to receive visitors, she changed rapidly into her own clothes and fled the theatre while, the door of his room slightly ajar, Vere watched her flight.

Approaching the following night's performance with even greater trepidation, Charley was unhappily aware of an element of capitulation. She took unusual pains over her own appearance, washing her hair and having it dressed with particular care, applying perfume strategically. More significant was the mingled fear and hope that the sexual chemistry would have dissolved overnight, and the terror and relief she experienced when she discovered that it was still there. Afterwards, and she could not imagine how he managed it, he was waiting in her dressing room, leaning against the wall with his arms crossed and a look of lazy appraisal in his eyes.

Without a word he reached out his arms and enfolded her, and his mouth devoured her. No stage kiss this, such as they had exchanged countless times, but hard, bruising, urgent. Clinging together, they sought to probe deep inside each other, breathing in short, sharp gasps, murmuring inarticulately as their bodies swivelled and it was Charley who was rammed against the wall. As their tongues intertwined, emulating the more intimate coupling they desired, Charley could feel the pressure of his erection against her groin, as his fingers slid from the small of her back to clasp the curve of her buttocks and pull her even closer and harder against him.

And then, still without saying a word, he released her and left her. Deserting the field? Charley thought not. Weak-kneed, she understood, or hoped she understood, his message. He was as strong, or stronger, than she. Last night she had fled, and therefore tonight he had repaid her in kind – just as Petruchio repaid Katharina – but he departed with the added message, the taunt, of that kiss.

That night, naked in her bed, she pressed her body into the mattress, aware of the swell of her breasts and the pointed peaks of the nipples, the flatness of her stomach and the jagged edge of the hip-bones, the long, long length of her legs. She wanted him so much that she knew she would have no peace until he touched her.

On the third night she looked at him and she knew that he knew, as the flame licked between them, that tonight she was his. While her mind was lulled into a half-dreaming state, her body felt extraordinarily sensitive. Her heart was thudding at the base of her throat and she struggled to control her breathing, but every inch of her was tactile, luxuriating in the swish of silk against her legs, her fingers lingering on the smoothness of a glass, aware of her own body as never before. When Petruchio bade her 'kiss me, Kate', their lips fused with such a passion for such an eternity that a *frisson* of shock rippled round the theatre.

'I will walk you home,' he said as they left the stage, and he was waiting outside her door after she had changed. Gripping her arm, he steered her swiftly into the street and along the Strand to her lodgings, clamping her so tightly against him that their bodies moved in unison. They did not speak or look at each other, not even when Charley fumbled blindly for her key before opening the door. Preceding him up the stairs, she was suddenly swamped by panic: suppose this was the most terrible mistake, what if . . . But then he was standing in front of her, easing off her cloak and his fingers brushed her breast, and they fell on each other ravenously.

Here, in this embrace, was no gentleness or tenderness, only raw hunger that demanded to be satisfied. Mouths wide and welded together, tongues deep, hands and fingers groping as they stripped each other of clothes, leaving the garments where they fell, they stumbled towards the bed. Tearing his lips from hers, he bent his head to kiss her breasts and take her nipples in his mouth, the big glossy brown tips peaking as his tongue swirled over them, and Charley stretched and arched her back as she felt that kick, that tug of desire, deep inside her.

Collapsing on the bed, she ran her hands over him,

through his dark hair, down his neck, across the broad shoulders and muscled back, down to the tight buttocks and firm thighs, all the time breathing in, drinking in, the individual erotic smell of him. Straining against him, their bodies growing hot and slippery with sweat, she thought she was aroused and ready, but then found that as yet she had only just begun to feel desire and to learn how deep desire could be. The hard sweetness of his erection moved against her thigh and she reached down to hold it. How beautiful it was, how immense and glorious, and she heard him gasp as her fingers caressed him. Squirming down in the bed, Charley tried to change position so that she could take him in her mouth, but he restrained her.

'If you do that, this is going to be over before it has begun,' he muttered harshly, 'and you and I have waited too long for this moment to waste it.'

Pinning her against the pillows, his fingertips traced an erotic outline, creeping down to the red-gold triangle and lingering there, tantalising her until she parted her legs and silently begged him to continue. The fingers probed along the moist cleft and, as they began to caress, she frantically sought his mouth again. She had not known that such a hunger, such a wanting, was possible. Her whole body was an aching, craving void crying out to be filled, by him and only by him. As the swirls of sensation spiralled within her, Charley could bear it no longer and, with a sudden thrust, she dislodged his hand.

'No, *no*, that isn't what I want. I want you inside me,' and she eased herself beneath him. For a moment she looked up into that dark face above her, into those midnight eyes as he leaned over her, positioning himself between her legs; and she stayed poised on a knife-edge of anticipation, before closing her eyes as she felt the tip of his penis and the rapture as he entered her in a long, slow slide, which penetrated her more deeply than anything she had experienced before. Abandoning herself to the agonising ecstasy of his thrusts, Charley wanted it to last, wanted to control it for as long as possible, but here Vere was in command, driving deeper and deeper and lifting her to an early shuddering, screaming orgasm, her vaginal muscles squeezing and clamping on him so violently that it seemed impossible he could continue. But he stayed hard, almost implacable inside her, and as she went limp he began to move again and Charley responded to his rhythm, their slippery bodies slapping together, their mouths meeting as hungrily as their groins, each amazed by the uniqueness of the other. For just as Charley had never known such a lover before, neither had Vere experienced a woman with Charley's uninhibited passion.

She came again, and again, in a tumultuous series of orgasms, exploding in his arms, but never did she ask him to stop, not once did she indicate that she had had enough. Her hair dark with sweat, that long, white, blue-veined body pulsing beneath him, she challenged him to defeat her. Once he paused, in order to wrap her legs around him and he kissed her inner thighs and ran his hands down her calves, before renewing his assault. Then she sensed a change in him, and his breathing and those remorseless thrusts quickened, driving her to a peak so all-encompassing that she screamed and dug her nails into his flesh, and she felt his body tense as he gathered himself and the ensuing convulsion flung them both into momentary blackness.

Charley accepted his weight as he collapsed against her and lay limp, breathing hard, dripping sweat. She lifted her hands and pushed some damp, bedraggled strands of hair out of her eyes and then did the same for him, tenderly but with a matter-of-factness as well. These were no sentimental lovers. Being sexually mature, they were aware of the uniqueness of the experience they had shared, which their bodies had created, and yet they did not cling together with sweet murmurings of love. They knew, Vere and Charley, exactly what they had done, and they knew that they would do it again, and again, but neither of them knew where it led, this road, this relationship they had embarked upon.

'It's like a death, isn't it,' Charley murmured thoughtfully, tracing the contour of his cheek with her forefinger, 'an orgasm, I mean. A little death, of course, but do you suppose a lot of little deaths add up to one big one?'

Vere smiled at her indulgently but, suddenly, Charley shivered as an icy chill of foreboding ran through her. In response to his inquiry, she only laughed and shook her head.

'Nothing's the matter. It was just someone walking over my grave.'

But she lay back on the pillow and kissed him with an urgency and a tenderness that betrayed an unprecedented depth of emotion.

Chapter Twenty-Two

The worst of the tears and recriminations was over by the time Peter arrived, but the atmosphere reeked of bitterness and hostility. Marion and Frances received him in the sitting room at the back of the house, comfortably furnished with shabby sofas and chairs, where the family gathered in the evenings and where specialist teachers were welcomed for tea. The two sisters listened in silence to his faltering explanation and, despite Vere's stricture, to his apology.

'The Mannerings and the Courtenay-Hardys attended a party at The Cavendish,' Frances exclaimed, her face deathly pale, 'and you did not try to stop them!'

'I didn't think . . .'

'And Charley was there. You fool!'

'Frances, please . . .' begged Marion.

'Probably Charley told them, on purpose and out of sheer spite.'

'Charley said nothing,' Peter lied desperately. 'The Mannerings sort of jumped to conclusions.'

'Did they jump or were they pushed?' Frances asked scornfully.

'Does it really matter?' Marion said wearily. 'The end result is the same, no matter how the damage was done.'

'It might not matter to you, because you never wanted

this school, but my dreams have been smashed, my hard work has come to nothing, and my happiness is ruined. So, yes, it does matter, it matters to me very much indeed.'

A timid knock at the door announced the entrance of a small maid, her face streaked with tears over her imminent loss of employment, who informed them that a carriage had come to collect one of the boarding pupils.

Frances rose and smoothed her skirt, her back ramrod-straight. 'I will say goodbye to Anne and see her off. It means enduring the patronising stare of the servant or minor relative who has been sent to escort her home, but one must do these things properly.'

Peter was standing at the window, staring out at the rainswept garden as the wind sent little flurries of fallen leaves scudding across the grass. In the dusk of the late afternoon, light glowed in a nearby window and, pressing his face close to the windowpane, he strained to detect any signs of activity in the room.

'Maria Scarlatti,' Marion explained, joining him at the window, 'is giving an Italian lesson.'

'I thought all the pupils had gone.'

'After Anne's departure today, only one girl will be left. Maria is teaching Italian to the twins.'

'I would love to meet the twins some day,' Peter remarked, turning away from the window and walking back to the fire. 'You make such a mystery of them, keeping them out of sight, as though there is something terribly wrong with one of them.'

'It is what is *right* about one of them that makes the mystery! Believe me, Peter, if I had a garret in which I could lock Arabella, or if I could put her to sleep until the prince kisses her awake, then I would. That is what terrifies me most about our present predicament: what on earth am I going to do with the twins?'

'It was you I wanted to talk about.'

'Me? Oh, I'm past hope. Don't worry about me.'

'They still talk about you at The Cavendish.'

'You don't have to flatter me, and try to make me feel better by saying all the right things. Frances is right – I never wanted this school. In fact, as she is not here to hear me say it, I will admit that I have detested every day. But I owed Frances a debt of gratitude and it was a living, and a roof . . .'

'The Cavendish would have you back like a shot. You need only say the word.'

'To whom?'

'To me. And I will tell Cavendish that you are available.'

'Available.' Marion laughed harshly. 'Yes, that about sums it up. I am not going to pretend that I haven't thought about going back to the stage – I have thought about it every day since I left! But The Cavendish! I don't know about that. Vere and Charley . . . Oh no, Peter, I'm not at all sure about that.'

'You can be sure that I will protect your interests. Your money worries would be over – I'd see to that. And in all fairness, Vere is a very reasonable man and the roles are perfect for you. They are doing the *Shrew* . . .'

'I know,' Marion cut in. 'I sneaked a glance at the notices while Frances wasn't looking. Vere wants me for Bianca, I assume?'

Peter nodded. 'At the party on opening night, your name was on everyone's lips.'

'Was it? Was it *really*?' Her face lit up. 'But even if I agreed . . . Peter, look at me and tell me honestly: do I still look like Marion Leigh?'

Yes, he thought, and then again, no. His affection for her was undiminished and his continuous acquaintance with her made it difficult to judge in any detached and analytical fashion. Her hair had not regained its former glory but, on the stage, wigs would conceal its deficiencies. The face was still lovely, the brilliant eyes and the glorious complexion overcoming a weariness and sadness of expression. It was her figure that had altered most; the breasts were voluptuous but the waist had thickened, making her appear shorter and dumpier than before.

'You are as lovely as ever,' he said.

But his brief hesitation had not passed unnoticed. 'I will lose weight as soon as I start acting again,' Marion said quickly.

'So I can tell Cavendish that you are avail . . . willing to return?'

'I have no choice. The theatre is my only means of earning a living.'

Having waved a dignified farewell to Anne, Frances crossed the hall and started up the stairs. Halfway up she paused and looked around her, her fingers stroking the smooth wood of the carved balustrade. It was not only the loss of her beloved academy that she felt so keenly, but the loss of this house as well. At times, particularly during the school holidays when only a couple of pupils remained on the premises, she had almost been able to believe that this was her own home, with rooms arranged elegantly for entertaining, visited only by family and friends. Although the closure of the school had meant many things to many people, for a number of reasons Frances was devastated and no one felt the loss as acutely as she did.

Yet there was one possible exception; there was one person in the house who, in her way, felt as lost, lonely and afraid as Frances.

When Frances found her in the empty classroom,

having first searched the deserted dormitories, the girl was kneeling on the window seat, her nose squashed against the glass as she stared at the gates through which Anne's carriage had driven. Lucia Gresham was ten years old, stick-thin and very pale, with abundant chestnut hair and immense, solemn brown eyes. Alone of all the pupils, she had not been sent for by her family. Her father, a widower, lived in the country and as yet he had not replied to Frances's letter advising him of the closure of the school.

'There's only me left now, isn't there?' Lucia asked, with a wobble in her voice.

Frances nodded, trying to smile. 'I have not heard from your father, but perhaps he is away. He travels a lot, doesn't he, which is why he wanted you to be a boarder here.'

'He wanted to get rid of me, and he won't want me to go home because I'll only be in the way again.'

'Nonsense, Lucia,' Frances exclaimed. 'I am sure that he loves you dearly and wants only the best for you.'

'Please can't I stay with you? I will be very good, and very quiet, and you will hardly know I'm here.'

'But no one can stay here, not even me.'

'Then take me with you,' Lucia begged. 'You don't know what it's like at home. There is no one to talk to, and nothing to do, and I don't have any friends.'

'I am sure that you are exaggerating,' said Frances firmly, but her heart ached and when Lucia burst into tears, she put her arms around the girl and hugged her close.

Lucia's mother had studied singing with Maria Scarlatti and, after her marriage to Thomas Gresham, she had kept in touch with her former teacher until her death five years ago. The girl had inherited her mother's musical gifts but, although she sang well, her true talent was for the piano.

Out of all the pupils she had ever taught, Lucia had become Frances's firm favourite. She had tried not to let her preference for this gifted, sweet-tempered, lonely child be noticed, but Lucia responded so warmly to the rapport between them that there was no denying their mutual affection. Lucia's lessons were the high point of Frances's day, and the holidays were all the more enjoyable because Lucia, due to her father's frequent absences from home, usually remained at school. Frances felt closer to Lucia, in body and spirit, than she did to her sisters and part of Frances's overwhelming desolation was due to her forthcoming separation from the child and to the guilt she felt at somehow having let her down.

Life could be a real bastard, thought Frances fiercely, as she tried to comfort the weeping girl. It was so unfair that one worked hard and tried to do the right thing and found someone to love and then, through no fault of one's own, one lost everything.

Hand in hand, Frances and Lucia went to the kitchen to order tea to be served in the sitting room.

'There will be seven for tea,' Frances told the maid and, still referring to Marion by the name that she used at the school, she went on: 'including Miss Mary's guest.'

'The gentleman has just left, miss.'

Frances thought for a moment and, sending Lucia to join Maria and the twins, she rejoined her sister. One look at Marion's face, at the light in her eyes and the sudden energy and life in her movements, was enough.

'You are going back to the theatre, aren't you!' Frances said bitterly. 'He has persuaded you – not that you needed much persuading! But not to The Cavendish . . . Please God, Marion, tell me that you are not going back to The Cavendish!'

'I must . . .'

There was no need to say more. Both knew the arguments for and against, both had heard the other's viewpoint a thousand times. In the ensuing silence Frances's eyes alighted on a heap of letters lying on the table.

'You didn't tell me that the post had come,' and she crossed the room and began riffling through the envelopes.

'It arrived earlier. You were too busy being beastly to Peter to notice.'

With trembling hands Frances held a letter she had been expecting, addressed in a firm, masculine hand, and after a moment's hesitation she opened it.

'From Lucia Gresham's father, I hope?' Marion inquired.

'He expresses regret at the unfortunate turn of events and says that he will be in a position to receive Lucia at the weekend. He would be grateful if a school representative could escort her on the train as far as his local station, where a carriage will be waiting, and offers overnight accommodation at his home to that representative before she makes the return journey.'

'I couldn't possibly . . .' Marion began.

'I shall travel with Lucia,' Frances cut in, 'naturally.'

'He doesn't know about . . . What did you tell him?'

'I simply said that the school was closing down due to unforeseen financial difficulties. Perfectly true, in its way. Fortunately, his way of life, and the distance between here and his home, make it unlikely that the rumours concerning our lurid past need ever reach him.'

'You hope.'

'Don't you?'

But Marion only shrugged and turned away, her thoughts already in the West End with Vere and Charley.

Frances crossed her fingers and offered up a silent prayer. Please, let Mr Gresham and his daughter remain in ignorance of the truth behind the closing of the school. Please, let her rescue something from this fiasco, even if it was only the affection and respect of one ten-year-old girl.

'*Cara*,' Maria murmured, kissing Lucia extravagantly on both cheeks. 'So pale and sad . . . come, come, where is that lovely smile, so like your mother's?'

'There is nothing to smile about.' Carefully Lucia kept her back turned to the twins.

'You will see your father soon. Isn't that something to smile about?'

'Papa does not smile when he sees me, so why should I smile when I see him? He doesn't want me, no one wants me, I'm just a nuisance.'

'He does want you, but you are old enough to understand that your father loved your mother very much,' Maria said. 'When she died, he was very upset.'

Lucia's memories of her mother were few and vague. She could not remember a time when she had not felt alone, and each time she formed an attachment to a maid or a governess, that person was taken from her. There was always a good reason for their going, but she could understand only that something else had been more important than her, and so she shrank a little more and became less willing to give her affection. Until she met Miss Frances and felt safe.

'I love Miss Frances and it makes me very upset that she is being taken away from me, like all the others.' Lucia, still conscious of the silent presence of the twins, fought valiantly against tears.

Maria was fond of the child, but she belonged strictly to the 'little girls should be seen and not heard' school and genuinely believed that Lucia had no cause for complaint. 'Don't be silly. You should spend less time feeling sorry for yourself and more time counting your blessings. Most girls would be glad to be going home to such a beautiful house and such a privileged existence.' And, picking up her books, she swept out of the room.

Maria Scarlatti in full sail was an impressive sight and the twins watched her departure in awed silence, while Lucia tried to sink into the floor in the vain hope that they might not notice she was still there. Timid at the best of times, she was absolutely terrified of Imogen and Arabella, the sisters of the Miss Leighs, the oldest girls in the school, the prettiest and cleverest girls in the school, one of whom everyone worshipped and one of whom everyone feared.

'Anyone who loves Frances,' Imogen said thoughtfully, 'does have an indisputable right to feel sorry for herself. In fact, I would say that self-pity was both a prerequisite and a product of her condition.'

Lucia did not understand a word, but she knew enough to realise that she was being ridiculed. However, as her eyes began to fill, it occurred to her that one advantage of her present position was that she need never see Arabella and Imogen again.

'You don't know anything about it,' she said loudly, as if volume gave her words emphasis and herself courage to continue. 'You don't know what it's like to be all alone.'

'One can dream,' Arabella murmured, so quietly that not even Imogen caught the words, although she cast a sharp, suspicious glance at her sister.

'There are so many of you, and you two are twins and so have each other. You two are always together.'

'Aren't we just,' Arabella agreed. 'Some people believe we are joined at the hip.'

This time Imogen heard perfectly, catching the caustic

note in the remark and blaming Lucia for starting the subject. 'I'm not surprised that you are alone,' she said cruelly. 'No one would want to be friends with you, you pathetic little creep.'

Tears began spilling down Lucia's cheeks.

'Look at you, you're not even pretty,' Imogen taunted, walking around the girl, eyeing her scornfully from top to toe. 'Plain face, dull hair, and a body that's straight up and down, thin as a matchstick. You don't have a bulge anywhere, do you!' And Imogen prodded the girl's flat chest with a jabbing forefinger.

'Ginny, she's only ten years old,' Arabella protested quietly. 'And even though she is so young, she is by far the best pianist the school ever had. Aren't you, Lucia?' And Arabella gave the girl an encouraging smile.

Arabella was kind, Lucia thought. Everyone at the school was in love with her and would do anything for her. *Imogen* would do anything for her. So why did not Arabella stop Imogen being so beastly?

'You are not alone,' Arabella went on. 'You have a father, and presumably you have aunts, uncles, cousins and so on.'

'Not so as you'd notice,' Lucia replied. 'There is an aunt, but she is terribly old and my cousins are grown up. As for my father . . .' she paused. 'What happened to your own father?' she inquired innocently.

The effect of this remark was astonishing. Arabella and Imogen went very still and very white.

'He died,' Arabella said shortly.

'Were you sorry?'

'Sorry about what?' Imogen interjected sharply, taking a step towards Lucia. 'What should we be sorry about?'

'Sorry that he was dead,' Lucia stammered. '*Sad* that he was dead.'

'Why should it mean anything to us? Why should it mean more to us than to anyone else – what are you implying?' Imogen caught hold of Lucia's long hair and gave a vicious tug.

'I'm not implying anything.' Lucia struggled to free herself and backed away. 'Only I was sort of sorry and sad when my mother died.'

'Of course you were,' Arabella said soothingly, laying a restraining hand on Imogen's arm, 'and we felt exactly the same when our parents died. It's only natural. We really are awfully sorry that you are unhappy at home.'

Lucia had her back pressed firmly against the door, having retreated as far as she could without actually leaving the room. From this position of relative safety she said: 'You two are very peculiar, you know.'

'No,' said Imogen in a dangerously quiet voice, 'we didn't know.'

'You are the wrong way round,' and as Lucia said it she wondered why she had never realised it before.

'Oughtn't you to be somewhere else, with Frances or Signorina Scarlatti?' Arabella asked quickly. 'In fact, isn't it time we went next door for tea?'

'No one is going to have any tea before this revolting child has explained herself,' Imogen snarled.

'In the stories I've read, the beautiful sister receives all the attention, but inside she is mean and selfish and unkind, while the plain sister is overlooked, but inside she is good and kind and clever. With you two, it's the other way round.'

'Imogen is just as clever as, in fact cleverer than, me,' Arabella protested hastily.

'But she is nasty and evil to everyone – everyone except you.' Lucia's hand groped for the door knob. 'And I hate her, and I don't care who knows it, because I'm leaving here and I don't have to see either of you ever again!' She opened the door and backed out. 'Cross-eyes,' she spat at Imogen as a parting shot.

'The little . . .' Imogen lunged at the door but was held back by her sister. 'What does she mean – cross-eyes?'

'You have a slight squint,' Arabella replied calmly. 'It's nothing. Lots of people have one.'

There being no mirror in the room, or in the immediate vicinity, Imogen went to the window and peered into the glass, trying to position herself so that the light illuminated her face. She inspected her eyes intently.

'You never mentioned it before,' she said at last, accusingly.

'It isn't worth mentioning. I hardly notice it. I don't suppose anyone else has ever noticed it.'

'Lucia did.'

'Oh, Lucia.' Arabella made a dismissive gesture. 'What does she know!'

'A lot, apparently. About you, and me, and Father . . .'

'She knows nothing,' and Arabella grasped Imogen by the shoulders. 'It is all in your mind. You are giving her credit for more knowledge and intelligence than she really has, you and your . . .' She did not finish the sentence.

'Me and my guilty conscience,' Imogen supplied, with a harsh laugh. 'But she described you and me as we used to be before . . . You, beautiful and spoiled rotten, and me when I was clever and the leader that Nature intended me to be, until *it* happened.'

'Only you and I know the truth about what happened,' Arabella said urgently, 'and neither of us is ever going to tell anyone else.'

'Promise?'

'Need you ask? The truth, not the accident of our birth, is what joins us at the hip.'

They moved apart, Imogen still grimacing at her reflection in the windowpane.

'Lucia is upset about leaving here,' Arabella said, watching her sister carefully. 'Was it you, Ginny? Did you do it again?'

'I don't know what you mean.'

'Tell someone about The Cavendish. A little word in the ear of a girl with influential parents, perhaps? Like you did before.'

Imogen did not reply.

'Just because I did not say anything about it before,' Arabella went on quietly, 'does not mean that I did not know exactly what you had done, and why.'

'You were beginning to love her more than you loved me.'

'I loved Sarah, but not more than you. She was my friend and my love for her was something extra, something in addition to loving you, not *instead* of . . . Ginny, in my life there will be other people I will meet, other friends I will make, and other places I will have to go, without you.'

'I do not want to be separated from you for a single moment,' Imogen said fiercely.

'Then there will be times when you will be disappointed and unhappy,' Arabella responded calmly. 'Now, did you tell someone here about The Cavendish or didn't you?'

'No, I did not. There was no reason why I should. Funnily enough, I have rather liked it here.'

Because there were no girls with whom I was likely to form an attachment, thought Arabella, but she let it pass. 'It must have been Charley who let the cat out of the bag.'

'It could have been anyone,' Imogen objected. 'Lots of people could have made the connection between Marion and Frances Leigh of The Cavendish, and Mary and Frances Leigh of this school.'

'No, it was bound to be one of us. Nothing much happens by chance in this family and we always end up hurting each other, haven't you noticed?'

Or are you too busy trying to hurt other people?

Arabella was uncomfortable about the way her sister bullied the girls. It had been bad enough at their previous school but it was much worse here, where Imogen felt more powerful and where so many of the pupils were younger and more vulnerable. Yet, as Lucia had astutely observed, Arabella made no real attempt to stop it. Why not? But, to that question, only Arabella and Imogen knew the answer.

Chapter Twenty-Three

Five miles from Gloucester, the carriage turned through a pair of wrought-iron gates and up a broad avenue, which traversed an area of thick woodland before entering the park. As they crested a small rise, Frances glimpsed Lucia's home in the distance and craned her neck for a better view. A pale gleam of autumn sunshine escaped the lowering grey clouds and illumined the house of her dreams. A perfectly proportioned but originally modest Georgian manor house had been tastefully extended with matching east and west wings, the whole built in a local stone that glowed golden in that brief burst of sunlight. Then the road dipped and widened, lined by ancient elms that framed the view of the house ahead, and the carriage rolled on to gravel and pulled up at the front door.

For a moment Frances sat back, her hands shaking suddenly with a mixture of excitement and trepidation. She was only the schoolmistress delivering a pupil, but to enter such a mansion, to eat here and sleep here, of such were her fantasies made. Lucky Lucia to have such a home. But, and she glanced curiously at the girl beside her, evidently Lucia did not share this sentiment. As the carriage door was opened and a servant helped them down, the girl's face remained pinched into an expression of apprehensive misery. What sort of ogre, Frances wondered as she smiled graciously at their helper, awaited them within?

Entering the hall, Frances's eyes darted from the ornate ceiling to the opulent carpet, from the elegant chairs and tables to an arrangement of fresh flowers that seemed an impossible achievement in autumn, and to an antique sculpture which, being either Greek or Roman – Frances could not tell the difference – ought to have been out of place in this quintessentially English environment and yet seemed perfectly at home.

The manservant opened the door into the library and stood aside for them to enter, but Lucia hung back, looking up at Frances with such desperate appeal in her eyes that Frances placed her arm around the girl's shoulders and guided her into the room. So it was that they entered together, side by side, unconsciously presenting a harmonious picture, Lucia in brown leaning towards the taller but slightly built figure of Frances in her best coat of dark blue cloth trimmed with black, and a matching hat.

Thomas Gresham had been seated at a desk near the window at the far end of the room, but he stood up as they came in and watched their slow advance across what seemed, to Lucia's faltering footsteps, an acre of carpet. His face revealed neither pleasure nor displeasure at his daughter's arrival, and when Frances gently pushed the girl forward, Lucia bobbed a little curtsy and kissed the impassive cheek that was offered to her.

'Well, Lucia, I hope you are . . . er, well?' he asked awkwardly.

'Yes, thank you, Papa. Quite well.'

'And you have been a good girl on the journey, I trust? Not made a nuisance of yourself and been a burden to Miss Leigh?'

'No, Papa. I mean, yes . . .' Flustered as to which question she was answering, Lucia floundered into silence, backing away from her father until she nearly trod on Frances's feet.

'If you cannot make up your mind, I will have to ask Miss Leigh,' and he looked straight at Frances for the first time.

She saw a broad-shouldered man of medium height, older than she had expected, with a thick mass of silvered hair, deep brown eyes and the healthy, ruddy complexion of a man who loved the outdoors. He had very beautiful hands, she noticed, big and well shaped with long, sensitive fingers. Something in his manner gave the impression that she, too, ought to curtsy, but she resisted the initial impulse to comply, feeling that submission would lower her status. Instead she extended a gloved hand.

'How do you do, Mr Gresham. I can assure you that Lucia has behaved beautifully today, as indeed she does every day.'

He saw a highly attractive woman, much younger than he had expected, whose black hair gleamed beneath a charming blue hat, whose complexion radiated youth and beauty, whose pink lips and white teeth were most unschoolma'am-like, and whose blue eyes met his with the frank and intelligent stare of someone who was not expecting anything of him, or criticising him, or getting at him in the indefinable ways that women had of getting at him. And the voice, that beautifully modulated voice, so much more refined than he had anticipated! Grasping Frances's hand, Thomas Gresham regretted that this undoubted influence for good on his daughter would be unable to see her task through to the end.

'You had a comfortable journey?' he asked.

'Indeed we did and we enjoyed ourselves, didn't we,

Lucia, eating more than was good for us and playing games so that the journey seemed over before it had begun.'

'Playing games?' He looked puzzled, glancing doubtfully at his daughter. Obviously, to Thomas Gresham, children's games were a foreign country.

'Our only regret was that the season is not conducive to educational entertainment,' Frances said sweetly. 'One can learn a certain amount from shapes and colours, but flowers and leaves are both helpful and decorative.'

'Quite.' He shifted uncomfortably, his hands behind his back, and nodded.

Frances looked at him again. Far from being an ogre, this was an intelligent man who would be highly articulate when on the home ground of his work, friends and interests. He was awkward and embarrassed with his daughter, because he did not know how to talk to her or how to relate to her. Probably he was not accustomed to children and his discomfort manifested itself as an uncaring, unloving harshness.

'We are disturbing your work,' Frances exclaimed, gesturing at the desk littered with books and papers. 'I will take Lucia upstairs to freshen up after the journey. If I do not see you again before I return to London, I . . .'

'But we will dine tonight,' he said quickly. 'And Lucia can join us, it being a special occasion.'

He was rewarded with two genuinely happy smiles, and in response his own expression softened.

'We will look forward to that,' and Frances smiled down at her charge, 'but now there is unpacking to be done, and faces to be washed. Come, Lucia.'

'The servants will . . .' A thought seemed to strike him. He hesitated for a moment, frowning, and then rang the bell. The butler materialised in the doorway.

'On second thoughts, Parker, Miss Leigh will be in the Blue Room.'

As the man dematerialised, Frances turned to Gresham with a worried look. 'I do not wish to be any trouble to anyone during my stay.'

'No trouble, Miss Leigh. Originally I gave orders that you should be accommodated in the quarters occupied by Lucia's former governess but, having met you, I feel the Blue Room would be more appropriate.'

Frances opened her mouth, in order to protest that she would be perfectly happy being treated as a governess, but then her mouth snapped shut. Her status had risen and, even though the other quarters would be closer to Lucia's room, she preferred to let matters stand.

'And, of course, the servants will do any unpacking,' Thomas Gresham added.

Surely it was unusual for such a matter to be mentioned? Was it a test, was he assessing her reaction? Did he imagine that a schoolmistress possessed only darned and humble garments, which she would be ashamed for servants to see? Doubtless, with the majority, this would indeed be the case, but Frances had not wasted the time she had spent at The Cavendish or the money she had earned there. She had an eye for quality, and the clothes purchased during that brief period of plenty had been carefully stored and laundered and kept 'for best'. No, Frances had no need to be concerned that the contents of her valise would demean her in the eyes of the staff.

Several hours later, completing her toilette for dinner, Frances surveyed herself in the mirror and was satisfied that she had struck precisely the right note. Not only had her experience at The Cavendish provided the wherewithal for a fine wardrobe, but it had provided the expertise with which to make the most of herself in any role she chose to play. Her hair was brushed back smoothly from her face, because Frances disliked the fashionable fringe, and swept up into a knot on the crown of her head, a simple style that suited her admirably. Simplicity was also the keynote of her gown, the bodice V-necked at the front and back with elbow-length sleeves, the draped 'apron' front of the skirt gathered back over a small bustle, while the folds of figured blue silk flowed into the merest suggestion of a train.

Yes, she thought as she inspected herself carefully, she had chosen right; too elaborate an ensemble would have appeared presumptuous, too modest would have seemed subservient. A station somewhere between governess and wife was her aim, and she felt that she had judged it to a nicety.

Having asked Lucia to show her the former governess's quarters and compared the accommodation with the Blue Room, her self-confidence had risen another notch. And she had wasted no time in establishing a rapport with the nurserymaid, a relationship that discouraged overfamiliarity on the girl's side and emphasised Frances's superiority while maintaining the domestic courtesies. The Frances who had set off from London this morning would cheerfully have unpacked and helped Lucia to bathe and dress for dinner; the Frances who thoughtfully surveyed the Gresham household this evening surrendered her charge into the care of the nursery staff and made a dignified withdrawal to her own room. One must start as one intended to go on.

Deliberately she waited until Lucia was taken downstairs and had spent fully ten minutes alone with her father – ten minutes which, Frances guessed, would seem more like an hour to both parties. As she expected, father and daughter were sitting in tense silence and both looked up eagerly when she entered the room.

'Lucia, how pretty you look,' she exclaimed with an enthusiasm and surprise that belied the fact that she had helped Lucia to choose which dress to wear. 'You should always wear that colour – it brings out the red-and-gold lights in your hair. And, oh, such flowers, how heavenly . . .' She bent over the bowl, inhaling the scent, as Lucia and her father beamed at the compliments.

'That's the last of the roses from the garden and the begonias come from the hothouse. A little hobby of mine.' Thomas Gresham coughed and added diffidently: 'I could show you, if you are interested.'

'If it isn't too much trouble, I can think of nothing I would like more.' And, taking Lucia's hand, Frances followed him out of the room, down the hall to the south-west corner of the house and into the conservatory.

This was no fashionable extension to a society house, where a few potted palms or wilting ferns provided a background to romantic trysts, but a large-scale working hothouse that provided a year-round supply of flowers and greenery for interior decoration. Apart from the begonias and other autumnal plants, there were hyacinths and cyclamen being prepared for Christmas, while the lilacs, tulips, primulas and camellias would, Thomas Gresham assured his audience, be in full bloom by February. In addition there were many rare plants that he had brought back from his travels and which he was trying to propagate, some, he admitted, more successfully than others.

Even Lucia was interested, actually asking questions and initiating conversation with her father to which he responded with animated explanations. His home ground, thought Frances . . .

'I don't believe it,' and Frances gazed in astonishment at a display of strawberry plants, glistening with scarlet fruit.

'A second crop, which we lifted from the beds last week

and brought inside. I tell you what we'll do – we'll have them for dinner, why not!'

'But surely other arrangements have been made for dinner,' Frances protested politely, 'and you were saving the fruit for a more important occasion.'

'What could be more important than *this* occasion?' he replied gallantly. 'And, whatever the arrangements for dinner, I never knew a woman yet who could not find room for a strawberry or two.'

'You are very kind, Mr Gresham. Strawberries would help to turn a sad occasion into a celebration.'

'Why should this evening be sad?' he asked as they sat down to dinner.

'Lucia and I are very fond of each other. Both of us are dreading the moment of parting, perhaps never to see each other again; but I have tried to explain that one cannot have everything one wants in this world, that there are bad times as well as good, and that everyone's life comprises a bit of both.'

'How very true,' he said, watching his daughter's eyes fill with tears.

'And I have told her that bad times are always followed by good, so she must bear her unhappiness bravely. No tears, please, Lucia! The courageous smile through their adversity.'

It was the most fearful nonsense, Frances thought privately, indeed it was priggish, sanctimonious rubbish, but if she was any judge of character, it was just the sort of pious sentiment that Thomas Gresham would like imbued into his daughter. It even had the desired effect on Lucia, who gulped back a sob and forced a wan smile. With her host looking immensely impressed at the transformation, Frances proceeded to guide the conversation along lines that showed Lucia to advantage, talking earnestly about the girl's education and abilities, but injecting a note of humour every once in a while.

'I am sure Lucia would like to show you how far she has progressed on the pianoforte,' Frances said as the meal drew to a close.

Lucia, whose demeanour had brightened during dinner, blanched. 'No, I couldn't,' she whispered. 'I'll make mistakes.'

'All you have to do is pretend that you are playing for me in the music room as usual,' Frances said firmly. 'I will come to the piano and sit where you can see me, like I always do.'

Meekly Lucia allowed herself to be led to the piano. Frances began by treating the little recital rather like a lesson, choosing the pieces to be played, standing beside her pupil and turning the sheets of music, but as Lucia warmed to her task and forgot her fear of her father, she relaxed. Soon Frances was able to sit down and confine herself to a few nods of encouragement, as Lucia played her favourite pieces from memory and Thomas Gresham sat in attentive silence on the other side of the room. However, there was no doubting the sincerity of his applause when Lucia's recital was over and the young girl flushed with pleasure, her face glowing with praise from this unaccustomed quarter.

'You must hear Miss Frances play, Papa. She is much better than me. In fact I think she is much better than *anyone*.'

Frances laughed and exchanged a conspiratorial glance with her host. 'Far be it from me to disillusion you, my dear Lucia! However, I fear that as you grow older, my deficiencies will become all too clear to you!'

But Lucia took her hand and pulled her to the piano and, after a few moments of playful prevarication, Frances sat down and began to play. Knowing the effect her musicianship had on people hearing her for the first time, she could *feel* Thomas Gresham's surprise and heightened attention as he leaned forward in his chair. But she knew not to overdo it – always leave them wanting more. So, after an effortless and faultless rendition of several of her 'showpieces', she stood up and walked across to where Lucia was sitting.

'You will practise, won't you, darling? You have a great talent and I want you to promise that you will practise, and that you will remember all I have told you and . . .'

She was interrupted by an outburst of tears from Lucia, who flung herself into Frances's arms.

'I wish that you didn't have to go,' Lucia sobbed, 'or I wish that I could go back to the school with you.'

'So do I, darling, but it is not possible, so both of us must be brave and promise to write to each other.'

The idea that letters could be a substitute for the love and care of Miss Frances only provoked another storm of weeping. Out of the corner of one eye, as she hugged the girl, Frances saw that Thomas Gresham was watching them anxiously.

'Now,' said Frances, 'you can accompany me in a song.'

With Lucia perched on the piano stool, Frances arranged herself in an attractive pose by the instrument, backlit becomingly by the lamp and, facing her host, was able to see his full reaction to her singing. If anything her voice had matured during her years with The Cavendish, while the comparative rest during the school year, coupled with extra tuition from Maria, had brought further improvement. It was indeed a glorious sound that streamed into the room, and she made a lovely picture in her blue dress against the pale gold of the curtains, which shut out the dankness of the autumn night. Thomas

Gresham's eyes remained on her long after the last note had died away.

Again she left him wanting more, suggesting to Lucia that they sing together. She let Lucia choose the songs, hoping in this way to avoid selecting pieces that had been Mrs Gresham's favourites.

'It is long past Lucia's bedtime,' she said when the songs were finished. 'Perhaps I should go upstairs and inquire if the nursery staff are ready for her, while you say good night,' and she began to walk towards the door.

'No, no,' he said hurriedly. 'I will ring for them. No need for you to go.'

He is terrified of being left alone with Lucia, Frances thought, simply because he does not know what to say to her.

'Sleep well,' and she kissed Lucia's forehead.

'You will still be here in the morning when I wake up?'

'I will see you before I leave.'

'Promise!'

'I promise,' and Frances kissed her again, before the child said good night to her father with another kiss on the cheek. Was it her imagination or was the salutation less stiff and formal than the one exchanged when they arrived?

'You have a way with her,' Gresham said when they were alone, 'and I am more sorry than I can say that you cannot continue her education.'

'So am I. However, doubtless you will enjoy the opportunity to get to know her better. Or are you planning to travel again in the near future?'

'Not in the immediate future, no. I intend to winter here, enjoying my books and devoting some time to the estate. Much as I enjoy travelling, I have missed the hunting season in recent years. In addition I am under pressure, and an obligation, to resume my duties as a local magistrate.'

'I quite understand.' Frances paused tactfully. 'There has not been much to keep you here in the last few years,' she suggested.

'Nothing. When Lucia's mother died . . . Well, local society and friends were very kind, and my sister had a great many suggestions as to what I should do – I'm sure she meant well,' he added hastily, 'but to be honest I preferred my own company. When I was not travelling, I holed up in my villa in Florence. That's it there,' and he pointed at a charming watercolour on the wall.

Frances rose and inspected the picture. 'I cannot imagine anything more perfect,' she said truthfully.

'I have been very happy there, in a quiet way. I wish that . . .' He stopped and watched as she resumed her seat. 'What about you? Is there absolutely no chance of rescuing the school?'

'I fear not. The financial situation was irretrievable, despite the school being fully subscribed and the fees coming in regularly. I am afraid that we set our sights and our standards too high, and borrowed too much when starting the enterprise. Obviously my sister and I were not intended to be in business!'

'What are you going to do?'

Frances shrugged. 'I must look for suitable employment as soon as I return to London. Fortunately my sister is already settled – she is returning to a former employer who was anxious to have her back.'

'Do you mean that you have no position waiting for you, that your future is uncertain? But why didn't you say so before?' he exclaimed.

'I really did not imagine that my future plans were of the slightest interest to anyone but myself,' she replied with disarming frankness.

'But if that is the case, there is no need for you to go, you could stay . . .' His agitation was, Frances thought, rather sweet. 'But no, of course not, what am I thinking of! As if a woman of your breeding and qualifications would want to be governess to one ten-year-old child!'

'If,' Frances said, 'that child was Lucia, I would consider it. I love her very much, you see.'

'Yes, I do see, and that is another reason why I would like you to stay. Miss Leigh, you need only name your terms . . . Naturally, in addition to a generous salary, I would not want you to think of yourself as a governess – more as a friend of the family. Is the Blue Room comfortable enough for you? And of course you would dine with me and any guests who are entertained here, and if you would condescend to play and sing a little in the evenings, I can promise you an attentive and appreciative audience.'

'It seems, Mr Gresham, as if you have named my terms more fully and generously than I could ever have done. I accept those terms and I hope, and indeed I believe, that we can provide a happy and harmonious environment for Lucia.'

'Would you care to give Lucia the good news? I am sure she would sleep better knowing that you will be staying for good.'

'I must return to London tomorrow as planned, in order to close down the school and collect my belongings.' Frances smiled at him. 'But I think *you* should give Lucia the news. I like to think that she is as fond of me as I am of her, and if you were to go to her now and tell her that you have persuaded me to stay, why, I think you might be surprised at the heroic status you achieve in that single moment!'

He left the room immediately and Frances leaned back in her chair, her fingers caressing the gold-and-blue silk of

the upholstery. It had been almost too easy. And this was
only the beginning . . .

Charley was lying in bed with Vere, sexually replete after
love-making and happier than she had ever been in her
life. Usually they went to bed in her room, but this
evening he was entertaining her in an establishment that
Charley could only assume was a bordello. Not that she
was offended by being brought here – on the contrary,
she felt pampered and distinctly wicked. Besides, it was a
very up-market bordello, their suite reached by way of a
curved staircase and furnished in pale-green and gilt
Louis XV.

'Are you asleep?' She leaned across and kissed Vere's
nose.

'Just thinking,' he said, opening his eyes. 'I saw Peter
Frith-Tempest today.'

She drew away from him. 'Rather you than me,' she
said tartly.

'Come back here,' and he reached out for her, drawing
her close so that her head nestled on his shoulder. 'Don't
be so prickly, darling. We cannot shut everyone else out of
our world for ever, much as I would like to.'

'There is a time and a place for dragging up names from
the past and somehow, for me anyway, this isn't it.'

'I agree,' he murmured, kissing her uplifted face tenderly, 'but I have a decision to make by tomorrow – a
business decision – and only you can help me to make it.'

Charley groaned, but the magic word 'business' stilled
any protest.

'We must do something, and soon, about Bianca and
the casting of Esther Eccles in *Caste*. Have you any suggestions?'

'Only negative ones, in that no one in the company is

suitable. Obviously we must look elsewhere. Where does Peter come into this?'

'He visited your sisters.' Feeling Charley stiffen and try to pull away from him, Vere tightened his grip on her. 'Calm down and hear me out. Apparently Marion is in rather a poor way . . .'

'Oh dear, I *am* sorry,' she said sarcastically.

'Frances is leaving. She has a position as a governess and Marion is pretty cut up about it. According to Peter, Frances says that she has her own life to lead and that the rest of the family can jolly well manage without her.'

'Good for her. I know exactly how she feels.'

'Which leaves Marion with no home and no job, and the entire responsibility for your younger sisters.'

'Damn it, Vere, as this is obviously leading up to a proposal that Marion returns to The Cavendish, are you bloody well suggesting that the twins come, too?'

'Of course not, only Marion, and only if . . .'

'If she comes, I go. I have made that very clear, time and time again.'

'Listen, no one is suggesting that you should shoulder any family responsibilities or take an active part in looking after the twins, but surely you do not want to stand in the way of your three sisters achieving a reasonable standard of living? Particularly when the school was closed down because you . . .'

'I know,' she interrupted, 'you don't have to rub it in.'

'And you have nothing to lose. It is Marion who must put her pride in her pocket and return to The Cavendish in a more humble role than in the past. You are the leading lady now, not her. It is you whom I consult over policy decisions and you who will receive top billing and the best parts.'

'In actual fact, I will get the roles that are best for me and Marion those that are best for her,' Charley said shrewdly.

'You complement each other. Together you will be the perfect combination, one that could be crucial to the survival of The Cavendish and the company. That is what you want, isn't it?'

'Yes,' Charley replied, thinking of her intervention over the matter of Peter's investment, 'but I never dreamed that I would have to make the ultimate sacrifice in order to achieve it!'

He laughed, stroking his fingers up and down her bare back. 'Most people would think that the ultimate sacrifice was going to bed with me!'

'No, they wouldn't and you know it. Being in bed with you is the ultimate ecstasy, and don't think that you are fooling me by raising such a thorny question at this particular juncture, because you aren't. You are taking advantage of me shamelessly, because you know that when I am in bed with you – oh God, do that again, *please* – I go to jelly, and that includes going soft in the head.'

'Now, would I do a thing like that?' His fingers were creeping between her legs and his mouth stabbed hers as he spoke.

Charley opened her eyes wide and looked at him. 'Yes, you would but, then, in your position I would do exactly the same.'

'The only position I want is the one I am in right now,' and he moved on top of her.

Oh, what the hell, thought Charley as she abandoned herself to him. What did Marion matter compared with this? And in any competition, she, Charley was bound to win: she was younger and stronger, she was the leading lady at The Cavendish and she had what Marion had never had: Vere.

A run-through of the *Shrew* was called for Marion's first day so that she could familiarise herself with the play. Charley arrived at the theatre a good half-hour early and went straight to the stage. As she had anticipated, Marion was standing there alone, staring out into the darkened auditorium. Hearing Charley's footsteps, she turned and faced her sister.

'Are we going to be friends, Charley?'

'I shouldn't think so,' Charley replied crisply. 'Why change the habit of a lifetime?'

'First you, and now Frances,' Marion said slowly. 'You will not be aware of this, but not only did Frances go away, she flatly forbade any communication with her. None of us is to write to her, let alone visit, on pain of death. She is terrified that the taint of the theatre will waft towards Gloucestershire and foul her new nest.'

'She will be happy to know that I have not the slightest desire to write to her, and I would not visit if she paid me. Which is saying something, because I will do almost any-thing for money.' And Charley shrugged carelessly as these pointless, and untrue, words fell from her lips.

'So,' Marion continued, 'even though I gave the best years of my life to looking after the family, and putting the interests of my sisters before my own, only the twins are speaking to me.'

'They are very young. Give them time.'

'This isn't going to work, is it? You and me on the same stage?'

'I will work with you. I will not try to upstage you and I will co-operate in any way that will contribute to the success of the production. On the stage you may be confident that I will be sweetness and light. Offstage I intend to keep my distance.'

'Don't you even want to know where we are living? Or what I have done with the twins?'

'You see, that phrase sums it up exactly. You never treated any of us as individuals. We were just the recipients of your munificence, and puppets for you to manipulate.'

'I wasn't your mother,' Marion flashed. 'I could only try to do my best in very difficult circumstances.'

'What *have* you done with the twins?'

'Enrolled them at a finishing school in Kensington,' at the cost of another piece of Lord Melton's munificence, Marion reflected, 'and Maria Scarlatti will keep an eye on them while I am at the theatre.'

'Arabella and Imogen will soon qualify as the most highly educated young ladies in the country,' Charley drawled. 'I assume you have their names down for a place at university.'

'I will do anything that will keep them away from the theatre.'

A sudden noise diverted their attention. As a piece of scenery was being moved into position, it shuddered to a halt, tilted and fell over.

'My God, the old place hasn't changed much,' Marion remarked. 'I see that Vere has not overcome his reluctance to spend money on anything that is not in full view of the audience.'

'The Cavendish productions run like clockwork,' Charley said defensively, 'but I have told him that more investment in the invisibles is required.'

'Have you indeed! Unfortunately he does not appear to have taken your advice.'

'He takes my advice on every aspect of the production!'

'Just like he used to take mine,' Marion said softly. 'Oh, don't worry, I do not intend to interfere. Onstage I intend to fight my corner, but offstage he is all yours.'

At that moment Vere appeared in the wings and had the grace to hesitate before approaching the two sisters. In that light, there was something dark and forbidding about him.

'You were saying that you intended to steer the twins away from the theatre?' Charley inquired, watching Vere closely.

'Arabella in particular.'

Charley had only two clear impressions of Arabella, the first being of an almost inhuman beauty, the second of the curiously comforting warmth of a handkerchief waving in a window after the ejection of the prodigal sister. As Vere walked towards them, a cold hand clutched at her heart.

'I do agree that Arabella should pursue a different path,' Charley said, 'and that at all costs she must never set foot in The Cavendish.'

Part Four

Chapter Twenty-Four

Arabella walked through the stage door, past the door-keeper, who opened his mouth to challenge her but stood in silent, slack-jawed astonishment, and made her way to the greenroom. Her entrance aroused two very different reactions: the dazed expression of the impressionable young prompter with the clipboard reflected his evident belief that she was an angel from heaven, whereas the malevolent glances of the assembled young ladies clearly wished her in hell.

Superbly dressed in a tight-waisted black velvet jacket over an indigo silk skirt, her golden hair swept back under a high-crowned black felt hat trimmed with indigo ribbon, Arabella leaned gracefully on her long-handled umbrella and waited.

'N . . . n . . . name?' stammered the young prompter.

The young ladies held their breath, willing the vision to ruin the effect by the way she spoke.

'Arabella Leigh.' The voice was low and soft, while retaining total clarity, beautifully modulated and impeccably vowelled.

'You're not here. I mean,' and he blushed abjectly, 'that I cannot find your name on the list.'

'An oversight, doubtless. Don't worry, I quite understand.'

'But if your name is not on the list, you cannot audition.'

'Do you really think that the manager will not want to see me?'

'I think,' and he swallowed hard, 'that he would like to see you very much.'

'So,' and Arabella glided past him into the room, 'do I.'

She sat down, apparently oblivious of the fact that every eye in the room was trained on her. In reality, she was perfectly aware of being the focus of attention, but she was used to it. All her life she had been stared at, her personal appearance bestowing many advantages and, although some would find it hard to believe, disadvantages. So Arabella returned the stares of her rivals with perfect poise and equanimity. This was no contest. They knew it, and so did she. The part in this play was hers; the moment she walked on to the stage and the manager and his associates saw her for the first time, it was hers.

Her lovely face remained expressionless, giving no clue to her feelings. She would be, *was*, labelled proud and vain, but this was to misunderstand and underestimate her. Vanity had no place in Arabella's emotional composition. On the contrary, she possessed a down-to-earth assessment of her looks, their effect on others and how little this effect owed to any effort or virtue on her part. Her coolness, her total *sang-froid*, sprang from that vital self-confidence and self-containment that had characterised her since childhood. Arabella had never failed, with anyone or anything.

'Miss Leigh,' the prompter called.

And Arabella rose and walked on to the stage.

*

If Marion could have displayed this passion on the stage, controlling it, repeating it performance after performance, she would have been a great actress instead of a competent one and would have achieved the very pinnacle of her ambition. So thought Arabella as she waited for the first storm of her sister's fury to pass.

'I absolutely forbid it,' shouted Marion, pausing for breath.

'You cannot keep me away from the theatre for ever,' Arabella pointed out in an eminently reasonable tone.

'While you are under age, I can. And what's more, I will. God, when I think of all I have done for you, of all the sacrifices I made for you . . .' And she was off again.

'Why,' Arabella asked during the next lull, 'is it all right for you to be in the theatre and not for me?'

'Because you can do anything, be anyone. Think about it, darling, please,' and Marion caught hold of her sister's hands in a last attempt at persuasion. 'With your looks and talent, there is a place for you, a role for you, in real life. Don't waste yourself on the stage.'

'If you are still dreaming of dukes and princes sweeping me off to their castles, forget it,' Arabella said drily. 'If these hypothetical noblemen believe an actress to be unsuitable marriage material, I dare say they might apply the same criteria to an actress's sister.'

Marion was silent. This had always been the fatal flaw in her plans for Arabella and she had no logical answer to it.

'Has it never occurred to you,' Arabella went on, 'that I might not want to be a duchess or a princess? That I might find such an existence jolly boring and that I might, just once in my life, want to achieve something by my own efforts and not because I was given a pretty face.'

'That face has made life too easy for you and now it

makes you think that you can be a successful actress. I'm telling you straight, my girl, that it takes a damn sight more than a pretty face to succeed on the London stage!'

'I know,' Arabella said patiently. 'That is what I have been trying to say to you.'

'It would serve you right if I allowed you to go ahead with this ridiculous scheme and take this part. You would soon learn, the hard way, that you have looks but no talent.'

Arabella's face hardened imperceptibly. 'I ought to be allowed the opportunity to prove you wrong,' she said steadily.

'You could escape the stigma of the stage,' Marion said eagerly. 'Frances has done it. She simply cut herself off and, indeed, would deny all knowledge of us. We would not dream of imposing. All your sisters would be content to admire your success from afar.'

'You have Imogen's consent to this plan, have you? And I assume that Frances has sworn Lucia to silence over the existence of three sisters – I exclude Charley from this sororial maelstrom, her having perfected the art of keeping her distance.'

At the mention of Charley, it was the turn of Marion's lips to tighten. 'I will not permit you to take up this part,' she said flatly. 'You must go away, leave London, do something completely different until you come to your senses.'

'Very well.'

Arabella's ready acceptance took Marion by surprise. 'Don't you care about losing the part?'

'There will be plenty of other parts.'

'You arrogant little bitch,' Marion flashed. 'How dare you dismiss your good fortune in winning a role in a West End play in so cavalier a fashion, and how dare you assume that you will walk into another with the same ease!'

'Because it is a fact of life,' Arabella replied, 'and there is no use railing against it. However, I would point out that even the most beautiful "stick" might find it more difficult to secure a third, fourth or fifth role.'

Arabella had always been different, been 'special', but until now Marion had not realised how immensely self-aware, analytic and intelligent the girl was. But she was not a girl, she was a young woman, and in that instant Marion's attitude changed from protective, loving elder sister to a most unladylike and unsisterly jealousy. Here was someone, ten years Marion's junior, with her life still before her, with her slate clean, her mistakes unmade, with everything to play for and the sky the limit. And Marion felt that if Arabella had the slightest talent as an actress, she would never forgive her.

'Where do you want me to go?' Arabella inquired politely.

Marion could think only of Frances, and clearly that was not a good idea.

'I could go to Sal,' and, as Marion looked puzzled, Arabella went on, 'Sarah Vale, my friend at school. She invites me to stay in every letter she writes.'

'She writes?'

'You don't imagine I would have her write here, do you? Imogen would go mad. I used to bribe the maid to slip me the letters secretly, but since the school closed she has written to me at Charley's address.'

Charley's complicity was galling, but Arabella's continued friendship with Lady Sarah was exactly what Marion wanted to hear.

'Do her parents know about this?'

'Of course, although I should explain that they are

unaware of my theatrical connections. Sarah knows and doesn't care, but she concedes that her folk might have reservations.'

'Lady Sarah does not care that your sisters are in the theatre,' Marion said it very slowly and very clearly, just so that there could be no misunderstanding.

'There is a new generation in the aristocracy, just as there is in other walks of life, and young people see things differently. Your problem, Marion, is that you were born a decade too soon.'

Her thirtieth birthday was not imminent but it was sufficiently in sight to make Marion wince. 'If Sarah will have you, then of course you and Imogen must go there.'

'I don't think that Imogen is invited.'

Yet again Marion was caught off-balance. 'But you and she are . . .'

'Inseparable,' Arabella agreed, 'in everyone's eyes but mine. Arabella-and-Imogen, *the twins* . . . For heaven's sake, we do not look alike, we do not think alike and we are *not* alike! We are separate individuals, and thank God Sarah realises that, even if no one else does.'

For a brief moment a very real passion was revealed, raw and naked, in Arabella's face. But then it was gone, as quickly as it came, as Marion said: 'But Imogen must go with you. I cannot have Imogen on my hands, here, when you are gone.'

'Would Imogen be in the way? Would Grace disapprove?'

Marion flushed. 'Grace has nothing to do with it. I would appreciate a little time to myself, that's all.'

Again Arabella surprised her. 'Imogen is my responsibility and Sarah will accept her, if it is the only way she can have me. I will write today and tell her that we are coming.'

'But for how long? It is April – won't Sarah be coming to London for the Season?'

'One of her brothers just died,' Arabella replied laconically, 'and her début has been postponed.'

'How sad.'

'Not really. Brothers are not something she is short of.'

Marion looked at her with concern. Was there any feeling beneath that perfect exterior? Or was this cold, hard truth, this certainty when applied to her own affairs, this detachment from the triumphs and tragedies of others, the real Arabella? And if so, was it the product of Marion's care and fostering? She shuddered and, for the first time, was conscious of the distance – mental and physical – that existed between the five sisters, of just how little they liked each other, and how they were beginning to turn against one another.

'Don't move,' Marion's companion admonished, 'not a muscle, not the minutest twitch. Supper will be ready in ten minutes and I will call you when it is on the table.'

Marion closed her eyes, the delicious smell from the kitchen wafting into her nostrils, and allowed the work and worries of the day to slip away. The luxury of having a meal prepared for one, she thought sleepily, was a joy that should never be underestimated or taken for granted. Conveniently forgetting the months when Frances had done the housekeeping, it seemed to Marion that all her life she had cooked and cleaned for others and that only now was someone taking care of her.

'So,' said Grace as she served a nourishing consommé in delicate porcelain bowls, 'you are free at last.'

'I suppose I am. Funny, I had not looked at it like that before.'

'You should. All the time. The only pity is that you did

not push both those young ladies through the nearest stage door and tell them to shift for themselves, and then your freedom would have been permanent.'

'I couldn't do that.'

'*Couldn't* is not the same as *wouldn't*, my dear.'

'I am going to miss them terribly.'

'No, you aren't. You are going to enjoy yourself – by God, you deserve it, after wasting the best years of your life on being mother and father, carer and provider, to a collection of ungrateful brats. You are coming into your prime, Marion, and you must make the most of it.'

Marion laughed. 'It's terribly sweet of you to say so, but I think "over the hill" is a more accurate description of my current status!'

'What rubbish you talk! Of course men are notorious for chasing virgins barely out of the schoolroom and leaving the mature, intelligent women to languish on the shelf, but surely this sad, if predictable, state of affairs does not apply to you?'

The keen glance that accompanied Grace's seemingly innocuous question passed Marion by. 'It most certainly does. This is delicious soup, by the way, thank you . . . What was I saying? Oh yes, in the eighteen months since I returned to The Cavendish, I have noticed a marked cooling-off in men's attention towards me.'

'They need their heads read, or a new pair of spectacles. And although I am the last person to defend the bastards, you still wade knee-deep in bouquets every evening.'

'Ankle-deep,' replied Marion, 'and only occasionally.'

'I was in the audience tonight, and they loved you. Quite rightly. Your Olivia is a wonder to behold.'

'But not as wondrous as Charley's Viola. She is very good, although I still think that Rosalind is her finest role.'

'Do you mind that Charley has a higher profile than you?'

'I mind that she plays women who have spirit, verve and vivacity, while I'm landed with the prigs as usual. But I have to accept that I could not play Viola, for instance. I am not the right shape, for a start!'

'There is nothing wrong with your shape, believe me,' Grace said firmly. 'My God, the rest of us should be so lucky!'

Standing up, she gestured dramatically and wryly at her own person. Grace Norton was tall and angular, big-boned, plain-faced, her hair dressed simply and severely. However, her dress revealed that there might be more to this woman than first appearances would suggest. The design was deliberately understated, but the fabric was sumptuous and the cut so perfect that 'expensive' was emblazoned on every fold, dart and tuck. It was a dress that indicated the style, and strength of character, of its wearer.

'All the same,' and Marion pinched a generous inch from the plump roll at her waist, 'I must stick to the diet.'

'Plain grilled chicken and steamed vegetables for the next course,' Grace assured her, clearing the soup plates. 'I did make a cream sauce but it is served separately, so you can ignore it.'

Marion watched wistfully as the sauce-boat was placed on the table. 'Perhaps just a drop wouldn't hurt,' she said, weakening.

'It would do you good. You must keep up your strength,' and Grace poured a cascade of creamy white sauce on to Marion's plate. 'Are you in the mood for confidences tonight? Because, if so, tell me whether the roles are all that you envy Charley.'

'You mean, am I jealous of her relationship with Vere?

I was at first, when I rejoined the company and found out that they were lovers. Oh, I minded *dreadfully*.'

'Had you hoped to resume your former relationship with him?'

'I don't know.' Marion toyed thoughtfully with a piece of chicken. 'No, I don't think so, not really. Perhaps if his current mistress had been anyone else, the impact would have been less. But to think of him sleeping with Charley, making love to my sister . . . Somehow that made it worse. And then of course there were the others.'

'Others?'

'Peter, for one. He has always been a good friend to me, but as time went on I noticed such definite undercurrents between him and Charley that I am absolutely certain she went to bed with him, too. And then there is Edward Druce – you know, he was Sebastian this evening. My dear, he was *wild* about me at one time.'

'You didn't . . . ?'

'No, and now he treats me like his *mother*! He has a girlfriend, a little blonde at the Haymarket, but any fool can see he is crazy about Charley. He watches her with a yearning, hangdog look which is unmistakable.'

'Does he know about her and Vere?'

'Everyone knows. Discretion is not Charley's strong point, although I will say that she doesn't crow about the relationship or take undue advantage of her position.'

'So you are completely over Vere. No regrets.'

'I don't think that I will ever be completely over him,' Marion said slowly, 'and there are plenty of regrets. At times I still wish that it could have worked out between us, that we could have been married and formed our own company . . . had a family . . .' And her voice trembled and trailed away. 'Perhaps it is that which is most difficult to forgive and forget,' she went on, when she had regained control, 'the abortion and my barrenness. Sometimes I think that I still love him, and then I think of that and I hate him. He is that kind of man – you either love him or hate him, and sometimes both at once.'

'I can understand that losing the baby, and then finding out that you could not have any more, was a terrible thing, but it isn't the end of the world.' Grace leaned across the table and covered one of Marion's hands with hers. 'Being childless is not a sentence to a sterile life. Look at me – go on, force yourself, I know I'm no oil painting! I am older than you, as well as being unattractive to men, and I am resigned to a childless existence, but I have a wonderful life. I go places and meet people, I travel to the Continent and to America, I have work and friends, and I am happy. In fact, I have been particularly happy since I met you,' and she gave Marion's hand a slight squeeze before withdrawing her own and resuming her meal.

'Your friendship has meant a great deal to me,' Marion assured her earnestly, 'and the people I have met through you have opened my eyes to a whole new world and a fresh view of the theatre. But, Grace, forgive me for saying this, but your circumstances are different from mine.'

'I have a private income,' Grace agreed promptly, 'but I still work.'

'You work because you want to, not because you have to, and that work does not depend on your personal appearance. As a writer, you can toil away in seclusion for as long as you want. You do not have to fear old age and loss of looks, like I do.'

'You really are frightened, aren't you!' Grace looked at her, horrified. 'How dreadful, I never realised . . . Come on, buck up. There are two solutions to your problem and two moves you can make. Number one, move into a theatrical sphere where superficial good looks are less important than the truth and beauty portrayed in the play.'

'The only dramatists writing those sort of plays, with those sort of parts, are you and Henrik Ibsen!'

'Don't speak of me in the same breath as Ibsen,' Grace implored. 'It's like being compared with Shakespeare! My paltry efforts pale into insignificance beside those of the master. I swear that if someone does not stage a decent production of *A Doll's House* soon, I will do it myself.'

'Do, and find a part for me.' Marion's tone was deliberately light. 'If you think I am good enough.'

'You would be brilliant,' Grace said firmly. 'Perhaps a little more maturity is needed before you could tackle Nora, but you would be perfect as Christine.'

'I thought as much – I'm not good enough for the lead.'

'Heavens, but these men have been grinding down your self-esteem for years and your sisters haven't done a bad job, either! Look, there is no use in arguing over a hypothetical production, but take my word for it that you can be Nora. You need to work your way into entirely different feelings and technique from the goody-goody girls you usually play.'

Marion drank in the praise and encouragement, her interest in the theatre becoming ever more intense and serious as she grew increasingly dissatisfied with what she saw as the triviality of the range of roles offered to her. Shakespeare apart, what was there? A few Robertson revivals to show Vere Cavendish at his best, Charlotte Leigh as second best, and Marion Leigh as the dull but devoted puritan trailing in a bad third.

'In my humble way I am trying to interpret Ibsen's message for modern London,' Grace was saying. 'It is high time that women were portrayed as human beings with minds and wills of their own and that we dealt with moral conflict, social values, the stress that convention places on behaviour, petty social values versus social responsibility. And now is the ideal time to launch such a revolution. People are delving deeply into human nature from every angle, in science as well as art, and as we investigate each trait . . .'

Marion drained her wine glass and tried to concentrate, but most of Grace's dissertation washed over her head. She was very tired. 'Wonderful,' she murmured when her friend paused for breath.

'You are exhausted,' Grace said contritely, 'and here I am, rambling on about my own preoccupations.'

'It's been fascinating.' And Marion made a valiant effort to rouse herself. 'You know that I am always interested in the theatre, and in your work especially. But what was the other solution to my original problem – heavens, I've forgotten what the problem was!'

'Your other move, in order to counteract your morbid fear of old age, loss of looks and employment, is to move in with me.'

Marion looked at her blankly.

'I may be rich,' Grace said with a gaiety she did not feel, 'but hand in hand with riches goes guilt. I know that you will say that you could not afford to contribute, say, half of my living expenses here. The whole point is that I can pay my living expenses ten times over and still have money in the bank at the end of each month. You could alleviate the guilt by letting me help you.'

Marion said nothing but continued to gaze at her companion in wide-eyed and disconcerted surprise.

'And in return,' Grace continued in that same half-joking, half-serious tone, 'I could provide financial security and a lee-tle bit of encouragement that might slay the dragon of your lack of self-esteem – if we persevere for a thousand years, that is!'

'The bargain is too one-sided,' said Marion at last.

'But I adore you.'

There was a long pause.

'The twins . . .' Marion said, from long habit.

'Ought to be self-supporting soon, and ought never to have been your sole responsibility in the first place. Think of it – without them you could give up that wretched flat and lead your own life.' Grace watched Marion's head drooping over the table. 'Well, that is all in the future but, whatever else you do, you are staying here tonight.'

Marion's head jerked up. 'I couldn't . . .'

'What is to stop you?' Grace demanded. 'There is no one expecting you at home. There is no one *there*. Besides, you will do as you are told.' And Grace smiled as Marion's eyes blinked in astonishment. 'When is the last time someone said that to you! You need someone to look after you, don't you, my dear, my darling girl . . .'

Vere had called an understudies rehearsal, something he did regularly and which the company found a crashing bore. Not only were these occasions a source of irritation but they tended to be time-consuming, as Vere ran through the play with all the understudies and then repeated scenes mixing the regular cast with the stand-ins. This was his eighth season at The Cavendish but, surprisingly in one with his ultimate ambitions and predilection for a lavish lifestyle, he had lost none of his desire for perfection.

'What's up with the Chief this morning?' Edward Druce demanded, throwing himself into the chair next to Charley in the greenroom.

'Nothing, as far as I know,' she replied without lifting

her gaze from the newspaper she was reading. 'Why?'

'He's in a foul mood and distinctly pale around the gills. Don't tell me that you haven't noticed!'

'Probably an attack of indigestion. Look, don't cross-examine me about his health and temper. I'm not his bloody keeper!'

'No, but you are his . . . Well, if you don't know what's put him out of sorts, no one will.' He stole a glance at her absorbed face. 'You haven't fallen out with him, have you?' he suggested optimistically.

'I refuse to answer that question, on the grounds that it may incriminate me.'

'Ah, you mean that if you have quarrelled with the Chief, you won't have a cast-iron excuse for refusing to have supper with me tonight.'

Charley lowered the newspaper slightly, gave him an infinitely weary look and then returned her attention to the page in front of her.

'I know,' he agreed. 'I'm a thundering nuisance, aren't I!'

'That is putting it mildly.'

'I am persistent, you see. Won't take no for an answer. It runs in the family.'

'And here I was thinking that you would grow out of it.'

'I say, you can be jolly patronising about my youth and apparent naivety sometimes, Charley,' he protested. 'I'll have you know that I'm not far off thirty.'

'Honestly?' She looked at him in surprise.

'Truly. I cannot help it if I'm cursed with the appearance of eternal youth.'

'Trust a man to call it a curse rather than a blessing,' Charley said drily, still inspecting his face. It was a remarkably handsome face and he had lovely eyes framed by the amazing, almost girlish, sweep of those long lashes.

She was accustomed to this face but, scrutinising him carefully, close up and without greasepaint, she realised that it did contain and convey more maturity than she had previously credited. 'I tell you what I'll do: I will have supper with you when you reach thirty, or if I break with Vere, whichever comes first. Now, *go away*.'

'I'll hold you to that,' he exclaimed and was about to say more when Marion came in.

As usual she took a seat on the opposite side of the room from the one where Charley was sitting and neither sister greeted the other or acknowledged her presence. Edward, old loyalties struggling with new, sank lower in his chair with embarrassment and closed his eyes.

Shortly afterwards Charley was called to rehearse a scene with Marion's understudy. After only a few lines, she understood what Edward meant about Vere's mood.

'We all know that you can play Viola in your sleep, Charley, so there is no need to prove it,' he drawled. 'Go back to the beginning, and this time put a little life into it.'

Compressing her lips, Charley complied, but the atmosphere was not helped by the excessive nervousness of Marion's stand-in, a sensitive girl who was reacting to the bad vibes between Charley and Vere, as well as to her own feelings of inadequacy.

The sharp, peremptory clap of Vere's hands halted proceedings yet again. 'Take a ten-minute break,' he ordered, 'and use that ten minutes to think about the scene and what you are trying to achieve in it. Either come back refreshed or don't come back at all.'

As he stalked off, the understudy broke down in tears, but a furious Charley followed Vere to his dressing room.

'What the hell has got into you today?'

He was pouring a whisky, even though it was only

noon, and looked at her coldly. 'I do not remember asking to speak to you.'

'Oh, I see. Little girls should only speak when spoken to,' Charley mocked. 'Everything has to be done at your convenience, doesn't it, and arranged to your timetable, and relationships run along lines that suit you.'

'If you want to put it that way, yes,' he snapped.

'And of course it is permissible for you to dance the night away, drink London dry and get to bed so late that next morning you are short of sleep, hungover, and take it out on the rest of us.'

'What I do with my time is my business.'

'When you behave as badly as you are this morning, it becomes the business of the entire company, and me in particular. What were you doing last night?'

'You are getting into very dangerous territory, Charley. Stop now before one of us says something we will regret.'

'Drinking, certainly,' Charley went on reflectively, 'but, on second thoughts, not dancing . . . Cards, that's it! You were gambling and you lost, which is why . . .'

'That's enough.' His voice cut in with a sharpness and finality that sounded a clear warning that she was going too far. Unfortunately Charley was in no mood to heed such signals.

'Good God, man, aren't you in enough financial trouble without making matters worse! The Cavendish is barely breaking even, and neither Ernest Meyer nor Peter Frith-Tempest will stay on board unless we show a thundering great profit, and soon.'

Vere was leaning against the dressing-table, his whisky glass in one hand, staring at her. His expression showed an implacability that she had never seen before.

'Don't you think that the time has come to put that brilliant brain and undoubted intelligence of yours to better use than this perpetual interference in my affairs?'

'I *am* one of your affairs,' she retorted wittily, or so she thought.

'Indeed you are, and very delightful it has been. But you are not my wife, Charley, and therefore you have no right to inquire into my private life. And you are not my business partner, so neither do you have the right to question my financial status. Do I make myself clear?'

'Perfectly,' she spat back defiantly. 'So clear that I would not be your wife or your business partner, if you were the last man and the last theatre manager on earth!'

'Good, because neither position is likely to be offered to you. Close the door on your way out and be back on stage at the appointed time.' When she had gone Vere let out a long sigh, poured another drink and sat down. Why, he wondered for the thousandth time, did women always want more than a man was prepared to give?

In her dressing room Charley sank down on a chair, her head in her hands. Of course it could be just a lover's tiff. She and Vere had had plenty, and they always made it up, but the very number and nature of these arguments only provided a yardstick by which to measure today's quarrel, and she knew that this was different. This time he meant it. This time she had gone too far. She had to face the unpalatable fact that all he had ever wanted from her was a leading lady for his theatre and a body in his bed.

Which was exactly what she had wanted from him. At the start.

Vere had been right about her, after all. He had seen into the future more percipiently than she, that day by the river, when he had predicted that in the end even she would want love.

She stood up shakily and, after straightening her tunic, inspected the breeches that she wore for rehearsals. Go on,

Charley, she told herself, flash your legs a little and he'll come running back. No man can resist your legs. And on the stage she performed with a flair and flamboyance that sent Edward Druce's heart hammering in his chest and one of Vere Cavendish's eyebrows twitching in wry appreciation.

In the galleries high above, the stage staff were 'flying' a piece of scenery into position, hauling on ropes and windlasses as they did innumerable times each day.

Charley moved to her next position, so accustomed to rehearsing amid the creaks and groans of stage machinery that she was able to ignore the noise completely.

But then one of the stagehands saw the old, frayed rope break and he yelled a warning.

Below, Charley looked up, puzzled. She saw it coming but a strange paralysis seemed to seize her, gluing her feet to the boards. She was vaguely aware of pressure on her shoulders and some movement in her body, before a heavy chunk of Illyria smashed her to the floor.

Chapter Twenty-Five

Arabella and Imogen were in Gloucestershire, staying at the country house of Earl and Countess Westlake. While the utter subjugation of the entire county to Arabella's blonde beauty was taken for granted, the charm and popularity of Imogen came as a complete surprise.

Imogen was making an effort, and the first improvement was in her appearance. All her life she had been 'the plain one' and, while comparison with her twin's exceptional good looks was inevitable, she also suffered from being the least attractive of five lovely sisters. Now she stopped worrying about that slight squint and swept up her abundant black hair, revealing a strong resemblance to Marion and Frances; her eyes and expression showed an intelligence akin to Charley's; and the brilliance of her smile proclaimed her as Arabella's sister.

She stopped being an aggressive, resentful figure on the fringe of every gathering and became the Imogen she might have been, had not fate dealt her a severe test when she was too young to handle it and also given her Arabella as a twin sister. Here was a very formidable young person and there were those in Gloucestershire that season who recognised and appreciated her individuality.

A warning from Arabella had played an important part

in this transformation. Imogen had been badly shocked to find that her sister had been conducting a secret correspondence with Sarah for three years. She was not quite sure which was worse: Arabella keeping a secret from her or the threat that, if crossed, her sister would go on the stage. In that event, Imogen was certain that she would lose Arabella for good.

'The alternative to staying with Sarah is for you to do something by yourself,' Arabella had said, 'instead of tagging along behind me all the time.'

'I'm no good at anything,' Imogen had protested. 'That's why I need you so much.'

'You are as clever as a cartload of monkeys, Imogen, and you do not fool me for a moment. I'm warning you: at Sarah's you will be on your best behaviour. One unkind word or sulky look and I will never speak to you again, and you ought to know, better than anyone, that I am perfectly capable of keeping my threats as well as my promises.'

Although the Vale family had eschewed the Season, they did not cut themselves off entirely from local society. The lost son and brother had been an invalid since birth and his passing, while deeply mourned, was seen as a merciful release from his suffering. Therefore the Vales wore black and kept to the country, neither attended nor gave balls and parties, but did join in everyday country pursuits and duties. The bishop and his lady came to dine, as did other acquaintances in the neighbourhood, but when the annual exodus to London took place, the castle took on an echoing desolation. This the countess tried to counteract by using the gardens and park for the benefit and enjoyment of others. Convalescents from the nearby hospital were driven over for a day in the fresh air; schoolchildren were entertained to games and tea; estate workers were treated to an extra feast; workers for the countess's local charities were rewarded with a tea party.

Arabella and Imogen were expected to participate in all these activities, and Imogen found that she enjoyed dispensing tea to invalids and children, and lending a sympathetic ear to earnest purveyors of charity to the disadvantaged. She was rather good at it, better than Arabella who, while being perfectly polite, never quite managed to vanquish her general air of detachment.

As spring turned to summer, Imogen's sense of well-being grew. She even shared with Sarah a mutual delight in Arabella's conquests, the two girls giggling together as Arabella daily deflated male egos and remained immune to the most ardent advances. Perhaps she did single out Sarah's brother, Henry, for rather more encouragement than the rest, but this could be ascribed to courtesy to her hosts, and Imogen did not begrudge him that.

Then, in early June, the earl entertained his business and professional neighbours – the diocesan staff, legal and medical men, the magistrates and squirearchy – to a modest supper party. It was a beautiful, balmy evening and the French windows were open to the terrace where the twins stood, peering into the brightly lit drawing room to watch the earl and the black-gowned countess receiving their guests. Suddenly Imogen grasped Arabella's arm tightly, squeezing the tender flesh so hard that her sister winced.

'Look,' Imogen said softly, 'over there with that old man – it's Frances.'

It had taken Thomas Gresham a year to propose marriage, long enough for Frances to begin to worry that he might shrink from taking the plunge and be content to allow the relationship to continue on its existing basis.

During that year she had become much more than Lucia's governess and mentor, although caring for the girl remained her first priority. Gradually Frances had insinuated herself into the very fabric of the household and its master's life, becoming indispensable to his daily routine, his work and his leisure. It was no more trouble to Frances to help with his dissertation on classical architecture than it was for her to entertain his dinner guests with her singing, liaise with the cook over the ordering of that dinner, and ensure that his little girl went to bed at a suitable hour afterwards. The only time that nerves nearly got the better of her was during her first meeting with Gresham's sister, a formidable matron of ample proportions, iron-grey hair and a pince-nez. Through these she subjected Frances to a lengthy and minute inspection, convincing Frances that she had been instantly identified as a lower-class schemer intent on trapping the lady's brother into matrimony. Frances kept cool, was polite but not too deferential, friendly with just the right amount of formality, made a huge fuss of Lucia and none of her employer, sang like an angel and passed the test. The lady thawed by degrees, until one day she indicated which way the wind was blowing by asking some very searching questions.

'You have a family, Miss Leigh?'

'No, not any more.'

'Everyone has someone.'

'With respect, I believe that there are people who are all alone in the world but, yes, in my case you are right. I do have a sister.'

'Mr Gresham mentioned her to me, in connection with the school that apparently you ran as a joint venture. What was her name now, I forget . . .'

Just as well she had owned up to the existence of one sister. 'Mary,' Frances replied. They were walking in the garden, admiring the roses, and Lucia was a few steps ahead of them. Frances willed her not to listen.

'She is also in service as a governess?'

In service. That put her in her place! 'She returned to a previous employer, who was anxious to have her back. I have not heard from her since and do not expect to do so.'

'How very odd.'

'We are not close and, although naturally we wish each other every success, we do not believe that we can contribute to each other's happiness.'

'Hm.' Clearly unconvinced, the lady gave Frances another long stare. 'Sounds more as if you have something to hide.'

Frances's heart lurched. 'I simply see no point in wasting time and energy on arid relationships on the grounds of consanguinity alone. If that sounds hard, forgive me.'

It did sound hard but, knowing her brother's intentions towards the young woman, the former Miss Gresham was by no means displeased to ascertain that no unsuitable or embarrassing Leigh relatives were likely to descend on them.

'And where did you come from?'

Believing that biology was not at the root of this question, Frances was grateful that she had anticipated such an interrogation. 'My father was a London businessman but he died young, leaving us greatly impoverished. My mother was a . . .' and she named Fanny's family and home, 'but, like me, she was proud and independent and did not care to ask for help. After she died, Mary and I managed to find suitable work, but it meant that we drifted apart.'

It was sufficiently close to the truth to be convincing and apparently her inquisitor was satisfied, because she asked no more questions. However, that night Lucia clung to Frances's hand longer than usual when she went to say good night.

'You did not tell Aunt about Arabella and Imogen,' she whispered.

Frances looked at her, worried by this weak link in her fabrication of lies, and was astonished to see fear in Lucia's eyes.

'I am so glad that you didn't tell her,' Lucia went on.

'Why?'

'They frighten me. I know that it's silly, that they are your sisters, but at school they frightened me, and if I think about them now I feel afraid all over again.'

Then Frances did something that she knew to be very wrong, but which was expedient: instead of dispelling the child's irrational fear, she used it for her own ends.

'In that case we will not let Arabella or Imogen come near us again or ever mention them to anyone. You haven't told anyone about them, have you?'

Lucia shook her head. 'But won't you miss them?'

'Not in the least. I do not like them either, and you are much more important to me than any of my sisters. The twins will be our secret, just yours and mine.'

Thomas Gresham proposed after supper one evening while Lucia played the piano in the music room.

'Pleasant, this,' he said awkwardly, 'being together, the three of us. You are more like a mother to Lucia than a governess. Do you think, my dear, that you could bear to take on the position permanently, be a mother to Lucia and a wife to me?'

'I would like it above all things, Thomas,' Frances said simply, raising her face to be kissed.

He pressed his lips to her cheek and then, after a moment's hesitation, to her mouth. A gentle, even per-functory, kiss, without passion and almost without emotion. Against Frances's closed eyelids there rose the forbidden, banished face of Vere Cavendish, a searing reminder of what she was missing but, with a constriction in chest and throat, she pushed it from her mind. Vere Cavendish was the stuff of dreams and fantasies, while this was real; this was money and position and security.

'I suggest that we have a Christmas wedding,' Thomas said later, 'after the banns are read at the local church. We could have the cathedral, of course . . . No? I do so agree, my dear, that a quiet, intimate service would be more appropriate, as well as more to our liking. In which case we will keep the guest list to a minimum. My sister, of course, and her husband . . . And what about your sister? Surely you would like a member of your family to attend?'

Sitting within the embrace of Frances's encircling arm after being told the good news, Lucia stiffened and Frances felt it and understood, and thanked providence for whatever the twins had said or done to the child in the past.

'My family is here,' she said clearly, 'with you and Lucia. I do not need anyone else.' And she felt Lucia relax.

So when, with Lucia in attendance, Frances married Thomas Gresham on Christmas Eve 1887 she came to the church alone, without any of her sisters knowing that she was a bride. That night she lay with her husband in the big double bed formerly occupied by his first wife, and accommodated him. Thanks to the theatre and to Marion, she was fully *au fait* with the facts of life and knew what to expect, but she did insist that it was done in the dark. She gasped involuntarily with the pain of his entry but thereafter made no sound or movement. It was what he expected, she judged correctly; the response, or lack of it, of an archetypal Victorian wife, who did her duty but was not expected to enjoy it. Indeed, had she enjoyed it, the likes of Thomas Gresham would have found that enthusiasm suspect. Happily, he was unlikely to be a demanding man. Three times a week would do him nicely, and when the honeymoon was over twice would become routine, lapsing slowly to Saturday nights only. After all, Frances thought as she settled down to sleep, he had lived without apparent discomfort since the death of her predecessor.

Next morning she crept out of bed and sat by the window, watching a winter dawn gradually illumine the landscape. As the garden and the park were revealed, she contemplated the life that lay ahead: Lucia and this lovely house; entertaining their neighbours to dinner and musical evenings; drives in the brougham; garden parties and horticultural shows; social links with the hunt and the diocese, and the Three Choirs Festival; her husband's position as a magistrate and its links with the courts, judges and the prison; her position as lady of the manor and the charitable work she would do with schools, hospitals and musical societies. And, when Lucia was eighteen, the London Season.

Then there was Florence. She had looked at the picture in the music room so often that she could see it as clearly as the view out of the window of an English Christmas Day. Frances longed for Florence, feeling that it was her spiritual home, although she was practical enough to concede that this was a romantic notion. The villa was real enough, in her mind's eye, but what did Tuscany mean to her, what did the name convey, what did she expect? Warmth and sunshine stole over Frances that Christmas morning; she saw cypress trees, vines and olives, the pure white gleam of classic sculpture, a vista of towers and domes; she heard the clang of bells and the buzz of insects; and she smelled an aromatic perfume and something sharper – lemons, perhaps?

In her heart she still remembered Vere on the lawn of that lovely house on the day of the garden party and she ached with the longing that this was their home and that he was here beside her. However, she had the next best thing, and she was determined to be a good wife and mother. She would do anything to keep what she had won, and she would kill anyone who threatened to take it away from her.

'She hasn't seen us.'

Fascinated, the twins edged into the room and, over-hearing the introduction 'Mr and Mrs Thomas Gresham', exchanged a look of wicked delight.

'Do you suppose that Mr Gresham knows about us?' Arabella murmured as they withdrew to the terrace again in order to discuss their strategy.

'Unlikely, unless Lucia told him.'

'Lucia would do anything Frances told her to do, so my guess is that Frances has disowned her entire family.'

'Which means,' Imogen said thoughtfully, 'that our presence here tonight might come as something of a shock.'

'I think it would be proper to pretend that we have never seen her before.'

Imogen sighed wistfully. 'I suppose you are right, but couldn't we tease her, just a little bit?'

Arabella grinned. 'Absolutely but, Ginny, promise me that you will not go too far.'

'Would I wreck my sister's marriage?' Imogen looked injured.

'Yes, if you thought that you could gain by it. So this is your opportunity to prove that your reformation is not only skin deep.'

Arm in arm, the twins advanced into the drawing room

and, manoeuvring themselves into a position adjacent to the group with whom Frances was talking, stood in her direct line of vision.

She was much lovelier than they remembered. Happiness had made her innate beauty bloom, filling out the contours of her figure, softening the sharp angles of her face, widening her sparkling eyes and curving the generous lines of her mouth. Maturity had dealt with her more kindly than it had Marion. Now, should they stand side by side, Frances would be deemed the more beautiful.

Then Frances looked up and saw her sisters. The colour draining from her face, she swayed and clutched her husband's arm for support, her eyes never leaving the nightmare vision of those two radiant young faces.

'I say, are you feeling unwell?' Gresham asked anxiously and the group, knowing that Mrs Gresham was virtually a bride, looked at each other knowingly and started counting the months back to the wedding.

'A little air . . . I do apologise,' and Frances walked unsteadily to the nearly deserted terrace where, watched by the twins, her husband fanned her stricken face.

'Can we help?' Faces composed into suitably solicitous expressions, the twins approached with tactful discretion. 'We are staying at the castle and I'm sure the countess would want us to assist her guests,' Arabella said sweetly.

Worried about his wife and not having the first idea how to assist her, Gresham looked at them gratefully.

'What you need, Mrs Gresham,' Imogen suggested, 'is a few deep breaths of fresh air and then a sit-down in the supper room with a reviving drink. Mr Gresham, if we stay with your wife, won't you reserve a supper table and we will escort her there in a few minutes.'

'I need to go home,' Frances protested, but her husband was already hurrying back into the house.

'Mrs Gresham, you could not possibly desert the earl's reception so early,' Arabella exclaimed. 'He and the countess would be very offended.'

'Go away, go away the pair of you,' Frances said in a low voice. 'I never want to see you again. If you say one word about who you are, about who I am, I swear . . .'

'Why, Mrs Gresham, what can you mean?' Imogen looked puzzled. 'What have we done to offend you?'

'Don't play games with me, Imogen,' Frances hissed. 'What are you doing here, anyway? Is Marion here as well, and Charley? Oh God, I cannot *bear* it. It just isn't *fair*!'

'Come inside and sit down, Mrs Gresham,' Arabella said kindly, taking one arm while Imogen took the other.

They virtually frog-marched her across the terrace, their grip so tight that it hurt, but short of trying to struggle free and thereby causing a scene, there was nothing Frances could do.

'If you say anything, I'll kill you,' she whispered. 'I mean it, I swear I do . . .'

They found Gresham at a small table in the supper room, and a sip of brandy soon revived the colour in Frances's cheeks. The initial shock over, she began to regain control.

'You have been most kind,' she said firmly, 'but we need not detain you further.'

'It's no trouble,' and Arabella sat down next to her. 'We have nothing better to do. Ginny, fetch some champagne.'

'Did you say that you are house guests here?' Gresham inquired, mightily impressed by the beauty and good manners of their new friends.

'Yes. I am Arabella Leigh, by the way, and this is my sister Imogen.'

'What a coincidence!' Gresham exclaimed. 'Did you hear that, my dear? You see, my wife's maiden name was Leigh.'

'It is a small world,' smiled Arabella.

'How very true,' Frances said tartly. 'Unfortunately, members of my family were never likely to be guests of the aristocracy. Do tell us, Miss Leigh, how you come to know the earl and countess.'

'We were at school with their daughter, Lady Sarah.'

Of course. Frances could have kicked herself for not making the connection but, even had she done so, she could hardly have refused the invitation on the vague off-chance that the twins would be there. But then another aspect of the affair dawned on her and was immediately voiced by Arabella.

'We are very good friends with the whole family and expect to be here frequently, so I am sure we will have the pleasure of seeing you often.'

Frances took a deep gulp of brandy. Oh, the injustice of it, the downright bloody-mindedness of it, that the local aristocracy, whom she had wanted to meet so much, should be the parents of Arabella's best friend. Now it was spoiled, this evening and any other invitation to the castle, spoiled because she would always fear the presence of the twins.

They were joined by two other couples, neighbours of Gresham, come to inquire after Frances's health. Introductions were made amid more exclamations of surprise over the Leigh name.

'Frances disclaims all knowledge of them,' Gresham said jovially, 'but, looking at this charming young lady,' and he bowed to Imogen, 'I fancy I can discern a resemblance.'

'They might be sisters,' affirmed one of the newcomers,

while Frances went from white to scarlet and back to white again.

'I am terribly flattered,' Imogen said, 'but I fear that I am far inferior in looks to Mrs Gresham. Oh, don't worry,' she protested at the chorus of reassurance, 'Arabella and I are twins and I am perfectly accustomed to being "the plain one".'

'Do you have any other family?' someone asked.

'We have two sisters in London . . .' Deliberately, and very cleverly, Imogen's voice trailed away, as if she was hesitating whether or not to add to the family tree or embellish the bare facts.

Frances felt faint again and asked for another brandy.

At that moment Sarah stopped by their table and spoke softly to Arabella. During their brief exchange, one of the newcomers asked Gresham if he was planning a visit to his villa in Florence. He proceeded to explain at some length that he and Frances had decided not to travel to Italy that year, but planned an extended visit next spring.

'Italy,' Imogen exclaimed. 'Arabella, did you hear that? Mr and Mrs Gresham have a villa in Florence,' and without missing a beat both sisters broke into a torrent of fluent Italian.

'You should take the Miss Leighs with you to Florence,' someone remarked, laughing. 'They would make extremely efficient, and immensely decorative, interpreters.'

'Oh yes, do take us,' Arabella pleaded. 'We have never been to Italy and we positively yearn to see Florence, and Rome and Venice . . .'

'Did you learn Italian at school?' Gresham inquired.

'Yes, but also we took lessons in London. From Maria Scarlatti, although I doubt you will have heard of her.'

'But this is astonishing,' and Gresham grew positively

pink with excitement. 'Maria is an old friend of the first Mrs Gresham and it was through her that Lucia went to school in London, and that Lucia and I met Frances.'

'*No!*' exclaimed both twins in unison, 'Well, I'll be . . .'

'And does your acquaintance with Maria mean that you sing, Mrs Gresham?' Imogen went on.

'A little,' Frances replied.

'Apparently Mrs Gresham sings more than a little,' Arabella remarked. 'Sarah has just whispered to me that the countess would be delighted if she would entertain the gathering with her music after supper.'

'I couldn't possibly,' Frances flushed, partly with pleasure, partly with nervousness, and more than a little because she believed that Arabella had engineered the invitation and suspected that some frightful fate was in store for her. Of course she was persuaded – indeed, there was no way she could refuse – and when supper was over, Frances prepared to take her seat at the piano.

But Imogen stood up, too. 'I will accompany you.'

'I can accompany myself, thank you very much.'

'I'm quite reliable. I had a frightfully good teacher.' And Imogen marched determinedly to the piano followed by Frances, fearing the worst.

Standing by the instrument while Imogen ostentatiously shuffled the sheet music, Frances was taken back to the old front parlour and Imogen creating havoc with the piano keys, while Frances pressed her hands to her ears in a vain attempt to ward off a headache. However, as Imogen struck up the opening chords, Frances launched herself into the song and tried to lose herself in it. What else could she do, but her best? And, to her relief, Imogen played accurately and kept time with her beautifully. They were an immense success. Then, as Frances embarked on her fourth song, Arabella walked across the room and joined in with her strong, sweet soprano. And Imogen took up the refrain, she and Arabella harmonising effortlessly while Frances's voice soared above with true, trained clarity.

The result was electrifying and they sang again, songs that Frances had taught the twins in those innocent days, which seemed so very long ago. To her horror Frances felt tears pricking at her eyelids, not out of emotion at the huge swell of applause that greeted them but because it had not been in vain, all that toil and struggle over the years. She really had taught them something, and they were talented, and they were her sisters; but she could never acknowledge them as such, never, not any more.

Fortunately, in one way, they made it easy for her to turn her back on them.

Arabella and Imogen were curtsying with exaggerated, almost comic, flamboyance.

'We are nearly good enough to go on the stage,' Arabella said wickedly, the remark bringing another thunder of applause.

'While on the subject of the stage, why don't we play charades?' suggested Imogen.

'Yes, let's,' and Sarah stepped forward eagerly. 'Couldn't we, Mama? Arabella and Imogen are terribly good at charades.'

'Bags us Mrs Gresham for our team,' Arabella declared, 'because she used to be a Leigh. Let's have the Leighs versus the Vales.'

'The Leighs will win easily,' and Henry Vale clasped his forehead in mock dismay. 'They always do. Arabella and Imogen ought to be in the professional theatre – Ellen Terry wouldn't stand a chance against that kind of competition.'

'Perhaps we will go on the stage,' Arabella teased, 'but

'if we do, you must promise to take a box every night.'

'Can you doubt it?' and he sketched an extravagant bow.

Everyone was laughing, everyone except Frances, but she need not have worried. Every eye was on the tall, graceful figure of Arabella, and no one was looking at Frances.

'I think,' she said in a low voice as she rejoined her husband, 'that I would like to go home. I really do not feel up to charades.'

'Of course,' and he was on his feet immediately, apologising to his hosts for their early departure and ushering his wife to their carriage, perfectly content with her musical success and secretly rather glad to be going home at a respectable hour.

'Don't mention those Leigh girls to Lucia,' Frances said as they drove home. 'She is highly sensitive and very reliant on me. For some reason she seems to fear that I will leave her – do you think that it could be because her mother died? I do not want her upset by a story of some mythical sisters who, she might imagine, could be more important to me than she is. Nothing and no one is more dear to me than Lucia!'

And Thomas Gresham, who would not have thought of mentioning those lovely girls to his daughter, squeezed Frances's hand reassuringly.

'Are you feeling better?' he asked. 'You do not think that your indisposition might be due to . . . ?'

'No,' said Frances, 'but I continue to hope . . .'

Several days later, Imogen offered to deliver a basket of food to a tenant on the earl's estate and persuaded the coachman to make a detour past the Gresham property.

Sitting in an open carriage, a parasol shading her

against the sun, Imogen noted the location of the gates and, further on, saw the house in the setting of its gracious park.

Frances had done very well for herself, very well indeed, thought Imogen, settling back in her seat. And, who knows, that information could prove very useful one day.

When Imogen returned to the castle, a letter addressed to the twins was lying on the hall table. It was from Marion, summoning them urgently to London.

Chapter Twenty-Six

M arion had been sitting in the greenroom when she heard the crash and, like everyone else in the theatre, she had run to the stage and cried out in horror at the sight of Charley pinned to the floor beneath the heavy flat. While the stage staff, under Vere's direction, lifted the burden from Charley's body, Marion pushed her way through the crowd and knelt beside her sister, too shocked to speak. And when the full extent of Charley's injuries was revealed, Marion's face went as white as that of the victim and she fainted.

Charley had taken the full force of the impact on her lower body, so that her head and upper torso were unhurt but her legs were a bloody, mangled mess.

By the time Marion recovered consciousness, Charley had been taken to hospital and Edward Druce was hovering anxiously in the background.

'I must go to her,' and Marion scrambled unsteadily to her feet.

'That is why I waited,' Edward said quietly. 'I thought that we could go together – you are in no fit state to go anywhere on your own.'

'Has Vere gone with her?'

'Of course.'

'It's all his fault.' Marion's voice began to rise hysterically. 'I said there would be an accident here one day, because he spends money on front-of-house luxuries instead of backstage necessities.'

'There is something in what you say,' Edward returned gravely. 'But if Charley survives, it is Vere Cavendish whom she must thank. I'll never know how he crossed the stage so quickly, but he grabbed Charley's shoulders and tried to pull her clear. Another split-second and he might have succeeded. As it was, the flat caught her a glancing blow and knocked her down – Vere, too, incidentally, although he appears to be unhurt – but if it had smashed into her skull . . .'

'I don't care how much of a hero he was. It ought never to have happened in the first place and if Charley doesn't make a full recovery, I will hold him personally responsible.'

Edward did not comment. He did not want to point out that, from what he had seen, it was not a matter of whether Charley made a full or partial recovery, but simply whether she lived or died.

There began for Marion long days and weeks by her sister's bed while Charley fought for life. The loss of blood was so severe that for a time she seemed to be sinking, slipping away from them, leaving those who watched over her with a fearful sense of helplessness. But each time she rallied again and the spark of life within her burned a little brighter. Lapsing in and out of consciousness, she brought welcome moments of hope by recognising her visitors, but wakefulness also brought appalling pain from the injuries to her shattered limbs. Marion would stumble back to Grace's apartment, to try to sleep, with the sounds of her sister's screams echoing in her ears.

'Send for the twins,' both Edward and Grace urged.

'They could sit with Charley while you get some rest.'

But this Marion stubbornly refused to do. 'My place is at Charley's side and the twins would only be another source of worry. Better they stay where they are and enjoy themselves while they can. I will tell them about the accident when I know the outcome.'

Slowly it became apparent that Charley would live and, much against Grace's advice, Marion went back to The Cavendish. She had a public and a contract to satisfy and, besides, working took her mind off the tragedy. First, she sought a private interview with Vere.

'You have been conspicuous by your absence at Charley's sickbed,' she said scornfully, 'but you might be interested to know that her spine is believed to be undamaged and that the doctors have decided not to amputate.'

'I am relieved to hear it,' he said quietly.

'Of course, we do not yet know whether she will ever walk again – her legs . . . Oh my God, her beautiful, beautiful legs!'

His hands clenched, whitening the knuckles, but he said nothing.

'It's all your fault,' Marion screamed. 'How many times do you have to be told to take care of basic repairs but, oh no, if it is out of public sight, it is right out of your mind.'

'Naturally The Cavendish accepts full responsibility for this unfortunate incident,' he said formally. 'Charley will receive full pay during her convalescence and I have already informed the doctors that I will meet all medical expenses.'

'You have?' Marion was taken aback. She stared at him, at that impenetrable face, wondering what – if anything – he was feeling. 'She doesn't want to see you,' Marion said suddenly, 'not ever again. She says so often.'

It was not true. Charley had not mentioned Vere when

she was conscious; however, she cried out his name constantly when delirious and drugged against the pain.

'Whatever Charley wants, she shall have,' he said in that same toneless voice. 'I would not dream of intruding where I was not wanted.'

'Stay away from her, stay away from all of us! You bring death and destruction wherever you go and to whoever you touch!'

'A mite melodramatic, Marion. But perhaps melodrama is your mark, after all.'

She hated him, then; hated him more than ever; for her, loss of professional pride was nearly as acute as losing her baby. Yet, had he thrown himself at her feet, begging forgiveness and declaring his everlasting love for her, she would have succumbed. Despite everything, she would have married him, given the chance. She knew it, and hated him all the more.

'I will stay at The Cavendish until the end of the season but no longer,' she declared.

'Your departure, and Charley's continuing absence, have been anticipated and suitable replacements hired.'

With the sound of the slamming door reverberating around the theatre, Vere leaned back in his chair and sank into quiet contemplation. He had not felt this bad since Marion's botched abortion. Goddamn it, what was it about these Leigh sisters that managed to get to him, to crawl under his skin and prick him with the barbs of a thousand thorns? He had told Marion a pack of lies, said a host of things he had not intended to say, and the result was the mess that he invariably made of his private life.

Why had he said that he had hired replacements for Marion and Charley? He had done no such thing. Furthermore, there were no obvious candidates for the positions, although he had heard that his old flame, Arlene

Sidley, was free. Arlene . . . Oh my God, and Vere groaned.

Even more important, why hadn't he told Marion that he had visited the hospital every day in order to inquire after Charley's progress? Why hadn't he admitted to the nights he had spent at her side, long after Marion, Grace and Edward had gone home, simply sitting there in silent vigil by Charley's unconscious form, willing her to live and silently begging her forgiveness?

Pride, he supposed. The same pride that would lead him into obeying Marion's command not to see Charley again, while not allowing himself to admit that, in so doing, he was taking the easy way out. He knew that he needed Charley's forgiveness, that without it he would never rid himself of the guilt he felt about the accident. He was haunted by the memory of Charley's broken body and that frayed rope, and yet he lacked the courage to confront it. Had just one person encouraged him to go to Charley and ask her forgiveness, then he might have done so, and so many lives and circumstances would have taken a different turn. But Vere had no one to talk to, no one in whom to confide, no close friend who had his best interests at heart. So, instead of dealing with the emotional and personal residue of the tragedy, he turned his attention to the practical implications and, much too late, embarked on a programme of backstage repairs, renovations and improvements, which he could ill-afford.

So here she was, back in the bosom of her family. Seated in a basket chair by the window in Marion's apartment, Charley felt that this imprisonment, with her sisters as jailors, was the worst aspect of her present sorry state. But, a few minutes from now, she would feel that another condition was the hardest to endure, and an hour later it

would be something else, as her moods fluctuated wildly
between anger, frustration and self-pity.

At this moment she was obsessed with her sisters. To be
dependent on them was more than she could bear:
Marion, so smug and self-sacrificial after her cold, unforgiving silence at The Cavendish; Arabella, whose perfect
beauty was like a physical hurt, a constant reminder of
what Charley had lost; and Imogen whom, however irrational it seemed, she could not entirely trust. To be thrown
back among them, as a helpless invalid, when all she had
ever wanted was to put as much distance as possible
between herself and them, was a cruel joke for fate to
play. Or was it a punishment for selfishly deserting her
responsibilities and leading such an immoral life? Or had
she died after all and this was hell?

The pain was creeping back into her limbs as the morphine wore off, only a dull ache now, but a reminder that
it would intensify slowly until she reached screaming
pitch. She glanced at her watch; nearly an hour before
her next dose . . . Oh God . . .

In the street people were walking, some slowly, some
quickly, some elegantly, some comically; everyone in the
world seemed to have two perfect legs on which to walk,
everyone except her. A sob rose in her throat, to be
checked instantly. Another punishment – for being so vain
about her legs, for showing them off in tights for men to
leer at, for flaunting them so shamelessly? Well, she would
not be doing that again. No one, bar doctors and nurses,
would look at her legs again. Not even *she* would look at
them again, because she simply did not have the courage –
when the dressings were changed, she closed her eyes.
Sitting in the basket chair, she insisted on having a light
rug wrapped around her lower body so that the outline of
her legs was not visible.

Without her legs, she could never act again. If she could not act, how would she earn a living? She must earn a living, she must! She could not stay here, dependent on the charity of her sisters for ever, and, besides, without her work she would go mad. Of course, she could go back to the printshop. Uncle John had mentioned it again during his visit this morning. 'My accounts are in a terrible mess,' he had said casually. 'Do you think that you could look at them? I'd be very grateful for your help.' But he didn't fool her – he didn't really need her help, he just felt sorry for her. She did not want a job on those terms. She wanted a proper job, won on merit, not to be an object of pity.

Better if Vere had not intervened and the flat had fallen on her head and killed her. Charley looked at the window, gauging whether she would be able to stand upright unaided, open the window and throw herself down into the street. No, on second thoughts, perhaps not. Terribly messy, even if she could manage it, and horrid for those who would have to clean up after her. The medicine would be best – quick and painless, she imagined, and possibly quite pleasant – but even if the bottle contained sufficient for suicide, Marion insisted on it being kept out of Charley's reach. Bugger Marion. Bugger the whole bloody lot of them, particularly Vere.

Here Charley's thoughts tended to shy away from the subject, as if it were too painful to contemplate. He had not been to see her, or sent a personal message, although her wages were delivered each week. Evidently that dreadful quarrel had been the end of the relationship. Anyway, if she were realistic, it was obvious that Vere Cavendish was not a man who would have any use for a cripple. No man would, no man would want to sleep with her again, because no one would be able to bear the sight of her legs.

Yet sometimes she felt a memory stirring within her, of the hospital late at night, when the lights were low and all was quiet but for a few muffled sobs or snores, and she opened her eyes and saw the hazy, blurred vision of Vere's face bending over her before she sank into unconsciousness again. Wishful thinking, she thought, angrily brushing away the beginning of a tear. But he had tried to save her – how like Edward to have told her, and how like Marion to have kept quiet about it! Then again Marion was right – the accident had been Vere's fault, that damn rope . . .

The thoughts crowded in on her, tumultuous, teeming, throbbing in her head like hammers on angry anvils, discordant and disruptive, and Charley pressed her hands to her forehead in despair. I am going mad, she thought, but only because I have nothing to do but sit here and think.

The pain was getting worse and she must have the morphine. Where was everyone? Matinée day, so Marion was at the theatre. Arabella had gone out, looking determined yet furtive, and the nurse would be back at five to dress Charley's legs and undress the rest of her.

'Imogen,' bellowed Charley peremptorily. 'Where the hell are you?'

'Doing the ironing,' said a distinctly martyred Imogen, walking into the room and eyeing her sister belligerently.

'Don't sound so hard done by. Thank your lucky stars that you have legs to stand on while you are doing the ironing. It's time for my medicine, so look sharp.'

'No, it isn't. Half an hour to go, then you may rely on me to down tools, doff the pinny and minister unto you.'

'Sarcastic little so-and-so, aren't you! Don't argue with me. If anyone knows when the medicine is due, it's me.'

'I take orders from Marion, not from anyone else.'

'Don't we all! Story of our bloody lives. Oh, very well, give me a brandy instead.'

Imogen looked at her doubtfully. 'I am not sure that you ought to drink liquor during the afternoon.'

'It is my brandy and I will drink it when I bloody please. Fetch the bottle and a glass and, so as not to offend your finer feelings, I will pour it myself. Your hands can remain clean.'

With a sigh, Imogen fetched the brandy and a glass and placed them on a table beside Charley's chair. 'I don't understand what you see in that stuff,' she remarked.

'You aren't supposed to understand. Suffice it to say that it makes me feel better. Now, go away, but make sure that you come back, with the medicine, in thirty minutes prompt.'

The brandy slipped down, raw fire into her stomach. It did not really banish the pain. It just made that pain easier to endure.

Precisely on time, Imogen brought in the morphine and watched as Charley swallowed it. She lingered, observing the change in her sister's features, the creases gradually smoothing out, and peace replacing the ravages on that lovely face.

'What does it do exactly?' she asked.

'It makes all the pain go away.'

'I know that, but do you mean only the physical pain, or mental pain as well?'

Charley was too far gone, sliding blissfully into oblivion to wonder that Imogen should be aware of mental pain. 'Both,' she said. 'Right now I do not have a care in the world.'

In the kitchen Imogen replaced the medicine on the shelf but, before closing the cupboard door, she paused for a moment, looking at the bottle. Then, thoughtfully, she tiptoed into the living room in order to remove the brandy and dirty glass from Charley's side. A little brandy was left in the bottom of the glass and, after sniffing it suspiciously, Imogen drank it, grimacing horribly at the taste. Another, unopened, bottle stood on the dresser, a gift from Vere Cavendish, and Imogen stood the half-full bottle beside it.

Then she sat down at the kitchen table, twirling the dirty glass between her hands. If Arabella was not back in ten minutes, she would have another brandy. Just a little one, of course . . .

Edward Druce visited Charley every day but one afternoon, towards the end of July, he burst into the room with a distinctly jaunty air and a spring in his step.

'You're late,' Charley said morosely, 'and I do wish that you would not look so bloody cheerful.'

'Good afternoon, Edward. How nice to see you, Edward. How kind of you to come, Edward,' he said mockingly. 'I see that there is no danger of *you* being cheerful.'

'Some of us do not have anything to be cheerful about.'

'Ah, still playing the helpless invalid to a captive audience.'

'It is *me* who is the captive.'

'Not entirely, dear girl. The rest of us are suffering along with you – you are making very sure of that. What is top of the list of complaints today – reliance on your sisters, loss of independence, loss of legs, loss of work, or love, or Vere . . . ?'

'If you intend to continue in this vein, you can bloody well turn round and go straight out again.'

'There was a time,' he said, sitting down next to her, 'when I thought your anger was a good thing, that all the bloody-this and bloody-that was a sign of defiance, but instead it is degenerating into a destructive bitterness.'

'Oh, just tell me that the whole thing is my fault, why don't you! And then throw me down the stairs on your way out, so that I can break my neck – you might as well, I'm neither use nor ornament.'

'A destructive bitterness,' he went on inexorably, 'mixed with a most un-Charley-like self-pity. Come on, you are a fighter and you can do better than this.'

'Don't you think that if I could pick up my bed and walk, I damned well would!'

'You are too reliant on that nurse coming in every morning and evening,' he said craftily. 'Of course, it is very generous of Vere Cavendish to provide the service, but . . .'

'*What?*' shrieked Charley, hands on the arms of the chair, levering herself forward. 'Is *Vere* paying that woman's wages? Why the hell didn't someone say so before – she is not setting foot in this place again, and she is most certainly not laying a finger on me again. I'll change my own blasted dressings before I am beholden to that man!'

'That's my girl!' Edward exclaimed, smiling. 'And if you start by changing the dressings, you can continue doing other things.'

A shadow passed over her face. 'Such as?' and the bitterness was back in her voice.

'Get out of that chair.'

'I can't,' she shouted. 'You know that I can't!'

'Have you tried to stand up? Because if not, you should. A bit of self-will and determination instead of all this self-pity could work wonders.'

Charley stared at him resentfully and then looked away.

'I was late today because I went to the hospital and had a long chat with your doctor. My cheerfulness is the result of that conversation.'

'You had no right to discuss me behind my back, and the doctor had no right to breach the laws of confidentiality! You are not even family!'

'I told him that I was your fiancé,' he said calmly. 'Now, some might consider that to be a blatant untruth. I consider it merely an anticipation of the inevitable.'

Charley stared at him, dumbstruck.

'Perseverance is my family motto, remember? We never take no for an answer. My romantic aspirations have not changed, even though they are temporarily superseded by an iron determination to get you on your feet again.'

A faint flush was warming Charley's cheeks. 'You have not seen my legs,' she whispered.

'No time like the present. Your sisters are out, leaving you unchaperoned.' And he raised an eyebrow in mock consternation.

'Don't take that as a compliment to your gentlemanly instincts. It is merely an acknowledgement of my status as an object of pity, not desire.'

'How little they know,' he said softly, and lifted the rug from her legs. 'Shall we take off the dressings together?'

'What did the doctor say?' she prevaricated, trying to grab the rug, but he tossed it out of reach.

'He said what, in your heart, you already know. That one leg – the right – has healed remarkably well, that the broken bones have mended and the muscles, though wasted, are not irreparable. You took the full force of the blow on your left side, and it is the left leg that is the most damaged. That leg will never recover its full use, although in time the pain and discomfort will subside to reasonable proportions.'

'So the best I can hope for is one good-ish leg and one bad. What am I supposed do – *hop*?'

'You are supposed to take one step at a time – literally and metaphorically. Look at your legs and confront the reality of your condition. Stand up, with my help. Walk a few steps, with the aid of crutches. After that ... Well, we will have to find out if your perseverance matches mine.'

'I am going to put a stop to this nonsense right now,' Charley said decisively, pulling up her skirt. 'One look at my legs and you will be out of that door so fast that all this crap will be irrelevant.'

'Let's start with the right leg, shall we?'

'What would the little blonde at the Haymarket think about this?'

'The little blonde at the Haymarket had one, very physical, function, which I dare to think you understand all too well. Her thoughts, about anything or anyone, are not exactly germane, and anyway she's history.' He had removed her shoe and was rolling down her stocking with an expertise that, in different circumstances, would have been erotic. 'As I expected – one thin layer of bandage, to protect your sensibilities, not your leg.'

Charley was staring over his head, at the bright square of the window, feeling the unravelling of the protective layer as if it was the baring of her soul. She could not look at him and she could not look at *it*. But then she felt his lips, unmistakably his lips, pressing against her foot and her ankle, and travelling tenderly up her calf to her knee. Instinctively Charley reached out a hand and smoothed his hair and, in so doing, she looked down and saw his cheek resting against her leg. He drew back and looked up at her, holding her leg, cradling it and stretching it out for her to see in all its glory.

Some glory! The leg was straight enough, its former curves vaguely discernible, but the translucent white flesh of former years was riven by slashes of scarlet and valleys

of purple. The foot looked strong though, and Charley
flexed it cautiously, seeing the ripples of response and
feeling a twinge – no more – of pain.

'That isn't so bad, is it?' Edward asked encouragingly.
'Let's look at the other one.'

'Must we? Couldn't we do one at a time and leave it
until another day?'

But he pretended not to hear and went on unwinding
bandages with the concentration and gentleness of a
fervent archaeologist unwrapping an ancient Egyptian
mummy. When he had finished there was a long pause,
during which Charley stared over his head before forcing
her eyes down to her left leg. And when she did look, a
great choking sob consumed her and she let out a heart-
rending wail of despair.

The bones of the mangled, misshapen limb, which had
barely escaped amputation, had been too splintered to
knit together properly, while flesh, muscle and tissue had
been pulped, leaving a leg barely recognisable as such,
purplish-red in hue, with weals of rough scarred tissue
and open, ulcerating sores. Blinded by tears, Charley
buried her face in her hands, but then she felt the soft,
healing touch of his lips on what had been her knee.

'How can you do that?' she whispered. 'How can you
bear to touch it?'

'It is part of you,' he answered gently. 'My God,
Charley, if you only knew how many times I have
dreamed of kissing you!'

'But not like this.'

'Like even your little toe has been the subject of my
fevered imagination,' Edward assured her with mock seriousness. 'The point is, Charley, that this leg is not going to
walk again even if it can be coaxed into taking your
weight. The sores will heal and the pain will pass,

although you may suffer a dull ache on damp days! Exercise is the thing, and that is where I can help.'

'Now?'

'No, you've had enough trauma for one day. We will start exercising tomorrow.'

'Can we keep it a secret from the others? I do not want to be seen trying to do something and failing.'

'We will not fail! Now, where are the clean dressings? We might as well complete the job while we're at it, if you are giving the nurse her marching orders. Mind you, I reckon the right leg can stay unbandaged – you can exercise it more easily without any restriction.'

When it was done and she sat back in her chair again, her skirts rearranged but the rug permanently discarded, she smiled at Edward for the first time in months.

'You are so good to me. Why, when I behave like such a bitch?'

'You know why. And don't succumb to exhaustion because you have work to do – you must write a note for the nurse.'

'I do not need to write. I can send her away with a verbal flea in her ear quite satisfactorily, thank you!'

'You must write a polite note to Vere Cavendish, thanking him for his courtesy in providing the nurse, but advising that you are sufficiently recovered not to need her services any longer.'

'I must *what* . . . ?' Charley choked over the words and the very idea. 'You are a perfect gentleman, Edward,' she said at last, 'but don't waste your time trying to turn me into a lady.'

'I will spend my time as I wish, and nothing will disillusion me from the belief that under that tough exterior lurks the very flower of femininity.'

Fumbling behind her, Charley extricated a cushion,

which she flung at him and which he dodged, laughing, before wheeling her to the table and finding her writing materials.

Edward helped her to stand and take her weight on her right foot, and then to hop unsteadily with her left arm around his neck and his right arm around her waist. Sitting in her chair, Charley constantly stretched and flexed the right leg, strengthening the muscles, and so good was her progress that it seemed that the chief barrier to further advancement was the cramped conditions of the apartment.

'The crutches are ready,' Edward announced, 'but you cannot take two steps in here without bumping into something. Anyway, you don't want your sisters to see. So I think it is time to implement Plan B. You must come to the country with me.'

'Come to the . . .' With Edward, Charley was falling into habitually incomplete sentences. She grasped at the practicalities. 'Your holiday is nearly over – what about The Cavendish tour?'

'I am not going. Told the Chief ages ago that I was opting out. He did not seem surprised and did not try to persuade me to change my mind.'

'Marion has said nothing about it.'

'I don't suppose that she knows. She hardly speaks to me these days and of course she is not touring either. So, how about it? Long, lazy days in the quiet of the country, with an enormous lawn on which to practise walking and on which to find a soft landing if you fall.'

'What do your parents say? They can hardly be thrilled at the prospect of having an out-of-work crippled actress for a house guest.'

'I do wish that you would stop seeing yourself as a

cripple – it is a horrid word, for a start, and I continue to maintain that the mental battle is more important than the physical. I shall not pretend that my people were over-joyed; indeed they were somewhat taken aback, but they warmed to the idea, particularly when I pointed out that they would be in Scotland for the duration of your sojourn in our midst.'

'I won't have to meet them?' Immensely relieved, Charley began to warm to the idea herself. 'How would I get there?'

'Cab, train and carriage. And, in between, a lot of hopping, and hanging on to me, and being pushed in your chair, and bumping downstairs on your bottom.'

Charley's eyes sparkled at the prospect of leaving her prison. 'Sounds like fun.'

'We will have to travel light. I don't think we need take the brandy and the morphine, do you?' His tone was steady but deliberately casual. 'Our local quack will oblige if you have a relapse.'

She hesitated, knowing that her dose of morphine had been diluted but still finding it as much of a crutch as the wooden aids that awaited her in the country. 'Very well,' she said, 'leave it here.'

The journey took a lot out of Charley and for forty-eight hours she did not emerge from the Garden Room in which she had been installed. When she was rested, Edward wheeled her out to the terrace and down the steps to the lawn. She still needed help in levering herself out of the chair and into an upright position, but now she steadied herself on the crutches instead of on him. Slowly, with him close enough to catch her if she fell, she moved the crutches forward and swung her body after them, paused and repeated the manoeuvre, until she was making un-certain but effective progress across the grass. She tired quickly and therefore they restricted the sessions, gradually extending them until she was stronger and more skilled.

In the evenings he pushed her chair to a small drawing room, where they sat and talked and ate their meals, not wanting to trouble the staff by using the main reception rooms in the house. After dinner they usually adjourned to the music room and fooled about on the piano, with Charley freely admitting that Edward was a better pianist and singer than she.

'Have you thought about what you are going to do next season?' she asked.

'I thought I might approach the Haymarket – no, not because of her, idiot! I happen to think that Herbert Beerbohm Tree, despite his preposterous name, is the up-and-coming man. He is doing what Vere Cavendish set out to do, only doing it rather better.'

'He would be lucky to have you,' Charley said sincerely. 'You really are frightfully good – good enough to succeed at anything you wanted to do. Have you thought about going into management yourself?'

He pulled a face and rippled his fingers haphazardly across the piano keys. 'No,' he said finally, 'I don't think management is for me. Too much hard work and worry. I want to act, pure and simple.'

'Being the great actor-manager seems to be the only way to reach the top of the profession,' Charley remarked guardedly.

He turned and laid a finger across her lips. 'We ought to be discussing your future, not mine.'

'What future? Oh, sorry, sorry . . . no bitterness or self-pity, I promise! Tell me, is there a part written for a tall, thin redhead on crutches?'

'Yes, the role of Mrs Edward Druce.'

She stared into his eyes, her heart thumping. 'You must not say these things just because you feel sorry for me.'

'Sorry for you, am I?' He pushed the piano stool close to her chair and pulled her towards him, his lips finding hers, forcing her mouth open and devouring her, his former gentleness crushed by passion. 'You know what I feel for you,' he murmured huskily, 'and sympathy is a very funny word for it.'

Soon she could get around on her crutches with swiftness and expertise, but she disliked the awkward inelegance of the movement.

'The problem is,' she complained, 'that my left leg is too floppy to be any use at all.'

Edward thought for a moment. 'I remember,' he said slowly, 'as a small boy, seeing one of the village children with crutches and then, when we were both older, he was walking with a stick and a sort of wooden brace on his leg. Stay where you are – I'm going to see the local quack.'

He returned with an air of excitement and a tape measure. 'Don't ask,' he advised Charley. 'Cross your fingers, pray, and place your faith in rustic ingenuity.'

Within forty-eight hours Charley, attended by Edward, the doctor and the carpenter, was fitted with a wooden brace, which stiffened and supported the lower portion of her left leg. Then Edward produced a pair of silver-headed walking sticks from the house. Her left leg still dragged but, leaning on the sticks, Charley found that she could walk and, although the motion was a trifle twisted and curiously one-sided, she could move more gracefully than before.

'I cannot take your father's sticks,' she protested.

'For heaven's sake, we have enough canes and walking sticks to stock a shop!'

'Why am I doing this, Edward? What the hell am I trying to achieve?'

'You wanted independence, didn't you? And you wanted to earn a living.'

'I am replacing dependence on my sisters with dependence on you. And, even with walking sticks, I am still unemployable.'

'As an actress, possibly,' he said evenly. 'But is that your only option? Nothing wrong with your head, as far as I can make out, brain unimpaired . . . And you always did take an unusual interest in management and backstage affairs.'

'Yes, I did, didn't I . . .' She paused, remembering old George Allen's argument that the actor was king, that without a great actor even the best efforts of management and dramatist were wasted, and she remembered her ambition to be the best actress-manager in the land. She could never be that, but she could learn to settle for second-best, and a calculating, speculative spark of hope gleamed in her eyes. As if to prove a point, she reached for her sticks, stood up unaided and *walked* to the window.

Edward followed, standing behind her and running his hands over her body. 'You have not lost your independence or your legs, or the possibility of work . . . Let me prove that you have not lost love, either.'

Charley leaned back against him, allowing him to kiss her cheeks and neck, not sexually aroused but desiring reassurance. Sensing her lack of resistance, Edward lifted her and carried her to the bedroom.

Afterwards, while he slept, Charley lay wakeful in the darkness. Of course she was fond of Edward, and she intended to return to London and find work but, when the chips were down, there had been one dominating motivation behind her rise from the wheelchair.

She would show Vere Cavendish the stuff she was made of, and if there was one thing he would regret, it was his shabby treatment of her. He should have loved her, like Edward loved her. It ought to have been Vere who was lying here beside her and who had helped her to walk. Revenge was an emotive word, but it was the sentiment in Charley's heart that night as she took another step back to life and vowed that Vere Cavendish would regret not only his part in her accident but his failure to be her saviour.

Yet, driving past The Cavendish when they returned to London, Charley wondered whether Vere really deserved these vows of vengeance or if she was succumbing to the petty resentments of a woman scorned. She took no immediate action, being busy putting her own affairs in order. First, she had to explain to Edward that she could neither marry him nor live with him – not yet. She had an overwhelming need to put her independence to the test and to prove, to herself if to no one else, that she could live alone and earn a wage. Edward accepted this disappointment with his customary good grace and took himself off to the Haymarket and Beerbohm Tree's interesting repertory, while passing as many of his leisure hours with Charley as she would permit.

Second, Charley embarked on a round of the West End theatres, seeking backstage work. The combination of gender, youth and disability proved too much for most managements but she persisted, resisting Edward's hardheaded advice to go to The Cavendish, where Vere was hardly likely to turn her away. Eventually she was given a trial by Charles Hawtrey at the Comedy.

Third, she found ground-floor lodgings which, in early October, Marion came to inspect.

'It isn't what one would call homely,' Marion remarked doubtfully.

'I cannot afford anything better, and anyway I never was much of a home-maker,' Charley retorted. 'As long as I have a roof over my head, I am perfectly happy.'

'I did not mean to sound disapproving,' Marion said hastily. 'In fact, I am full of admiration for the way you have fought back after the accident and for all you have achieved.'

'Thank you, Marion. Do you know, I believe that is the first time you have ever praised anything I have said or done.'

'Really? No, you must be mistaken. I distinctly remember praising your Rosalind to the skies.'

'To the skies, maybe, but not to me.'

'You didn't need me to tell you how good you were,' Marion said briskly. 'Apart from your adoring public, you had Vere bolstering your self-esteem and we both know how uplifting that can be.'

'Do we?'

'I think we are both old enough and wise enough to face facts and admit that we have shared so many identical experiences with Vere Cavendish that there is little we do not know about him.'

'On the contrary,' Charley said slowly, 'I feel that I do not know him at all. Except in the Biblical sense, of course, and you don't mean that . . . Do you?'

The sheer astonishment on Marion's face was answer enough. 'Do you honestly mean that you never suspected I was Vere's mistress while I was at The Cavendish?' she asked incredulously.

'I never thought about it. I knew you were Lord

Melton's mistress and I was too busy trying to counteract other comparisons with you, without . . . Oh God, it's disgusting. I knew that he must have had heaps of lovers, but why does it seem so much worse that one of them was my sister?'

Marion shook her head. 'Don't ask me. I have been trying to find an answer to that since I found out that you were in his bed, but I haven't succeeded.'

'Where did he take you?' Charley asked suddenly. 'Not to that bordello!'

'Heaps of times. A room decorated rather tastefully in pale green and Louis XV gilt.'

'The snake, that piece of slime, I'll kill him!'

'Join the queue,' Marion retorted. 'The stairway to that room is probably littered with maidenheads.'

'Not mine,' and Charley felt a certain satisfaction at having denied him that. 'Why did you break up with him?'

Marion told her about the abortion.

'He must be stopped,' Charley said violently, 'before he destroys some other poor girl.'

'I think the present incumbent can look after herself. Arlene Sidley is back in the company and she has weathered worse storms than Vere Cavendish.' Marion stood up and prepared to take her leave. 'You will get over him Charley, and so will I.'

But Charley noted the future tense and took little comfort in it.

'You have heard about Arabella,' Marion went on, buttoning her gloves. 'She has walked straight into a part in the new Pinero play. Only a couple of lines, but that girl has the luck of the devil.'

'How do you feel about that? You were always so set against the twins having anything to do with the theatre.'

'I feel nothing, absolutely nothing. I wash my hands of the pair of them,' Marion announced. 'I am moving in with Grace, and leaving Arabella and Imogen to their own devices. A few months of paying her own rent and buying her own food might teach Arabella more of a lesson than anything I say.'

'You are not working at the moment?'

'No. I am waiting for a really challenging part in a production worthy of one's time and interest.'

Charley decided not to comment on that. 'It will be interesting to see if Arabella has inherited the family talent.'

'Yes,' Marion said thoughtfully, 'won't it just.'

Responding to the note she sent him, Peter Frith-Tempest was Charley's next visitor. They had not been alone together since their quarrel two years before and the atmosphere was strained.

'It's awfully good of you to come.'

'I am glad to see you making such an excellent recovery,' Peter responded sincerely.

'This is embarrassing, because I want to ask you a favour and I am afraid that I have done that too often in the past and given precious little in return.'

'That's nonsense and you know it. If there is anything I can do for you, Charley, anything . . . I mean it.'

'It is The Cavendish, of course, and Vere. Tell me, Peter, you and I quarrelled about Marion, didn't we? I was angry because you had been seeing her, behind my back as I saw it, and then I became involved with Vere. Yet, even though you knew I detested her, you never told me that Marion had been Vere's mistress.'

Peter stared at her, the pain like a physical blow. He had thought that he was over Marion. It seemed so long ago, those days when he wanted her so badly and had to endure Uncle Reggie's lewd remarks over the port, but having his suspicions about her and Cavendish confirmed hurt like hell. He had admitted that he still cared about Marion, as a friend, and had even conceded that he had felt more for her than he had ever felt for Charley, but now he knew that he still loved her. He ought to have had the courage to ask her to marry him, he thought suddenly, at the start of her career, before making her name as an actress had made marriage impossible. But he hadn't had the courage, and never would, and in all probability he would never marry anyone now.

'I was never entirely sure,' he said at last. 'They were very discreet, more discreet than . . . Sorry.'

'Than I was.' Charley completed the sentence for him. 'And it is I who should apologise, for behaving so childishly and treating you so shabbily. I really am sorry, Peter. You were always a good friend to me, as well as a lover, and you deserved better than that.'

'All over and forgotten,' he assured her.

'Friends?' And they shook hands. 'Then I will come straight to the point. After the Celia Melton episode, I asked you not to withdraw your backing from The Cavendish. Now I am asking you to do exactly that.'

'I guessed as much. Did you know that Ernest Meyer has backed out? You can imagine the ultimate effect on The Cavendish if I do the same?'

Charley nodded.

'And, knowing that, you still want me to disinvest?'

'Yes. I cannot stop him acquiring new backers but, believe me, I will ruin him if I can.'

'A trifle drastic, isn't it?' he suggested quietly. 'Of course, the man is a philanderer, but surely falling in love with the leading lady is an occupational hazard.'

'He does not fall in love. He uses people.'

'Like you used me, and are using Edward Druce now, and used Cavendish a little bit, in your own way?' When no reply came, Peter sighed. 'I will withdraw my backing from The Cavendish, Charley, but not only because you have convinced me of the manager's wicked ways. The man's finances are in a parlous state and I doubt if the current company and repertoire can salvage the situation.'

'You sound as if you are writing his obituary.'

'And you sound as if you would dance on his grave! Don't be so bitter, Charley. It doesn't suit you.' Peter stood up, watching with concern and sympathy as Charley struggled out of her chair. 'The London theatre is not the same without you and Marion, but I shall attend the next première at the Comedy with additional interest.'

'There is another first night that ought to attract you, one that launches a fourth Leigh sister on an unsuspecting world.'

'I hope that the play will be an unparalleled success.'

'Oh, the *play* doesn't matter two hoots. It is Arabella who is the thing. The burning question is: can she act?'

Chapter Twenty-Seven

Imogen was alone almost all the time now. Arabella was rehearsing and Marion was home so seldom that it came as little surprise when gradually her clothes were transported to Grace's flat and Marion moved out. Bored and angry, regressing into her old self, Imogen's only companion became the brandy bottle. The solitary drinking started slowly: an occasional tot on evenings when Arabella came home late; but one drink became two and then three, and soon Imogen was looking at the clock, trying to stave off the hour when she took the first glass.

As the habit grew, supply became a problem. The bottles donated by Vere, and forgotten by Charley, diminished at an alarming rate and, having no money of her own, Imogen was forced into devious ways. She manipulated the housekeeping accounts, lying about food prices; she stole from Arabella's purse and, when the opportunity arose, from Marion. She took to dropping in at Grace's apartment on odd pretexts, her sharp eyes soon discovering where Grace kept her spare cash. Taking it and creeping home guiltily, she was reminded of the arguments about money overheard in her childhood, of Marion berating their father for stealing the housekeeping in order to buy liquor, and Imogen shuddered and for a little while cut down on the drink.

When Marion and Grace called to collect her for Arabella's première, outwardly Imogen was composed and looking extremely attractive, but inwardly she was tense and feeling nauseous with stress. She feared Arabella's involvement with the theatre as much as her sister's involvement with a man. She knew that she could lose Arabella to the stage, that if Arabella was successful she, Imogen, would be surplus to requirements. Imogen had not heard Vere Cavendish's description of the theatre as 'my beautiful mistress' but she would have understood it perfectly.

Settling into her seat, Imogen discovered that she was not alone in wishing her sister's career curtailed.

'I do not see why you are so agitated, Marion,' Grace was saying. 'The girl has such a small part that she will hardly be noticed, and certainly no one will be able to evaluate her performance.'

'She has little to say but is on the stage quite a lot, and you would be surprised how much one can tell about an actor merely from one entrance and exit.'

'One did not expect Frances to attend, but one would have thought that Charley could have made the effort.'

Grace's disapproval – or was it jealousy? – of her sisters was not as obvious to Marion as it was to others. To Marion, Grace was a sister-substitute. Her friend was older than Frances but had taken her sister's place completely, as kind and loving as Frances had become cold and distant.

'Charley is working tonight,' Marion replied equably. 'She and Edward are coming round afterwards.'

The curtain rose and the three women waited nervously for Arabella's entrance and, when it came, the tension gripped more tightly and turned to aching despair. For a short while they hoped they were mistaken, that their personal interest was influencing and clouding their judgement, but that illusion faded fast. Marion, in particular, with her professional expertise, was able to assess the situation accurately. Yet, as she tried to do so, logic collapsed under the sheer impact of Arabella's stage presence.

She did not have much to do, or much to say, but one simply could not take one's eyes off her. Arabella shone. Her beauty was incredible, enhanced by the lights, and although excluded from the limelight focused on the principals, she seemed to exude an inner glow. When she did speak, the soft sweetness of her voice reached the back of the gallery, and when she moved – even an eyelid – several hundred hearts missed a beat. The audience knew that they were seeing someone exceptional and they wanted to see her again; and they knew that when they did see her again, they would want her on the stage for the duration of the play because, when she left it, the light went with her.

Afterwards Arabella was mobbed. Arriving late after working on their own productions, Charley and Edward had only to look at the crowd surrounding her, and at the expressions on the faces of Marion and Imogen, to know what had transpired.

The emotions of the three sisters were difficult to define. Marion was jealous of so quick and easy a success in such a shallow play, and bitter about having wasted time, money and effort on preparing Arabella for a very different role. Imogen was lonely, resentful and afraid. And Charley . . . Charley, too, was jealous, envious of an unblemished body and the ability to act. However, for Charley, the evening took a different turn as she watched Arabella dealing with the crush of admirers. Some, evidently, she knew: Henry Vale was allowed to kiss her hand, although his friends warranted only a polite nod; others were treated with cold disdain; and the least welcome were demolished, swatted like flies on a summer afternoon. They meant nothing to her. Not one of them, even the most handsome or influential, warranted a second glance. On the stage Arabella was a siren, warm and enticing, fascinating and full of personality; in real life she was an ice-queen with a heart of stone. Why? Had her beauty spoiled her, making attention too cheap and easy, or was there another reason?

Watching Arabella that night, Charley began to see her as the focus of the entire family – to realise that, indeed, Arabella always had been – and as a catalyst and nemesis.

A plan stirred into life at the back of Charley's mind.

The public was more taken with Arabella than with the play and the production did not seem destined for a long run. However, one of London's most popular playwrights announced that he was reshaping the leading role in his new *oeuvre* especially for Arabella Leigh and that rehearsals would start before Christmas.

At home the rise in the brandy bill was in direct relation to Arabella's ascending star. Suspicious about increasing costs, missing cash and certain aspects of her sister's behaviour, Arabella returned unexpectedly to the flat after a matinée. Imogen was slumped over the kitchen table, with the brandy bottle to hand.

'You've been drinking,' Arabella exclaimed, shocked.

'Nothing gets past you, does it! Not content with being the pretty one, you have to be the clever one, too!'

'Imogen, it is five o'clock in the afternoon.'

'Half-past, actually, but who cares?'

'I care that you are drinking yourself senseless at this

hour of the day, or at any hour of the day! And I care that this is how you have been spending my money. Good God,' and Arabella looked at her sister bitterly, 'like father like daughter!'

Imogen's head jerked up and she stared her sister full in the face. 'You ought not to have said that,' and her voice rose hysterically. 'You, of all people, ought not to have compared me with *him*.'

'Sorry,' Arabella said contritely. 'But why are you drinking?'

'Nothing else to do.'

'Find something to do.'

'Can't.'

'If Charley can work, in her condition, I fail to see what is stopping you.'

'A pre . . . prerequisite . . .' Imogen stumbled over the word, '. . . for finding work is to know of a job that one can do and that someone will pay one to perform, and preferably to know of a job that one would like to do. I fail on all counts.'

'You cannot spend your life sitting at this table in an alcoholic haze. Surely there must be something you want to achieve, some goal, even if it is only finding a hus-band?'

Imogen's expression changed subtly and the blue of her eyes seemed to deepen. 'No, that's the trouble,' she said, still slurring her words but conveying a desolate sincerity. 'I cannot think of anything that I can or want to do. There is no aim in my life and nothing to look forward to. All of you have these busy, colourful lives but I only have a huge black hole. So I fill the hole with brandy. Cheers,' and she raised her glass in mock salute before draining it. 'What are you doing here anyway, at this hour?'

'I was worried about you.'

The look on Imogen's face changed again, to a mixture of satisfaction and cunning. 'This brandy cannot be all bad, then, if it brings you home.'

Arabella could see where this was leading and her heart sank. 'Somehow we must get you out of the house and into a worthwhile job,' she said resolutely. 'I will help you. We will sort this out together.'

'I wouldn't mind doing something at your new theatre.'

The price was going to be even higher than Arabella had expected. 'I do not think that they are looking for anyone,' she said warily, 'not even front-of-house.'

'But you are the star. If you said that you wanted me there, they would have to agree, otherwise you would walk out of the production.'

'Ginny, I am *not* walking out for you or for anyone else,' Arabella began, and watched her sister's hand grope for the brandy bottle. 'Let me think about it,' she prevaricated, 'and test the water. The script does not call for supers, but there might be a niche. Would you be prepared to . . .'

'I will do anything,' Imogen affirmed quickly, pushing away the brandy ostentatiously and making the bargain perfectly clear, 'as long as I can be with you.'

It transpired that the management was only too happy to accommodate Arabella by acceding to any, reasonable, request and Imogen was installed as her sister's dresser and general factotum. Caring for Arabella's wardrobe, dressing her hair as she had done so often in their lives and, best of all, mounting guard over Arabella's dressing-room door like Cerberus, Imogen was in her element.

The unspoken bargain seemed to work. Imogen reduced her brandy intake to one bottle a week, while Arabella cut down her personal and professional engagements in order to spend more time with her sister. She was unhappy about it, feeling Imogen dragging on her like an anchor staying a schooner in full sail, but it was this or having the image of a drunken Imogen weighing on her conscience. At the theatre, during rehearsals for the new play, there was little direct contact between them, but Imogen did not mind; she was there, under the same roof, watching, involved, ensuring that no one usurped her position. At home the time passed quickly, with Imogen cooking while Arabella worked on the script, and later sitting together while Imogen heard Arabella's lines. This sense of participation was what Imogen wanted, what gave strength and direction and meaning to her life. If they could have gone on like this, perhaps all would have been well.

Therefore at this, Arabella's second première, Imogen's feelings were very different from those at the first. Instead of sitting in the audience, she had duties to perform, although these were not so onerous that she could not snatch a few moments in the wings in which to witness her sister's success. Yet her pride in that performance was still mixed with a deep desire for Arabella's ultimate failure. If Arabella failed, Imogen could pick up the pieces and comfort her and they could be really close again – equal, as Nature had intended.

Marion, who was still 'resting', and Grace were in the audience again that evening. Leaving before the applause had subsided, because otherwise they could have been there all night, they also shunned the opening-night party. 'She is nothing but a nine-days wonder,' declared Grace scathingly during the drive home. 'Any actress with a pretty face could have done as well. A trivial plot and a puerile script, and a part that kept her on the stage for virtually two and a half hours . . . My dear Marion, it is just too, too *easy*. Try her with a Shakespeare speech or a few meaningful lines from Ibsen, and see how far she gets!'

Marion agreed fervently, but the professional actress in her knew that the fact that it looked so easy probably meant that it wasn't, that making it look easy was the most difficult and skilful trick of all.

Charley had taken a night off from her duties at the Comedy and, as luck would have it, the repertory rota at the Haymarket allowed Edward to accompany her. They sat side by side with the relaxed relationship of an old married couple merging with their professional expertise. When Charley glanced at her companion during Arabella's strongest scene, she was gauging his reaction to the performance, not wondering if he would rather be sleeping with her sister than with her. Turning her head slightly to the left, Charley could see Marion's face – the auditorium conforming to current practice by being dimly lit – but for the most part Charley watched her youngest sister with amazement.

It was absolutely true: there was no justice, and life was a bitch. Arabella was not only the most beautiful of the Leigh sisters but the most talented as well. Put her on the same stage as Marion, Frances and Charley – a tempting prospect for any West End theatre manager, although he might as well have sighed for the moon – and Arabella would have outshone and out-acted them all. Charley's sensations were complex: did her disability increase or decrease her envy of Arabella? Comparing that beautiful body with her own disfigurement was understandable but, had she still been on the stage in full competition with her sister, would she have resented the rivalry more?

Pushing aside her private thoughts, Charley knew that the time had come to implement her plan. She was virtually certain that Vere had not seen Arabella. The programme at The Cavendish – *Henry V* – would have precluded his attendance at another theatre. However, advance publicity for a revival of *The Woman in White*, starring Arlene Sidley, indicated that Vere was not acting in that production. After some consideration, Charley decided that Richard Ramsey, Vere's business manager, was her best contact at The Cavendish and she asked him to call. For a while she pretended to pick his brains about problems encountered in her job, but he knew her too well to be fooled by this façade.

'Come on, Charley, level with me. What is the real reason behind this meeting?'

She feigned embarrassment. 'I was wondering how things are with Vere and The Cavendish. Oh, I suppose I blame him for the accident, but one does not forget all that shared experience and happiness.'

Succinctly Ramsey filled her in on the current state of affairs at The Cavendish. *Henry V* had been playing to good houses, but advance bookings for *The Woman in White* were virtually non-existent. However, Vere was adamant that he was reducing his acting role and that he intended to concentrate on management.

'But he is the main attraction,' Charley exclaimed. 'It is seeing Vere Cavendish on the stage that puts bums on seats.'

'Precisely,' Ramsey agreed grimly, 'but there is no one who can tell him that. At least, there is no one who can make him listen! He does not want to act. I think that he wants to play to a different audience, in the restaurants and casinos, and,' here Ramsey paused, before sighing and continuing, 'he is drinking too much. Keeping the Scottish distillers in business, as far as I can see.'

'Poor Vere,' said Charley, and almost meant it. 'The Cavendish certainly seems to need an injection of new blood. Tell me, has Vere seen my sister – Arabella, I mean?'

'You do not need to elaborate,' Ramsey assured her. 'With due deference to past reputations, there is only one Leigh sister who counts these days. And, no, I do not believe that the Chief has seen her, although obviously he must have heard of her.'

'Give him these tickets,' and Charley passed them across. 'I think you will find that he is not onstage that night, and it will do him good to see another production. Don't tell him that this was my idea or you may prejudice him against it from the start, but I believe that if he could persuade Arabella to join him at The Cavendish, it could be his saving grace and the making of them both.'

'A nine-days wonder, I expect,' Vere said in a bored voice, unconsciously echoing Grace Norton's verdict.

'More like the eighth and ninth wonders of the world,' his companion replied, 'and I'm surprised that you have not seen the phenomenon before.'

'Haven't had the time or, to be honest, the inclination. I seem to have been beset by Leigh sisters since time immemorial. How many more of them *are* there, for God's sake?'

'You have had the others, by all accounts, so when you see the fair Arabella you may feel like completing the set.'

Vere smiled cynically. 'I think that I will conserve my energy for a more rewarding exercise. I'm only here because Ramsey reckons the girl might do for The Cavendish. He even talked some claptrap about the Leighs being "lucky" for us.'

'Perhaps so, but The Cavendish was not that lucky for the redhead, was it!'

The remark was made jocularly, the young man being unaware of Vere's sensitivity on the subject of Charley's accident, and he did not notice the pain that twisted Vere's mouth at mention of it. A brash young man, the younger son of a minor peer, who had latched on to Vere in the hope of gaining introductions to charming and accommodating actresses, he was one of a group of sycophants with whom Vere socialised these days. His presence here tonight was a sign of the times: in the past Vere might have cultivated the youth's father, in the hope that the acquaintance proved fruitful for business, but he would barely have given the son the time of day.

The 'joke' about Charley hit hard, but Vere was too dispirited to respond. What did it matter? In the end, in the great scheme of things, what did anything matter? He looked at the programme, stared at the safety curtain, glanced unsmilingly around the auditorium and sank a little lower in his chair. His boredom seemed bottomless and without end; it encompassed this production, his own productions and performances, his social life, and induced a lethargy that made him wonder if it was worth getting out of bed in the morning. He drank, in the misplaced hope that alcohol might bring about the return of happiness, energy and a sense of purpose, but instead he rediscovered every day that the whisky only depressed him further. Occasionally, struggling to wake in mid-morning, he wondered whether the whisky was cause or effect: was he drinking because he felt so awful, or did he feel so awful because he drank?

But, really, there seemed less and less to get out of bed for. He had tried everything, made endless sacrifices, and still he was not winning. Indeed, he was losing ground; he knew it and, if he forgot for a few moments, there was always a balance sheet or an unpaid bill to remind him. He could feel it all – his career, his theatre, his status – slipping away from him and he seemed powerless to prevent it. So stultifying was this ennui that he could not raise the energy, the will-power or the determination to fight back. Outwardly unchanged, inwardly this extraordinarily ambitious man was searching his soul, feeling that he had aimed high and failed, and that he was unable to adjust to a more modest rank or status.

All he needed in his life, he thought as the curtain rose, was another blasted Leigh sister to complicate matters further. And then he saw Arabella for the first time . . .

His heart was thumping so loudly that he actually wondered if his companion could hear it. At the interval he drank a whisky in the bar, agreed laconically that 'the girl has possibilities' and, yes, he 'supposed she might do for The Cavendish', while hardly knowing how to contain his impatience for the performance to resume.

At the final curtain, he was reminded that friends and dinner were waiting for them at a gaming club they frequented.

'Go ahead without me,' Vere said carelessly. 'I'll be along later.'

In the street he took a few deep breaths of air and paused, trying to steady his mind which reeled with unexpected and unfamiliar thoughts. Vere Cavendish had never felt like this before, never experienced such an intense longing for a woman, or felt such an extraordinary conviction that Fate or the gods, or both, had fashioned her especially for him.

At the stage door he asked for the manager and in the office he observed the niceties, offering congratulations on a splendid production before inquiring if he could present his compliments to the leading lady.

'Good God, man,' said the manager, 'you don't seriously imagine that I have any influence there, do you?'

Vere was genuinely taken aback. 'I have found it usual for a member of my cast to receive visitors after the performance, particularly at my invitation or request.'

'So have I, until now. However, there is one rule for Miss Arabella Leigh and one for the rest of us poor mortals. Carry on by all means, my dear fellow. Go to her dressing room with my blessing, but if you get past the gorgon at the gate, you are a better man than I and most of London.'

Laughing, Vere left the office and headed for the dressing rooms, as confident in his way as Arabella was in hers. He had never failed to win any woman he wanted. Indeed, his personal problems had largely emanated from women wanting him more than he wanted them, and certainly wanting more than he was prepared to give. He was forty years old but still the most handsome man on the London stage, an impressive, towering figure in full evening dress covered by a dramatic black cloak, with a shiny black top hat and a silver-headed cane. Using the cane to rap on the door, he reached into his jacket pocket and found a business card. When a small, dark-haired person opened the door, Vere handed her the card and asked to speak to Miss Leigh.

'She is not receiving visitors.' The young woman edged through the crack of the open door and closed it behind her, so that she and Vere were standing in the draughty passage.

'She will receive me,' and he indicated the card in her hand.

'No, she won't.'

'How do you know if you do not ask her?' His irritation was beginning to show.

'Because she never makes exceptions for anyone, least of all for you, Mr Cavendish. And even if she did feel inclined to change her mind, I would soon change it back again.'

'Just who the hell do you think you are to speak to me like that, and to dictate to Miss Leigh . . .'

'I am her sister.'

'Bloody hell . . . *another* one!' The exclamation was so sincere and so appalled that even Imogen, confronting one of her most dreaded demons, nearly smiled. 'The twins,' he said suddenly, 'of course. I had forgotten Marion's twins. But you and your sister do not look alike.'

'I had noticed.'

Cursing himself for his lack of tact, Vere said smoothly: 'I still think that Miss Arabella would find it advantageous to permit me the courtesy of introducing myself.'

But Imogen backed towards the door, leaning against it protectively, and Vere conceded defeat – temporarily.

'Please give my card to Miss Leigh and tell her that I will seek to make her acquaintance on another occasion.'

Imogen did not reply and remained, leaning against the dressing-room door, as Vere made his departure. Going past the office he was sufficiently in control to put his head round the door and feign morose disappointment.

'Losing my touch,' he said ruefully before laughing, tipping his hat to the manager, and leaving the theatre.

Outside he did not feel greatly disappointed or rejected, being too exhilarated at this new lease of life and the sense that suddenly there was everything to play for. Besides, it was obvious that the dark sister was keeping him and Arabella apart and that as soon as he could put his case to Arabella personally, she would recognise the situation for what it was: she would see that Vere Cavendish and Arabella Leigh was a personal and professional marriage made in heaven.

Chapter Twenty-Eight

Vere laid siege to Arabella, at first with an enthusiastic, reckless romanticism, deluging her with notes and flowers in what he believed to be the accepted manner. When these gestures went unacknowledged, he ascribed the silence not to indifference on Arabella's part but to Imogen's malevolence. In all probability, he thought, the notes had been destroyed before Arabella saw them and the cards removed from the bouquets.

Vere changed tack, from the personal to the professional, and substituted scripts for flowers. Instead of drinking and gambling in the evenings, he spent hours in his rooms going through the mountain of plays sent to him by aspiring dramatists, as well as his stock of tried and tested works, seeking a vehicle that would display him and Arabella to advantage. He sent her modern plays, staged or unstaged; he sent Victorian, Georgian, Jacobean and Elizabethan favourites; he sent letters detailing proposals for Shakespeare productions. Whatever he did, the result was the same: admittedly Arabella acknowledged these advances, but her brief notes merely thanked Mr Cavendish for his suggestions and advised that Miss Leigh felt that the proposed production was not suitable for her. What really rankled was that the reply was always the same, word for word *exactly* the same, even down to the spacing and placing of the words on the page. He could not even be sure that she had written it.

It could be that every advance from every lovesick admirer and every West End manager met with the same indifference, or it could be that he was being singled out for rejection and humiliation. He *had* to know. He had to meet her face to face and see her reaction for himself. However, if Miss Arabella Leigh thought that he, Vere Cavendish, would hang around like a stage-struck stage-door Johnny, she was very much mistaken!

Vere waited. He spent more evenings watching Arabella than overseeing productions in his own theatre, and The Cavendish box-office receipts reflected this neglect, but he made no attempt to meet her. He resumed his social round in the hope that reports of his popularity and good spirits would filter back to her. He perused every newspaper and magazine for references to her, and kept every picture of her and every paragraph that mentioned her name, but he told no one. A photograph of Arabella adorned his living room, another taunted him from the chest in his bedroom, a third smiled from the table beside his bed, but these were private places, because no one except his domestic staff set foot in Vere Cavendish's rooms. His obsession was his, and his alone.

So enthralled was he that everything else in his life suddenly made sense. Everything that had happened to him had been leading up to this, to Arabella, to his reward and his happy ending. Now he understood why the Melton marriage was not to be and why none of his other relationships had felt right. Even his involvement with the various Leigh sisters made sense, when viewed as a quest for the perfect partner.

The drawback, the temporary flaw, was that Arabella

was unaware of her destiny and Vere had not yet found a means of enlightening her. By now he knew her routine as well as she did, and knew that the chances of waylaying her casually and seemingly by chance were practically nil: she rarely left the apartment except to drive to the theatre and she was always escorted by Imogen. However, Vere bided his time because he was sure that, under the pressure of Arabella's overwhelming popularity, this state of affairs could not continue indefinitely.

He was right. Arabella *was* finding it more and more difficult to refuse the invitations that flooded through her letterbox and under her dressing-room door. With the play running smoothly and successfully, and without the added duty of rehearsals, she began to chafe at the hours wasted at home, trapped in her rooms with Imogen. There were things she wanted to do, people she wanted to see; she had an innate individuality that she wished to express, and that aspect of her personality was wrestling with a strong desire to live alone – not with her sister, not with a friend, especially not with a man, but alone. And she had a very clear idea about how her career as an actress ought to develop, and progress in that direction necessitated exploiting her current success to the full.

One Sunday in spring Arabella went out to a luncheon party and returned to find Imogen drunk. She decided to ignore it. She felt that she had done her duty and was not prepared to allow Imogen to continue relying on her so heavily. Arabella recognised emotional blackmail when she saw it.

After making discreet inquiries about Arabella's movements, Vere was rewarded with an invitation to a Sunday evening soirée at which she was to be present. Dressing, he was in such a state of excitement that he fumbled the tying of his white tie and cursed himself for a moonstruck youth in love for the first time. But he *was* in love for the first time, the first and only time . . .

Being introduced to her at long last, he summoned all his charm and *savoir-faire*, but he was as nervous as a schoolboy and Arabella did nothing to restore his confidence, merely nodding politely and murmuring 'Mr Cavendish' before gliding off to the next slavering suitor. And, of course, she was even more beautiful off the stage than on – that flawless complexion, gleaming hair, white teeth, those eyes . . . Vere groaned and took a determined grip on himself. He was still the best-looking man in the room and, he convinced himself, one of the most influential men in the English theatre. Clearly Arabella was playing hard to get.

'You are a most elusive young lady, Miss Leigh,' he said when he finally cornered her, 'but well worth the wait.'

'Just what have you been waiting *for*, Mr Cavendish?'

'To see you, of course,' he said eagerly. 'We have so much to discuss. Obviously you have not received all my letters . . .'

'Why should you think that?'

'Because you did not reply.'

'But if I replied to all the letters I receive, I would have no time to eat or sleep or act. And,' she added gently, just as he was beginning to seek consolation in his letters having met a universal fate, 'there are so many messages that do not deserve a reply.'

'We must talk – there is so much to discuss.'

'There is no *must* about it, and I fail to foresee any discussion between us that could last for longer than five minutes.'

'Perhaps we could dine together, as I suggested in those ill-fated letters,' he coaxed, with his most seductive smile, 'and I could prove to you that we would never run out of conversation, not even if we talked for the rest of our lives.'

'I would not bet your life savings on that – if you have any savings, of course.'

The sly comment passed him by. 'A private dinner would be best,' he continued, following a path he had trodden so many times, and with such singular success, before. 'That way we will not be troubled with interruptions and unwanted attention from our many admirers.'

'If you think, Mr Cavendish, that I would dine alone with you, anywhere, at any time, then you are either grossly arrogant or irredeemably stupid.'

'In a restaurant, then,' he pressed desperately. 'The Savoy, for instance, after the theatre one evening.'

'Do you think that I ought to be seen with a man of your reputation?'

He stared at her. 'What's wrong with my reputation?'

'It isn't for me to comment but I dare say that you could work it out for yourself. I will give you a hint, though: your reputation has been around for a long time, Mr Cavendish. Like you.'

And she was gone, dematerialising effortlessly to emerge on the other side of the room in the midst of an adoring circle, leaving Vere stunned and confused.

His dilemma was a thousand times worse than before. There was no Imogen to blame for keeping them apart, and the meeting had only intensified his longing for her. Now Arabella was a creature of flesh and blood; he could see the sheen on her skin and the gleam of her hair, *smell* her, and the urge to touch her was becoming uncontrollable. He knew that he was a good lover, a considerate, tender and satisfying lover, and more than anything in the world – at that moment more than any ambition for his career or his theatre – Vere wanted to make Arabella happy and show her how wonderful physical love could be.

Abruptly he left the party and headed for the West End. Never before had he paid for sex but this evening he went to a brothel where, he understood, the girls were good, attractive and clean. Of course he could have found a willing, unprofessional partner, but he knew from long experience that such relationships were never entirely free. All he wanted this evening was immediate, uncomplicated, physical release, with someone who would not complain if he called out 'Arabella' when he came.

He remained convinced that they were a perfect match, physically and professionally; that his mature, dark good looks set off her youthful blonde beauty, that his experience could hone and channel the natural, bubbling spring of her talent. His difficulty was to persuade Arabella of what, to him, was so obvious.

On the one hand, he bombarded her with notes, beseeching her to meet him; on the other, he threw himself into a frenetic round of activity, working hard in an attempt to reinstate his image at The Cavendish, and playing hard in the vain hope that he could forget her for a few hours. He gambled more frequently and for higher stakes, trying to make money because the future of The Cavendish and his chances with Arabella depended on it.

Richard Ramsey, witnessing every stage of Vere's decline, wished that Arabella Leigh had never been born. 'It was a good idea in theory,' he told Charley, 'but in practice it is not working.'

Charley had known that it would not work. She had never intended that it should work. She had intended Vere to fall in love with Arabella and be rejected. She wanted him to suffer as he had made others suffer. But when

Ramsey told her how Vere's behaviour was affecting the company as a whole, she conceded that it might be time to call a halt.

'I will speak to her,' Charley assured him.

She called at the twins' lodgings at mid-morning the next day on her way to work and looked with distaste at the room in which she had been confined after her accident.

'I am surprised you stay here,' she remarked. 'I always found the place gloomy and depressing.'

'So do I,' answered Arabella, 'but it will do until I have the time and money to acquire a home of my own.'

'I would not have imagined that time is a problem. Even if you are busy, Imogen is hardly overworked.'

'Imogen is not included in my future plans, although I would prefer that she did not know it.'

Charley raised an eyebrow but then shrugged. The relationship between the twins was none of her business. 'Where is Imogen?'

'Shopping. She insists on cooking a proper luncheon, especially on matinée days.'

'She was under Marion's influence for too long,' Charley remarked, with the grimace of someone who ate if, and when, she felt like it.

'You did not come here to talk about our sisters,' Arabella remarked.

'I wanted a word about Vere Cavendish. The word is that you are being beastly to him.'

'It was not my intention to be *anything* to him.'

Charley smiled appreciatively. 'Quite, but I gather the man is so besotted that his concentration has deserted him and that is bad news for The Cavendish company. At least hear what he has to say, and put him out of his misery once and for all.'

'You are an unlikely champion, Charley, all things considered. Do you wish me to follow in the noble tradition laid down by you and Marion?'

'More to the point, do you?'

'I am not leaping into bed with any man, thank you, least of all with someone twice my age, who has been sleeping his way systematically through my family tree. As for a professional partnership, The Cavendish is said to be on the skids and I am in the business of promoting my own career, not rescuing someone else's from terminal decline.'

'You really are not attracted to him?' And, seeing the answer in Arabella's face, Charley shook her head. 'I remember wanting that man, sexually, so much that I *burned* . . . Ah well, one man's meat and all that . . . Speak to him, Arabella. Listen to him. For the sake of The Cavendish company, sort it out.'

Arabella sighed but, as Charley had expected, she did not want to be the cause of trouble for other members of the profession. 'I am spending Easter with Sarah's people in Gloucestershire. He can come to luncheon on, say, the Monday and receive his *congé*.'

'How will your aristocratic hosts react to that?'

'They think actors are frightfully glamorous, and they are enormously thrilled that I'm a success. What's more, the countess thinks that Vere Cavendish used to be the bee's-knees, but I expect that is because they are the same generation.'

Charley, only four years older than Arabella but feeling forty, looked at her sister sharply. Was her sister being bitchy or was she teasing? Arabella's face remained a mask of innocence, but Charley thought she could detect the faintest gleam of amusement in those sapphire eyes.

'By the way,' Arabella went on, 'Imogen does not know

where I am going for Easter and I want it to stay that way. If she comes banging on your door, demanding my address, you won't know where I am, right?'

'Right,' Charley agreed and took her leave, relieved that as soon as Arabella's demolition of Vere was done, she need have little more to do with that young woman.

A surge of euphoria lifted Vere's spirits so high that his body, too, seemed to float several inches above the ground and he knew what it was to walk on air. He took a train to Gloucester on the evening of Easter Saturday and booked into an hotel in the centre of the city.

On Sunday morning he breakfasted early and walked the short distance to the cathedral, roaming restlessly around the ancient building in order to pass the time, trying unsuccessfully to take in the grandeur of the massive pillars and Romanesque arches, the riot of carving on the lierne vaults and the glory of the great east window. He selected an aisle seat in order to gain a clear view of the earl's party as it passed up the nave and, waiting for them to appear, he ignored the rest of the congregation and did not notice the arrival of a certain family group comprising a grey-haired man, a slender dark-haired woman and a twelve-year-old girl. Behind him a rustle among the congregation heralded the earl's party, but Vere stared rigidly in front, resisting the temptation to turn his head and look at her, although from the moment she glided past, his eyes followed her up the nave and into the choir, where for the duration of the service she was out of sight.

He had hoped that she might offer him a smile on her way out but she looked neither to left nor right, her face expressionless, her poise unruffled, even though she must have known that every eye in the cathedral was trained on

her. He was about to stand up, to follow her, to keep her
in view for as long as possible, when suddenly another
face caught his attention. Walking towards him was
Frances Leigh. Surely it couldn't be? Yet it was, yes, definitely Frances, although she looked sleeker and more
self-assured than before. She had her arm around a young
girl who seemed upset about something, and they were
accompanied by a grey-haired man whose bronzed complexion testified to a winter in the sun. Following at a
discreet distance, Vere was just in time to see Arabella
drive off and then he had ample opportunity to observe
the other sister. She was still comforting her young companion and Vere edged close enough to catch the tail-end
of their conversation.

'Stop worrying,' Frances was saying. 'No one is going to
force you to speak to Arabella if you don't want to. Look,
she has gone already and I do not suppose she will ever
come back. And there isn't a sign of Imogen. Do try to
compose yourself, or your father will wonder what is
wrong and we promised to keep the twins a secret from
him, didn't we!'

Idly Vere wondered why the existence of the twins
should be a secret, but Frances had never held any interest
for him and, his mind full of Arabella, he dismissed the
incident.

Presenting himself at the castle for luncheon the next
day, he took it in good part that he was not seated next to
Arabella. The countess's reception of him was immensely
flattering and he accepted as a compliment his position next
to Lady Sarah, on whom he turned the full battery of his
debonair charm. In fact so smitten was Sarah that it could
have been Celia Melton all over again, and she relinquished
him reluctantly to her friend when the meal was over.

The day was bright but there was little warmth in the

sun as Arabella led the way into the garden. Strolling down a gravel path that twisted through a landscaped woodland towards the lake, Vere waited until they were well out of earshot of the house before he spoke. Then it was like a dam bursting, as a torrent of pent-up words flooded out, and Vere enthusiastically began outlining his plans for their future artistic collaboration. At one point he tried to take hold of her arm, more a matter of habit with him than a sexual approach, but Arabella angrily shook him off. She said nothing but let him go on talking, most of his questions being rhetorical or in the nature of exclamations, and they had nearly reached the lake before he paused for breath and Arabella spoke.

'Your time is nearly up, Mr Cavendish, so perhaps I should point out that you have completely misunderstood the situation. I did not ask you here in order to arrange any kind of collaboration. This meeting is intended purely as an exorcism, to enable you to get this nonsense out of your system. When it is over, I never want to see you again.'

'You do not know what you are saying!' Rejection by a woman was so foreign to Vere's experience that he did not recognise it. 'I have just told you that you can name your own price, choose your own roles, anything . . . I want you as my leading lady.'

'So does every theatre manager in London. Why should I choose The Cavendish? What is so special about you?'

'I should have thought that was obvious!'

'What is obvious, Mr Cavendish, is that I can do a great deal for your – flagging – career, while you can do precious little for mine.'

'But can't you see that we are made for each other? That we are two of a kind, two halves of a perfect whole? I am not merely asking you to join me at The Cavendish, on the stage and in management, but I am asking you to marry me. You see, I love you. I love you more than anything, more than The Cavendish, more than life itself.'

He had not intended to say that. He had not known that he did love her that much. But, as he said it, he realised that he meant it.

'Oh Lord, not another proposal,' and Arabella sighed wearily. 'Really, it becomes so boring.'

There flashed before Vere's eyes a swift mental montage of all the women who had prayed to hear him declare his love and propose marriage – among them, prominently, Marion and Charley – and he gazed at Arabella in utter bewilderment. A change came over him. A strand of Arabella's hair was blowing in the breeze and, very gently, he lifted his hand and stroked it away from her face, the tips of his fingers lightly brushing her cheek.

'You are so very young,' he said, slowly and sadly. 'Too young, perhaps, to know good from bad, right from wrong, the wheat from the chaff. And certainly too young to choose, let alone recognise, a true, lasting relationship over the cheap thrills and excitement of the fleeting moment of success.'

The timbre of his voice tingled down Arabella's spine. She looked up into his face, silhouetted against the sky, and into such infinite weariness and despair that, almost, her heart misgave her. His skin was marked with the effects of too much liquor and greasepaint, and the raven hair was flecked with grey, but it remained a beautiful face, stamped with experience and authority. The fathomless, midnight eyes seemed to stare into her, penetrating to the very core of her being.

'I wanted to love you,' he said softly. 'I wanted you to be my partner in the theatre, to be my wife and the mother of my children. In all my life I have never believed so much and so fervently that something was meant to be. I still believe it. The tragedy is that I believe one day you will look at your life, reflect on it, and know that I was right. You will come to the conclusion, too late, that you ought to have married me.'

Arabella had known what it was to lack control over the actions and emotions of others, but never had she felt so powerless to control herself. His eyes were hypnotic, telling her something, telling her something she did not wish to hear. And his hands were resting on her shoulders and they were drawing her towards him, inexorably, effortlessly, and still she was unable to resist.

'I wanted to make love to you,' he went on in that same deep, dreamy voice, using his voice unconsciously from long habit and experience. 'It would have been so wonderful, our love-making, every touch for your pleasure, until together we experienced ecstasy, blessed as few in this world are blessed . . .'

His arms were encircling her, cradling her against his chest. She shivered violently. 'You are cold,' and he opened his jacket and clasped her close again, with the jacket wrapped around her, her cheek against his shirt. Through the thin material she could feel the warmth of his body and hear the wild beating of his heart. Something was sliding inside her, like a piece of ice melting, and his lips were on hers, gently at first, wondering and afraid, and then hard and hungry. For a moment Arabella was too shocked and surprised to move. Her body seemed to have a mind of its own, responding to him, but after his tongue slipped between her lips and drew her into an intimacy in which she felt she could lose herself for ever, something snapped. Memory surfaced, raw and cruel, and she lashed out, twisting away from him, pushing him, beating him with her fists.

'Don't touch me,' she screamed, 'don't touch me. I cannot bear it!'

Vere let her go immediately, releasing her at the first sign of distress, standing back with dismay and incomprehension etched deep into his features.

'I never want to see you again,' she said, her back turned towards him. 'If you as much as speak to me, I swear I will report you to the police. As far as I am concerned, you and your theatre can go to hell. You, Mr Cavendish, have nothing to offer me.'

He bowed and walked away. He knew he had been close to touching her, to awakening and winning her, but Vere Cavendish never knew just how close he had been. And he certainly never knew why he had failed.

Chapter Twenty-Nine

Driving to his rooms, Vere directed the cabby to take him via Gower Street because, despite all that had happened, he was still drawn to anything and anywhere that had a connection with Arabella. The street was quiet, indeed London seemed deserted this Easter Monday evening, when suddenly a movement caught his eye. Signalling to the driver to stop, Vere got out of the cab.

A girl was stumbling along the pavement, occasionally diverting from the footpath to execute exaggeratedly cautious steps in the gutter, as if trying to prove that she could walk in a straight line, then lifting her skirts and circling in an old-fashioned dance before launching herself at a lamp-post and swinging round it. He had been right in his initial assessment: it was Imogen and she was very drunk, but not lightheartedly so. The dancing was sad, leaden-footed and full of desolation.

He knew exactly how she felt.

She reached the step to her front door and stood for a moment, swaying, before subsiding slowly to the ground.

Swiftly paying off the cab, Vere hurried across the street and bent down to look at her. She was unconscious but, as far as he could see, unhurt. The door was ajar, perhaps an indication that she had been drunk when leaving the premises, so Vere lifted the slight figure and carried her inside and up the stairs.

The living room was in darkness, but enough light streamed in from the kitchen and landing to enable him to locate a sofa and lower Imogen on to it. After lighting the lamp and closing the outer door, he looked around him. The room was tidy but he noticed a film of dust on tables and ornaments and there was an unlived-in air about the place. Where did Imogen pass the time and why did the sisters apparently do without domestic help?

Vere walked into the kitchen and, the table being bare but for a cluster of empty brandy bottles and a dirty glass, found the answers to both questions. Vere was a social drinker as well as having a whisky bottle available at the office and at home but, being a man and living alone, he did not need to conceal his habit from the world. However, he could understand that the situation was very different for Imogen and, going back into the living room and looking down at the recumbent figure on the sofa, he felt a pang of sympathy. Here she was, alone in this shabby room while her sister . . . And with intense pain he pictured Arabella in her jewel-like silks at the glittering gathering at the castle that night. Poor Imogen, and it helped a little to know that he was not the only one who suffered.

He supported her head on a cushion and fetched a blanket to cover her, but he was unable to resist the temptation to discover which of the bedrooms was Arabella's, and to go in there and sit down on her bed. Prowling round the room, feeling a guilty but intense excitement, he opened cupboards and drawers and probed among her intimate garments, holding the delicate scented silks against his cheek. A hairbrush lay on the dressing-table, rather old and plain-backed, so presumably Arabella owned a smarter brush that she had taken to Gloucestershire. A fine web of blonde hairs was meshed in its bristles and carefully, taking infinite pains not to break them, Vere disentangled them and rolled them into a ball, which he placed in his empty cigarette case. Then he picked up a monogrammed lace handkerchief and pressed it to his nostrils, inhaling the scent of her, and he took that, too.

He had intended to leave without revealing his presence but, in the living room, he hesitated. To avoid any risk of fire, the lamps ought to be extinguished, and if in the morning Imogen remembered anything about tonight, she would wonder how she came to be sleeping on the sofa. So Vere scribbled a quick note, saying that he had found her in a distressed condition in the street and brought her home. If he could be of future service to her, he added – hardly knowing why he did so – Miss Leigh must not hesitate to approach him.

Then, checking once more to ensure that she was comfortable and warm, he put out the lamps and closed the door softly behind him.

He did not expect to hear from Imogen and dismissed both her and the incident from his mind. If he did think of her it was only occasionally, when he was drinking alone in his rooms and wondered casually if she was doing the same.

It was impossible to avoid news of Arabella, even if he had wanted to stay in ignorance of her movements, because she remained very much the current favourite. She would appear in a new play for the same management when the current production closed, it was reported, while gossip said that she was receiving such an enormous salary that she was moving to a very smart new address.

Therefore he was surprised when, sitting in his office

one June afternoon, he was asked if he would see Miss Imogen Leigh.

In a high-collared dress of striped silk and a jaunty straw hat, she was not bad-looking and it occurred to him that Imogen's looks suffered from constant comparison with her sisters. However, she was very pale and the dark circles under her eyes did not bode well for her sleeping and drinking habits.

'I never expected you to set foot in The Cavendish, Miss Leigh,' he said, observing her somewhat cynically. 'You have contrived to give the impression that I number among your least favourite people.'

'You do, but I did not know who else to ask. You did say that I could ask . . .' And at this obscure reference to their last encounter, of which she had absolutely no recollection, a faint pink flush tinged her cheeks.

'So I did, and I was perfectly sincere.' Leaning back, in a withdrawn, almost defensive posture, he waited to hear her request. 'Well, go on,' he said impatiently. 'What is it you want?'

'I must find a job and somewhere to live . . . Oh Lord, this is embarrassing. And the fact is, Mr Cavendish, that I don't know where to start. I know it is feeble of me but there we are, or rather I am.'

'There is no need to be embarrassed – lots of young ladies would be confused and nervous in such a situation. However, I must confess to being a trifle taken aback at hearing such sentiments from a member of the Leigh family! A most forthright, determined and energetic group of young ladies, it has always seemed to me, who know exactly what they want and where they are going, and who promptly go out and achieve it.'

'Don't rub it in.'

'Surely one of your sisters would be in a better

position . . . Four of them, aren't there, making five in all? Or is there a sixth, hidden in the attic?'

A suggestion of a smile tugged at Imogen's sullen mouth. 'No, I'm the youngest and the last.'

'What a relief. I don't think that my constitution or my sanity could have withstood a sixth.' He spoke lightly, feeling his way in this difficult interview. Five of them, but each so different from the others; five individuals whom one would not take for members of the same family, let alone sisters. 'I was about to say, Miss Leigh, with three of those sisters involved in the theatre, all leading independent lives, surely they are ideally placed to smooth your path towards employment and accommodation?'

'I will starve in the gutter before I ask *them* for help.' The bitterness in her voice was sharp, stinging and sincere.

'You are a strange family,' Vere said slowly. 'I am an only child and when I was little I used to wonder what it would be like to have brothers and sisters. I always imagined that it would be warm and stimulating – combative at times of course, but that there would be a sense of shared experience and, above all, loyalty.'

Imogen laughed harshly. 'Real life is not like that.'

'No. I have discovered, quite recently, that happy endings are a figment of a dramatist's imagination. But if you want a job, I can find a niche for you here at The Cavendish. I cannot promise how long it will last,' and he winced, 'but it would be a start.'

'Doing what?'

'This and that,' he said vaguely. 'Bert Harding will fix you up with something.'

'As long as it pays enough to live on – with a little left over.'

For your expensive habits, Vere thought, feeling a qualm at the prospect of her lurching into the theatre with a hangover and in no fit state to work. 'As for accommodation, I am not sure that I can solve that problem quite so easily. Hold on a minute, and I'll have a word . . .' He stood up and then hesitated. 'May I offer you some refreshment, Miss Leigh?'

'Do call me Imogen. You must wake up shouting "Miss Leigh" in all your best dreams and worst nightmares.'

'Tea, perhaps, or would you prefer something stronger?'

'I would kill for a brandy.'

After pouring her drink, Vere left the room and went into a huddle with Will Tucker, who had stayed the course at The Cavendish as prompter and assistant stage manager. When he returned, Vere was looking genuinely pleased.

'The gods are with you, Imogen. The young woman who took over Charley's room after she . . . after the accident . . . is vacating the same at the end of the season. If you can wait until August, and if you approve of the place, there is no reason why it should not be yours.'

Imogen tossed back the brandy and stood up. 'Thank you, Mr Cavendish. I never thought I would live to see the day when I was grateful to you but, then, I never thought I would see the day when Arabella . . . Goodbye,' and she held out her hand. 'I will see you at the start of the season.'

'I will look forward to it.'

'Liar,' she said, and left.

Arabella was decorating her new home. 'Come and see it,' she urged Imogen. 'You can help to choose the curtains.'

'I don't give a damn about *your* curtains in *your* flat. As far as I am concerned, the curtains and the flat and you can go to hell.'

But she did care. The problem was that she cared too much. Imogen did not dare to see Arabella's new home. If she did, the images would rise before her constantly and she would be unable to banish them from her mind. What she did not know could not hurt her.

Packing her belongings, she sorted through the rubble of the last vestiges of Leigh family life and in the kitchen cupboard found the bottle of morphine abandoned by Charley a year ago. Not that Imogen had forgotten its existence – there had been times when she had consciously resisted the impulse to try a tiny sip. Now she packed it very carefully, ensuring that the top was secure and the glass protected against breakage.

Braving the stares at The Cavendish was nearly as difficult as asking for Vere's help. Imogen had seen it before: the eager anticipation of meeting Arabella Leigh's twin sister and then the visible disappointment when she appeared, about as different from Arabella as it was possible to be. At first her duties comprised helping Will Tucker with the supers and running errands for Vere but, when she proved reliable, and sober, Vere began to contemplate the seemingly impossible: putting another Leigh sister on The Cavendish stage.

Why not, he wondered, watching Imogen drill the supers? She must have picked up something from the atmosphere in the house and the character of the family. All the others did. And even if she had not inherited the Leigh talent, she was Arabella's twin sister and the public would come to gawp at her out of sheer curiosity, if nothing else. He might as well cash in on her novelty value while he had the chance.

He was reviving *A Midsummer Night's Dream* for the Christmas season and, reflecting that the high-spirited

Hermia was short and dark, decided to give Imogen a try.

Somehow it was not a surprise that she was delightful in the part and a complete natural on the stage. Watching her as Hermia, Vere recognised that here, despite her abrasive offstage personality, was the comedienne of the five sisters, and he began to cast around for a light comedy or farce in which she could star in the spring.

Trying to be worthy of her employment, working willingly and hard, and cutting down on the drink, Imogen held her own through the autumn. She was a success in the *Dream* and enjoyed the plaudits and bouquets, and the congratulations of her sisters. Arabella, playing her current production at night and rehearsing a new play by day, made time to catch a matinée and was overwhelmed with relief that Imogen had at last found a purpose in life.

But Imogen was unsettled by her sister's visit. Afterwards her little room seemed smaller, shabbier and more lonely, and for the next few days the brandy consumption soared. It was only a temporary wobble and no one noticed anything amiss, but then Arabella opened in her new play.

A note from Arabella invited Imogen to the party after the first night of the show, but Imogen went to work as usual that evening and went straight home afterwards. The letter was lying on the table where she had left it and, with a bottle of brandy and a glass, she sat down and stared at it. In her mind's eye she could visualise Arabella at the party, the centre of attention and the toast of the town, but she could not define exactly why she stayed away instead of sharing her sister's success. Partly it was pride, not wanting others to see her as Arabella's cast-off. Partly it was jealousy, being unable to share her with anyone else. But mainly it was the hurt at what she saw as Arabella's rejection of her, which cut so deep that the sight and sound of her sister only served to reopen the wound and make it bleed afresh. Only by keeping a physical distance between them could Imogen maintain a semblance of normality.

That night she drank until she became maudlin. After all we were to each other, she sobbed as the memories overwhelmed her, after everything I did for her . . . And then suddenly the brandy bottle was empty and she did not have another. Too late to go out and buy more, and yet she must have something to deaden the agony and drive away the pain. Unsteadily Imogen stood up, negotiated the few steps to the cupboard and took out the bottle of morphine. It cannot do any harm, she assured herself; indeed, it had done Charley nothing but good. It makes the pain go away, Imogen recalled Charley saying, and, weaving her way back to the table, she set down the bottle tenderly. Her hands shaking, she poured a measure into the glass – a dose that she gauged to be the same as that prescribed for Charley when she first came out of hospital – and drank it.

'You look terrible,' Vere said, about a week after Imogen had taken the morphine. They were sitting in his office, as he wanted to discuss with her the possibility of reviving a Pinero comedy and, ascribing her condition to an excess of alcohol, felt a twinge of anxiety for his plans. 'Perhaps a hair of the dog . . .' and he poured a small brandy.

'Thanks. You look a bit rough yourself.'

'A late night,' Vere admitted, 'or, rather, an early morning. Unwise, of course, but it would have been even more foolish to abandon a winning streak of those proportions.'

'Were you playing cards?'

'Roulette. I had been drinking and in those circumstances I know better than to risk my luck at a game requiring the slightest element of skill.'

'Do you gamble for fun or for the money?'

'Now there is a question fit for a philosopher!' He was considering his answer when the door burst open and a young man walked in, the same young man who had accompanied Vere to the theatre on the night he saw Arabella for the first time. Vere effected the introductions, but Imogen failed to register the newcomer's name, her attention being diverted by his reaction to her. Instead of talking about Arabella, he seemed really interested in *her* and gave her his full attention, until Vere interrupted with a pointed reminder that he and Miss Leigh were trying to work.

'Sorry.' The young man looked abashed. 'Only called in to pay my debts. I think that this should square our recent transactions,' and he handed Vere a bundle of banknotes.

Vere opened a drawer in his desk, dropped the notes in it without counting them, and withdrew a small sheaf of IOUs, which he passed to the visitor.

'So he does win sometimes,' Imogen remarked. 'I always thought that gambling was a mug's game.'

'It is, when viewed in the cold light of day. However, it looks entirely different in the enticing cocoon of a well-appointed salon, when the cards or the dice are falling your way.' The newcomer was watching her speculatively, noting the brandy bottle on the desk and the glass at Imogen's elbow. 'Why don't you come along and see for yourself?'

'Me? Go to a gambling club?'

'Why not? We'll take care of you, won't we, Cavendish? And you can have dinner, and a few drinks . . .'

The prospect of a free meal and drinks was a powerful incentive, because Imogen was not earning as much as her sisters had been paid at The Cavendish. Equally persuasive was the way this man treated her as *someone*, an individual with whom he chose to spend his time. Imogen had received other invitations but had refused all of them, suspecting that they originated from her celebrity status as Arabella's sister, rather than from a desire for her own company.

'Thank you,' said Imogen. 'I would like to do that very much.'

'I'll pick you up after the show.'

'No need,' Vere said. 'She can come with me.'

'I think it would be best if you and I were not seen leaving the theatre together, Mr Cavendish,' Imogen told him. 'As your friend suggests, I will travel with him.'

And so it was settled although Vere looked, and felt, a trifle perturbed. There were those among his acquaintance who might not treat Imogen with the care and respect she deserved, and during a cab ride to the club he could have sounded a word of warning. Still, she probably would not have listened, and even more probably could look after herself. Her sisters, he reflected, had required very little guidance.

At the start, despite her hopes to the contrary, it was her relationship with Arabella and the other Leigh sisters that was Imogen's attraction. All night she was fêted and fussed over; nothing was too much trouble or too expensive for the sister of Arabella Leigh. She drank champagne and watched the tables, the centre of a jolly and increasingly drunken group of admirers. But it soon became evident that she could hold her own in such company with surprising ease, delivering a deadpan put-down or a witty riposte with flair and timing.

Watching from a distance, Vere's hopes for his new production revived. She had the talent and could attract a following. As long as the liquor did not make her unreliable, all should be well. Therefore it was concern for her

professional career, as well as for her personal reputation, that made him step in when the party reached the
rowdy stage. He was not popular with Imogen's would-be
seducers when he insisted on seeing her home and safely to
her bed.

Despite the fact that the anticipated sexual favours were
not forthcoming, Imogen was still welcome at the club.
She was entertaining and could be relied upon to be good
company and good for a laugh. Some of her friends, in an
odd reflection of Vere's old superstition, even considered
that she brought them luck at the tables and would happily pay for her food and drink if she sat with them while
they played. They descended on The Cavendish in the
afternoons, arguing their way past the doorman and sitting in the stalls, from where they proceeded to disrupt the
rehearsal, heckling Vere or calling out silly suggestions, to
the despair and distraction of the cast and stage staff. The
mystery was that Vere put up with it. The old Vere, that
grim unrelenting perfectionist, would have given them
short shrift, ejecting them from the premises and banning
them from setting foot in the place again. This Vere, the
Vere of 1890, seemed to encourage the intrusion, playing
along with it, responding to their sallies with ripostes of
his own, which produced howls of laughter from his
drunken cronies in the stalls. All too often, he and Imogen
left the theatre with them, leaving Bert Harding and Will
Tucker to take over the rehearsal and carry on as best they
could without the manager and one of the female leads. It
was as if Vere were treating the group as an escape from
the theatre; as if being there, going through the motions in
what he must have known was an increasingly futile exercise, was too painful.

Against all the odds, Vere and Imogen were becoming
friends. Every now and again, when one of them was low

in spirits or Vere was low in funds, they spent the evening together in Imogen's room. They would sit, drinking, playing cards for matches, or just talking. He encouraged her to talk about her sisters, feeling a pang of guilt at his enjoyment and amusement at her tart tales about Marion, Frances and Charley, and drawing from her every possible scrap of information about Arabella.

There were nights when he was too drunk or too tired to go home and he fell asleep on Imogen's bed, which long ago had been Charley's bed. But this relationship and these nights were very different from those shared with that passionate redhead. Now he woke with his arms protectively around Imogen, cradling her as if she were the sister he had longed for in his youth. He thought that he knew everything about her: her past and her present, her obsession with Arabella, her addiction to brandy. He did not know, until it was too late, that the ruling passion of Imogen's life was her increasing craving for morphine.

Charley's medicine had been consumed long ago, but Imogen was possessed by the need to obtain more, and preferably a permanent source of supply. Oh, the brandy was fine, and good, and as necessary to her now as breathing, but the *morphine* . . . She had found nothing else that made her feel remotely as good, nothing else that could make her forget Arabella, or simply not care about Arabella, that could make Arabella totally irrelevant. Thanks to the generosity of her friends, Imogen's living expenses had been reduced to the bare minimum. She had money to buy what she wanted but, short of suffering a very nasty accident, had no means of obtaining the drug she now needed.

Matters took an unexpected turn one night at the club, approximately three months after Imogen's introduction to these surroundings. She was sitting at the bar, feeling faintly out of sorts, while her escorts wandered among the tables. Vere was standing nearby, watching the spin of a wheel, smoking a cigarette, his face and demeanour conveying a restless dissatisfaction.

A man approached the bar, ordered a whisky and inspected Imogen from top to toe with open, brash approval.

'Have a drink, darling,' he suggested.

'Go to hell,' Imogen answered laconically.

'That's not very friendly,' he admonished, 'and here's me with a night off and money in my pocket to spend on one lucky lady.'

'And I am lucky enough to be a lady who is not that desperate.'

'I'll show you a good time if you'll show me one,' and he took a step closer, turning round and leaning one elbow on the counter so that he was facing her. In so doing, he had an uninterrupted view over Imogen's bare shoulder. 'Well, I'll be . . .' and he choked back an expletive. 'Harry . . . Harry Dobbs, or I'm a Dutchman!' And he shot past Imogen and clapped Vere on the shoulder.

Harry . . . Harry *Dobbs . . .* Imogen swivelled slowly in her chair in order to gain full advantage of her ringside seat. Clearly Vere was appalled.

'Dick,' she heard him say, 'is it really you, after all these years?'

'In the flesh, my old son,' and they moved away, Vere obviously shaken and pulling nervously on his cigarette, the newcomer, Dick, displaying the same cheerful cheekiness that had marked his approach to Imogen. She could not hear what they were saying, but the exchange did not last long. After only five minutes Vere broke away abruptly and strode out of the room.

'He didn't seem very pleased to see you,' Imogen remarked as Dick returned to the bar.

'Can't blame him, I suppose. Too grand for the likes of me these days. Are you sure you won't join me in a wee dram or a smidgen of mother's ruin?'

'I'll have a brandy.' Usually she stuck to champagne this early in the evening, but Dick did not look the champagne type. 'So Vere Cavendish is really Harry Dobbs?'

'Not surprising that he changed his handle – Dobbs doesn't have quite the same ring to it! We always knew he would make something of himself, of course. The funny thing is that I thought he would look a bit better on it, and I didn't expect to find him in a dump like this.'

Imogen glared at him indignantly. 'This happens to be a very exclusive club.'

'So exclusive that they let me in? Come off it, darling, these debs' delights are getting a cheap thrill out of slumming it. I'll guarantee that their fathers patronise a very different class of establishment, and that Harry is here because it is one of the few places in town that will accept his credit.'

She had not thought of it like that but, glancing round the room, she saw what he meant. 'How do you come to know Vere?'

'Grew up together. Next-door neighbours, near as makes no difference . . . But you don't want to hear about that. History, ain't it!'

'If there is one thing that has a total fascination for me, it is history.'

'Tell you what – I'll give you the guided tour: "The life and times of Vere Cavendish". A whole morning – or afternoon, you say. Your wish is my command, Princess – in exchange for you having supper with me this evening.'

Vere had gone. There was no one to interfere or haul

her back from the brink. 'Very well,' Imogen agreed cautiously. 'And what do you do to pass the time, Dick, when you are not looking up old friends or chatting up girls in bars?'

'Oh, I do a bit of this and a bit of that,' he said vaguely.

He was quite different from anyone else in the bar; indeed he was different from anyone else Imogen had ever met, with one notable exception: looking at him, the slicked-back hair, the moustache, the execrable suit, Imogen was reminded, revoltingly, of her father. A 'spiv' was how some people would have described Dick and that handle could also have been attached to James Leigh.

'What does that mean,' Imogen asked. 'Are you a salesman?'

'That's one way of putting it. A salesman, a dealer, a purveyor of goods – if there is something for sale, I will find a buyer for it. If a punter wants a certain commodity, I'll find it for him.'

'How very interesting.' Imogen leaned forward, subjecting him to the battery of her deep blue eyes and the full impact of her décolletage revealed by her low-cut bodice. 'Can you supply those certain commodities, even if the items are not strictly legal?'

'If the punter has the money to pay, I'll fulfil his, or her, requirements. As I said before,' and Dick smiled into Imogen's eyes, 'your wish is my command, Princess.'

Chapter Thirty

At first this area of north London bore a resemblance to the districts where the Leighs had lived long ago, a neighbourhood of modest homes occupied by the lower middle class, but as Dick guided Imogen to the east, the streets grew narrower and the buildings more cramped.

'We are still in Canonbury, but only just,' Dick said cheerfully, 'and here is our first port of call: Harry's birth-place.'

It was a dingy two-up two-down terrace, the front door opening on to the street.

'Difficult to imagine, isn't it,' Imogen said slowly, 'Vere going in and out of that door, sleeping in one of those tiny rooms. I don't suppose that he even remembers it.'

'Of course he remembers. His old mum still lives here. We can go across and give her a shout, if you like.'

'No,' Imogen said hastily. 'That won't be necessary.'

'Probably just as well. She'd keep us there all day, nattering on about her beloved Harry. Keeps a scrapbook, I'm told, of every press cutting and theatre programme. Lives for him, she does, although naturally she never goes up west to see him act. He wouldn't like that.'

'I think that is terribly sad.'

Dick looked surprised, considered the situation and

then judiciously shook his head. 'She's happy enough. Better off than many another mum round here. He visits her regular and sends cash – she don't go short of anything and she's dead proud of him. What more could she want?'

Imogen could have made several suggestions but conceded that, within the confines and demands of his position, Vere was good to his mother. They walked on, Dick pointing out the house, identical to 'that of the Dobbs, where he had been brought up.

'Mrs Dobbs worshipped Harry from day one,' he went on, 'but *Mr* Dobbs, now that was a different story, and this is one of the reasons why.' He stopped again by a school building, watching a group of small boys kicking a ball around the playground. '"Could do better" was the general verdict on Harry's academic record and it drove his dad wild. Lazy, that was Harry, and not interested, except when it came to English and he was always the one chosen to read aloud in class. But he was big and good-looking, popular with the masters as well as the boys, and our Harry learned from an early age that he could get by on his charm.'

'If he was that popular with the boys, I imagine that the girls were throwing themselves at his feet.'

'Are you kidding? Our Harry's success with the ladies was legendary, my darling. The rest of us looked on and marvelled. I can show you the house where he lost his virginity, if you feel up to a slight detour – no? As you like. It was my sister, you see, who was granted the honour of undertaking his tuition. She was married, of course. Harry had a penchant for married ladies, right through to the time he left home. Thought they were safer, if you know what I mean.'

'Did this famous charm continue to have the desired effect when he started work?'

'Same as me, Harry left school at sixteen and he went into the City office where his father worked, but it wasn't what you'd call a howling success. He had a bit of an attitude problem and the good looks counted against him. The top brass were constantly down on him like a ton of bricks and he felt that his father was always looking over his shoulder.' Dick paused and stared south, down the main road that eventually led into Bishopsgate and the heart of the City. 'We used to walk some mornings,' he said reminiscently, 'in the summer when it was fine. It saved a few pence, which could be put to better use . . . Where was I? We used to meet up at lunch time, a crowd of us, all working in offices and warehouses in the City, and let off a bit of steam. That's how Harry met this other fellow who became his bosom – if you'll pardon the expression – pal.'

'I thought that you were his best friend.'

'I was, until then. Not that I minded being supplanted in his affections, as you might say. Harry was a useful mate when it came to attracting the ladies, the trouble was that all the ladies wanted him and left yours truly in no doubt that he was distinctly second-best. No, this new fellow was much more Harry's style. More educated, a bit more up-market. Not only did he find Harry a vacant berth in the firm where he worked – fibre, it was, import-export merchants in Mincing Lane – but he introduced Harry to a whole new world.'

'The theatre.'

'Got it in one, Princess. At a stroke Harry had found his vocation. He discovered something that interested him and therefore he was willing to concentrate on it, and learn about it and work at it. All it takes, isn't it, a bit of interest? He and this chap were off up west at every available opportunity, spending their last penny – and the last pennies of their nearest and dearest – on seeing every show in town.'

'What was on in those days?'

'Gawd, don't ask me! I only went to a fraction of the shows that Harry saw. Henry Irving was in *The Belle's Stratagem* at the St James; Kate Terry was at the Adelphi; and I remember seeing Sothern at the Haymarket in Tom Taylor's *Lesson for Love*. And then there was Marie Wilton – I was in love with her for years – at the Prince of Wales.'

'And that is how Harry Dobbs became Vere Cavendish?'

'Not quite. There was another little incident in between. A woman, of course.' Dick stopped again, this time outside a public house in which, he informed Imogen, he and Harry used to drink. 'Now, by this time Harry had got ideas above his station. The fibre merchant had a daughter and, well, you know what I'm going to say. Harry cultivated her, she fell for his good looks, and her daddy put a stop to it smartish.'

'I assume that he courted her for her money and not for love?'

Dick looked at her approvingly. 'Harry had long believed that life held a lot more than clerking in a boring office, and he knew that he needed money for the lifestyle he wanted. His looks were his only asset, and this incident with the boss's daughter showed him that he needed to impress the fathers as well as the daughters. He learned that he had to find another way to make money, and he learned that his background counted against him and his climb up the social ladder. So Harry enrolled for elocution lessons.'

'And by now Squire Bancroft had married Marie Wilton and proved that the theatre could bring financial success as well as fame. By the way, was he still living in that awful little house?'

'How else would he pay for his elocution lessons and his theatre tickets? *And* his travelling expenses, because he had joined an amateur dramatic club and getting to the various theatres at which they appeared involved a fair outlay on train tickets. His mother was delighted that he still lived at home – she saw it as filial devotion – but Mr Dobbs was less than enchanted.'

'Thank God, it's opening time,' Imogen said with relief, heading for the pub. 'Knowing all this,' she said, sipping her brandy, 'weren't you ever tempted to . . . well, threaten to reveal all to Vere Cavendish's adoring public and his aristocratic connections?'

'Blackmail him? Yes, I thought about it. Who wouldn't? But then I thought, I don't know, he dragged himself up from nothing. His looks were the linchpin, naturally, but the rest he did himself and he worked damn hard. Why spoil it, for God's sake? He didn't hurt anyone on the way up, not that I know of.'

'He must have hurt someone,' Imogen said with total conviction, 'otherwise he would not have climbed as high as he did. There is always a price to pay.'

'Talking about prices, I got the distinct impression that you were in the market for a little something.'

'Morphine,' Imogen said without prevarication.

Dick's eyebrows disappeared into his thick dark hair. 'Honest? Well, I'll be . . . Say no more, I'll make a few inquiries.'

'But do you think that you could find some? It isn't easy, I know, but I'll pay . . .'

He patted her hand reassuringly. 'A pharmacist of my acquaintance is a very friendly fellow, and he knows a doctor whose sympathy for the suffering knows no bounds. Leave it to me, Imogen, and I'll be in touch.'

They finished their drinks and prepared to leave.

'Just one more thing,' Imogen said suddenly. 'In your opinion, did Vere Cavendish sincerely love the theatre or was it a means to an end, a means of winning fame and fortune?'

Dick thought for a moment and then gave an eloquent shrug. 'Chicken and egg, ain't it, Princess. Who knows? I doubt if even old Harry himself knows.'

That night Imogen went home after the performance and, when a knock sounded at the door, she instinctively knew that it was Vere.

'Did you have an interesting day?' he inquired, avoiding her eyes.

'You know, don't you! How?'

'I saw you, walking down the street with Dick. I was on the way to visit my mother.' His voice was even, with a touch of defiance.

'There is nothing to be ashamed of,' Imogen said with surprising gentleness.

'Yes, there is, if you have aspired to the heights to which I have aspired. Twice in my life I tried to better myself through marriage; twice I had a girl picked out and persuaded; and on each occasion I knew that if I did pull it off, I could never allow my wife to meet my mother. I was ashamed of her, and ashamed of myself for feeling that way. As it happened, both fathers threw me out on my neck.' A bitter smile twisted his mouth. 'In the end your "sins" will always find you out.'

'Your past nearly caught up with you sooner than you think. Your friend was mightily tempted by a spot of blackmail at one time.'

'I was always afraid of that. If you have tried to make yourself into something that you are not, it will always catch up with you.'

Imogen thought of Frances and nodded. 'I know some-one else who lives in fear of that,' she said slowly, 'but I think what you have done is splendid. It takes guts to pull yourself up by your boot-straps and achieve what you have achieved.'

'But it doesn't work – merit and brains do not triumph over class prejudice. If I had studied the Robertson plays more astutely, I would have seen that economic difficulties and humble status are not overcome by effort.'

'It is working for Arabella.'

'Yes.' He looked pained and also puzzled. 'Is it easier for a woman, I wonder? The irony is that the similarity in our backgrounds was one of the factors that made me sure Arabella and I were made for each other. She would not have despised my mother.'

Imogen looked at him sympathetically. She doubted very much if Arabella would have wasted two minutes on Mrs Dobbs but, then, she was unlikely to waste time on Harry Dobbs either. Best leave him with his illusions.

'You sound so defeatist. Are things that bad at The Cavendish?'

'We can see out this season. After that . . .' He shrugged and shook his head.

'You cannot give up,' Imogen exclaimed. 'You cannot allow The Cavendish to collapse around your ears. You've put too much into it, ten years of your life. You must fight!'

'It has been one long fight, Imogen, from the very begin-ning, and I'm tired and I'm not enjoying it any more.'

'You need a backer,' Imogen said firmly. 'A new backer, a new company and a fresh start and, who knows, Arabella may relent.'

'I won't hold my breath.'

'Who do we know with money to burn? You will have

tried everyone at the club, I suppose? Hey, wait a minute, I've got the perfect answer.' Her eyes shone with excitement. 'Frances has money. Her husband is filthy rich.'

'I never knew Frances very well, but I seem to recall that she detested the theatre.'

'She did. Still does. Will do until her dying day.'

'So why should she finance my humble efforts?'

'Because if she doesn't, we will tell her husband about her shady past.'

'Come off it, Imogen! Discussing blackmail with Dick has put silly ideas in your head.'

'It would work,' Imogen said stubbornly, 'and it is definitely worth a try. One last throw of the dice in order to save The Cavendish. Oh, do let's, it would be huge fun. I dare you!'

She made it sound like a lighthearted escapade, not a sinister plot. Heavily in debt from his expenses at The Cavendish and the gambling debts accrued from his attempts to rescue the situation, Vere was tempted to agree with her proposition and make one last attempt to save his theatre. It was probably a waste of time, because surely Frances would refuse to co-operate and they would not really call her bluff by implementing the blackmail threats, but it could not do any harm to try.

'Very well,' he agreed. 'If my guardian angel has not come up with the necessary finance by the end of the season, we will approach Frances, but in a proper businesslike way, mind.'

'Scaring her to death would be much more amusing.'

'Imogen, my dear, you are drunk as usual and I am worried about you. Talking about death, you will drink yourself into that state if you are not careful.'

'You are so sweet to me, Vere. Why are you so sweet to me?'

'I would like to be a father to you, or perhaps a brother.'

'Not a father,' Imogen said sharply, 'but, yes, a brother would be nice. There were some, you know, little boy Leighs, but all of them,' and she turned to Vere with a startled look in her eyes, 'all my brothers died.'

She kept her relationship with Dick secret, even from Vere. When Vere asked her if she had seen his old friend, Imogen assured him that she had no intention of pursuing the acquaintance beyond exchanging the occasional pleasantry at the club. In fact, Dick called at Imogen's room at discreet intervals, delivering parcels of essential supplies and receiving cash in payment. Rather to Imogen's surprise, he did not try to bargain the morphine for sex or to take advantage of their dealings in any way. She assumed that some old loyalty to Vere caused this display of good manners, but the truth was different: Dick found drug addiction offensive and dangerous, and did not wish to be more involved than was absolutely necessary.

At first Imogen controlled the drug. The effects could even be deemed beneficial, as she appeared more pleasant to her colleagues and several of her pharmaceutically assisted appearances in the Pinero play were astonishingly good. But gradually, and inevitably, the combination of brandy and morphine began to control her. Her behaviour became erratic. On some days she could seem perfectly rational and continue with the daily routine as if nothing was wrong, but at other times she shut herself away and drank and drugged herself into oblivion. Several times she missed a performance and Vere, after sending on her understudy, would try to rouse her in her room. But his knocks went unanswered and, blaming the brandy, he would walk slowly back to the theatre, wondering if he dared risk her for another season. If there was another season . . .

As her condition deteriorated, Imogen began to consider every drink of brandy or dose of morphine as a punishment aimed at her sisters, to make them sorry for what they were making her do, for what they had made her do in the past. Then she worked out that they could not be sorry if they did not know. So, in fits and starts and at extremely inconvenient moments, Imogen resumed contact with her family.

She barged into Grace Norton's flat, screaming abuse at Marion for having 'fucked up my life', and that she was dying, but no one cared and that they would be glad when she was gone, because no one had wanted her, not ever. Then she vomited over Grace's new rug, went white as a ghost and subsided into a conscious but inert heap. A grim-faced, tight-lipped Marion cleared up, took her home and reported the incident to Arabella.

Charley was next on Imogen's visiting list. In this instance she chose to corner her quarry at work, and an irritated but unembarrassed Charley pushed her into the wings, ordered her to pull herself together, and asked Imogen what made her think that she was so badly done by, because her lot in life was a bed of roses compared with a few others whom Charley could mention.

'I'll kill myself,' Imogen threatened, 'and then you will be sorry.'

'The weak point in that plan is that you will not be around to find out if I am sorry, glad or indifferent to your demise,' Charley retorted. 'I gather you are still at The Cavendish. Are you sleeping with the man himself?'

Imogen nodded defiantly.

'Oh well, that is enough to drive anyone to drink,' Charley snapped. But after Imogen had gone she sat down to write a note, and another letter dropped through Arabella's door.

So Imogen succeeded in manipulating Arabella into paying her an unsolicited visit.

'What is it you want, Imogen?'

'You know what I want. I want to see you, and be with you and be part of your life.'

'There is nothing to prevent that but your own stubbornness. Of course you can be part of my life, but you must accept that other people and other obligations occasionally take priority. Why must it always be all or nothing with you?'

'You say that, but you would be furious if I turned up at your new home.'

'I would be furious if you threw up over my new carpet.'

'And you would not want me to meet your friends.' Imogen was reminded suddenly of Mrs Dobbs. 'You are ashamed of me. You think that I would ruin your image and tarnish your reputation.'

'I think that you are drinking too much and, by the look of you, not eating enough. How are you managing for money?' and Arabella opened her bag.

It was on the tip of Imogen's tongue to refuse the money, but the need to finance her addiction overcame her pride. Arabella was right: Imogen wasn't eating enough, because she no longer went to the club regularly for free meals and most of her salary went on liquor and drugs.

'I need more than that,' she complained, grabbing the notes from Arabella's hand.

Arabella looked at the row of empty brandy bottles which, unlike the morphine, Imogen made no attempt to hide.

'That money is for food,' she said firmly, 'and it is all you are getting. I really cannot encourage this terrible drinking habit.'

'As you like,' Imogen shrugged. 'I can always get what I want another way.'

'What sort of way?' Arabella asked wearily.

'This room could be a gold mine, don't you think? So private. So convenient. This is where Charley used to fuck Vere Cavendish. He doesn't think I know, but he lets things slip every now and again and I can picture the scene perfectly. They talk about sex all the time at the theatre, and at the club I used to go to . . .'

In a slurred, sing-song voice Imogen went on and on about sex while Arabella, the colour drained from her face, sat tensely on the upright chair, her hands gripping her bag so tightly that the knuckles were white. But when Imogen began to describe a man's hands fumbling feverishly in a girl's private parts and a girl's lips and tongue performing fellatio, she was not talking about experiences discussed by the girls at the theatre or by the men at the club, but acts performed in a childhood home. Subtly her language changed to childish words and phrases, as she acted out both roles convincingly and with agonising slowness until Arabella made a gagging sound and, unable to bear it any longer, ran out of the room.

Imogen had another drink. Punishment, that was what she wanted to hand out to her sisters; punishment for what they were making her do now and what they had made her do in the past. And Frances needn't think that she was getting off scot-free, because she wasn't.

Arabella had once described Imogen as being as clever as a cartload of monkeys. Now Imogen was adding to that native craftiness the cunning of the addict, who can deceive even his family or friends and conceal his condition from the world. Setting off to Gloucestershire that warm August day, the only indications of Imogen's mental and physical deterioration were her extreme pallor and thinness, the emptiness in her eyes, and the tremble of her hands. Not the sort of signs that Vere would have noticed, even if he hadn't been preoccupied with his own troubles.

He had not been able to raise one penny with which to finance another season. Yet, confronting the unpalatable truth that he was a bad risk with no friends, he had picked up other signals: an uneasiness was swirling through the City, a caution, a holding-back. Something was up, but he was not sufficiently in the swim to know what it was. However, it was enough to hint to him that his personal status might not be the sole factor in his lack of success, and that all hope was not lost.

Therefore, his moods veering from wild optimism to darkest despair, he clutched at the faint possibility of Frances and pinned greater hopes on this encounter than he had intended, when agreeing half-heartedly to Imogen's plan. If he lost his theatre, what would become of him? Would another manager hire him as a jobbing actor? Could he take orders again, instead of giving them? Over and over again he struggled to divine how he had come to this, where he had gone wrong, and how he could salvage the situation. If only he could start again and relaunch his great enterprise! He had made mistakes, but he had learned his lesson and he would not make the same mistakes again. One more chance. He deserved that. And perhaps Imogen was right when she observed that Arabella might relent. Even in his wildest dreams Vere no longer dared to envisage Arabella as his wife and business partner, but every now and again he entertained the niggling hope that she might consent to appear at The Cavendish for a season . . . or two seasons, or three . . . And then who knows what might happen!

With their plans and hopes dancing in their heads, they spoke little during the journey and at Gloucester Vere left the initiative to Imogen to organise transport to the Gresham estate.

Frances was sitting in the shade on the terrace, languidly fanning herself against the heat of the day. She was in the early stages of pregnancy and felt limp and exhausted. Fortunately, Thomas was most understanding about the delicacy of her condition and had taken Lucia to visit his sister, leaving Frances to rest. She would be all right, she thought, if only this oppressive heat would pass, but, and she looked down at the open workbasket beside her, which revealed a pile of tiny white garments and cottons and embroidery silk, her hands were so hot and sticky that she could not even sew.

'Excuse me, madam, but there is a lady and gentleman to see you. On family business, the lady says.'

Frances's heart lurched. Marion. What had happened, and could she manoeuvre her sister out of the house before Thomas and Lucia returned? Taking the card that the butler handed to her, she saw the name Vere Cavendish and nearly fainted. When her female visitor turned out to be not Marion but Imogen, the terrace and the garden revolved dizzily for several seconds until Frances exerted an almost superhuman control and, for the sake of what the servants might think, managed to stand up and shake hands. Terrified that a member of staff might overhear their conversation through the open windows of the house, she suggested moving to the summerhouse in the garden.

'Say what you have to say, Imogen, as quickly as you can and then go.'

'But Mr Gresham is not here and I was so looking forward to seeing him again,' Imogen protested. 'Aren't you going to offer us a cup of tea?'

'No.'

'That is not very polite, when we have travelled all the way from London to see you, and on such a hot day, too.'

'Damn you, Imogen, will you get to the point and *go!*'

'Mr Cavendish and I have a little business proposition for you. It is very simple. What we want you . . .'

'Thank you, Imogen,' Vere cut in quickly. 'I think that I am best qualified to explain our proposals to Mrs Gresham,' and he outlined, courteously and succinctly, his plans for another season at The Cavendish.

Frances listened, an expression of sheer disbelief on her face. 'You want me to give you money for your theatre? Are you mad? Even if I had any money, which I don't, how could you imagine that I would put it to such a purpose? I detest the theatre, Mr Cavendish, and I detest yours most of all.'

'Do not make a hasty decision,' Vere pleaded. 'Think about it, sleep on it; I could come back tomorrow or, if you prefer, next week.'

'Under no circumstances will you set foot in this house again. Now go, before I have the pair of you thrown out!'

'And how will you explain that to Mr Gresham?' asked Imogen innocently. 'You can hardly ask that pompous old butler to keep our abrupt departure a secret from his lord and master.'

'Perhaps it would be better if I approached Mr Gresham direct,' Vere suggested, tightening the screw despite his reservations.

'But if we did that,' Imogen went on, 'it might be

necessary for us to expand on the theatrical background of the Leigh sisters, and, of course, we could not overlook your own contribution. I remember you, as if it were yesterday, as the singing fairy in the *Dream*, a particularly titillating costume as I recall, virtually transparent in places,' and she broke into a passable rendition of the fairy's song.

Frances moved towards Imogen, raising her hand as if to strike her, but Vere caught her arm in an iron grip and, with his free hand, motioned to Imogen to stand further away.

'Go away, Mr Cavendish, I want to speak to my sister alone,' Frances said at last.

Vere released her arm and, after a brief glance at Imogen, bowed and left the summerhouse.

'Was this blackmail plot his idea or yours?' Frances demanded. 'I would prefer to believe that he is behind it, but frankly I wouldn't put anything past you. Lucia is right: you really are a thoroughly nasty piece of work.'

'Darling Lucia,' Imogen murmured. 'I am sure she would be as riveted as her father by my glowing account of your stage career.'

But it was not Lucia who worried Frances most, nor was it her husband; it was the reaction of her sister-in-law that terrified her. She remembered, with utter clarity, the exclamation: 'And you knew that this person was on the stage, and you introduced her into my son's family?' – the words of a grandmother who, in a story by Thackeray, discovers that the virtuous family governess used to be on the stage. 'Pack your trunks, viper! and quit the house this instant,' she tells the governess; and the girl's admirer, a respectable doctor, breaks off the relationship immediately. Oh yes, Frances was certain that Thomas's sister would find a way of driving a wedge between her and her husband, and of driving her away from this house for ever.

'I could not pay you, even if I wanted to do so,' she said flatly. 'My husband gives me a dress allowance, of course, but it would not provide a fraction of the lavish costumes that are Vere's speciality. Imogen, be reasonable. We are sisters, after all. I virtually brought you up, with a bit of help from Marion . . .'

'In that case you ought to ask yourself where you went wrong – how did I turn out to be such a nasty piece of work!'

'I am sorry, I spoke hastily and without thinking. Darling Imogen, if you drop this terrible idea and persuade Vere Cavendish to do the same, I could stretch my dress allowance to allow a modest monthly sum for you.'

'You cannot buy me that cheaply,' Imogen said scornfully. 'And it is a trifle late in the day for *darling* Imogen, isn't it? You resented me just as much as Marion did, the only difference being that you also resented Arabella. Yet when there was a crisis, it was me who had to cope. It was me who had to manage when mother was taken bad that day and then . . . None of you even knew what was going on – but you should have known, you have eyes in your head, don't you, and ears that can hear footsteps on the stairs . . . Yes, I am a nasty piece of work, Frances, but I have had some very nasty pieces of work to do!'

She walked towards the summerhouse door, but paused and turned to give Frances one long last, look.

'It is your choice. Either you find the finance for The Cavendish or your husband will hear the full story. And don't make the mistake of underestimating me, because someone else did that, many years ago, and he paid the price.'

'And you should be warned, Imogen, not to under-estimate me or the lengths to which I will go in order to protect my position and my family.'

Soon after that, the letters began arriving: angry, abusive letters filled with threats and obscure references to something that, apparently, Frances had forced Imogen to do in the past. Frances tore up the letters, terrified that Thomas would query this sudden avalanche of mail; petrified that Imogen and Vere would reappear.

She might have found slight reassurance in the fact that she was not the only recipient of Imogen's poisonous diatribes. Marion, Charley and Arabella were receiving letters, too.

Marion was recovering from her disappointment at not being chosen the previous year to appear with Janet Achurch in a production of *A Doll's House* and was now entering wholeheartedly into plans to stage *Hedda Gabler* – only as matinées, because Ibsen did not pay, but part of the excitement was the feeling of being in the vanguard of a new movement, a pioneer of New Drama. Totally under the influence of Grace Norton, professionally and personally, Marion read Imogen's letters and recoiled at their contents and at the language in which the sentiments were expressed. After receiving the first letter she wrote again to Arabella, demanding that she make the time and the effort to see her twin and put a stop to Imogen's behaviour. When the nuisance continued unabated, Marion merely glanced wearily at each missive, threw it away and forgot about it. Really, Imogen was not her responsibility, not any longer. She had done her best with the girl and had received precious little thanks in return. Her conscience was clear.

Charley was even less inclined to give her attention to

Imogen's drunken ravings. At this moment Charley had only one object in life – to go into theatre management on her own account. Work at two West End theatres had convinced her that other managers had nothing to teach her and that it was time to put her own theories to the test. Yes, she agreed that in all probability she would learn the hard way and end up destitute, but if she did not try, she would always wonder what would have happened if she had.

'I do understand,' Edward said gently. 'Yes, damn it, go for it. Why not?'

'There are lots of reasons why not,' Charley replied wryly, 'chief among them being the indisputable and immutable facts that I am young and a woman and, to add injury to insult, I am a young woman with a gammy leg. Not exactly a financier's dream.'

'You know that The Cavendish is dark?'

'Yes, I had heard.' Charley tried to sound off-hand. 'What does your grapevine say about that?'

'Only that there is no sign of a new company being formed and it looks as if Vere Cavendish will have to sell the lease.'

So Charley had other matters on her mind when unsolicited letters from Imogen arrived on her desk. What the hell is she going on about, Charley muttered, reading Imogen's incoherent declarations that she was an outcast – an outcast from the family and from society, and from life hereafter – and all because Charley and her other sisters had done nothing. For God's sake, it is Imogen who does nothing, Charley thought irritably. The rest of us, even Frances, got off our backsides and did something with our lives and, believe me, Imogen my sweet, there were times when it wasn't easy. It still isn't easy, but we get out of bed every morning and go into battle, because what is the alternative – to lounge around and drink oneself to death? If that is what you want, go ahead and do it, no one is stopping you, but do not have the effrontery to place the blame for your weakness on the minds and consciences of others.

The letters that dropped through Arabella's door were accumulating on the hall table, where her maid had placed them. Arabella was out of town, taking her play to the provinces, but when she returned she pushed aside the envelopes addressed in Imogen's familiar scrawl and left them unopened. She had a new play going into rehearsal and a script to study, but pressure of work was not the reason why the letters were left unread. Arabella had not forgotten, or forgiven, the scene Imogen had made at their last meeting.

And then, suddenly, the letters stopped. For a day or two each of the four sisters looked upon this as a temporary relief, but when one week stretched into two and then into three, they decided that Imogen had seen the error of her ways. In fact, three of the four were convinced that – at last and quite rightly too – Arabella had shouldered the responsibility.

They only discovered their mistake when the police knocked on Arabella's door and told her that Imogen was dead.

Chapter Thirty-One

Arabella held a handkerchief to her nose and gazed in disbelief at the squalor of Imogen's room.

'I knew that she was drinking,' she said, 'but I had no idea things were this bad.'

The inspector trod cautiously through the brandy bottles and less mentionable debris on the floor and picked up a small glass container. 'Did you know about this?'

'What is it? My God, it isn't poison, is it? My sister didn't kill herself?'

'Poison of a different kind. Morphine. Lethal if taken in large doses.'

'Is that what killed her?'

'It is very difficult to say, Miss Leigh. Your sister had been dead for some time . . .'

Arabella winced, seeing in her mind's eye Imogen lying dead in this room and no one knowing.

'I see,' she said after what seemed an endless pause. 'I am very sorry, I have been away . . . Who found her?'

'Mr Cavendish. Of The Cavendish Theatre, of course. He was unable to obtain a reply from your sister when he called and therefore he raised the alarm. He and the proprietor of the shop downstairs broke open the door.'

'I see,' Arabella repeated tonelessly. 'Where . . . where is she now?'

'At the mortuary. Normally we would want a member of the family to identify the body formally but in this instance we are prepared to take Mr Cavendish's word for it. We could not possibly expect a young lady like yourself to see . . .' He was frowning, looking at her intently. 'Have we met before?'

'I shouldn't think so, would you? May I go now? I ought to inform my other sisters.'

'Certainly, but I must warn you that there will be an inquest. A sudden death, you see, and a young woman. However, I don't think that there are any suspicious circumstances. A brandy and morphine addict . . .' The inspector gave a slight shrug and then added: 'The only question is: did she do it on purpose or was the overdose accidental?'

'Are you likely to provide the answer to that question?'

'I very much doubt it.'

'Then it is a question that I shall be asking myself for the rest of my life,' and very quietly Arabella left the room.

They buried Imogen a week later, after the coroner had recorded the anticipated open verdict. The three sisters walked to her grave together, Arabella in the centre, flanked on one side by Marion and on the other by Charley, with Grace Norton and Edward Druce a few steps behind. Opposite them, on the other side of the open grave, stood Vere Cavendish, his eyes only leaving Arabella's white face in order to look down at Imogen's coffin. Behind him stood the police inspector.

Got it, the inspector murmured to himself, now that I see three of them together. Father got drunk and fell on a knife. Looks as if drinking yourself to death runs in the family.

When Imogen's body had been committed to the grave,

Vere raised his hat and bowed silently to the sisters before turning on his heel and striding swiftly away. They watched him go, sensing rather than seeing the sag in his shoulders.

'An open verdict is all very well,' Marion maintained later at Arabella's flat, 'but whether Imogen's death was suicide or an accident, the fact remains that someone supplied her with that morphine.'

Charley agreed. 'She probably started ages ago by taking some of my medicine, but obviously she has been obtaining illicit supplies from somewhere.'

'Imogen does not know anyone,' Marion expostulated, 'except the company at The Cavendish . . . Of course, why didn't I see it from the start! It's as plain as the nose on my face: Vere got it for her. He is exactly the sort of person who would have shady acquaintances, a chemist or a doctor who would sell drugs for money. After all, he knew a doctor who . . .' She broke off, colouring.

'He would not discourage the brandy,' Charley said, frowning. 'Word has it that he is sozzled in Scotch most of the time himself. But morphine? And the police are bound to have questioned him. Oh, I suppose you are right. Who else could it have been?'

'What do you think, Arabella?'

'I think that one of us ought to have known about it and stopped it. What the hell do you think I think?'

They were sitting at the dining table, the three of them, Edward having tactfully taken Grace to lunch elsewhere. The room was charming: blue and white like the rest of the apartment, the walls covered in shimmering brocade; flowers everywhere; books bound in gold-tooled white vellum in the alcoves; and, among the pictures, a portrait of Arabella in the extravagantly beautiful costume worn in a recent production.

'But do you think that Vere Cavendish supplied the morphine to Imogen?' Marion asked impatiently. 'It means he virtually killed her, for God's sake!'

'As Charley said, who else could it have been? Yes, why not, let's blame him by all means. Much more satisfactory than blaming ourselves.'

'The pity is that she ever became involved with that man.'

'Yes, Marion, but let us not forget that you were the one who brought him into our lives in the first place,' Charley retorted tartly.

'I didn't notice you turning down any of his offers,' Marion snapped. 'I suppose we must be grateful that he has not tried his charm on Arabella – yet.'

'But he has,' Arabella said calmly. 'Tried it on with me. Only I turned him down. Didn't I, Charley?'

'You knew about this?' Marion glared furiously at Charley. 'Why was all this going on behind my back? Why wasn't I told?'

'I turned down all his offers,' Arabella continued. 'I could have been his leading lady and co-manager of The Cavendish. In addition, he wanted me to be his wife and the mother of his children. He was virtually on bended knee. Really, my dears, can you *imagine*!' And she gave a tinkling laugh, so blatantly insincere that it ought to have sounded a warning note, but neither of her sisters noticed.

'Leading lady *and* a business partnership,' gasped Charley, her eyes flashing. 'I would have given anything for that, anything . . . the bastard!'

'Wife and mother.' Marion was sitting very still, her eyes fixed on Arabella. 'Did he specifically mention children? Are you sure? You must be absolutely sure. Don't answer until you are . . .'

'I am absolutely sure. Why are you so interested? You

surely do not imagine that I would have accepted him. Good Lord, Marion, you spent half your life educating me and cultivating my many gifts and talents. You did not expect me to waste all that effort on him?'

Tears were pouring down Marion's cheeks but she could not explain; she could not tell Arabella why she was so upset, or why her hatred – that intense love-hate she felt for Vere Cavendish – was rising uncontrollably within her. But she could and did respond to the supercilious note in Arabella's voice, not realising that her sister's attitude was all an act.

'It is all so easy for you, isn't it? Crook your little finger and every man comes running to prostrate himself at your feet! Just because you have a pretty face. I have told you before, and I will tell you again, that the day will come when your pretty face will not be enough!'

'Thank you for that prophecy, Marion, but in the meantime I seem to be doing tolerably well. A damn sight better than you ever did, anyway.'

'Try even the smallest Shakespeare part and you would be laughed off the stage!'

'My dear Marion, why should I exert myself to that extent? Your classical tradition did not carry you to the heights that I have scaled. Besides, I really do not have the time to study Shakespeare. My social diary is so full, so many dinners and parties in London society, and so many weekends in the country with the Duke of this and the Earl of that . . .'

Marion rose to her feet, walked around the table and slapped Arabella full in the face. Against the pallor of Arabella's cheek, the mark of Marion's hand showed clearly. The ugly red weal smarted uncomfortably, but Arabella was damned if she would acknowledge it.

'That is the other thing you cannot stand, isn't it,

Marion? Not only do you envy the proposals made to me by Vere Cavendish, but you are jealous of my upper-class friends. You were never invited to society gatherings on equal terms, as I am.'

'I always wanted you to be part of that society. That is what I planned for you. That is why I educated you.'

Arabella stood up, an inch or two taller than Marion and a great deal slimmer. 'You wanted me to *marry* into that society,' she said softly. 'What drives you crazy is the fact that I gained my entrée through the theatre. And you didn't. You have been going over old territory today, so you must allow me the same luxury: you were born a decade too soon.'

For a moment Marion hesitated, apparently fighting the urge to hit Arabella again, but instead she chose to leave the room, banging the door behind her.

'Phew!' said Charley. 'You might have overdone that just the teeniest bit. Poor Marion, her maternal instincts frustrated and her social ambitions thwarted. Still, I expect Grace will pick up the pieces and put her back together again.'

'Do you think that Marion and Grace . . . ?'

'Not for a moment' Charley shook her head vigorously. 'Marion would die from shock. No, it is separate rooms and all good, healthy, girlish fun. But give Grace time – she's working on it.'

'She is certainly feeding Marion well,' Arabella said waspishly and then caught Charley's eye and tried to smile. 'Lord, I am being a bitch today. I can't seem to help it. There is something about my sisters that brings out the worst in me. There's Marion gone off in a huff; Frances in her country house; and Imogen in her grave.' Arabella's voice wobbled, but she quelled the weakness and eyed Charley speculatively. 'That is three down and one to go.'

'Don't worry about me,' Charley advised. 'None of you ever did, and it is much too late to start now. Strewth, this leg is giving me hell.' Leaning forward she pulled the adjacent chair closer and hoisted her gammy leg on to it. 'That's better. Are we going to finish that wine or are you saving it for later, you stingy bitch?'

Arabella filled Charley's glass and her own and watched Charley light a cigarette. 'You wanted Vere Cavendish just as much as Marion did,' she observed shrewdly, 'but for the fulfilment of your professional ambitions, rather than your maternal instincts.'

'Someone really ought to tell Marion that you are not just a pretty face,' Charley said admiringly. 'I believe I could safely say that I detest him as much as Marion does, and that I have an equal right – or should we say left,' and she tapped her shrivelled left leg, 'to string him up from the nearest yard-arm. However, unlike Marion, I do not collapse into tears and vituperations. I plan a sensitive and apt act of revenge.'

'You always were the brains of the family. If you'd had the advantages of my education, you could have been prime minister by now.'

'No amount of education would change me into a boy,' Charley said drily. 'Do you know – of course you don't, but perhaps you can imagine – how much I wanted to be a boy? Just *how* hard I tried to be the son that Father wanted? I loved him so much. I waited desperately for him to come home every time he went away, but somehow he never quite lived up to expectations.'

'We were talking about Vere Cavendish,' Arabella said harshly.

'So we were.' Charley paused and drew on her cigarette. 'Marion's tears and emotional reactions would be water off a duck's back to a man like that. Oh no, I'm working on a much more subtle plan. The problem is that the plan needs money, and I have about as much chance of finding that as I do of changing into Charles overnight.'

Arabella leaned forward, resting her chin on her hands. 'I have a little money,' she said. 'Not as much as you might think, because you would be surprised at the cost of living up to one's reputation. The frocks, Charley, the money I have to spend on frocks! Still, one must speculate in order to accumulate, as the saying goes. However, I do have a little spare cash, which could be put to good use.'

'Your name would be more useful than your cash. Hey,' and Charley sat up sharply, 'we are not talking much about Imogen, are we? It was her funeral that brought us together today and, instead of mourning her, all we have done is squabble and quarrel, and plot and plan!'

'But Imogen is not forgotten,' and a spasm of pain crossed Arabella's face. 'If she did commit suicide – and I will never know and always wonder – then she wreaked the perfect revenge. Now she is always with me, whatever I do and wherever I go, the monkey on my back! But tell me, what is this subtle plan for revenge on Vere?'

'I want to buy the lease of The Cavendish Theatre.'

That autumn of 1890 ought to have seen Vere Cavendish launching his eleventh season. Instead, Charley limped around the City, shouting into deaf ears and banging on doors to no avail: no one wanted to invest in the expertise and acumen of a young red-haired woman with a gammy leg, particularly at a time when rumours of the imminent collapse of Barings Bank were sweeping the boardrooms. Using her knowledge of The Cavendish, pleading shame-lessly for information from Bert Harding and Richard Ramsey, both of whom were seeking other employment, Charley calculated the sum required to buy the lease and launch an initial season. She had some savings of her own, in the bank account opened with this very aim in mind when she first arrived in London, and Arabella put up what she could. Still far from her goal, Charley steeled herself to approach Lord Melton and found him receptive. Peter Frith-Tempest was next on her list – years ago he had said he would be first in the queue to provide finance for her theatre – and Arabella coerced Henry Vale into putting up some cash. However, old loyalties were all very well, and the lure of Arabella Leigh's participation in the venture was tempting indeed, but the contributions still did not reach Charley's target.

'Grace' suggested Arabella. 'She isn't Croesus, but every little helps.'

Cautiously Charley approached Marion, who listened attentively. 'I don't want you to bother Grace with this,' Marion said, 'not under any circumstances but . . .' She thought about the residue of her gifts from Reggie, the jewellery that she had not been prepared to pledge in order to save the school, her 'pension' lying in the bank vault. 'There might be a way round this, as long as I can be there when Vere finds out who is buying his precious theatre.'

'We will stage the signing in the best tradition of The Cavendish,' Charley assured her.

Determined to keep the identity of the buyer secret from Vere until the last moment, she asked Peter Frith-Tempest to make the preliminary approach and he reported that Cavendish seemed resigned to his fate.

'Was he curious about who was behind the deal?' Charley asked.

'He did not press me for details, but he looked at me . . . Well, he looked odd.'

'But he did agree to meet – he will sign?'

'He has no choice,' Peter assured her. 'Without finance of his own, he must sell and ours is the only offer.'

'Arrange the meeting for next Sunday.'

'What time'

'Eight in the evening – the time that the curtain went up on Cavendish productions.'

After Peter Frith-Tempest left the office, Vere walked out on to the empty stage and lit a small gas batten. The memories crowded in on him, the many triumphs and the few disasters, the comedy, the tragedy and the histrionics, the heat of the lights on his face and the roar of the applause in his ears.

Lose his theatre and he might as well lose his life.

Dimly he began to perceive where he had gone wrong. He had treated the profession too lightly. His beautiful mistress had been slighted and had exacted her revenge.

But, if he was given a second chance, he would not make the same mistake again. This time the work would be all that mattered, an end in itself. He would live for his theatre and for nothing else, touring the provinces in summer, touring America . . . His hands clenched as the plans teemed in his head and a sudden burst of hope surged through him.

If only he could scrape together sufficient funds to finance another season! The debts would wait – his creditors were pressing him because they saw him as having no future. Seeing him back in business, with income flowing into The Cavendish coffers, they could be persuaded to extend the repayment period. Breathing space, that was what he needed. And he could think of only one way to obtain it.

What's more, if he could pull it off, it would be an apt development. He could not be sure, but he suspected that either Marion or Charley was involved in Frith-Tempest's consortium. Both of them had been thick as thieves with the man, and both had grudges against *him*. If he had to bet on which sister was masterminding the takeover, he would put his money on Charley . . .

Vere left the stage, returned to his office and wrote a letter.

The letter from Marion, advising her about the death of Imogen, had brought Frances such an overwhelming sense of relief that, that evening, she sang for the first time in weeks. Fortunately, Thomas believed that her tense, anxious state had been caused by her pregnancy and therefore she had not been obliged to explain her lack of spirits or her sudden improvement. As the days passed, she felt as if she were coming back to life, anticipating the birth of her baby, appreciating her husband, Lucia and her home all the more for having so nearly lost them.

However, slowly, she began to realise that although the threat from Imogen had been removed, the one from Vere Cavendish remained.

When she received Vere's letter, and the blow fell, she felt surprisingly calm. Looking down at her body, she held her stomach protectively. She had meant what she said: no one should underestimate the lengths to which she was prepared to go in order to save her position and her family.

Telling a concerned but acquiescent Thomas that she wished to spend a few days in London with Maria Scarlatti, Frances took the train to town. After a night's rest she replied to Vere's letter, telling him that she was prepared to meet his terms and that she was arranging to raise the money, in cash and securities.

He wrote back, telling her to bring the money to The

Cavendish at a quarter to eight on Sunday evening.

It seemed a strange hour for a business meeting, but Frances supposed that he must have his reasons and, when she discovered that The Cavendish was dark, she realised that his choice of time and venue would suit her very well.

'The plan,' Charley explained to Marion on Sunday afternoon, 'is for you and me to get there early and set up. Arabella has promised not to be later than quarter to eight.'

'The doorman might tell Vere that we are there and spoil the surprise.'

'There isn't a doorman. There is no one there at all – Vere cannot pay the wages.'

'Then how do we get in?'

Charley produced a key and waved it under Marion's nose. 'I swiped the spare key from the board in the doorkeeper's cubby-hole while Peter spoke to Vere about the meeting. Honestly, Marion, have a little faith – I'm not likely to overlook something as basic as that. I've even managed to remember the champagne.'

'It will get warm.'

'In that theatre, when it has been dark for weeks? The place will be an ice-house.'

To be on the safe side, they set out soon after seven o'clock, having the hansom drop them near the Lyceum and walking back along the Strand and round the corner to the stage door.

'It's locked,' Charley whispered, reaching for the key, 'so he isn't here yet. I must admit that I did worry in case he was early.'

The cold, dank chill of the deserted theatre hit them like a physical blow and, shivering, the sisters felt their way along the dark corridor, both women familiar with every inch of their path.

'Will Tucker always kept some hurricane lamps on the floor by the gas table,' Charley whispered and began groping in the appropriate area. 'Oh God, I hope there aren't any rats, I keep thinking that I'll touch something furry at any moment . . . Ah, here we are. Matches, Marion . . .'

Eyes growing accustomed to the dark, they lit the lamp and Marion held it aloft as they walked to the stage. Halting by mutual unspoken consent at a particular spot, they illumined Vere's chair, table and screen, which had been such essential features of his rehearsals.

'It needs to be centre-stage. Can you shove it across a bit, Marion? This damn leg . . .' And Charley watched critically as her sister pushed the table into position. 'And the chair, facing stage right so that we can make our entrance OP. Yes, that's fine. Leave the screen where it is, we don't need it.' She limped forward and perched on the chair while she rummaged in a capacious bag, hanging from her wrist, for the champagne.

'I'll fetch the glasses,' Marion said, 'but shall I light a batten first? I don't want to leave you in the dark.'

'No, we mustn't risk any stage lighting. It is feasible that Vere might forget to lock the door, but it is highly unlikely that he would believe he had forgotten to put out the lights as well.'

When four glasses had been placed on the table beside the champagne, the only remaining task was for Marion to move a chair into the wings for Charley to sit on while they waited. Five minutes passed very slowly.

'Come on, Arabella, come on,' muttered Charley. 'We'll have to put out the lamp – we're running the risk of Vere arriving before her.'

'It will be difficult for Arabella in the dark. She doesn't know The Cavendish like we do.'

'Tough luck. She should have been here by now.'

'It isn't quarter to eight yet.' Marion paused as a door slammed. 'There she is now.'

'No,' and Charley swiftly extinguished the lamp. 'That isn't Arabella's footstep. Damn and blast, the whole effect is going to be ruined.'

'He might wait in his office,' Marion whispered.

'When he has found the door open? I doubt it.'

Sure enough, the footsteps came closer. A match flared by the gas table and then a batten leaped into life, revealing the tall figure of Vere in full evening dress, top hat and cape. He turned, his shadow etched eerily against the wall and looked around him.

'Shit,' hissed Charley through clenched teeth.

Vere stood, staring at the table, the chair and the champagne as if mesmerised. Then he raised his head. 'Come out, whoever you are.' His voice echoed around the theatre, bouncing off the ceiling, reverberating from the back of the gallery. 'Charley, is that you?'

Charley clutched at Marion and choked on an expletive.

'Or is it you, Marion, seeking revenge for past wrongs?' He tipped his hat to the empty stalls.

'Peter?' whispered Marion.

'No, he wouldn't . . . Vere has worked it out for himself. He is cleverer than we thought.'

Pressing back into the shadows, they waited but then, suddenly, without sound or any prior warning, a figure appeared in the wings on the opposite side of the stage. Arabella, both sisters immediately thought, but when the woman folded back the hood of her cloak, they gasped audibly. *Frances!* What the hell . . . ?

'Ah, there you are,' Vere said, turning towards her. 'My dear Frances, do come in and sit down. Have a glass of this excellent champagne.'

Frances shook her head, advancing only a few steps towards him.

'Let me take your cloak,' Vere suggested politely. When Frances again shook her head, he divested himself of his own cloak and hat, throwing them to the side of the stage, and then uncorked the champagne with a pop that made Marion and Charley start nervously, and poured the wine, fizzing, into two glasses. He held out one glass to Frances but, when she made no move to take it, Vere drank it himself. 'Your health, Frances, and that of your family. Did you bring the money?'

'Of course.' The cloak that she was hugging around her parted slightly and with her left hand she deposited a rough paper parcel on the table. Then both hands disappeared again under the black velvet folds.

'Are you sure that you won't sit down? Very well,' and Vere took the chair himself, setting down his glass and beginning to unwrap the parcel. 'On reflection, a little contribution to my coffers is only fair, Frances. You have done very well for yourself and it is all thanks to me. I closed that school of yours . . .'

Frances was standing behind him and, in terrifying slow motion, her right hand emerged from under the cloak and in the subdued lighting Marion and Charley saw the flash of the knife blade.

Then everything happened very quickly. Another figure appeared in the wings. Sensing the movement, Vere turned but saw the knife in Frances's hand and reached up to grab it from her. His hand closed on it, easily forcing her to relinquish it, but Frances reacted swiftly, picking up the champagne bottle and smashing it down on his skull.

And it was not a bit like any of the death scenes he had
enacted on the stage. There was no speech, no last
reproach, no lingering glance. Vere Cavendish went down
like a felled tree, slumping over the table and sliding to the
stage, blood oozing from the wound in his head, flowing
to the floor to mingle with the shards of the champagne
bottle.

For a moment they stood frozen: Marion and Charley,
having started to her feet, in the wings; Arabella closer to
the grisly tableau on the opposite side of the stage, Frances
still holding the neck of the bottle. Then Charley limped
forward, bent down to hold her fingers to Vere's pulse and
straightened up again.

'I am going to lock the outer door, just in case Vere
asked anyone else to the party. Marion, make sure that
Frances sits down before she falls down.'

They heard Frances's story, Charley prompting her and
pushing her to tell the tale as quickly as she could, Marion
wiping blood from her sister's hands and face and clothes
while Arabella, herself spattered in Vere's blood, so close
had she been at the crucial moment, sat quietly and listened. When Frances had finished, her three sisters stared
at her, at her white, shocked face and at the pregnant
bump of her stomach.

'You killed him because he was blackmailing you?'
Charley said.

'I couldn't lose it all – Thomas, Lucia, the house, a life
for my baby. You do understand, don't you? And then he
told me he had closed the school, and yet . . .' Frances hesitated, her defences broken by the dreadful thing she had
done. 'I could have stopped. I nearly stopped when he
grabbed the knife. He was still so beautiful, you see, and
in that split-second I knew that I still loved him.'

'But,' Charley prompted.

'I looked at the champagne and I thought of all the champagne and love that he had lavished on all my sisters. All of you, but never on me. I was the only one he never wanted and so I picked up the champagne bottle and . . .'

For a moment no one spoke, but then Marion asked harshly: 'Are you hoping for a boy or a girl?'

'I think it is going to be a boy. It is a very active child – there, it just kicked me again.'

Marion placed her hand on her sister's stomach. 'I can feel it,' she whispered, her eyes filling with tears.

'Right,' Charley said decisively. 'This is what we are going to do . . .'

The inspector stood by the front row of the stalls, looking up at that perfectly posed tableau on the stage.

'I did not expect to have the pleasure again so soon,' he remarked. 'Your sister so recently in her grave and now another unfortunate death. First your father, then Miss Imogen and now Mr Cavendish. It is to be hoped that these things go in threes, as the old saying has it, and not in fours or fives.'

'If you want to come up on to the stage, Inspector, you will have to use that side door,' and Charley pointed the way, 'and go through the office.'

'I expected to find the stage door open.'

'So did we but, like you, we came in through the front entrance.'

'Still,' the inspector went on, 'if I had come in from the side, I would have missed the full impact of the Leigh sisters on stage. Miss Marion, isn't it, and Miss Charlotte and Miss Arabella. Now, before I do join you, let us clarify the situation. Even from the back of the stalls it is clear that Mr Cavendish collided with a bottle. It would save a lot of time if you told me which of you ladies hit him over the head with it.'

There was a slight pause and then the young woman slumped on the floor raised her head.

'I did,' said Arabella.

Chapter Thirty-Two

Spring came late that year and it snowed on the day that Arabella was brought to trial for the murder of Vere Cavendish, causing Charley to brush the flakes from her dark green coat when she gained the safety of the court. Marion was already there, sitting in the waiting area set aside for them, while Edward Druce joined Grace Norton in the public gallery. Pale and thin, having lost weight through sheer anxiety, Marion was shaking with nerves.

'This was your bloody silly idea,' she hissed at Charley under her breath. 'We ought to have run away from The Cavendish that night and no one would have been any the wiser.'

'That isn't true and you know it. Other people – Peter, and Lord Melton, for instance – knew that we were meeting Vere.'

'Then we should have said that he was dead when we arrived.'

'Someone might have seen us entering the theatre before Vere arrived. The cab driver could testify to the time he picked us up at my rooms . . .'

'He still might,' Marion said grimly, 'and then what do we do?'

'Marion, just concentrate on remembering your lines. Today the Leigh sisters are going to give the greatest performance of their lives, and the drama will have a happy ending. No one is going to send Arabella to the gallows.'

Marion's face went a shade whiter. 'Only if the three of us can perjure ourselves convincingly.'

The arrival of Peter Frith-Tempest saved Charley from replying. This was a Peter she had never seen before, black-gowned and bewigged, holding two great leather-bound books and a thick sheaf of the notes he had prepared for Arabella's defence. A Peter who believed, implicitly, the story that the sisters had told him about what happened at The Cavendish Theatre that fateful night, and who never suspected for a moment that Frances had been involved.

'It will be all right, won't it?' and Marion clutched at his hand.

'I cannot promise that Arabella will walk free from this court,' Peter said gravely, 'but on the available evidence there is a very good chance that she will.'

'I still cannot believe that she is accused of murder. I thought that, at the very worst, the charge would be manslaughter.'

'It is possible that she could be found guilty of manslaughter, but Arabella is not guilty of murder and I continue to maintain that no jury will convict her.'

'How is she?' Charley asked.

'Holding up bravely, but one would expect such courage of Arabella. Now, we have been through the procedure several times and you know what to expect: the prosecution will parade the medical evidence first and establish to the court how Cavendish died then they will call the police witnesses. During my cross-examination, I must establish grounds for the jury to believe that

Cavendish's death was an accident. The prosecution, of course, will attempt to prove that it was murder, and that it was premeditated and executed with malice afore-thought.' Peter smiled weakly, trying with his melodramatic phraseology to lighten the atmosphere, but failing badly. 'Charley, I will call you as first witness for the defence, in order to establish the reason for the meeting at The Cavendish, but I'm afraid it might be some time before we reach that stage. Marion, you will have even longer to wait.'

'I'd rather get it over,' Marion wailed.

'There is no need to be afraid,' Peter said encouragingly. 'All you have to do is tell the truth.'

At that, Marion exchanged a bitter and appalled look with Charley and sank into the nearest chair, covering her eyes with her hand.

A noise like a dull rumble of thunder reached their ears from the street, followed by a murmur from the adjacent court room.

'Nothing to worry about,' Peter reassured them. 'I expect the hubbub heralds the arrival of Mrs Dobbs, Cavendish's mother.'

'His *mother* . . . is she here?' and Charley groaned as Peter walked away. 'Why is it, Marion, that until this ghastly thing happened, I never even considered that Vere was some woman's son?'

'I did consider it, but he wouldn't talk about it. He never wanted to talk about himself at all. His mother . . . Oh, Charley, what are we doing? Why did we protect Frances? They would not have hanged a pregnant woman!'

'Not until she had given birth to the baby, but afterwards . . . ?'

Marion shuddered. 'I know, but I keep worrying that

the police will remember that there were five of us and bring it up in court. Of all the damnable luck – that they should send the same man each time!'

'Not so surprising really. There aren't many plain-clothes detectives in London.' Charley tried to sound calm and sensible, but inside she was as worried as Marion. 'Damn it, Marion, we made a decision and we must stick to it. We are doing this for Frances and the baby – for God's sake, *you* were the one who always said that the family must stick together and make sacrifices for each other. It was *you* who preached loyalty and so you cannot back out now. It is Arabella's neck that is on the line – all you are risking is your conscience . . .'

Charley broke off abruptly because a crescendo of sound swelled from the court and drowned her words. Arabella had been brought up from the cells.

In the court room Arabella stood in the dock, dressed in black, a haunted expression in those great sapphire eyes. Her tense, ashen face betrayed the strain she was under but, if anything, the pallor served only to enhance her beauty. The members of the jury were staring at her, with a blend of curiosity and fascination. They had read about her in the newspapers, seen her picture, but nothing had prepared them for this moment when they saw her in the flesh for the first time. Surely, *surely*, no man could con-demn to death such extraordinary loveliness? In the packed gallery Edward and Grace looked down at the dock, in as much ignorance of the real facts as Peter, because the sisters had decided that the fewer people who knew the truth, the better. There, too, was Sarah Vale, her eyes never leaving Arabella's face, and Maria Scarlatti – how much did *she* know? Frances had returned to Maria's home when she left the theatre that night. Had she been able to conceal her emotional state? Had Maria noted the coincidence between Frances's sudden visit and the death of Vere Cavendish?

And there was another pair of eyes that did not waver from Arabella. Neatly but shabbily dressed in a black coat and a black hat from which a few wisps of grey hair escaped, the tiny, birdlike figure of Vere's mother gazed at the incomparably beautiful young woman accused of killing her only son.

Counsel for the Crown was addressing the court. 'The fact that the defendant struck the deceased on the head with a bottle, inflicting an injury that caused his death, is not in dispute. The defendant admitted as much to the investigating officer. What is in dispute is *why* she struck that blow. She claims it was because the deceased, Vere Cavendish, attempted to violate her.

'Anyone who saw Mr Cavendish on the stage will know that he played opposite some of the most attractive leading ladies of our time. Women who are well known for their beauty, popularity and, er . . . *sociability*. Yet we are asked by the accused to believe that Mr Cavendish met her at his theatre on a Sunday evening – at her own request – and then attacked her. She claims that she fought him off and that when he did not cease his advances, she struck him on the head with the bottle.

'This story may sound plausible when you look at the prisoner at the bar, because there is no denying that she is exceptionally beautiful. However, I will put before you another reason why the accused wanted to kill Vere Cavendish. That reason has nothing to do with self-defence or the possible violation of her body by a man who, let's face it, could have had almost any woman he wanted. No, that reason was revenge – revenge for what he had done to her sisters, and to one sister in particular.'

Most of the medical evidence was of a technical nature,

but there was one point that Peter needed to establish in cross-examination.

'How many blows to the head did the deceased receive?' Peter asked the pathologist.

'One.'

'And that single blow was enough to cause death?'

'Yes.'

'Would you say that the blow was powerful and delivered with considerable force?'

'In most cases such a blow might not have proved fatal, but would merely have caused concussion. However, the skull of the deceased was particularly thin and therefore death would have been virtually instantaneous.'

It was more than Peter could have hoped for. Perhaps even the pathologist had been caught off-guard, captivated by the allure of Arabella, because he had volunteered information that had not been included in his initial report and this evidence could help to convince the jury that Vere Cavendish's death had been accidental.

Then the police inspector took the stand. Outside the court, waiting their turn to give evidence, Marion and Charley struggled to maintain an outward calm; Marion, fluttery and feminine, played with her handkerchief and was glad that she could not hear what was going on in court, while Charley, shifting in her seat because her leg was uncomfortable, strained her ears in the hope of catching a word or a sense of the atmosphere. In the dock Arabella tensed.

All went well while the inspector described the scene at The Cavendish Theatre on the night of Vere's death, but then the prosecutor asked him: 'Was this the first time you met the Leigh sisters?'

A muscle twitched in Arabella's cheek, but the reaction was fleeting and went unnoticed.

'I met them on two previous occasions,' the inspector replied, 'the first time being when their father died.'

'Why were the police called in that instance?'

'It was a sudden death. Apparently Mr Leigh slipped and fell on a knife after a bout of heavy drinking.'

'You say *apparently* he slipped and fell on a knife. Did you have doubts about the circumstances of Mr Leigh's death?'

A rushing noise sounded in Arabella's ears and the room began to tilt alarmingly, but with a supreme effort of will she concentrated on one fixed point ahead of her and managed to stay upright.

'Not at the time,' the inspector replied, that slight qualification doing little to restore Arabella's equilibrium.

'Where did this incident take place?'

'At the Leigh home. In the bedroom shared by the defendant and her twin sister.'

There was a gasp from the crowded gallery and the prosecutor paused before asking: 'When did you meet the accused for the second time?'

'After her twin sister, Imogen, died from an overdose of morphine and alcohol.'

Again there was an involuntary intake of breath from the gallery and a sudden murmur of conversation, but Arabella relaxed slightly as the line of questioning moved away from two problem areas – one that her sisters shared, another that was her burden alone. However, now it was Peter who scented danger. The Crown case hinged on revenge as a motive for murder, and the prosecutor was trying to assert that Arabella had lured Vere Cavendish to the theatre, not to purchase the lease, as she maintained, but to murder him.

'An inquest into the death of Miss Imogen Leigh recorded an open verdict,' Peter protested. 'There was no suggestion of foul play. I submit that the circumstances of Miss Imogen's death are irrelevant.'

'Miss Imogen and the defendant were twins,' the prosecutor replied, 'and were very close. It is the Crown's contention that the accused considered that the deceased was in some way responsible for the death of her sister.'

The judge overruled the objection and Peter's heart sank.

In the next few minutes the inspector told of the relationship that had existed between Imogen and Vere Cavendish and that it had been Cavendish who found her body. One of the mysteries of the case, he said, concerned the person who had sold the morphine to Imogen. The police had been unable to discover the identity of the supplier, but Cavendish had come under suspicion and Arabella must have been aware of this.

'So, in your opinion, Inspector, the defendant might have harboured a grudge against the deceased because she believed, rightly or wrongly, that he was, directly or indirectly, responsible for her twin sister's death?'

'Yes,' the inspector agreed.

At the outset of the trial Peter had felt that there was an enormous amount of sympathy for Arabella, but now he was not so sure. The inspector's evidence might have sown the first seeds of doubt in the jury's mind about her innocence. Was it coincidence that she had been involved in three violent deaths? It was Peter's task to win back that sympathy, to try to shift the minds of the jury from pondering how and why tragedy was seemingly stalking the life of one so beautiful. He had to produce new evidence.

In his cross-examination Peter drew out of the inspector details of what he had found in Vere's office at the theatre – the exact number of whisky bottles and dirty glasses. He asked the policeman to describe his visit to

Vere's rooms and to list – along with revealing another cache of whisky bottles – the number of photographs of Arabella that adorned the establishment, the piles of newspaper cuttings about her, the formal acknowledgements of his notes to her and, most significantly, a handkerchief monogrammed with the initials AL and a twist of long blonde hair which, as the jury could see, matched Arabella's.

Gradually Peter was building up a picture of a man who was a drunkard, down on his luck and losing his theatre, and obsessed with the greatest beauty on the London stage. When the jury looked across at Arabella, so quiet and still in the dock, that picture was irrefutable. All Vere's hard work, the almost ascetic existence he had lived at one time, went unmentioned, unnoticed and unrecorded.

The inspector resumed his seat, curiously dissatisfied with his evidence and the entire case. He did not know what to believe. He *had* believed Arabella Leigh's assertion that she accidentally killed Vere Cavendish in self-defence, just as he had believed that Imogen Leigh died by an accidental overdose of morphine and alcohol, and that a drunken James Leigh had accidentally fallen on that knife.

But Arabella Leigh was a very young woman and three accidents, of such a violent nature, seemed altogether too much of a coincidence. Bits of conversation kept floating into his head, along with shadowy recollections of a fifth sister, and he kept wondering if he ought to try to locate the file on the death of James Leigh. But there wasn't a file, or nothing much to speak of anyway, because he had accepted Leigh's death as an accident and had not written up detailed notes of his investigation. Investigation! The inspector was uncomfortably aware that his approach to the sisters – whether there had been four or five of them – hardly merited that description. At this distance it appeared that he might have been somewhat less than professional in his handling of the case, yet to contemplate an alternative to that 'accident' was to uncover something so ugly that . . . The inspector shook his head in an attempt to clear the images that crowded his mind. No, he wanted to believe that James Leigh had died accidentally and, because he was just as susceptible as the next man to the vision of loveliness in the dock, he wanted Arabella Leigh to get off. He leaned back in his seat, watched the red-haired sister take the oath and willed the jury to reach a verdict of not guilty.

'Perhaps, Miss Charlotte,' Peter began, 'you would tell the court why you and your sisters were present at The Cavendish Theatre on the night in question.'

'We had an appointment with Mr Cavendish. He had been in financial difficulties and I and my sisters, Marion and Arabella, had pooled our resources to form a consortium in order to buy the lease of the theatre.'

'At what hour were you due to meet Mr Cavendish?'

'Half past eight.' Charley did not meet Peter's eye.

'It was a Sunday evening,' he went on quickly. 'Surely Sunday is an unusual day for a business meeting?'

'It was the only time when Arabella was free. She was performing six nights a week, with two matinées, and rehearsing a new production.'

'You were the initiator of this proposal?'

'Yes, I undertook the preparatory negotiations and the lease, if and when it was acquired, was to be in my name. My name appears on the legal documents, which I took to The Cavendish that night for signature by myself and Mr Cavendish, and which I handed to the police at the theatre that same evening.'

The documents were submitted as evidence and scrutinised by the jury, and then Peter questioned Charley about her acting career.

'It came to an abrupt and unfortunate end, did it not?' Peter asked eventually.

Charley gave an honest, but understated, account of her accident.

'Did you blame Mr Cavendish for the accident?'

She and Peter had rehearsed this part of her evidence and had decided that the jury would be impressed by the appearance of absolute frankness.

'At first I suppose I did, yes. In fact, I know that I did. For a while I hated him. You see, I thought that I had lost everything – my ability to work, in particular. Later, when I had recovered sufficiently to be able to make a more sober assessment of what had happened, I came to realise that I was blaming him unfairly.'

Deliberately Charley did not mention that her life had been saved by Vere's intervention. Let her keep that part of her testimony to offset anything that the prosecution might care to suggest. Indeed, the prosecutor was on his feet immediately Peter sat down, anxious to destroy any favourable impression that Charley might have made by her apparent veracity and candour.

'Miss Charlotte, do you expect this court to believe that Mr Cavendish would seriously entertain a business proposition made by three *actresses*.' He emphasised the word deliberately, knowing that in the minds of most men 'actress' was synonymous with 'whore'. Out of the corner of his eye he saw several members of the jury smile knowingly.

Charley kept her temper. 'Certainly, when those three actresses are the Leigh sisters,' she said sweetly. 'If the other members of the consortium – Lord Melton and Lord

Henry Vale, for example – could take us seriously, why not Mr Cavendish?'

Peter relaxed a little, knowing that the defence was in capable hands. Charley would give as good as she got. It was something the prosecutor would discover, if he had not already learned his lesson.

'You did say that initially you blamed Mr Cavendish for your accident?'

'Yes, until on reflection I realised that it was more like an act of God than an act of negligence.'

'Nevertheless, it was negligence of a sort, was it not? There was reason to believe that insufficient attention had been paid to backstage fixtures and fittings?'

'These things happen,' Charley said, with a slight shrug. 'The manager of a theatre cannot be expected personally to inspect every square inch of the place and everything in it. I repeat, it was an accident.'

'But that accident destroyed your acting career and left you crippled for life. I suggest that, as a result, you hated Mr Cavendish. You hated him enough to bide your time and plot your revenge. In fact, this so-called consortium was only an excuse to lure Mr Cavendish to the theatre, and you planned, with your sisters, to kill him.'

A collective gasp rose from the gallery but Charley did not flinch. Instead she suppressed a smile. He had walked into her trap.

She waited until the court was quiet and then said, slowly and clearly: 'Why should I want to take his life when he saved mine?' Again the spectators murmured. 'In fact, he risked his life in trying to save me. He saw the danger and almost managed to pull me clear – but for his selfless and brave act, the flat would almost certainly have hit my head. Anyone who was there that day could have told you this – just as they told me, much later, because

Vere Cavendish was too modest to mention it himself.'

She could have said more, but Peter had warned her that in a court of law it was better to say too little than too much. And the prosecutor's line of questioning enabled Peter to counter-attack.

'Can you tell the court the current situation regarding your consortium and the lease of The Cavendish Theatre?' he asked in re-examination.

'I saw my solicitor yesterday and he assured me that everything is ready for my signature.'

'Your backers have not withdrawn their finance due to the unfortunate circumstances of Mr Cavendish's death and your involvement in it?'

'My backers have been immensely supportive and continue to express their confidence in me and my sisters.' Charley did not mention that her backers' support was conditional on Arabella being found not guilty and therefore being in a position to act in her productions.

'Well?' Marion hissed urgently as Charley rejoined her.

'It went better than we could have hoped,' Charley assured her. 'You should be fine as long as you keep your head.'

A buzz of conversation greeted Marion as, dressed in deep blue velvet, she entered the court, and secretly she was pleased that she still had her admirers. Leading her through the evidence slowly and methodically, Peter began by questioning her gently about the family background and Marion told of their mother's delicate health and early death; of their father's unstable character, his drinking habits and sudden, self-inflicted end. She described how she had earned money in order to feed and house her little sisters and how she had struggled to keep the family together. As they had arranged, ostensibly to protect the marriage, Frances was not mentioned.

'At what time did you and Miss Charlotte arrive at the theatre that night?' Peter asked eventually.

'Shortly after half past eight,' Marion replied, praying that Arabella's confession had made it unnecessary for the police and prosecution to try to prove or disprove this statement. 'I am afraid that we did not check the exact time. The stage door was shut, so we walked round to the front again. Inside it was dark, but Charley and I know every inch of The Cavendish so we found the stairs without difficulty.'

'What were your feelings at the time?'

'We were rather amused by the situation. "Vere is staging this like one of his major productions," I said and Charley laughed. "His last in this theatre," she said.' Marion paused, looking upset. 'It seems a dreadful thing to have said, but how were we to know that . . . ?'

'What was the first thing you saw when you entered the auditorium?'

'The stage – quite brightly lit – and Vere lying on the floor. Arabella was sitting, huddled up, hugging her knees and shivering, near the footlights. I ran down the aisle, through Vere's office and on to the stage, while Charley followed as quickly as she could. I went to Arabella first and tried to comfort her.'

'What was her condition?'

'She was very distressed. She wasn't crying, just sitting there, staring into space and shaking. Her dress was torn and spattered with blood.'

'Didn't you go to Mr Cavendish, in order to ascertain if he required medical help?'

'Charley felt his pulse and told me that he was dead. I am afraid that I was too upset to look at him closely.'

'What did you do next?'

'We tried to find out what had happened, but Arabella

was too shocked to speak. So I left her with Charley and went out into the street to fetch help. Luckily a policeman was walking up the Strand and he was able to send for assistance, while I went back into the theatre. By the time the police arrived, Arabella was a little better and more coherent.'

The prosecutor, who may have noticed how nervous she was when she entered the witness box, seemed to sense that Marion might be the sister who would crack under sustained questioning. As he stood up, Arabella tensed as if she, too, doubted her sister's ability to cope.

'Like Miss Charlotte,' the prosecutor began, 'you also acted with Mr Cavendish for some years. Why did you leave his employ?'

'I was upset about Charley's accident. No, I don't mean . . .'

'I am sure that you do mean that, Miss Leigh. But that was the second time you had left The Cavendish, was it not? Why did you leave on the first occasion?'

'I suffered a bad attack of typhoid fever.'

'Typhoid, or enteric, fever is a very serious condition?'

'It is. In fact, I almost died,' Marion said, forgetting Peter's warning never to volunteer any additional information.

'Doubtless your illness was caused by the unhygienic conditions Cavendish allowed to prevail in his theatre.'

'Almost certainly,' Marion agreed. 'I had warned him several times about conditions backstage.'

'Did he do anything about it?'

'No,' Marion replied, and a look of anguish crossed Peter's face.

'So in effect, Miss Leigh, it could be said that your illness was the fault of Mr Cavendish.'

It was more a statement than a question and Marion

was not as sharp as Charley. However, she was beginning to comprehend the direction that his questioning was taking.

'Yes and no,' she answered, trying to be noncommittal.

'Come, come, Miss Leigh, you can do better than that.'

Marion remained silent, her brain spinning.

'Miss Leigh,' and the prosecutor's voice rose to a higher pitch, 'the jury and all of us are awaiting your reply. Let me repeat the question: did you not blame the deceased, Vere Cavendish, for your illness which, on your own admission, nearly killed you?'

But Marion was recovering her composure. 'Yes and no,' she replied in a stronger voice. 'Yes, I did think that conditions backstage were unhygienic and that Mr Cavendish could have made improvements. No, I did not hold a grudge against him, because I did not feel that conditions at The Cavendish were any worse than those at other theatres. In addition, I was tired and run down, struggling with a role for which I was not suited and which Mr Cavendish had not wanted me to attempt – he always did know what was best for me . . .' At this point Marion gulped back a sob, her expression reflecting the heartache she wished to convey. 'Anyway, I went back to The Cavendish for another season at a later date, so I cannot have thought that either the theatre or Mr Cavendish was *that* bad. And why are you asking me these questions? I did not cause his death.'

'We are not disputing who struck the actual blow,' the prosecutor said, 'but the circumstances in which that blow was struck. There is a great deal of difference between lashing out at someone in self-defence and planning a cold-blooded murder.'

Peter sprang to his feet in order to object to this 'statement to the jury', his intervention partly designed to give

Marion a respite. In those few moments she managed to regroup her thoughts and felt confident enough to respond.

'We did not plan anything,' she protested, 'except to buy the lease of the theatre. Charley and I were very fond of Mr Cavendish. He was good to us and made us what we are.'

'It is a good thing that you were fond of him, because he seemed to play a quite astonishingly important part in the lives of you all, did he not? One after the other, each of you seems to have been involved with him, even your other sister.'

Marion froze and, momentarily, Arabella stopped breathing.

'My other sister . . .' Marion repeated in a whisper, playing for time. Oh my God, did he know about Frances? And she wished that Charley were here to tell her what to do.

Not realising the raw nerve he had exposed, the prosecutor continued: 'We have already established that Mr Cavendish reported her death to the police.'

The relief was overwhelming. 'Imogen . . . Yes, she worked with him for a short time. He was always very kind. We were very grateful for everything he did for all of us.'

'Surely there must have been some jealousy among you? A good-looking man like Mr Cavendish . . . Did he never favour one of you over the others?'

'Only Arabella, and we did not realise the extent of his obsession with her until it was too late. As far as I was concerned – and I feel sure that this is true of Charley, too – my relationship with Mr Cavendish was of a professional nature and no personal feelings, except friendship, were involved.'

The bordello, Marion thought . . . If they had investigated Vere's lifestyle, they could not have failed to discover the bordello. Suppose they found the fat woman at the desk and she identified Marion and Charley as having accompanied Vere to the bedroom. And heaps of people knew that Charley had been having an affair with him. This case had more holes in it than a sieve . . . She began to shake again, but the prosecutor sat down, evidently feeling that he had managed to extract something from Marion that supported his case.

At last, after days of tension as the long procession of witnesses passed through the court, came the moment for which everyone had been waiting. Apart from her initial plea of 'not guilty' when the charge was put to her, Arabella had remained silent, her face barely revealing any emotion as the evidence swayed first against her, then for her. As she crossed the floor from the dock to the witness stand, all eyes were on her, this beauty who could enthrall an entire theatre. Could she do the same at the Old Bailey?

She took the oath and then, speaking softly but with a clarity that reached the back of the gallery, Arabella confirmed her part in the consortium and agreed that the Sunday evening meeting had been arranged for her convenience.

'As it happened, I got away from rehearsal a little earlier than I expected. Let me see, it must have been at half past seven and, as there was not enough time to go home first or do anything else worthwhile, I took a cab to The Cavendish. The stage door was locked, so I had to walk round to the front again.'

'Did that surprise you? The door being locked, I mean,' Peter asked.

'Yes, I was surprised and not very pleased. It took me

some time to find my way into the foyer. It was in pitch darkness and I was not familiar with the theatre, so I stumbled about trying to find the stairs. Eventually I groped my way into the auditorium and I saw Mr Cavendish on the stage.'

'What did you do then?'

'I sat down at the back of the stalls and watched him. He did not see me and I remember thinking that he wanted us to use the front entrance, so that we would get a good view of him on the stage. He was a remarkably handsome man, with a powerful stage presence. Perhaps he thought that we might have second thoughts, or offer him a better deal, or include him in our future plans.'

'What time was it by then?'

'I don't know . . . The cab ride, finding the door, finding the way in . . .' Arabella shook her head. 'I did not hurry at any point, so it must have been well after eight o'clock.'

'Presumably Mr Cavendish did see you eventually?'

'Yes, if he hadn't, I would probably have gone on sitting where I was, waiting for my sisters. Mr Cavendish was moving a table and chair into the centre of the stage, and then he fetched a bottle of champagne and four glasses and placed them on the table. I was thinking that this was rather a civilised gesture, when suddenly he seemed to sense someone's presence and he looked up and saw me.'

'Who spoke first?'

'He called out to me, to join him and have a glass of champagne while we waited for the others.' For the first time Arabella's voice trembled and her eyes filled with tears. 'And I did . . . Oh, if only I had not done so! If only I had waited for Marion and Charley . . .'

In his seat the prosecutor checked the police report, which confirmed that two glasses had been partly filled with wine, while the remaining two were unused.

'I knew as soon as I came close to him that he had been drinking. I could smell the whisky on his breath. I should have guessed – it's a well-known fact in the profession that Vere Cavendish had been drinking heavily for some time. He began . . . well, propositioning me even before he opened the champagne.'

'He had made advances to you before?'

'Ever since my first stage success. He simply would not take no for an answer. He pestered me with notes and flowers, and then with scripts and plans for us to star together at The Cavendish.'

'Did you keep any of the notes that he sent?'

'No. I receive a great many notes and some of them contain suggestions of which I do not wish to be reminded.'

'I refer you to exhibit number fourteen. These are notes found in Mr Cavendish's rooms.'

The court orderly took the bundle of papers to Arabella. She barely glanced at them.

'Are these in your handwriting?' Peter inquired.

'No. They were written by Imogen, who dealt with all my correspondence at that time.'

'Did you, at any time, give Mr Cavendish one of your handkerchiefs and a lock of your hair?'

'Certainly not.'

'So how,' Peter continued after Arabella had confirmed that the relevant items were hers, 'did Mr Cavendish come to have them in his possession?'

'I can only think that he took them from my bedroom.' Arabella grimaced with distaste. 'I suppose he must have gained access to my room at the time I was sharing an apartment with Imogen.'

'Did you tell Mr Cavendish to his face that his advances were unwelcome?'

'Several times. Indeed, I went out of my way to tell him. One such occasion was the Easter before last, when I was staying in Gloucestershire with the Earl and Countess Westlake.'

A rustle of interest greeted the introduction of this aristocratic acquaintance, and Arabella glanced up at the gallery, where Sarah had been joined by her brother, Henry.

'With their permission, I invited Vere Cavendish to luncheon and afterwards I took him into the garden and put the matter straight once and for all – or so I thought.'

'How did Mr Cavendish respond to what must have been an intense disappointment?'

'Very well. He behaved like a perfect gentleman. And he did not bother me again until . . . until . . .'

'So you did not hesitate to join him on the stage and have a drink with him?'

'I didn't exactly jump at the chance but I was not afraid of him, if that's what you mean. Besides, and I know this sounds silly, it would have been rude to refuse. I did not wish to be discourteous or to jeopardise our negotiations.'

'You expected him to behave like a perfect gentleman again. However, he had been drinking on this occasion, you say, and he propositioned you. Can you tell the court exactly what happened?'

'It is something I would prefer not to do,' she said, her voice faltering, her huge eyes filling with tears.

'I can understand your reluctance, Miss Arabella, but I am afraid that I must insist,' Peter said gently.

The gallery was sympathetic. Arabella's beauty, her youth and vulnerability pierced them all to the heart, but to a man, and woman, they wanted to know what Vere Cavendish had done to Arabella Leigh that winter night on the empty stage of The Cavendish Theatre.

Arabella's face was deathly pale against the black of her clothes. 'He helped me off with my coat and gave me a glass of wine. I took a small sip and held the glass, more because it gave me something to do than for any other reason. All the time he was saying how much he loved me and wanted me – in his theatre and in his bed. That was the way he put it. I said that he must not talk like that. We had discussed the matter before and nothing had changed. He kept saying that we were meant for each other, that we were two halves of a perfect whole, and while he said these things he was only inches away from me, breathing whisky fumes into my face.

'I wasn't frightened. He was obsessive, yes, but he had never appeared to be a violent man. My sisters had had their disagreements with him, but had always spoken of him with respect, as a manager who honoured his commitments, so I went on trying to be polite. And then he grabbed me and kissed me.'

She broke off, in a silence so absolute that her breathing, and her shudder, reverberated around the room. 'You must understand,' she said, with a sob in her voice, 'that no man had ever kissed me before, or touched me, not like that.'

She paused again, as if battling to find the words. 'The champagne in the glass I was holding spilled over my dress, and I groped for the table and managed to put down the glass as I tried to free myself.'

'I do appreciate that this is painful for you,' Peter said, 'but what happened next?'

'I fought to free myself,' Arabella repeated, her eyes blank, 'but it was no use. He was so much bigger and stronger than me. He said that he had lost everything – his money, his theatre and his reputation, and that he had nothing more to lose, and that if he was going down he would take me with him. Before he went down, he said, he intended to have me. He pulled me round so that my back was against him and he began feeling me all over . . .' Arabella wrapped her arms around herself and rocked back and forth, cringing at the memory.

'I had been rehearsing all day and was wearing an ordinary, everyday gown. Mr Cavendish undid some buttons at the back and tore the bodice and then, with both his hands, he began to feel . . .' She choked on a sob and stopped.

Peter walked to the table where the exhibits lay and picked up a blue, blood-spattered dress, holding it so that the tears in the bodice were clearly visible to judge and jury. Everyone stared at it, imagining Vere Cavendish caressing the white breasts of Arabella Leigh.

'No,' shouted a shrill voice suddenly, 'no, I don't believe it. She's lying! He wouldn't do that, not my Harry. He was a good boy. I brought him up to be a gentleman, even though we were humbly born.'

The little woman in the gallery was standing up, gripping the rail in front of her, dry-eyed but desperate. Arabella watched as she was silenced, her heart lurching with genuine emotion. For a while she had almost believed that she was telling the truth, that all this had happened, but his mother was right. Vere, or Harry, would not have done this. He had never forced himself on any woman. He had never needed to – except with her; and when, in the garden in Gloucestershire, she had told him not to touch her, he had released her without question. And Arabella hated herself for the damage done to his reputation, and for the pain caused to his poor mother. But she had to go on. For everyone's sake she must go on . . .

'I screamed,' she said dully, when Mrs Dobbs had subsided into her seat, 'but there was no one to hear. I tried to work out what time it was, and when Marion and Charley would arrive . . . And all the time he was touching me and kissing me and breathing heavily, and he started to lift me off the ground. I thought he was going to carry me into the wings and . . . well, you know what he was going to do.'

Very gently Peter asked: 'What did *you* think he was going to do?'

'*Must* I say it?'

'Yes, Miss Arabella. It is important to know what was in your mind at that moment.'

'I knew he was going to rape me.' The words were uttered in a whisper that penetrated every corner of the room. There was silence after she had spoken and then a long, deep sigh, as if everyone had held their breath and exhaled collectively.

'What happened then?' Peter asked.

'I saw the bottle. It was the only weapon to hand and I knew that I needed desperately to fend him off, to stop him. I sagged in his arms, suddenly, and went limp, and he was so surprised that he collapsed on a chair with me on his lap.'

'And then . . . ?'

'I managed to wriggle free and I picked up the bottle and . . . I didn't mean to kill him, you must believe me, please! I only wanted to stop him, to get his hands and his mouth off me, and stop him – that was all I ever intended.' She swayed in the dock.

'Did you hit him?'

'Yes.'

'How many times?'

'Once. Then everything went blank until Marion and Charley were there, bending over me. I was sitting on the stage and . . . I don't remember doing it, but apparently I was trying to cover myself up.'

'And your behaviour had not been provocative in any way?'

'No,' she said, as Peter sat down.

When the prosecutor rose to his feet, he stared at Arabella for a long time. 'You were close to your twin sister, I understand.'

'Of course.'

'Yet, when she died, it was Mr Cavendish who discovered the body. Where were you at the time of your sister's death?'

'I was away, working.'

'Were you aware that she was a morphine addict and drank brandy to excess?'

'I tried to help Imogen with her drink problem. I did not know about the morphine.'

'Who was her closest friend and associate at that time?'

'I was not aware of Imogen's social life. We were living apart.'

'But you knew that she was working at The Cavendish Theatre?'

'Yes.'

'And therefore, given the family history, it would be safe to assume that she was close to Mr Cavendish?'

'I suppose so.'

'If someone had told you that Mr Cavendish was supplying Imogen with morphine, what would your reaction have been?'

Nine witnesses out of ten might have been expected to reveal their hatred of anyone who obtained drugs for a much loved and vulnerable person. Arabella was the tenth.

'I would not have believed them,' she said firmly.

'Why not?'

'Because he was not that sort of person. He would not have done a thing like that.'

'Yet he was a person who was capable of rape?'

'I believe so, yes.'

'The person who supplied your sister with morphine was almost certainly responsible for her death. Do you not wish that, whoever that person was, he was dead, too? Like your sister.'

'No, I do not wish that.'

'So the death of your sister can pass unpunished, but an attempted rape on yourself deserves the death penalty?'

'You are forgetting,' Arabella said in a dangerously quiet voice, 'that I did not intend to kill Mr Cavendish. At no time did I wish him dead.'

The prosecutor switched to a new tack. 'During your evidence in chief, you mentioned that no man had ever kissed you before, or touched you *like that*. Have I understood you correctly?'

'Yes.'

'But you are an *actress*, are you not?' Again he placed undue emphasis on the word, leaving it to every man present to decide for himself what was meant. 'And actresses are often embraced and kissed on the stage.'

'A stage kiss is very different, a mere brush of the lips. I intended to indicate that no man has touched me off the stage.'

'Come, Miss Arabella, do you expect this court to believe that an *actress*, and one as beautiful as you, has not had a man admire her, embrace her, kiss her, even . . .' Deliberately he left the sentence unfinished.

She stared at him, an expression of cold fury on her face. 'Your insinuation is insulting, sir. I am an actress, not a whore. I repeat, no man has touched me off the stage – except for Mr Cavendish.'

Her words echoed into a tense silence, which was soon filled by witnesses attesting to the spotlessness of

Arabella's reputation. Under Peter's guidance, again and again her colleagues and acquaintances confirmed that Arabella Leigh never accepted invitations from male admirers, that she only attended gatherings at which a number of people would be present, and that her private life was above reproach.

In summing up, Peter contended that the death of Vere Cavendish was an accident, the blow only fatal because of the thinness of the man's skull. The prosecutor repeated his allegation that the three Leigh sisters each had cause to hate Vere Cavendish, that they could have been expected to wreak revenge on the man who had wronged each one of them at some time in their lives, and that Arabella Leigh had cold-bloodedly planned to kill him that night.

The jury retired to consider its verdict. The participants in the case, the spectators and the press waited.

'Peter says it will be a good sign if the jury comes to a quick decision,' Charley said, as confidently as she could.

'We ought to go out for a cup of tea,' Edward maintained. 'Silly to sit here for goodness knows how long.'

'You do not seriously think that I could leave here?' Marion demanded.

'I wonder how Arabella is feeling,' said Grace.

The others looked at her. They had been trying not to think about that, trying not to picture Arabella waiting in the cells below, with her escort of prison wardresses and police officers.

'Perhaps I could force down a small gin,' Marion said suddenly and so they went out for some refreshment, but were so on edge that within the hour they were hurrying back to court.

The gallery was filling up again, with friendly figures like the Vales and the Meltons, and with the poor, pinched face of Mrs Dobbs and her elderly female companion. Then suddenly there was a stir and a bustle as the officials took up their places and Arabella was brought in. She remained standing, holding on to the rail of the dock with black-gloved hands. The judge, with a sense of theatre that the Leigh sisters could appreciate, strode in with a twirl of his red robes and a tweak of his wig. And finally the jury filed in, twelve men of different height, hair colour and degree of prosperity, but all wearing the same grave, self-important expression.

'Do you find the defendant guilty or not guilty?' the foreman of the jury was asked after the preliminary formalities.

'Not guilty.'

And Arabella fainted.

Chapter Thirty-Three

'**D**id you really faint?' Charley asked Arabella in the cab as they drove away from the court after the tumultuous climax to the proceedings.

Arabella smiled wanly. 'I did feel very peculiar,' she said noncommittally, 'and extremely glad that it was over.'

'*Glad* – that is the understatement of the century! But we did it, we pulled it off! It just goes to show what the Leigh sisters can achieve when they work together, instead of against each other.'

'There is no such thing as "the Leigh sisters" any more. Imogen is dead, and Frances is dead to us – because we all promised that night never to see her or speak of her again. And Marion couldn't wait to rush off with Grace as soon as the trial was over.'

'Your performance at the trial, and at the theatre that night for the benefit of the police, was superb,' Charley said quietly. 'You do understand that it had to be you – that you are the most beautiful and the most talented of us all, and that you stood the best chance of getting away with it?'

'Of course. I offered, didn't I?'

There was a moment's silence and then Charley

laughed. 'You will never have a better script,' she said lightly.

'Next time I write my own script, and I will invent something a little less traumatic.'

'It was my fault. I invented that story and persuaded you and Marion to go along with it.'

'One of these days,' Arabella said thoughtfully, 'Peter will ask why we said we were meeting Vere at half past eight and not eight o'clock. After all, it was Peter who arranged the meeting, and the time and place.'

'He will not ask. He is too frightened of the answer.'

They were silent, remembering why the change of time had been necessary, and of the use to which those precious thirty minutes had been put: of the rapid invention of Charley's plan; sending Frances back to Maria's home; setting the stage; hiding the knife and the brown paper parcel in Charley's capacious bag; disarranging Vere's office, emptying bottles of liquor, dirtying glasses and putting the empty bottles in full view; opening the front entrance so that the police would receive the full impact of their artfully arranged tableau on the stage. And all the time, over and over again, they rehearsed their lines and drilled their performance so that no inconsistencies should occur. And, equally important, that half hour allowed time for Arabella to have been alone in the theatre with Vere, her departure from rehearsal having been witnessed by members of her company.

'Why did you do it?' Charley asked. 'Only for Frances and the child, or was there another reason?'

'I had to give something back, for Imogen's sake.' Seeing Charley's look of sheer incomprehension, Arabella went on: 'Imogen made a similar sacrifice for me, and in the end it killed her.'

'You cannot feel that you are to blame for Imogen's

death,' Charley protested, placing the simple, obvious interpretation on Arabella's words. 'We all received those ghastly letters from her and, if you are guilty, so are the rest of us.'

'I was not referring to the letters.' Arabella stared sightlessly out of the window. 'Imogen killed Father, and she did it for me.'

To Charley, the shock was greater than anything she had experienced before. She listened with horror and disbelief as Arabella, haltingly, with none of the fluency she had shown on the witness stand, described James Leigh's visits to her bedroom, the things he had said and the things he had made her do, while Imogen shivered in the other bed.

'That night was going to be different. He talked about it beforehand, describing exactly what we were going to do together . . .' A sob escaped her and she held herself tightly before she could go on. 'It was as if the talking, saying the dirty words aloud to me, was half the fun, but Imogen heard everything and that night, before he could do it, before he could rape me, she stabbed him.

'She must have got out of bed and found the knife in the drawer, but I did not hear her do it. I was not aware of her at all and neither was he. He was sitting on my bed, pulling up my nightdress, when Imogen pushed me away and got between us and stabbed him in the chest. And the peculiar thing was that, although Imogen went to pieces afterwards, I was calm. Like ice. Like you were, when Vere died. I thought of everything. I changed our nightdresses, because we were covered in blood, and I screamed only when we were ready for Marion to come into the room. I even remembered to button up his trousers.'

Charley, remembering her childhood adoration of her

father, felt as if her heart was breaking all over again. 'So that was what Imogen meant in her letters. She felt that the rest of us ought to have known what he was doing and that we ought to have stopped him.'

'Imogen never recovered. After that I took the lead and I had to protect her. The problem was that she used it, cleverly and consciously, against me. She had done that terrible thing *for me* and therefore, in return, I must give her all my time and attention for the rest of my life. And I tried, Charley, I really tried, but the burden of that gratitude was too great. In the end I came to think that it would have been preferable for Father to have had his way.'

'No,' and Charley reached out to hold her hand. 'No, not that . . .'

'As things are, I have Imogen with me for the rest of my life, always there, whatever I do and wherever I go, just as she wanted. And Vere Cavendish is coming along for the ride.'

'He will always be with me, too. *And* his mother . . .'

'Which one of us *did* kill him, Charley? Was it Frances, or was it me? I cannot help thinking that, but for me, he might not have been in danger of losing his theatre.'

'I arranged the consortium,' countered Charley, 'and I actively wanted revenge. As did Marion, who put up more money than both of us – heaven knows how she got it. I prefer not to inquire too closely.'

'Vere found Imogen after she died, and I genuinely do not think that he supplied her with the morphine. I believe that he loved me, and he would not have done that to my sister. I believe that he was Imogen's friend.'

'Don't dwell on it,' Charley urged gently. 'We must look to the future. I will see the solicitor tomorrow and sign the lease for The Cavendish. I plan to put on a few matinées while I find my feet, then a short summer season, and organise a full season to start in the autumn. You are with me, aren't you! I know that it is asking a lot, because you are in demand everywhere, but . . .'

'I will be your leading lady, Charley, if you will provide me with the leading man of my choice.'

'Hey, that isn't an easy thing to promise! Men aren't exactly queuing up to appear with you because they know that, however good they are, they will be totally eclipsed! Who do you have in mind, anyway?'

'Can't you guess – Edward Druce, of course, who else?'

'Edward?' Charley gazed at her in surprise.

'I think that he and I could have a splendid relationship – professionally, that is. Even without the example of Vere Cavendish, I would never trespass on a sister's territory!'

'He wants to marry me, but I haven't decided . . .'

'I think you should marry him. It would make touring much more pleasant.'

'I want to go to America,' Charley said eagerly. 'We'll take a train, the whole company, and go everywhere . . .'

'I know exactly the kind of plays I want to do, and the roles that are right for me, if only I can find a dramatist to write the stuff.' Arabella's eyes sparkled into life. 'Women who have *lived*, women with a *past*, women who live life to the full.'

'And I know how hard you work, and that the front you show to Marion is so much nonsense. Incidentally she knows it, too, but is too jealous to admit it. Arabella,' and Charley squeezed her sister's hand, 'these appalling memories will fade. You will be able to get up in the morning without thinking about Imogen and Vere. And you will overcome your fear of Father and of sex, if you want to. You never fail, Arabella, at anything. One day a man will come along and he will unlock the secrets of your heart, and of your body, too.'

By the time Arabella was acquitted, Frances had given birth to her first child. The happy event was a great relief to her husband and his family, because she had returned from London in a distressed state and had not risen from her bed from that time until her confinement. But the baby was not the boy she had expected. It was a little girl.

FLOWER OF SCOTLAND

Emma Blair

'Emma Blair is a dab hand at pulling heart strings'
Today

In the idyllic summer of 1912, all seems rosy for Murdo
Drummond and his four children. Charlotte is ecstatically in
love with her fiancée Geoffrey; Peter, the eldest, prepares for
the day when he will inherit the family whisky distillery, while
Andrew, gregarious and fun-loving, is already turning heads
and hearts. Nell, the youngest, contents herself with daydreams
of a handsome highlander. Even Murdo, their proud father,
though still mourning the death of his beloved wife, is
considering future happiness with Jean Richie, an old
family friend.

The Great War, however, has no respect for family life. As
those carefree pre-war days of the distillery fade, with death,
devastation, revenge, scandal and suicide brought in their
wake, the Drummonds are plunged to the horrors of
the trenches in France. Yet those who survive discover that
love can transcend class, creed and country . . .

HALF HIDDEN

Emma Blair

The news of her fiancée's death at Dunkirk was a cruel blow
for Holly Morgan to suffer. But for Holly – forced to nurse
enemy soldiers back to health while her beloved Jersey
ails beneath an epidemic of crime, rationing and the worst
excesses of Nazi occupation – the brutality of her war
has only just begun.

From the grim conditions of the hospital operating theatre
where Holly is compelled to work long hours alongside the
very people responsible for her grief, unexpected bonds of
resilience and tenderness are forged. When friendship turns
to love between Holly and a young German doctor, Peter
Schmidt, their forbidden passion finds sanctuary at
Half Hidden, a deserted house deep within the island
countryside. A refuge where traditional battle lines recede
from view in the face of more powerful emotions, it
nevertheless becomes the focus for the war Holly and Peter
must fight together – a war where every friend may
be an enemy . . .

THE ITALIAN HOUSE

Teresa Crane

Secretly treasured memories of her grandmother's Italian house, perched high upon a mountainside in Tuscany, are very special for Carrie Stowe; for not only do they recall and preserve the happy childhood summers of the golden years before the devastation of the Great War, they are her only escape from the mundane and suffocating routine of her life with Arthur, her repressive and parsimonious husband.

When she discovers that she has unexpectedly inherited the house Carrie sets her heart upon going to Tuscany alone to dispose of the effects of Beatrice Swann, her eccentric and much-loved grandmother.

Arriving late at night and in the teeth of a violent storm she discovers that she is not the only person to be interested in the Villa Castellini and its family connections. A young man, an enigmatic figure from the past, is there before her: and as the enchantment of the house exerts itself once more, Carrie finds herself irresistibly drawn to him . . .

COCKNEY FAMILY
Elizabeth Waite

London, 1936. There was a time when Patsy Kent thought she might never belong to a real family, when her mother died and she was nearly sent to the orphanage. But the market traders of Strathmore Street stood by her and Ollie, Florrie and all the others became the best relatives anyone could wish for.

And now Patsy has a husband and four children of her own, and life is full of the cares and joys of motherhood. Alex and David, her sons, always seem to be getting into scrapes while the twins, the prettiest little girls on Navy Street, are a constant source of delight. But war is in the air, and as the fateful events of September 1939 unfold, London will be shaken by air raids and food shortages, children evacuated, men called up. And though the cockney spirit never burns brighter than in times of trouble, Patsy wonders if her family can survive the war intact . . .

Tugging at the heart-strings throughout, Elizabeth Waite's moving portrayal of Patsy and realistic depiction of wartime London make *Cockney Family* a worthy sequel to *Cockney Waif*.

Other bestselling Warner titles available by mail:

☐	Flower of Scotland	Emma Blair	£5.99
☐	Half Hidden	Emma Blair	£5.99
☐	Jessie Gray	Emma Blair	£5.99
☐	The Italian House	Teresa Crane	£5.99
☐	The Raven Hovers	Teresa Crane	£5.99
☐	Icon of Gold	Teresa Crane	£5.99
☐	Cockney Family	Elizabeth Waite	£5.99
☐	Cockney Waif	Elizabeth Waite	£5.99
☐	Nippy	Elizabeth Waite	£5.99

The prices shown above are correct at time of going to press, however the publishers reserve the right to increase prices on covers from those previously advertised, without further notice.

WARNER BOOKS

WARNER BOOKS
Cash Sales Department, P.O. Box 11, Falmouth, Cornwall, TR10 9EN
Tel: +44 (0) 1326 372400, Fax: +44 (0) 1326 374888
Email: books@barni.avel.co.uk.

POST AND PACKING:
Payments can be made as follows: cheque, postal order (payable to Warner Books) or by credit cards. Do not send cash or currency.

All U.K. Orders	**FREE OF CHARGE**
E.E.C. & Overseas	25% of order value

Name (Block Letters) _____

Address_____

_____

Post/zip code:_____

☐ Please keep me in touch with future Warner publications

☐ I enclose my remittance £_____

☐ I wish to pay by Visa/Access/Mastercard/Eurocard

Card Expiry Date

_____